PRAISE FOR *RESERVATIONS*

"*Reservations* is the visceral, thought-provoking story of Samantha's pursuit of a serial killer her mentor had failed to catch before he died. The murder scenes become highly engaging, requiring the reader to be as methodical and deliberate in the reading of those scenes as the writer was in creating them. Five Stars."

—Vivian Stones for OnlineBookClub.org

"*Reservations* has a compelling and engaging mystery that begins immediately and makes it impossible to put the book down. As the audience, you're immediately drawn into the story and have to see it through to the end. Sam's character drew me into this story immediately. She is strong and endearing. Her intelligence is compelling, as is her kindness and overall charisma. The interesting writing style also captured my attention, and I enjoyed the shifting perspectives. The mesh of genres in this story is so unique, it's both a suspenseful thriller and passionate romance, and the thriller aspect affects the characters but does not impact their romance. The blend of genres makes this a rare gem. Made a TaleFlick Pick."

—TaleFlick Marketplace

"Janson offers a fast paced, gripping multiple murder mystery with an intense storyline that smartly reveals the protagonist's past personal traumas and present-day conflicts. Janson enriches this story with humor and sizzling romance. Prose is clear and often poetic, with well-integrated foreshadowing and authentic details relating to the work of an FBI agent and criminal profiler. Readers will be easily emotionally invested in Janson's unique, character-driven mystery that integrates questions of cultural identity and deftly explores the lasting impact of violence and abuse. *Reservations* is a must read."

—*Booklife Prize*

Lovers of mystery sleuth and murder novels blended with romantic intrigue, adventure, suspense, and thrill will find *Reservations* an enthralling read. Using a first-person perspective voice and introspective commentary, Janson unfolds the storyline with evocative depictions. The emotional depth of the storyline gave the prose an intimate touch. It felt like I was in every scene next to the dynamic cast, experiencing every moment. I could feel the electric sparks and adrenaline rush that comes with the magic of new love. I found myself caught in a storm of rescue operations, gunfights, drama, betrayal, healing, vengeance, and more. Janson juxtaposes the cast's complex traits, anchoring the story in reality. The conversations were raw and unfiltered, constantly shifting from playful to urgent and tense. This is the type of story that reminds you of the beauty and power of true love. It makes you want to experience it.

—Keith Mbuya, *Readers' Favorite*

RESERVATIONS

A SAMANTHA WRIGHT CRIME SERIES

THERESA JANSON

Once in a lifetime someone comes along and brings passion and true love into your life. Tom Moody, I thank you. You are a good man, my cheerleader, my life partner and the love of my life, inspiring me every day.

CHAPTER
ONE

There is peace in not forcing something that by nature will have a force of its own. What is the saying; that which does not kill you, makes you stronger? Having been an FBI Profiler for almost two decades, well, I would argue that my last case killed something in me that I will never get back. Stronger? Knowing my weaknesses is a sense of strength. Knowing how it happened, strength is relative. My name is Samantha Wright. Most people call me Sam and I am at a crossroads in my life. Death touches me every day and I haven't figured out how to live.

Dr. Edmond Sampson died a week ago at age sixty from a heart attack at his home in Georgetown, DC, while in the middle of the most difficult and publicized profile of his career, The RESERVATIONS Case. There was a fast-food wrapper on his desk the last time I saw him at work. He hadn't looked well for a few weeks prior to passing, and maybe I should have said something to him, but he was engrossed in this case. He just looked tired, I told myself. I was wrong, and now he is gone. I miss my friend, my father-figure. I miss the only family I'd had in my adult life. Sometimes at night, I hear him, "Sam, lead with your head and not your heart. Don't let others define you. To know you is to know the victims you strive to give a voice to. Never let them be quieted." I was having difficulty accepting the reality of his being dead. He wasn't dead to me, but he was dead to this plane of existence. Sleep eluded me and tears welled up but never flooded me. I was devastated without the outward signs of collapse. Laying him to rest was paramount but letting go was a struggle that I wanted to put off.

"Dr. Sampson's death caused me to reflect as to why I came to the Bureau. The last time in my mentor's presence reviewing case notes is when I noticed his sadness. His last words were not words at all, but a look that transcended everything, a look of complete and utter abhorrence as to what we as humans do to each other. His lifestyle and last case killed him.

His death left a hole in me, and the only way to fill it was to finish the case for him. I owed it to Dr. Sampson as a eulogy to him and the life he lived. I owed it to myself to prove I had learned what it is to be a human being while being a Profiler as he was every day of his life.

Dr. Edmond Sampson, a renowned Profiler, Medical Doctor, Forensic Psychologist, expert on all things alive, dead, and ever known in the universe, or so he thought. He was usually right. Dr. Sampson was a man of a lot of words. It was often tedious, and you had to listen to find the few words that were worth the wait. Those tidbits could be brilliant. I was put under Dr. Sampson's wing after being recruited right out of graduate school because no one else would work with him. The Bureau figured I was a challenge myself. I had the credentials with two Phd's; one in Forensics and one in Forensic Psychology and had the ability to see things that other people usually miss on the bodies of the deceased and in the minds of the living, but I lacked real time, on the job experience. I was a lab rat and had the sense to know that the dead will tell you everything, sometimes you can see the moment of death in their eyes. What I lacked was the connection where the death of the victim meets with the human emotion of those who experience the loss. I learned this from Dr. Sampson and until losing him did I really come to understand it.

Dr. Sampson not only did not take care of himself physically but was one fast-food meal away from a heart attack or stroke. He lived alone, and his appetite went to convenience of access. He dressed as if tweed were a staple no matter what the season and wore a clip-on tie over a white dress shirt. I guess it saved time not having to decide. One thing Dr. Sampson always ran out of was time. He had never married, except to his job, but never seemed lonely. I have never seen pictures of Dr. Sampson as a young man, but I sensed he was attractive as a shy, rumpled Paul Newman. There was a comfortable look about him making you feel at home with his presence. His glasses continually slipped down his nose, and his shoes had seen the last of their sole lives. I admired him, I was at ease with him, and he with me.

We had a relationship based on mutual respect of our minds, and he found me "refreshing." He would say, "Sam, don't let your physical being get in the way of your brilliance, your inner beauty will last long after your body is gone. I know how everyone looks at you, why you push yourself so hard, but they don't see what I do, your brain and your heart."

When things became stressful and difficult preparing a profile, generally on serial killers, I always endeavored to find some levity to ease the horror, but it had to be levity that was relevant to the case for him to laugh. He would make up words that I would write down in a notebook and smile when he would say them. His mind worked so fast he could create new words, for simple terms. I will cherish this notebook of his funny words. I always look at it when things are crashing in on me.

Working with Dr. Sampson for sixteen years at the Bureau was enlightening, rewarding, and I more than respected the man, I loved him like a father.

TWO

Having just returned to my old, federally, bureau-isk furnished office in downtown DC after Dr. Sampson's funeral, feeling sad and empty of all other emotion I collapsed into my chair. I'd lost a colleague, a friend, and so much more. I felt spent. The cemetery had been cold, icy, and made the process just that much more difficult. I wondered if he was dressed warmly, wearing his tweed. The black I was wearing was an outward reflection of how I felt inside and a sign of things to come. I could still smell his aftershave and looking at his empty office chair only deepened my sorrow. I learned a lot from Dr. Sampson, especially now, not to eat fast food. He would smile at my attempt at a joke.

Special Agent Charlie Falken walked into my office, shut the door, and stood with his hands clasped in front of himself, not looking at me directly. He was well dressed as usual and seemed somber, even for him.

"Are you up for it?"

"For what?" I was confused as to what "it" was. Sometimes "it" meant sex.

"Taking over the profile Dr. Sampson didn't finish on The RESERVATIONS Case. You familiar with it?" Special Agent Falken asked again, looking as though he was bewildered by my silence.

I could not seem to get my mind moving fast enough, having just buried my compass.

"Yes, I assumed I would inherit it." A bit of a whispered response came from my lips.

"Okay then, get on it because another victim has been discovered under similar circumstances." He urgently pushed me with his voice, "We fly out to Montana tomorrow. Be ready."

Special Agent Falken must have realized that I hadn't moved. He slightly turned where he stood. "Dr. Sampson thought you were brilliant, don't let him down."

I looked at Charlie who I have been intimately involved with the last six years, a tear slipped out of my eye and ran down my cheek as he stepped away. I wanted him to hold me, tell me he thought I could do this, but this relationship made things difficult since he was my superior. I was thirty-one when we started our affair, ten years into my job at the Bureau, and Charlie was forty-three. It started when we worked a case together that ended with more than just spilled blood. I think colleagues knew, but no one would say anything because they all had their own secrets. I juggled this relationship with him because often he was my boss, Special Agent Charlie Falken, and other times he was just Charlie.

I worked a profile on my own six years prior, just before Charlie and I were anything more than just coworkers. The BAKER'S DOZEN had fallen into my lap with a thud. The case being headed up by Special Agent Charlie Falken took us on a path neither of us expected. This elusive serial killer had killed thirteen young women the first time around. Each victim had been tortured and died within thirteen days of each other with the number of the killing cut into the palm of each woman's hand postmortem. The killer wanted us to keep track of how many he had gotten away with and how many we had not saved. I have had night sweats, nightmares, and flashbacks about the case that almost killed me and permanently left scars on my legs and my soul since it happened. This old case weighed heavily on my psyche because it had been the first case handed down to me from Dr. Sampson early on in my career here at the Bureau. I bungled it and I feared that could happen again with The RESERVATIONS Case.

I arrived home after a tediously long and draining day, dropped my briefcase and tote on the floor as I shuffled to the bedroom removing my clothing, creating a path of business discards to the bed where I crawled under the covers naked, free of the day. I wanted sleep to escape the sorrow my heart felt yet I feared sleep would take me back to the case that haunts me with emotional and physical pain on an almost nightly basis. I thought about having a beer but could not muster the strength to retrieve it from the fridge all the while pondering the dilemma. Sometimes I feel as though haunting dreams are just your guilt of failure or remorse reminding you of your weaknesses to things that go bump in the night. I felt myself drifting off despite my best efforts to delay sleep as it engulfed me.

It had gone quiet for a year. Initially, we thought the killer might be dead, ill and not able to continue killing in some way. It is not unusual that some serial killers stop and start for various reasons until something triggers them. He was back again after evading capture last time and was already on number twelve, his second set of The BAKER'S DOZEN.

He taunted us. I thought he knew us. Knew me. I worked night and day on the case, wondering if this person knew me because the victims had similarities to my physical appearance. Trying to reconcile all the facts, I looked at my murder boards, went over the profile details, and forensics to see if there were connections I just was not seeing. I went over the autopsies and photos to see if something was there, I just wasn't picking up on. I looked at everything I had access to. At the time, Dr. Sampson happened to be working a case out of state and left me on my own.

The victims were tortured on wooden tables, their feet tied into the stirrups you'd find in any gynecologist's office, with their shoes left on. The victims had been cut from the top of the inner thigh, down the inside of each leg to their knees, and again under each arm, armpit to wrist, as if the killer intended to undress them from their skin. None of the victims had been sexually violated. The victims also suffered burn marks from cigarettes in their genital areas.

The victims' breasts were never touched as though the killer had some affection or fascination for breasts, maybe having been nursed as a baby or longer, breasts were covered with strips of white cloth for what I assumed was modesty. Other than that, and the shoes, the victims were naked. Pieces of paper stuffed into each ear canal possibly prevented them from hearing their own screams except for what reverberated in their heads. The worst torture of all from my perspective, was the fact that they all were repeatedly strangled, just long enough each time for them to pass out, come to, and have it occur all over again until the hyoid bone broke.

The one piece of evidence that hadn't been for public consumption was the paper stuffed in each ear. Each, a piece torn from the daily newspaper showing the date of the killing. The killer didn't want us to miscalculate dates and times of death. He thought we were stupid, and I was starting to think that myself.

The killer, I profiled to be approximately thirty-five to forty years old, a white male with gender identification issues, a smoker, most likely with a religious upbringing, strict house rules, and looking for his mommy who he had probably killed first, years before when he was practicing his methods. We never found any cases matching this style of killing, but he may have evolved over time. He left DNA that wasn't in the system, but we knew he presented as male. He never left fingerprints at the scene, but what he did leave once, presumably by accident in the rush to exit the scene, a high heel shoe print, size twelve, an aroma in the air of cigarette smoke, and perfume. The victims all had smaller feet and from the investigation, none of them smoked. The women were all abducted and found within a couple blocks of Catholic churches.

Exhausted and fearful number thirteen was coming up in a few days, and I had nothing new, nothing to save the next one from this horrible fate. If we didn't stop him this time, he might go underground and retreat again for a while. He had to be stopped now.

Special Agent Falken was losing patience with me even though I had done everything I could, but it's never enough when lives are on the line. It wasn't looking good for my career, his career, or for number thirteen. We had let these victims down. I felt as though the killer has always been one step ahead as if he had insider knowledge. We had checked backgrounds on all those working on or near this case. Visitors were checked, including the cleaning staff. We came up empty. There had to be a leak or an accomplice. It was frustrating.

I had gone through the evidence, the data, and all related materials again, deciding to go out to the scene of number twelve to gain some perspective. Some of the crime scene photos hadn't shown all the angles I needed, leaving me with wanting a personal look around. It left questions in my mind. I left a text for Special Agent Falken that I was headed out to the scene since he didn't pick up his phone.

I was grasping at straws but had to try, since we were running out of time. Two uniforms accompanied me, and I felt safe enough despite the fact I was going to a gruesome crime scene, my weapon holstered in the middle of my back in my waistband. I wore a Kel-Tec P32, 8 shot pistol in my left boot, and a four-inch knife in my right boot. The Bureau frowns on carrying a knife, but I always have since my college days; it was a comfort thing for me. No one knew I had it. I wasn't used to this, being in the field, unnerved and needing comfort.

This locale had a scent of death and a feeling of darkness, evil even. The temperatures were dropping and the area, desolate. All locations had been similar; abandoned warehouses, tombs of concrete, and frigid.

The crime-scene tape was still up, and the scene had not yet been completely broken down. I looked around and in my mind's eye, I could see the last victim in these surroundings. I could feel the bile rise up in my throat. The room large, with concrete floors, walls, and ceilings felt claustrophobic. In the middle of the room stood a wooden table with stirrups set up, blood stains and bodily fluids that release when we no longer have control were on the floor, the table, and walls. Lighting came from the fixtures the crime scene crew brought in, but it still caused shadow casting, making it feel even more creepy.

Looking at the bodies in the ME's office never got to me because I could distance myself, but actually being at the scene was overwhelming, and too real for what the victims went through. I could feel the fear, the desperation, and I could hear their screams.

I was comparing the scene to the photos in my hands and laid out what happened in a time sequence. I was there for a couple of hours, trying to find something so number thirteen wouldn't happen. Squatting down on the floor, I looked up under the table and saw a dirty, faded, worn label from a rental store that had been missed in collection. My mind started working faster, and I couldn't remember any such evidence collected at the other scenes. I made a mental note to have all the other tables checked by the forensics team, and to have Agents check out this rental place. I collected and bagged the new evidence. Trying to call Special Agent Falken to assess him of the new information was futile since my phone didn't have any bars in this concrete box.

I finished my work and noticed the two uniforms were no longer there with me. I looked around the area, shouting for them, but all that was returned to me was silence. I felt ice-cold now, fear gripping me at the instant someone put their hands around my throat, and that was the last I remembered.

"They really do come back to the scene of their crimes," was my first thought when coming to, coughing, hacking, and trying to suck in air to breathe. My neck throbbed, and I was having trouble getting my vision clear. It seemed quiet, too still, until realizing something in my ears prevented me from hearing. Reality set in and I knew number thirteen now had been assigned to me unless I figured out a way to get out of this, grimacing for a second when I realized it was also Friday the thirteenth. The joke wasn't funny, but it was on me.

It's impossible to be calm in panic-mode, and it was impossible to hear if someone was coming or not. All I could hear was the pounding of my own heart. Needing a plan, choking back tears and trying to steady myself consumed me. My mind raced, to figure out my surroundings, my options while laying naked, hot, and tied into the stirrups with my boots on. Looking at my boots my thought came out in a whisper. "What's wrong with this picture? Only cowboys die with their boots on." Nothing seemed real to me. I didn't want to accept reality.

My wrists were tied to the sides of the table with elastic similar to what phlebotomists use to tie around your arm when taking blood. Same as the other scenes. My wrists were bound, and I was losing feeling in my hands. My breasts were covered, and my body was dripping with sweat. The last twelve scenes had the temperature of the winter outside, but this place was so warm. Why the change in scene? The smell now infiltrating my nose — my own fear.

Looking around I realized I wasn't at the scene of number twelve; this place was different. No one would know where I had been taken, heightening my anxiety. My clothes were in a pile on the floor, along with my gun.

This place felt like a humid day in July with temperatures in the nineties, but it had been in the thirties outside, and lightly snowing when leaving the office. There were vibrations as if something heavy was coming—a train, maybe trucks, or even heavy equipment turning on. The table I was tied to shook, a bit, or maybe it was just me shaking with fear. The light over the table glared and only added to the heat of the room. The odor of cigarette smoke mixed with perfume wafted into the room, and then, I felt a hand on my arm.

The hand on my arm belonged to the Bureau Medical Examiner Assistant Michelle Dean, who I later found out, had been born Michael Dean Kilpatrick. Michelle took the paper from my ears and spoke, as if we were having tea, "Let's have a talk before you can't." She continued to smile down at me. "I thought you would have figured this out by now. Everyone thinks you're so brilliant. I had to remove some of the photos from the file, so you would need to come back to the last scene."

I was still trying to get my head around the fact that it was Michelle. Cripes, Michelle is the killer? She stood over me wearing a blue sweater and pant combo. In any other setting, I would have thought, what a nice outfit. I couldn't see her feet, but wondered what she was wearing, maybe size twelve heels. Is this a dream, but it feels awfully real, too real. Michelle had makeup on, which in this heat was melting a bit, but I was not going to tell her that at this point. I didn't often wear makeup, and I didn't know why that would matter just now. My thoughts were all over the place for self-protection.

"We checked everyone close to the case, including you." Croaking out words, my voice hoarse, "No record, no problems in your file. The Bureau is going to look bad on this one."

Michelle laughed, "No problems on this current life of mine, but it would have been different had you known my prior one. It's not that hard to change your life or your identity. Easier than people think."

"You've been an accomplished ME's Assistant for years." My voice was shaking, "Why, why do this? I never knew you were transgender. I don't think anyone does." I was a bit surprised, my voice getting louder and shaking from fear.

She sighed with anticipation. "I've done everything except the last surgery, you know, putting the penis outside in, vaginoplasty. I wish I had your breasts; they're great and real too. Had to buy mine, but they are nice, don't you think?" Admiring herself, she said, "I appreciate breasts, they have such power over men, that's why I never hurt them, I cover them out of respect and regard. I also leave the ladies their shoes, the stirrups can be uncomfortable and cold."

"Funny, that's what my gynecologist says. Awkward if I ever go again."

Michelle was staring at me. "You look just like my mother did, except she had a harder look. You're softer. That's why you were always going to be my last. She's dead a long time now. Michael killed her. I pushed up the timing for you, Sam, opportunity knocked when you went to scene twelve."

It flashed in my mind that my profile had been essentially correct, but Michelle had fucked with the forensics just enough to throw me off, since the DNA and blood tests should have shown a male with elevated female hormone levels. I didn't miss the detail; the specimens had been altered. I've known Michelle for years, and I felt that maybe there was a chance I could talk my way out of this situation without being killed. If that didn't work, I hoped someone would be looking for me.

Michelle held a scalpel in her hand, tapping it on my leg as though assessing how to start. I've seen her in autopsy, and she is swift with a blade. I was hoping not to be on the receiving end of it.

Michelle was looking over my body. "Didn't know you went native, natural down there, Sam."

"I get busy."

I needed to distract her from cutting me. I needed time. "Michelle, didn't know you smoked."

She laughed, "Only in social situations." She regarded me, admiringly, "You have very long legs." Before I knew what was happening, she had cut me from the top inside of my thigh to my knee on my left leg, stopping just above my boot. The blade was so sharp I hardly felt pain for a couple of seconds, but then the pain set in, and the bleeding was profuse, making me reel.

She said in a matter-of-fact tone, "Go ahead and scream if you want, I know it hurts, but no one will hear you except me. I want us to have some quality time together tonight. I always wanted to have a friend like you, but you were always too busy, and I liked that you reminded me of Michael's mother." It was as though she were lamenting with old memories still fresh in her mind.

The pain was intense, and I tried to avoid thinking about how badly this was going for me. I think I missed this class in training, "How not to die."

"I didn't cut any arteries, it will be a slow bleed out," she said in a crazy comforting way.

Michelle could see I was in pain and put her hands on my throat. I tried to struggle, but she was strong and kept pressing until I passed out again.

I came to, blinking with the harsh light, trying to calculate how much time had passed, wondering if next time I would come back at all. I never thought about my own life and death before. My thoughts were always about the victims I dealt with every day, somebody else's human connection.

"I gave you a little time away from feeling the pain and your fears. Feel better?"

I coughed, then in a stammering, small voice, I asked, "Where did you learn this choke hold routine?"

"You know it's used in erotica sexual play—it heightens the orgasm. Well, if you live through it. I learned it from the ME when he explained a case he was working on. Who knew I'd use it one day. Pays to listen," Michelle explained, then looked at my natural hair down there and winked, "How's your sex life?"

I was a bit foggy and trying to gather myself together. I whispered, "Michelle, I've never been very religious, but maybe I should think about that now."

She laughed with a look on her face as if she were lost in memory. "Michael was brought up Catholic and was an altar boy until those priests decided he should be more than that to them. He tried to tell mother, but she believed the priests over Michael."

I could see tears in Michelle's eyes talking about Michael's difficult upbringing. I quipped to lighten things up. "I'm a POC."

She looked at me perplexed, "a POC?"

"Yeah, a pissed-off Catholic. I guess that's why I don't have a religious penchant in my life, but I'm thinking I should learn a prayer about now."

Michelle sadly smiled. "I hear you girl. I like that."

I was trying to stall, the more I talked to her and hoped that if someone was looking for me, they would have more time. "Michelle, what is the significance of thirteen killings?" I doubted she would answer but she did.

"Michael was thirteen when he killed mother. She should have listened about those priests. What kind of mother is it who won't believe her own kid?" Michelle was losing focus and sounding impatient.

Asking another question, just to postpone time moving forward. "Why the time delay between the sets of killings?"

"I was taking hormones, going through some surgeries, and getting my breasts. I couldn't do both, but now I'm back at my calling."

I was sweating and was feeling light-headed as though I was going to pass out from the blood loss. "Water?"

"You're in hell honey, there's no water here."

I was trying to focus on the profile I wrote so that I could find a way to sway her from continuing down the path that would eventually kill me. "What about your dad, Michelle?" Instantly, my right leg was cut as the left had been. I cried out, tears splashing out of my eyes. My breath coming in pants felt like suffocation.

Michelle raged, "Don't ever mention my father. It makes me angry. That man always told Michael he was weak, that he was ashamed of him, because he acted like a girl, not a man."

It's a crazy thing looking at your own legs, seeing the blood, and thinking, "Those can't be my legs." I could smell the blood now, sickly sweet mixed with acrid sweat, and possibly some urine, embarrassed that my body had betrayed me a bit, laughing to myself, "Dignity out the window."

My head wasn't held down by anything, but it felt weighted, and I was getting so weak and couldn't lift it. I needed to stay lucid. I needed to keep thinking how to save myself.

Tears streaming down my face because the pain was unbearable, and I didn't know for sure how long it would take me to bleed out or lose consciousness. It was so hot in this place that the sweat mixing with the blood was making the table slippery. I hoped I wouldn't pass out, but it wasn't my choice. Michelle had her hands on my neck again.

I slowly regained awareness, but kept my eyes closed. My head was spinning. I didn't know how much time had passed, and desperately needed to think. I could hear her, but she didn't sound close. Forcing myself to inventory my situation; bleeding, in a lot of pain, and sensing the inside of my throat constricting. Was I going into shock? I was shaking, sometimes even chilled in this hot place.

I had a gun in one boot, a knife in the other, and needing to get to one of them. I knew she hadn't found them because I could still feel their weight. I moved my wrists to see if I had any feeling in my hands, to have the ability to shoot or use a knife. I felt my right wrist move. The sweat and blood gave my bindings some wiggle room. If I could just get one wrist out, I might be able to save myself.

I opened my eyes and saw Michelle across the room smoking, looking away from me, and I knew what was next: cigarette burns. She hadn't noticed that I had come to yet; I had to make my move quickly and without screwing it up. I was so weak, my body shaking, but I only had one chance to muster up what was left of me and try to save myself, or at least stop her.

My service revolver was in Michelle's hand, as though she was admiring it. She held it up, looking at all sides of it as if she was figuring out how to use it. She was just buying time until I came to. It was also at that instant she saw I was awake.

I pulled my right wrist as hard and quickly as I could to release it from the binding. I reached for the knife in my right boot as Michelle pointed my gun at me. I chose a knife in a gunfight, and I was going to be killed by my own service revolver.

"Shit."

The blade was out and as Michelle took aim at me—in that instant, the door opened, and Special Agent Falken entered. Michelle spun around, startled, and pulled the trigger, hitting Charlie in the shoulder. He returned fire and shot her in the head.

You always must shoot them in the head, or they will come back. I learned that at the movies, I thought to myself, amused.

The look on her face was one of disbelief as she dropped to the floor. I was getting sleepy now, dropping the knife, not feeling pain any longer and the lighting was becoming dimmer.

Charlie staggered, slumping against the wall. Charlie's partner, John, ran in, kicked the gun away, and came over to me after checking to confirm the killer was dead. He didn't know it was Michelle at that point—that came later. I saw Charlie on the floor, his gray suit had a hole in it with blood coming out of it. "That is not going to come out," I said aloud. "I liked that suit." I was feeling faint and still bound to the table by my left wrist and both feet. I was looking at Charlie, he was looking at me, and at that instant, I gave up, and let myself go.

I woke with a start, covered in sweat, my sheets drenched with my emotions. I could feel I had been crying as I touched my cheeks, tears dried in place and as I attempted to raise myself from the bed, my body was heavy, filled with dread, insecurity, and sadness. The past made itself known again because I was vulnerable with raw feelings and dread, it had robbed me of myself in my sleep. Before I could steady myself on shaking legs, I fell to my knees sobbing and there I stayed until the alarm clock reminded me that it was another day to be without Dr. Sampson.

CHAPTER
THREE

Working in the office late into the night, tired and frustrated, attempting to get everything together to take out of town the next day for The RESERVATIONS Case, and I still had to go home to pack cold-weather clothing for the trip. I was trying to avoid home and sleep after last night's unrest. I knew I couldn't outrun the demons but hoped one day I'd give them the slip.

My home when I was there was a small apartment until the probate on Dr. Sampson's house was finalized having inherited his house. Apparently, he had no one else to leave his life to except me and had arranged it when he found out months earlier that he did not have long to live with the heart that he had. The house came with everything he owned, frozen in time and a treasure trove of findings while being amazingly tidy. The colonial townhouse was in Georgetown, DC, gray with white trim and a black door. I was still getting used to the idea of having my own house. Dr. Sampson had thought of me as family, a daughter, and that meant everything to me.

Back in the office at the Bureau I had shared with him, sometimes I could pick up the scent of his cologne and feel his presence when I used his books or sat in his big chair. He was still here amongst his things. These things gave me great comfort but still reminded me of the sadness of loss. Papers he wrote were here. His thoughts and insights hovered here. I would pick up a book to read and see the notations he made in the margins. Yesterday, I found a safe deposit box key in his desk but was not up to finding out what it contained. It was too soon.

Hearing footsteps coming down the hall to my dingy office, caused my heart to beat faster as I felt for my gun in the desk drawer. No one should be in the building at this hour. The footsteps stopped. There, shown a shadow in the glass of the door and then it opened.

"Fuck, Charlie, you scared me to death," I growled. "I could have shot you!"

"You should keep the door locked when you're here alone," Charlie shook his head with a soft retort. "I went by your place. I figured you'd be packing for tomorrow."

"What time is the flight and where are we going? Where was the body found?"

Charlie answered, looking preoccupied, "Ashland, Montana, details in the morning." His tie was undone, the top button of his shirt open. He looked as if he was on the prowl, he had a shadow beard and smelled of beer. To me, this night, he looked like he needed something. That something was me.

"I like your suit, new?" I mused not really knowing what to say, just filling in the awkward silence.

While sitting at my desk as Charlie slowly, deliberately walked over, and stood behind me putting his hands on my shoulders, massaging them, while making an observation, "You look tired. I haven't seen you alone for weeks."

"Just been working, you know that." I think he was wondering if I had a social life other than his visits. I didn't.

I rolled my head, trying to feel the benefit of the shoulder rub when his hands slid to my breasts. I was looking at his hands, his long, manicured fingers, teasing my breasts from on top of my sweater. Men's hands are one of my favorite things when they keep them groomed. My breath caught, and I knew this was going to go Charlie's way, whether I was tired or not. He slowly spun my chair around to face him, and there in my sightline was his maleness, already hard and trying to escape the restraints of his trousers. He instantly pulled me to my feet by my upper arms and began kissing my lips, teasing with his tongue. His need was increasing, frantic.

He kissed with his eyes closed, masking any emotion other than lust. Charlie tasted of beer. He must have stopped after work for one, maybe more. The first kiss was tender, lingering, but then I could feel the momentum of his urgency; the kisses became harder and deeper, a preview of other things to come. I could feel his tongue probing deeper into my mouth, and his hardness pushing against my leg. I was too tired to fight it, and at this point, I wanted it as much as he did. I wanted solace from my sadness and loss.

Charlie slipped a hand under my sweater and cupped my breast. A moan escaped. I think it came from me. Using his thumb, he softly played with my nipple. He pulled the front of my sweater up, unclasped my bra, and without missing a beat had his mouth on my opposite breast. His tongue was hot. I was getting warm, and my nipples were pronounced, seeking more attention. My breasts and nipples are my Achilles' heel, I go weak when it comes to them, and Charlie knew that. He loved my ample, natural breasts and spent a lot of time on them. That was just fine with me.

Just the touch from him on my breasts, I felt warmth and moisture at my clit as if these two parts of my body were physically connected and simultaneously reacting to each other. He was preparing me. I could already smell his sex.

He stopped and began taking his clothes off, looking at me as I attempted to pace my breathing, leaning against my desk. I liked watching him remove his clothes, revealing parts of himself, and making me hungry for other parts yet to come. Charlie was muscular, but it was subtle. He wore clothes well, but I liked it more when he didn't wear any at all.

It didn't take long. He was naked and hard. I stood there waiting for his move, his manhood, red purple with intensity. He stood there for a moment to let me take it all in. He looked so good, and I wanted him. I just wanted it. He touched himself to increase his size and to offer it to me. Charlie was above average, but tonight, maybe because we hadn't been together for a while, he looked larger, and I could see a pearl of moisture at the tip. He was already coming a little. He couldn't wait.

He came towards me and started removing my sweater and bra, biding his time, admiring what was there for his taking. Next came my pants. By the time he got to the panties, he tore them off. Had I waxed down there? Too late now.

"Sorry, I'll owe you a pair," he smiled. "God, your body is amazing, Sam, you're perfect." He moaned.

He had me naked, except for my boots. He ran his hands over my shape, admiring, wanting, and finding my wetness. He touched me and I shivered. My hands caressed him, but he liked being in charge and to make all the moves resisting any of mine.

"Musky." He smiled as he sniffed his finger. "You always just smell like you, real."

I went to remove my new boots, but he shook his head. "No, leave them on." A thought flashed through my mind. I kicked the boots off, left the lights on, and locked the door. For a moment, I thought of the old boots, years in a box in an evidence locker, never to be seen again. He looked at me, seemed to remember and winced for his insensitivity.

There was an old leather couch in my office, this office I had shared with Dr. Sampson, and in an instant, I was splayed on the couch with Charlie above me, my legs open to him, wrapped around his back. The head of him teasing me until I lost patience. "Just fuck me, will you?"

We didn't use a condom because Charlie had had a vasectomy and that saved a bit of time. As he got into his rhythm, the leather squeaked, gaining a cadence with us. The movement on the couch exhaled a familiar aftershave aroma, that of my mentor, Dr. Sampson. I thought to myself, he must be rolling over in his grave, shielding his eyes from what we are doing on his old couch. Things became a bit frenzied as Charlie's thrusts became more intense, and I was trying to get there, to reach my pleasure there.

Charlie was handsome, had blondish hair with just a dusting of vaguely visible gray he acquired since I came to the Bureau ten years ago. He had ample size to pleasure but never looked me in the eyes during sex as if there was a distance, he wanted to keep between us. It took a little of the excitement out, made it a little sad. I don't think he ever knew my eyes were two different colors.

He shifted my hips and was deep inside me now. I could feel his heat, and the pace was getting faster, more urgent. He came with such a rush of himself that he could barely speak. "Sorry, I couldn't wait," he apologized with a shortness of breath, his heart pounding. "Sorry." He laid his cheek on my breast.

I had almost been there, I thought. "Crap."

Charlie came fast and furious because it had been a while since we last had sex. He would sometimes finish for himself and then spend more time on my needs, which he did now. He hoped to have a second go at a slower pace for both of us later. It was his MO, his pattern of self-recrimination and my test of patience.

In a flash of movement, he sat me on his lap, facing him, my legs open so he could lick and kiss my nipples while fingering me. It was effective, and the surges came. He touched me tenderly, putting more fingers inside of me, adding more pressure with his thumb against my clit until he could feel me quake.

Charlie was the only one who had seen my scars, even though I think he tries to avoid looking at them. His emotions are complex. The scars were healed and faded a bit, but they were there on my legs and in my mind.

He arched me back using one hand to stroke me across my breasts and stomach while he was kissing me at my center. I was gasping and coming. I was wet with orgasm. For now, I had forgotten about the scars.

I hung my arms around Charlie's neck to steady myself. We were covered in sweat and wanting more. We stayed like this for a short while. No sweet whispers, no looking into each other's eyes, just a quieting of our panting, waiting for him to get hard again. My heart never beat in unison with Charlie's. It was a sequence so familiar to me. It was just carnal, plain and simple.

When he was ready again, he slipped into me smoothly, slowly, as I sat facing him. I held onto his shoulders, seeing the bullet scar I had cost him. He helped me accelerate with his hands on my waist, lifting me with each probe of himself. He took his time until we both came.

We disconnected, depleted, and tried to catch a breath. Sex with Charlie was always satisfying, but it wasn't love or passion. It was just sex with no commitment. A release. Charlie and I both had commitment issues, and this worked for us. I know he didn't see other people. He didn't have enough of himself to share with more than one person. Nor did I. There was no time in my life for additional complications. Charlie liked me, but I don't think he loved me, and I didn't love him. Sometimes I didn't even like him.

We were done and done in. Packing was still to be finished and now I needed a shower. I made a mental note to wipe down the couch before I left. We got dressed, and I went home. Charlie went to wherever he goes when he doesn't go home. He can't go home because they aren't there.

Charlie lives alone, and I have never seen his place. He doesn't like being there except to shower, sleep fitfully, and change clothes. In the six years, we've had this ritual, I've learned some things about Charlie's past. He lost his wife and two kids in a car accident eighteen years prior, the year before I was hired. He still hasn't gotten over it or through it. He may never. I don't think he can look into my eyes when we have sex because I believe he feels he is betraying her. Charlie's taken a bullet for me, but he will never give me his heart, it still belongs to her. He had the vasectomy so he would never have other children. The dead for Charlie, are never gone.

The morning came too soon, and packing was finally done. It was the middle of winter, and I packed for the cold. I stopped by the office and retrieved The RESERVATIONS Case files as well as my laptop, to check comparisons with the current crime scene. I would need the forensics and crime scene photos of the latest victim but would get those in Montana and put the briefing together there. I caught a cab and headed to the airport. I figured I could sleep a bit on the plane, at least I hoped. The Bureau's jet was loaded with equipment and personnel for the case. I settled into a comfortable seat, but sleep eluded me. All I could do was think about the case, last night with Charlie, and the fact that I had to go home without underwear on. I think I was pissed off.

The flight from DC to Montana was uneventful, and I had a lot of time to process my thoughts. Being alone with your thoughts for an extended length of time, well, you can either convince yourself that you're okay with how things are, or these pesky thoughts can convince you to change your life. I chose the latter.

Charlie sat on the other side of the plane directly across from me but hadn't looked my way. He managed to converse with the Agent next to him to avoid my eyes. I didn't know if it was avoidance, guilt, or maybe both. It was all business now, and that suited me.

It was fortuitous that Dr. Sampson and I had shared an office for sixteen years, so I knew his filing system and protocols. He was quirky in his own way, but precise in his note-taking, and explicit in details. He had been old-school, counting more on his brain than a computer. I had been working on The RESERVATIONS Case Profile with him, and it was an ugly case that made even Dr. Sampson comment, "This is the most abhorrent one I've seen in my career. We have to be perfect with this." Then with his eyes red and moist, he said, "We have to get this guy." Dr. Sampson never got emotionally invested in cases. "It will rob you of your life," he always reminded me, but this case gave him pause. This case killed him in a way the fast food alone couldn't. It robbed him of his hope about humanity.

Memories of him warmed me to the brilliant man he was, but the loss would catch in my throat from time to time. I would resist the urge to revisit those times again, and I would force my focus on the case, hoping to make him proud.

The RESERVATIONS Case is a serial killer profile that has been going on for months. Every time the FBI got close, the killer would evade capture, and nothing would happen. Then it would start up again at another reservation in another state without a trackable time frame that made any sense. The FBI called in Dr. Sampson a couple of months before his death since no one else had been able to get close to the killer's identity or his trail. If anyone could do this, Dr. Sampson could, but he was gone now. Now it was up to me. I have worked dozens of cases with Dr. Sampson, but this was only my second case solo in the last six years. The last one not having gone so well. I was not particularly confident.

Dr. Sampson had been to all the other reservations relating to the case, and the Tribes all had great affection for him because he treated them with respect and with a sense of awe. He had known all the details intimately. I now had to catch up and do the same. The last notation made by Dr. Sampson underlined in red asked, "How did the killer know the victims' birthdates?"

It was complicated, intricate. The murders were complex and had been occurring on Indian reservations all over the American Southwest, and now the latest one was in Montana on the Cheyenne Reservation near Ashland.

The victims were all boys who disappeared on or around their twelfth birthdays. Dr. Sampson had been the one who found that correlation. The victims lived on different reservations, yet the scenes were similar, and the methodology the same. Not even Dr. Sampson had come up with the motive. The why was always the most difficult to determine with serial killers. They can be motivated and triggered by slight, to us insignificant, switches. Sometimes the why is never found, but I had to get close enough with forensics and our profile, so that I could determine where the killer would strike next. My best bet was to find out which boys on what reservations had birthdays coming up, when they would turn twelve, and get there before the killer.

The reservations are large, and it is a huge undertaking to track and find people, much less any clues that nature in Montana can mess with. The Tribes resented having the Feds on their lands but were outraged by the killings. They all knew of Dr. Sampson, and that gave me an inside advantage since he had talked to them when he worked the scenes, and since he had worked with these people in the past, there was some trust established. I hoped that would be extended to me.

Uppermost in my mind was to respect their traditions, be mindful of their losses, but to do my job no matter who I had to bulldoze to get it done, and get it done fast.

It gets convoluted. The FBI must work with the Tribal Police because they can't work on felony cases on their own reservations, and local LEOs (Law Enforcement Officers) who aren't on the reservations, are needed as support to work a case like this in adjoining counties to clean up spillover when killers cross state lines and boundaries. We needed cooperation from everyone, egos in check. These were young boys being killed and anyone who couldn't put aside "who's in charge" would have to deal with me, even though Special Agent Falken was in command. This case made me angry for so many reasons that I needed to use this anger and focus it on the killer.

The plane landed in Ashland, Montana at a private airfield the Bureau could use. Ashland is a small town with a census population of around 460, some of which are Mennonite. It is east of the boundary of the Northern Cheyenne Reservation. The body had been found near the Custer National Forest on the Cheyenne Reservation. Without a minute to take stock of what the ramifications of this case would be for me, the work began in my head. Lives were on the line, and these lives belonged to young boys.

CHAPTER

FIVE

I exited the plane and stepped onto the tarmac. The frigid temperature hit me in the face so severely that I could barely catch my breath. Thankfully, there were cars waiting with heaters running, because I don't think I could have walked very far in such weather. The equipment and files were loaded, and we headed to The Lodge that would be the center of our operations. I was a city girl, and this was a bit out of my comfort range being in this part of the country.

This case, complex as it was, was going to be even more complicated by the weather conditions, which were expected to deteriorate, bringing high winds and freezing snow. I hoped the crime scene had been preserved, but it started looking doubtful to me. This was Montana in the dead of winter. The killings had been as cold as the weather. It was only a matter of time before the killer would strike again and this time, I had to stop him. My prayer was that the weather would slow the killer down and give me time to find him. December in Montana is relentless.

We were going to meet with a Cheyenne guide at The Lodge, (yes, it was called The Lodge, just outside of Ashland), one familiar with the reservation and who would hopefully take us to the scene where the remains were found. I would have to convince him to return there with me in tow since he was the one who found the body, along with a couple of hunters he had been guiding at the time. His Cheyenne culture would prevent the contamination of this now sacred site, sacred to his Tribe, sacred to him and his beliefs.

Dr. Sampson's notes had enlightened me as to the enormity of this case as it crossed cultural, religious, historical, scientific, and moral lines with the final duty being the takedown of the individual responsible for this reign of terror.

I don't know what men hunt or fish for in the dead of winter, but I would think it would flash freeze. This was the last of the hunters and gatherers for the year. The weather would soon keep everyone away.

As I walked through The Lodge and absorbed the surroundings, I made notes in my mind. Will Little Bear would be our guide. He was a guide, tracker, and the owner of The Lodge at the edge of the reservation. It boasted a karaoke bar and grille. I smiled. I like to sing, but another time. I shook my head as I realized my thoughts were not in sync with my reason for being here. I was trying to see the normality of this place and frame the killing around it.

You could hear the attempts at singing from the few hunters who were trying to get the mental pictures of the remains out of their memories by drinking way too much and being way too loud. I understood, but I knew it would never leave their minds. Despite Will Little Bear not wanting to go back there, I needed to convince him otherwise, regardless of spirits of the dead and it being a sacred place now. I wanted to be respectful and to understand his beliefs, but I also had to make sure nothing was missed or mishandled when they came across the site. The local Tribal Police had gotten to the area before the Bureau guys, and I wasn't sure what I would find. I needed to talk to everyone and visit the site myself.

This time of year, The Lodge wasn't crowded with tourists, just some die-hard hunters and people who must really like being alone in the cold. The Lodge was nice, clean, and rustic, just perfect for this location and decorated with forest trees, animal ornaments, the traditions of its owner, and the colors associated with the Christmas holidays that I had forgotten were coming. Always play to your clients' holiday beliefs and add in some souvenirs. The Lodge would be closed from the week before Christmas until the end of February. I could see myself in warmer weather taking in the scenery, but all I came here for was to look at a grave site where a boy had been buried, but who now occupied a drawer at the FBI's ME's lab. My task: try to catch a killer before another boy became a victim.

We all were given our own rooms and there was a Meeting Room available to set up as our "Murder Room." The Murder Room was where I would set up whiteboards with all the details of the murders, including photos, forensics, and anything of pertinence to use at the briefing for all of Law Enforcement coming tomorrow morning.

My room was small and cozy with log walls. A double bed took up the majority of the room with a dream catcher above the headboard. There was a small dresser and a desk, with a chair made from limbs and branches. I wasn't going to sit there. Limbs, my mind always went to the physical. My attention went to the down comforter on the bed while looking around for a fireplace or heater. The room was cool, and I didn't see a thermostat.

The bathroom was small, but nice, with a shower, but no tub. The towels were thick; there was a bar of soap and tiny bottles of shampoo and conditioner. Some stuffed fish were on the walls as decorations. The floor was hardwood, with an area rug that looked like an Indian blanket. I settled in and pulled a warm sweater out of my luggage, before I headed over to set up the Murder Room boards. It was early afternoon, but the sun wasn't out. It seemed as if darkness was right around the corner. I was hungry, but work needed to be the priority.

Charlie stopped by my room to see what my accommodations were like. "My room looks the same, except I have small animals mounted on my walls. If you get cold, I'm down the hall." He offered with the same look as our last time together.

I was here to work, and Charlie wanted to combine business with his pleasure. My only thought was on finding a killer and stopping him. "I don't think there will be much time for sleeping." What I really wanted to say was, it would be colder in his room than in mine.

"Who's talking about sleeping? By the way, we don't get to talk to the guide and owner of this establishment until morning when he gets back from town."

"That gives me time to set up for a morning briefing. I understand his name is Will Little Bear and he's the best around, or so I have been told, plus he's already been at the site."

Charlie asked while trying to move closer to me, "Is he the one who discovered the body?"

I backed up. "Yep, I hear he isn't too keen on going back based on his Reservation's religious beliefs." I wondered if Will Little Bear would work with us, if not, I'd have to figure out another way to get to the site.

I had Googled Will Little Bear, and he is the stuff legends are made of. Not only is he a world-class tracker, guide, and hunter, but a security expert as well. He is a marksman and sniper from his time in the Marines. As a Silver Star recipient, he saved two men from his unit by carrying them both out of a firefight. He earned a Purple Heart for shrapnel he took to the chest.

Google offered photos reflecting that he is quite the ladies' man and prefers them in their twenties. He is Cheyenne and a respected member of the Tribe. Will Little Bear has lived in the area his entire life, which is now nearing forty-two years. He never married, but considers all Cheyenne his family, and all Cheyenne children his own.

He is a Cheyenne traditionalist with progressive leanings. Some of the local news stories and posts reported he built The Lodge around ten years ago when he returned from Iraq. He has made a name for himself as an entrepreneur and as a pillar of the community. Everyone likes Will Little Bear, and from what I could tell in photos women seem to love him.

We were going to need him to get us to the site, and I hoped the hype was real. Foul weather was moving in—blizzard-like snow, high winds, and bitter cold. This was going to be difficult. I had no idea of what the site was going to look like now, or if we could even get there.

SIX

I had help from the other Agents on this case setting up the five white-boards in The Lodge's Meeting Room, our designated Murder Room. I needed to work alone now to set up the details for the meeting tomorrow morning. It was important that I communicated to everyone the classification of the killer, methods or modus operandi, the evidence, forensics, and the profile so that everyone understood what we were up against. I also needed them to know the faces and names of the victims, these boys, showing them the young lives that were lost, and why we were here. These boys were alive not so long ago, with dreams and desires, and I wasn't going to let that get lost in the grim details.

There was a whiteboard for each victim and one blank board for the one we were trying to prevent. The fifth board was for my conclusions and new "clues" I would endeavor to come up with on this trip. I made each board consistent, but individual to each victim, with photographs of the victims and the recovery sites. There were autopsy highlights, victim profiles, police reports, and witness statements. I needed to integrate all of this information into something the local LEOs, the Tribal Police, and even my own Agents would understand. How did this killer plan his crimes, display control over the victims? Perhaps, by using social skills. I needed to break it down, assimilating all of it into one plan to give them while trying to answer all their questions. Was this killer organized or simply taking advantage of circumstances? Were the murders opportunistic, impulsive, or well thought out? Were they premeditated? What was the killer's sexual behavior? What was the best information to go on? I had to have answers. I needed to give the team hope that this killer could and must be stopped.

I reconstructed the scenes, noting the similarities and differences. What was his signature? The signature is idiosyncratic; it is what the killer does to satisfy his psychological or sexual needs by committing the crime. His mental and physical need to want to continue to do it, repeatedly, committing additional killings, is the why.

I looked at the staging of the sites, the demographic details of the killer, physical characteristics and background if possible—anything and everything to make a mental image of this guy and what his next step would be. It was important to see if the locations and the murders linked, and what type of offender he was. Where was the impulse from?

My report to the Agents and Law Enforcement personnel the next day had to be reliable and empirically tested, giving them a profile that would stand up so they would have a clear focus of who we were looking for. It was critical to give them the smallest of details that might lead to someone not considered before.

I worked until two in the morning putting everything in order so that the briefing, even though it would be long, would be precise, and no time would be wasted. I printed out information for all sectors of law enforcement to take along and refer to in the field, and what tasks they would be assigned to help find the killer before he left us another victim. Everyone had like-minded skin in this game whether they were the Tribal Police, local LEOs, or my own troop of Feds.

While working, I had a feeling that someone had been peering into the room and watching me. I had felt something, but when I turned around, there was no one there. I figured I was feeling anxious, and my imagination was overworking. I hit the snack machines before heading to my room, hoping I would sleep. I had a headache, and this case was not going to give me any relief.

Will saw a light under the Meeting Room door and decided to check it out before turning in for the night. He had been out all-day getting supplies before the weather turned fouler. He was cold and tired. He also hated the fact that he had to get up early for some meeting with some Special Agent from the FBI, who wanted him to go back to that place. He opened the door a few inches and saw a woman standing in front of a bunch of whiteboards. She looked absorbed in what they said. She turned as if she felt his presence, and for a few seconds, he saw her face. He had never seen a more beautiful woman in his life. He didn't think she saw him. He noticed his breath was coming faster. He remembered when he saw "The Godfather" movie, where Al Pacino sees a woman and immediately falls in love. The men around him joked, "You just got struck by a thunderbolt." Will laughed to himself. "Women always ask, why do men always think of Godfather references?" He shook his head. Down deep he knew it wasn't a joke; he felt something for this woman he just saw.

Will Little Bear liked women, but most of them didn't fit his own sensibilities. He liked a natural woman; not much makeup, no fake nails, no plastic surgery enhancements, self-confident, not needy, and above all, hair down there. Why does a woman want to look prepubescent? Be a woman. He had a fitful sleep and had a vision that centered around this woman he had seen for only seconds. He needed to think about that. He believed in visions. It was early, and the meeting was set for eight a.m. Right now, he needed coffee.

Around seven a.m. the local LEOs, the Tribal Police, and my Agents were slowly showing up at The Lodge dining room for a quick breakfast before the meeting. Some had traveled far in this inclement weather to attend my briefing, and they hoped they weren't wasting their time. They wanted to get back to their counties before the weather deteriorated later in the day. The weather had been unusually harsh for this time of year, and it was causing havoc.

I thought, they better eat now. After I finish with my briefing, no one will be hungry.

They weren't sure what I was going to tell them, but they did know about the reservation murders and were anxious to prevent any more. They were here because they didn't want this killer breaking precedent and start killing in their counties. These guys were from rough country, and they had seen a lot of things in their careers, but they might not be ready for what I was about to describe.

I went back to my room with the same headache from last night and readied myself for the day. To top it off, I'd had strange dreams with an arithmetic trick of "1+1=1" in it. I decided to downplay what I wore so that the details of the crimes were the only things they would notice. I put on black jeans, a black thermal shirt, black boots, and fashioned my hair into a ponytail. I didn't put any makeup on and even though it was impossible, I tried to hide my physical assets. Why do I care about the image I project? I survive a man's world by being objective about myself and it goes to the essence of who I am because what I project to the world despite what is the reality of my soul enables me to do my job. I did wear the only pair of earrings I owned, my garnets. I didn't feel wearing the usual FBI suit attire would go far with these guys, and I didn't want to come across as too significant. I needed to relate to them, get them pulled into the case without feeling coerced by rank or Agency.

I entered the Meeting Room as people were starting to work their way in. I had set up four-to-a-table, so they could take notes and be comfortable for something that would take their comfort away. Coffee and water were available, and it was now time to ruin their day. This room was geared towards business with no niceties of decorative softness to take the sharp edges off why we were here. It seemed utilitarian in its effect. The last one to come in sat in the back alone. I assumed it was Will Little Bear, since he fit the description, I had seen in photos online. He was dressed all in black, mimicking my attire. I was glad he came to the briefing because I had to convince him to take me back to the site where the remains had been discovered.

Charlie and the other Agents were to my right. When I looked at Charlie, he signaled me to get started. His look gave me confidence in what I was about to do. Charlie was the Special Agent in Charge, but what I had to say was what everyone came here for.

"Hello, my name is Special Agent Samantha Wright. I'm a Profiler with the FBI, more precisely, the NCAVC, The National Center for Analysis of Violent Crime and I've been brought in with my colleagues and Agent in Charge, Special Agent Charlie Falken to brief you on what we've designated The RESERVATIONS Case." I continued, my voice strong and accustomed to giving these presentations. "In support positions are Special Agent John Thomas, in charge of Logistics and Agent Randall Johnson, our Technical Specialist and Communications Director. If you can hold your questions until the end, it would be appreciated. We have a lot to get through, all of it is important and essential to accomplishing our goal, which is to prevent another death—to find the killer and apprehend him. Your trip here will not be a waste of your time."

Will was in the back thinking it was going to be worthless talk. He decided to stick it out because he didn't want any more killings on his reservation. If she had the way for that not to happen, he would listen. It didn't hurt that she was eye candy and he had nothing better to do for the next four hours. He could tell Special

Agent Wright was trying to hide her physical assets, but it wasn't working. She had a great body and the men in the room noticed.

"I know some of you worked with and knew my mentor, Dr. Edmond Sampson. He worked with many of you in the past, and I am sure gained your respect for what a Profiler can add to make Law Enforcement's job have more clarity and focus on certain circumstances. Dr. Sampson was called in after other Profilers and Law Enforcement were unable to identify or stop this serial killer. He made significant strides, in a brief length of time on this case. I worked with Dr. Sampson for sixteen years and this case now falls to me to bring it to fruition."

I looked around the room, and knew I had to fill some big shoes and hopefully gain their respect. I was no Dr. Sampson but was the best the Bureau had. Without their respect, they would not accept my analysis and findings. They would not follow through if they didn't think I had the facts right. As a room full of men looked to me for clarity as to why they were here, I again realized I was the lone woman in a sea of male-dominated law enforcement. I have an audience of men that don't think a brain can exist in a beautiful vessel. It was hard to be taken seriously, and I was if anything, serious. It was this way here due to the rugged areas we were dealing with and the cowboy mindset in this part of the country. I looked at them and saw the history of this country and the men who settled it for good and for bad.

"I am going to introduce you to the victims first. (Say their names over and over again, to make them alive and real as possible was the mantra in my head, my prayer for these boys.) I will then go over autopsy findings, forensics, site descriptions, locations, and follow it up with a profile of the perp, since all the murders have similar characteristics."

I started. Board One. "The victim is Jon Eagle Fletcher, twelve years old, of the Arapahoe Tribe. The victim was found on the Arapahoe Reservation in the State of Colorado, on October 5th of this year. This killing took place approximately one month prior to that, based on the ME's estimation of time of death." This was going to be more agonizing than I thought. "Jon's body had not been found for almost a month after death due to the weather and the hostile environment it was found in. Please refer to your photos of Jon prior to the abduction, in his school photo and then in his autopsy photo.

"Jon had just turned twelve years old on September 3rd, was the pride of his local soccer team, and excelled in school. Jon wanted to be a gym teacher when he grew up. Jon was abducted four days before his birthday and was taken from his neighborhood while walking to the store for his mother. Jon comes from loving parents who want justice for their son."

I had to make these tough men in front of me know who these victims were so that they would work harder and faster to prevent another child from becoming a victim to the killer. They would have to relate to these boys and put everything from their experience into finding this killer. I had to make the lifeless photographs in their packets come to life. I had to make these young boys their young boys. I was going to drill these names into their memories, so they would never forget what these boys had given up, their young lives.

I could see Will Little Bear sit a little straighter in his chair. He was looking at the photos in his packet. His attention was now on these boys and how he could play a part in not letting this happen again. This is what I needed to happen for him to take me back to this recent site.

I continued. "The Tribal Police were called in when a neighbor informed them that he had seen a young man fitting Jon's description talking to a white man. The neighbor reported that white people don't come to his neighborhood, and it caught his attention. The neighbor lost sight of them at the edge of the woods and didn't know where they had gone. He remembered Jon wearing a brown coat, faded blue jeans, and a wool cap. He did not remember much about the white male except he was not much taller than Jon, who measured 5'4" and 105 pounds. The neighbor would have stopped but had to pick up his little girl from daycare. The witness gave a statement which is in your packet. There are no other witnesses nor has anyone else come forward despite efforts by the Tribal Police and the community to find Jon. At the time of discovering Jon's body, a month later, the Police concluded it was an isolated incident. We know now that Jon was the first victim."

I moved to Board Two. "The second victim is Chad Owens, twelve years old, a member of the Navajo Tribe. An extensive search on the Navajo Reservation in Arizona took place by the Tribal Police after Chad went missing five days prior to his twelfth birthday on October 18th of this year. Chad was taken from his backyard while playing with his dog. Chad was found October 25th, just two days after his birthday. Chad was found much sooner than the first victim, Jon, and left more available forensics at the scene than did the first murder victim, triggering a more thorough investigation by the Tribal Police and the FBI because of its similar feel. Again, please refer to your photos of Chad before the abduction and then his autopsy photo.

"Chad lived with his grandmother and was the light of her life. Chad took care of her and his dog, which was found dead in the yard. Chad was small for his age, 5'2" and 88 pounds. He was wearing a navy hoodie, and sweatpants. There were no witnesses to the abduction, but a car driving by heard the howl of a dog, or a wolf, that seemed to be in distress. The witness noted the howling ceased quickly and didn't pursue it further. Forensics did check the dog's teeth and nails for skin evidence as well as blood in case he had gotten ahold of the assailant, but nothing was detected. The dog's death was by strangulation with a wire noose. Chad's grandmother did not hear anything since she is almost completely deaf. Chad aspired to be a teacher for the deaf. He had learned sign language to communicate with his grandmother."

Will was sitting in the back watching Special Agent Wright talk about the young victims with such respect and humanity, making them real, more than just names on a whiteboard. When she spoke, no one made a sound in the room. Her voice wasn't mechanical; it was as though she knew these children. Will knew he had to be part of stopping this. He wanted to work with Special Agent Wright. He needed to. He was reluctant to step on hallowed ground, but his desire to prevent more of his children of the Tribe from dying overcame that.

Board Three and I was feeling the strain.

"Our third victim is Tommy Lee Jordans, twelve years old, a member of the Crow Tribe. Tommy was found on the Crow Reservation in Wyoming, November 5th after being reported missing on October 30th. Tommy was abducted two days prior to his twelfth birthday and was found after a state-wide search. An Amber Alert had gone out on a boy similar to Tommy's description, but later, was found not to be our victim. Tommy, 5'7" and 125 pounds, was wearing a red corduroy coat, black jeans, and a straw cowboy hat according to his father. Tommy played the guitar in a band. He was funny, his family said, and could always find the humor in things.

"There were no witnesses to the abduction. Tommy had dropped his cell phone during this assumed struggle, and we found a partial picture of the feet of the abductor. The perp was wearing hiking boots, size eight to nine, generic in nature, that can be found at any hunting or retail store, as well as online. A copy of the cell phone picture is in your packet. Tommy's picture is from the garage band he started, and you have the autopsy photo as well."

Board Four. My head was pounding. "Our fourth victim is Samuel Percy Little Star of the Cheyenne Tribe here in Montana. Samuel turned twelve on November 2nd and was reported missing after failing to return home from his surprise birthday party at a friend's house. Samuel had received a scooter as a gift and rode away alone. The scooter was later found on the ground at the scene of the abduction. Samuel was wearing a hooded, gray sweatshirt, blue jeans, and cowboy boots, according to his friends. Samuel was a strong boy, 5'5" and 130 pounds. Samuel was found November 7th on the Cheyenne Reservation, here in Montana. Everyone believed Samuel was destined to be a doctor—he cared for animals and people, and always carried Band-Aids with him. A Band-Aid was found at the abduction site with Samuel's print on it. Samuel's photo is a favorite of his mother's. You can see, the autopsy photo doesn't do him justice.

"This was the only recovery site that Dr. Sampson was not able to phys-ically visit. He had every intention to but fell seriously ill and died recently.

I am here to visit the area, and to fill in the missing information along with what we just received this morning from the FBI's ME regarding Samuel's autopsy. The forensics were rushed, but due to the condition of the remains, having been frozen for nearly a month, they are still tentative with more tests to be run. I intend to finish Dr. Sampson's work and follow the path he set out on."

When Will heard the name of the victim from Montana, the one he had stumbled upon, his eyes welled up with tears and he became physically sick. He had known Samuel. He felt the children of his Tribe were his children. He had not recognized the body when he first saw it, it had lain in the path of severe weather and wildlife. He knew Samuel's family and felt compelled to do this for them and for all the children—all the Tribes. He would take Special Agent Wright to the site even though his beliefs in spirits gave him pause. It was a sacred place now, but the spirits would have to understand. This had become personal now.

"**I** would suggest that if you need a break to take it now. When you come back, I'll go over the forensics, the recovery sites, and the profile."

Charlie came over, touching my arm in a knowing way. "You're doing great. I know this is only going to get harder but hold it together." He stood a little closer. "Give them what they need to get this guy. We can get a drink later tonight, maybe a stress reliever." I took a gulp of water and two aspirins, ignoring his idea.

Will Little Bear watched the interaction between Special Agent Wright and Special Agent Falken and saw something in the way Special Agent Falken looked at her, touched her arm, and got in her personal space. Will was a good reader of people and animals; really the same thing, according to him. He saw opposing desires between Special Agent Falken and Special Agent Wright. Falken wanted something, and Wright didn't. Her boss was using his power in the wrong way. It made him think back to the vision from the night before showing how she would have a significance in his life, and he wasn't going to let Falken get in the way of that.

The meeting started up again, and I focused on Board Five. The board was a composite of all similarities relating to the four boys. The overlapping details, by type, indicated to me, who the killer was, maybe not by name, but by facts, the boys told us through their deaths. This board said this is the guy we are looking for.

"Let's go over the forensics, the pathology, and ME reports, which you all have copies of in your packets. The FBI repeated all the autopsies that local MEs had done to verify results and to see if anything was missed. The Bureau's ME facility far exceeds those in most local hospitals and coroners' offices as to equipment and personnel. Since this case has a high priority for finding even the most insignificant gram of dirt, we felt we would be remiss if we did not perform a second autopsy on all victims. These boys deserve everything we can do to bring them justice." I didn't care if there were hurt feelings.

"All the victims were twelve years old, males, Native American; either Crow, Navajo, Arapahoe or of Cheyenne descent. All the boys had been well-nourished and healthy prior to abduction. Each had been tortured for several days after abduction—some of the wounds were older than others, some had healed over, and some were closer to the time of death. The boys' feet and hands had been cut with a sharp instrument, comparable to, or possibly a filet knife. The palms of their hands had been cut along the lifeline, and the bottoms of their feet had been sliced at the instep, making it difficult to walk, run, or to escape. Their feet also showed signs of frostbite. Their fingers had been broken one at a time, based on the bones mending slightly at different rates, and they also showed signs of frostbite and bruising. There were numerous bruises and lacerations all over their bodies, made at different intervals based on the stages of healing and color of bruising."

I had to take a drink of water. The glass shook in my hand. Charlie looked at me with concern. I proceeded. My voice cracked, and Will Little Bear noticed. He looked at me with sad eyes. I was trying to be professional, but the voice in my head was screaming in terror at the things I was saying out loud.

"The boys, while still alive, had their penises mutilated, left hanging by one end near their testicles. No sexual rape signs were visible. The MO or pattern indicates rage, sadism, and could relate back to some disfigurement of the killer's own anatomy; or indicate some form of religious rite. Their necks had lacerations deep enough to decapitate them, which had happened in all cases. Lacerations had been made with wire nooses, not unlike a dog choke collar attached to a leash, perhaps to keep them under control. If they tried to pull away, they would cut their own necks. Their hair had been shaved off to facilitate the noose more easily. There was no sexual abuse to their anuses, but the unpublished detail is that DNA was found on all victims, as if the killer ejaculated on them when they died. The DNA does not match anyone in our system but is consistent to all the murders. On each of the boys' faces were traces of tears that must have run down their faces for days. According to the Coroner's Report, cause of death, though hard to be certain, was most likely loss of blood due to the severed jugular vein in their necks. Decomp was extensive, in all cases, animals, time, and weather had disturbed the remains."

I didn't say it out loud, but my personal cause of death conclusion was suicide to stop the torture. I believed the boys pulled their own nooses. I would have.

"Particles of dirt, grass, rock, and animal feces specific to the area where each of the boys were found has been analyzed. We have not found a way to trace these to any individual who may be involved in the murders."

I could see discomfort and strain on the faces of the men here. They couldn't make eye contact with one another or with me.

I was nauseated at this point and requested a fifteen-minute break. I quickly headed for the ladies' room and threw up. I felt sweat running down my back and between my breasts. I took a towel, ran water on it, wiped my face my neck, and rinsed out my mouth. I knew I still had the scenes to go over, and to profile the perp. I was exhausted, and my head was pounding in sync with my accelerated heartbeat, but I had to keep going for the boys. Giving a briefing when everyone has packets with the same information is necessary to make the victims—the boys—human and alive, at least for today, to everyone in the room.

Will Little Bear saw me in the hall as I was heading back to the Meeting Room. He walked up to me and introduced himself. "Special Agent Wright, I'm Will Little Bear. I'm the guide you requested to take you to the grave here on the Cheyenne reservation—my reservation."

"Yes, I appreciate you being here. Call me Sam, please."

"Call me Will. Are you okay?"

"No. Not really," I answered, feeling the need for a mint.

I shook his hand. "I'd like to talk to you more in depth after the briefing if you have the time, Will." I noticed he kept his nails manicured. You can tell a lot about a man by his nails and how he shakes hands. He didn't hold back a firm handshake because I was a woman.

Will felt her hand tremble as they shook. She looked as if this briefing was taking a toll on her, but it didn't mask her beauty. He couldn't take his eyes off her. He couldn't breathe around her.

"I'll make the time," Will said emphatically. "I've never seen a room full of tough guys buckle to their knees by what you are telling them. How do you stay standing?"

"For the boys. For justice," my voice was shaking.

He walked me back to the room, holding the door open for me. I went back to my place at the front of the room, noticing that he was again towards the back of the room taking his seat.

The room was spinning around like the scene from *The Good, the Bad and the Ugly* movie where Eli Wallach was running in circles in the graveyard. I closed my eyes, regained my composure, and began, "Thanks for your patience. Let's talk about the discovery sites now. All the boys were found on their respective reservations at elevations between 3,000 and 6,000 feet. Please see the topographic photos in your packet for each specific site. They were found in shallow graves, as if the killer wanted them to be found, or perhaps because the ground was frozen and could not be dug deeper. There were dig marks from a shovel or something similar. The boys were found in the fetal position; their heads placed next to their necks. It was obvious their heads were detached. The boys were found without clothing. There was no significant physical evidence at the sites other than the boys' DNA, the DNA of the killer, and the items noted earlier. The weather and frigid temperatures may have put the times of death off slightly since their bodies were frozen, and wildlife had contaminated the remains considerably.

"The area around the graves were similar, trees, bushes, broken tree limbs, grasses, and rocks. The species are listed in your notes. All are indigenous to the regions they were found in. Photos of the scenes are in your packets. In all cases, torture and death happened at another location. The places where the murders occurred have not been discovered yet. Again, the weather and rugged landscapes have prevented continued exploration for the actual murder scenes. If any of you see something in the photos that may be out of sync or not true for the area, please bring it up to Special Agent Falken after we finish.

"One scene had two unshod horsehoof prints you can see in your photos. Things like this might tell us how the killer moved the bodies, since these areas are not accessible by car, snowmobile, or motorcycle. Horse, mule, or on foot seems to be the only mode of transportation in these areas.

"The profile that Dr. Sampson and I compiled, that I am giving as of today, along with the latest ME updates, is as follows. Anything else that comes in later based on toxicology tests may change things, and you will receive updates.

"The killer is a white male, close to forty-five or fifty years old, and small in stature. His appearance is non-threatening. He has knowledge of the reservations, is physically strong, though small in physicality. He is capable in harsh conditions, has anger issues, and more likely started killing and torturing animals as a child. This perp has racist tendencies and probably has some preconceived notions about Native Americans, or he has had run-ins with the Tribes sometime in his life. The killer must be experienced at hunting, hiking, riding, survival, and the like, in order to operate and feed his desires in these rugged and treacherous surroundings. He gets around easily in these areas. He finds hiding places to commit the crimes and yet the killings are so close in time frame, with such expansive distances in between. How does he get from reservation to reservation so quickly, in this extreme weather? We know from the DNA at all the scenes, we have one perp.

"The killer probably has experience with knives and guns. The perp knows his DNA is not in any database, so he is smug about not caring about leaving it behind. Skin cells have been found, DNA in semen, and spit. Killing, turns him on. Either he was twelve years old when something traumatic happened to him, or he simply relates to the age of his victims.

"The number one thing—he has knowledge of the boys' birthdates. Somehow the killer has access to this information for every reservation. Who would have this access? Each Tribal Police office is researching all personnel as we speak, and checking who has access to computers or passwords that would get them this information?

"The perp must have access to transportation. He must have a car, a van or some other kind of vehicle to get from state to state so quickly. He may have a small plane. He may pull a horse trailer but could easily steal a horse that hasn't been reported missing. He needs at least one horse, snowshoes, snow gear, guns, knives, food, and water.

"We need to find out the birthdates of all boys at all the reservations and see whose twelfth birthday is coming up. We can't let another boy become his victim. All reservations have been put on alert, and we will update all of you as current information comes in."

I took a breath and continued, "We have a lot to follow up on. Please use whatever resources you have access to that may enable you to find anything helpful. Let's stop this killer. He will kill again, and soon. Special Agent John Thomas will give you your assignments, so we're not wasting time duplicating efforts.

"If any of you have questions that have not been covered by me, or by the documents you have, please see Special Agent Falken. Thank you for your time today. Be safe out there. Remember, this briefing isn't just about strategies and a profile, it's about these murdered boys. This briefing is the moral authority for you to do your duty. Stop this killer before he again cuts short another life."

I walked over to Charlie. "If you will take the questions, I can have a conversation with our guide, Will Little Bear."

Charlie urged, "Try to get him on board."

"He already is." I confirmed he was, based on my impression in the hallway earlier in the day when he approached me. He had taken the first step, that had been critical to his change of perspective.

It was noon, and no one was in the mood for lunch, although they went through the motions. They needed food for the drive back to their respective counties. Will was waiting just outside the door of the Meeting Room and offered, "I could use a drink. Let's go into the bar. We can sit in the back corner and talk."

"I just need a minute. I'll see you in there." I needed to splash some water on my face and take a breath. I was nauseous, and repelled by this case, but it was mine, and I had to finish it. I'd finish it for Dr. Sampson—and for the boys.

Will saw Sam walk into the bar and watched as she approached the table where he was sitting. He watched her long legs stride and the soft movement of her hips and breasts. Will, hadn't seen such natural, unconceited beauty, ever. She walked as if she had no idea of her effect on every male in the place. They were all looking, and she was either unaware or didn't care. He saw her catch him watching, and he got up to wait for her to be seated.

The waitress came over, and I placed my order. "Just a soft drink for me. Pepsi if you have it."

Will ordered a beer and was curious, "You don't drink?"

"Not while I'm looking for a killer and trying to find him before he makes another boy his victim. I'm not much of a drinker normally, but I'll drink after we catch this guy."

Will was a one beer kind of guy; he liked to stay in control. The beer was a prop to keep his hands busy. He felt nervous around this woman, and he could feel her step into his space where he'd have to cede control.

While we waited for our drinks, Will, seemed to be alone with his thoughts, and it gave me time to see who I was dealing with. He was almost forty-two years old, tall, around 6'2", a muscled 210 pounds, with not an ounce of fat on him. His dark, almost black hair just hit the collar of his shirt. He was a cross between Lou Diamond Phillips and The Rock. He looked strong, with soft brown eyes that could give a person comfort, and the whitest teeth I'd ever seen. He might have an easy smile, but it wasn't going to be today. His voice was smooth and calming. He certainly outgrew his name, Will Little Bear. Flawless skin and a scar at his right eyebrow—flawed beauty. I smiled to myself, thinking of him as beautiful. Good manners and I'd heard from some of the staff that he didn't curse. Cursing was a weakness to him. He had presence, but didn't seem full of himself, even though women watched him, maybe not watched, but lusted for him.

He owned The Lodge, and when the waitress came over to bring our drinks, one could tell she had some sort of relationship with him—the way she touched his shoulder. He didn't seem to notice, and it obviously irritated her. I was surprised that it bothered me. She was twenty-something and was out of her league with a man like Will.

Will looked at me after the waitress left and asked in a soft voice, full of emotion, "How do you handle the work you do?"

I looked at him and explained, "I concentrate on the details so I can stop killers like this. There is no closure to something like this, even if you get the bad guy. It's not attainable and wouldn't give you any relief. Looking for closure is like looking for the proof of God in situations like this. The result is I don't sleep a lot."

He looked at me with soft eyes. "You were talking about those boys as if you knew them."

"I know more about them, their lives, and families than I do about most people I know. I need to be familiar with the boys to know their killer. I need to see through their eyes the final moment they were alive. I have to listen to what their remains say to me." My voice was a bit weak with my answer.

"You have a gift."

"No, it's more like a curse," I quipped, trying to lighten things up a bit.

"I have to help you to stop this guy," Will stated flatly. He had made his decision. "You know I was the one who found the last victim, Samuel, on a hunting trip I was guiding?"

"I know. That's why I need you to take me to the site. I need to see it through your eyes and Samuel's eyes."

"It's sacred ground now," he said sadly but with reverence.

"I feel like you know I will treat the grave with respect. I hope the spirits will let me see the site, so I can stop this for one of their own," I pleaded my case.

Will nodded. "That's rough country. Severe weather is rolling in, and it will be tough going, even for me."

"I don't care. I need to get to the grave site to see if there is anything I can find that was missed. I won't hold you back," I tried to reassure him and myself.

Will looked as though he could see right through me, sizing me up like he would an advancing animal. His eyes were on me, and I felt a bit uncomfortable, but I needed to stand my ground. I was the only woman on this case, and I had to get a step ahead of the killer. I needed him to help me.

"Okay," he said. "We leave at first light." It will be a day up and a day back, slower, if the weather worsens. Dress warm and carry light. I know the location but following a track in snow can be deceptive. Snow blindness can also make things hard, so be prepared with eye covering."

Charlie came into the bar and walked up to us, interrupting without an excuse me. "So, when do we leave for the site?" he blustered out.

Will looked directly at Charlie with disdain, "Not we. It will be just me and Special Agent Wright. I can't take more than one person with the turbulent weather rolling in. We need to be able to move quickly."

The truth was, Will wanted to tell Falken he was an impediment to his vision about Sam. There was no way he'd give up an opportunity to be with her alone and to see where his vision led.

Charlie looked at me and then back at Will. "If that is what it takes to do the job, that's fine. You're responsible for Special Agent Wright, and I expect her to come back without incident."

I had no qualms about being alone with Will out in the wilderness. My job was reading people, seeing who they were in the first few minutes of contact, and I prided myself on my gut.

Will stared at Charlie until Charlie was forced to look away.

CHAPTER
NINE

I needed a release from the tension after the four-hour briefing, and Will indicated there was a gym in The Lodge. He offered to spot me on the weights, and I thought it would be a good opportunity to get to know into whose hands I was putting my life, in heading out into rugged country.

I usually work out four days a week to stay in shape and find it a great reliever of stress. I showed up at the gym, but Will hadn't arrived yet. I decided to start on the treadmill until he did. I needed my muscles to relax so my nagging headache would subside.

Will walked in and saw me cooling down from a four-mile run on the treadmill. I usually do three miles at an easy pace, and then I go all out for the last mile. I was wearing my usual workout gear of tight tech pants and a sports bra.

He seemed to take notice. "I can see that you take care of yourself. It must be necessary for the job you have."

"I workout for the job, but also for myself to stay healthy. Stress is a big killer in Law Enforcement, well, in any line of work."

Will liked it that Sam was strong and in excellent shape. He would be respon-sible for getting her back in one piece from the trek he was taking her on tomorrow. He loved how she looked, with the sweat glistening on her skin, but he really liked who she was inside after hearing her give the briefing, and after their talk in the bar. She was the total package, and he was interested in her for way more than a one-night stand. The vision was in his thoughts, wrong, she was in his thoughts. He also noticed her eyes; one was hazel and the other a little darker brown. He knew he was quick to the realization that he was interested in her, but he wasn't a kid—he knew what he was starting to feel. He caught himself controlling his impulses and came back to reality. First things first. Find the killer.

"You'll do okay out on the trail," he said.

I slightly laughed, "Well, if you and I are out in the woods and a bear is coming after us, I want to be able to outrun you." To that he smiled and shook his head. I spent a couple of hours in the gym with him and saw that not only did he take care of himself, but he was strong, and agile. I thought he might outrun me, and the bear. Good thing bears are hibernating.

I wanted to hit the bag for a while, get the rest of my frustrations out, and then take a shower before trying to get some sleep for tomorrow. Will held the bag, while I did my boxing routine.

"Your boss, Special Agent Falken, doesn't seem to like me much. Why is that?"

"I'm not sure. Must be a guy thing," I answered, breathing hard through my routine. I didn't want to go down that road about Charlie. I was done with that part of my life, that kind of life, that lack of life.

Will and I talked about many things. I felt comfortable with him as if I'd known him for a long time. We worked out for two hours on the weights and the bag. He looked like he could go for two more hours, but I was dead on my feet.

"Thanks for working out with me, it made things easier. What time are we leaving tomorrow?"

"Six a.m. You should get some rest. The cold can really take your energy away fast out there. Eat something before we leave."

I arrived at my room, and the first thing I did was take a long, hot shower. I was a little nervous about tomorrow but had more confidence in Will after talking with him. I looked in the mirror, and was pleased with my body, but the scars really bothered me sometimes. They bothered me when I had thoughts that maybe someone other than Charlie might see them.

There was a knock on my door. I thought it might be Will with additional instructions for tomorrow, but when I opened it, Charlie was standing there in his workout gear. "I'm going down to the gym, do you want to come with me?"

"I already worked out for two hours with Will, and I just took a shower."

The look on Charlie's face was one of surprise, followed by pissed-off.

"Enjoy your workout." I smiled and closed the door. I didn't care that it was awkward. I was hungry and about to call room service.

Twenty minutes later and another knock at the door. I was starving. I hoped it was dinner. I opened the door, and it was my food—being delivered by Will. "You deliver room service, too?"

"Not usually, just short-handed in the kitchen this time of year. I added a little more protein to your plate to help you handle tomorrow. Make sure you have breakfast in the morning." He put the dinner down on the desk. It was cool in my room, and I was wearing sweatpants and a white thermal top. I forgot I had taken my bra off; my hair was in a ponytail, and I had no makeup on, as usual. Will had a half-smile and remarked, "You look about nineteen years old. How old are you? You must have started at the FBI as a child."

I was taken aback by the question but really didn't mind. "I'll be thirty-eight in a month, and I've been at the Bureau for seventeen years. I joined the FBI when I was young and didn't understand the ramifications—both physically and mentally. It's been challenging. Thanks for the compliment though, and thanks for bringing my dinner. I'll see you in the morning." I felt I had to move him along, or I might not let him leave. He smelled of nature, the good smelling nature of trees, leaves, fresh air, and pine. I was having thoughts that would only get me into trouble.

"Good night," I said while trying to close the door.

Will turned smiling, and as he was leaving suggested, "I think I should turn the thermostat up for you, you look a little cold."

I wasn't quick on the uptake but then I realized my nipples were showing through my thermal top.

"Oh shit," I said and shut the door.

"Damn it." Will chastised himself, "What am I thinking? I'm going to be alone in the woods with her. She is amazing, just the kind of woman I've been waiting for my whole life, a real woman a man can build a life with." Her flawless face would be in his thoughts all night, and probably those nipples, too.

Will had just left Sam's room when he saw Charlie coming down the hallway. The alpha males walked towards each other and had the look of two bulls ready to rumble. As they passed each other neither said a word, but each knew what the other was thinking. Will thought, "Not on my watch." He didn't like the idea that Falken wanted Sam. He didn't sleep well. The vision came to him again with greater clarity and intensity and was ebbing over into his life whether he was asleep or awake. Special Agent Samantha Wright had penetrated his subconscious.

Another knock at the door. "What is the deal?" I thought, as I was finishing my dinner.

It was Charlie again. "Hey, just checking in to see if you're ready for tomorrow."

"I am," I reassured him.

"Would you like me to stay, maybe help you relax?" Charlie was leaning against the doorjamb, looking entitled.

"I'm good. Had a workout and some food, but thanks," I replied with a stifled yawn, distracted. "I really just need some sleep. I'll see you before I leave in the morning. Good night."

"Night." Pushing himself off the doorjamb, he looked a bit put out.

Will stood at the end of the hall to Sam's room, saw her rebuff Charlie, and smiled.

While Sam was sleeping, Will, Googled her. He couldn't relax. He wanted to know more about Special Agent Wright before taking her out into the wild tomorrow. There were numerous newspaper articles, FBI press releases, and biographies about her. She had Doctorates in Forensics and Forensic Psychology. Top Profiler at the FBI. She was in Mensa with a 168 IQ. Six years before she had been seriously injured by a serial killer. She's single, never married, lives in DC, writes as a hobby, and likes to sing. An excellent marksman, she's competed and won several shooting competitions. He sat back in his chair with his hands locked behind his head and thought, "Certainly more than what meets the eye, and what meets the eye is a real beauty." He couldn't get her out of his head, either one.

TEN

The alarm went off at five a.m., but I had been awake for an hour. I was feeling anxious, thought I'd better get dressed, and have some breakfast before leaving for the site. I put my long underwear over my bra and panties. I decided on the flannel-lined jeans, a thermal shirt, and flannel shirt over that. I put on thermal socks and my fleece-lined hiking boots. I added a waterproof puffer coat, a wool cap, and gloves to finish my cold weather clothes ensemble. I hoped I would be warm enough. I ordered a quick breakfast in the dining room and thought about what I might need for my backpack. My mental list included sunglasses, camera, collection bags, cell phone, radio, Maglite, sleeping bag, water, jerky, protein bars, aspirin, and first-aid stuff. This was going to weigh too much. Carrying my shotgun which I always kept in my vehicle was too much. It would slow me down.

I finished breakfast and went to my room. Will was waiting in the hall outside my door. I was grateful, because I needed him to decide what I should take along.

"Good morning."

I smiled back. "Hi. Would you help me pack? I feel I'm overthinking this, and it's going to weigh me down."

"Sure, no problem."

He looked at what I had laid out on my bed to take and gestured. "You don't need the water, the jerky, the protein bars, or the first-aid supplies. I've got that covered. You won't need your cell phone either, since there is no service where we're going. I carry a satellite phone; your radio wouldn't even operate out there because of the cloud cover."

I put everything he allowed into my pack as he watched. I tucked my 9mm Glock with fifteen rounds in my waistband into the middle of my back, put my knife in my boot, and grabbed for the shotgun. Will looked at me and laughed, "Are you expecting an attack? I already carry a rifle in case of wildlife."

"No, just Bureau protocol for the car," I answered embarrassed. "Don't say anything about the knife. The Bureau frowns on that, but I like knowing it's there."

"Well, I don't think you'll need the shotgun, you don't have a car, and I won't mention the knife. Let's go. The weather is supposed to deteriorate later today or by tomorrow morning. It could bring in a lot of snow, and I'd like to beat it if we can."

"I'm ready." I followed Will to his car, wondering if I was up for this.

Charlie didn't come around to say goodbye. I figured he was still sleeping, and we'd just get going. Daylight was burning, as they say. I was hoping by the time we got back there would be information about any birthdates coming up for any boys, on any of the reservations. The Tribal Police were working on the information they had but still had to canvass for those on the reservation who may never have registered their children or were in isolated areas where births and deaths went by sometimes without notice. We had to stop the next murder, so I had left instructions for our team to oversee these efforts with information stored at the Bureau, so-called oversight on the reservations.

Will had a four-wheel drive black SUV. It had heated seats, chains on the snow tires, big spotlights on either side of the rearview mirrors, and an extra can of gas in the back, along with a lot of equipment and supplies.

"You seem to be prepared for just about anything."

Will looked at me. "If I'm not prepared, people won't survive out here."

"How far will we be able to take the car?" I asked hopefully.

"For about an hour, to the place where we'll pick up the horses," he answered. "Some of the roads have been closed due to the ice and snow. Depending on the weather, we may have to ride for about five hours before we get about a mile from the grave. After that, it gets too rocky for the horses to walk safely. From there we'll hoof it on snowshoes. It sounds like a long time, but the trails are snow-covered and icy. The rocks are hidden, so we'll have to go slowly, and visibility might be bad. In decent weather, we could do this in a day but not this time of year, especially when it gets dark early."

I looked at Will and nodded, I didn't know what to say, and hoped I wouldn't hold him back. This was not in my wheelhouse. So far, the weather was holding, just extremely cold in the single digits. It snowed a couple of days before, and there were a couple of feet of hard packed snow on the ground.

I saw stables in the distance after nearly an hour on rutted roads and sliding on ice. I figured the warmth of the car was going to be a distant memory very soon. I hadn't ridden a horse in years and hoped it would come back to me. The drive had been quiet, each of us with our thoughts.

Will parked under an overhang to somewhat protect the car from impending snow, but I imagined if there was wind it wouldn't matter. I got out of the car when he did and looked for him to give me some instruction. He walked over to the stables, unlocked the door, and went inside. I followed. He had been very quiet on the drive, and I wondered if he was worried or upset about something. I understood the gravity of this situation, and it was palpable, coming from him but I wondered if there was even more, he was internalizing.

I walked into the stables and saw him getting the horses ready, and asked, "Can I help?"

Will nodded at me, "Get your pack so I can put it on the back of the saddle. I'm giving you the easiest horse I have. She will know what to do even if you don't. Her name is Laney. Just be easy on the bit and let her lead."

"Got it." I went to get my stuff and brought it to him.

Will had the horses saddled and went to get his equipment for the ride. I went to introduce myself to my horse, so we would hopefully have a good relationship on this trip. I had heard that if you blow your breath into their nostrils, they'll remember who you are. I gave it a try. I was talking to her—Laney—and she was a beautiful paint. When Will came back in, I saw he smiled a bit, but immediately tried to hide it from me. I wondered what was going on with him, but I needed to focus on the job at hand.

"Are you dressed warm enough? You don't look like you wear many layers out here in the cold?"

"The cold doesn't really bother me, but I don't like the wind," he answered as he checked the horses one last time.

We led the horses out, locked the stables, and Will helped me mount Laney. His hand lingered a bit longer on my leg, adjusting the stirrups, but he caught himself, and moved on to mounting his own horse. His horse was named Bear Boy, a gelding with chestnut hair—about sixteen hands, maybe twelve hundred or more pounds. Bear Boy was big enough to handle Will.

"Are these your horses?"

"Yes, but if someone needs them, they can borrow them. We take care of each other around here. I hope to build a house around here one day. I like this area." He looked around and had a wistful look on his face.

"I think it's beautiful here. Hope you get to do that," I commented, trying to be pleasant, although I did mean it.

Will looked at me. "Ready?"

I shook my head to the affirmative.

It was going to be a quiet, long ride. The only sounds breaking the stillness were the horses breathing, the squeak of my saddle, and their hooves hitting the snow. I didn't even hear birds. Since no one was talking I decided to do a list in my head of what to look for at the grave. Based on other sites where evidence had been collected, I needed to look for similarities, or by a miracle, something that might give me a clue as to who the killer was. Laney kept up with Bear Boy and after a few hours Will stopped. He dismounted and explained, "We need to water the horses. There's a stream over behind those trees. If you need to use nature's facilities, this is the time."

I was okay for now.

I eased down from Laney and felt my legs buckle under me from being in one position for so long. My ass was asleep. I was glad I brought the aspirin along. We led the horses to the water, and I was surprised the stream wasn't frozen. I assumed because it was fast moving that it didn't freeze over. If it hadn't been so damn cold, this would have been a beautiful spot to enjoy. I looked at Will and asked, "So what's on your mind? You're quiet to the point I think I should take your pulse. Have I done something?"

He exhaled, "I apologize, I'm just trying to concentrate on the trail and to watch for anything I may have missed the last time I was here. I know how important this is and I want to help by doing what I do, better."

I saw his face was tense and advised, "Breathe. It helps to breathe deeply. When I've been in bad situations, breathing makes the difference. Sometimes we don't realize that when we stop breathing, it tenses up our muscles. We aren't as efficient with our mind or body—so just breathe."

Will studied me for a second. "Thanks. I think knowing this boy Samuel, has gotten to the core of my belief system. And you're right, I haven't been breathing since I found out it was him."

"Had I known, you were familiar with him, I would have told you prior to the briefing and not blindsided you like that. I'm sorry for your loss. It wasn't right, and that's on me not researching your possible connections within the Tribe or to Samuel."

Will half-smiled. "There was no way of you knowing, and thanks for that."

We mounted the horses, and Will said, "I'd say about two to three hours, and we'll get to where the hike begins. We will still have daylight, but you may have to work fast once we are there."

The snow was starting. Lightly at first, but in an hour's time it was coming down steady and heavy. The horses were having difficulty walking through the wet, heavy snow, but we finally made it to the clearing where we dismounted. Will pointed. "There's a small cave over there where the horses can stay until we get back. That's where we'll camp tonight. It'll be warmer and out of the weather."

I nodded, understanding him.

"I don't usually use caves this time of year because of the hibernating bears, but I know this one is empty. There will be no running required."

We unpacked the horses and tied them up in the cave with some grain and hay Will had brought for them. It looked good enough to eat. I was hungry, but we needed to hike about a mile further to do my work. Will handed me a bottle of water and I gratefully took a drink. We put on our backpacks, snowshoes, and started hiking the rocky terrain. A foot of snow hid the rocks and made walking difficult. I lost my footing once, but he was able to grab my arm and keep me from falling.

Will stopped short and pointed. "This is where I found Samuel." He pulled out a stick of sage, lit it, and blew it out so it would smoke. He blessed the area and cleansed both of us with the sage smoke while praying aloud in Cheyenne with a reverent and shaky voice. I found his trepidations about affronting the spirits, and his profound sorrow at the loss of this boy heartbreaking.

The crime scene crew had left a tarp over the site. It was held down by rocks and had a stake with a red flag on it. The remains were at the Bureau's ME's office, but the grave and its surroundings would hopefully still be intact. I knelt on the ground as Will help me remove the tarp. We moved it carefully, halfway only so we could keep the blowing snow out. I pulled my small flashlight out and started a tedious, inch by inch examination of the grave site, making notes as I went along. It was a shallow grave due to the frozen hardness of the ground, which made it accessible to the ravages of wildlife.

I bagged and tagged a few pieces of grass, and possibly a degraded string that was on the upper side of the grave. This could have blown in after the first team, or it had been missed. I took numerous pictures which I thought might give me some idea of the tool the killer had used to dig the grave if I could have it blown up in the lab. It could have been a shovel or something else; there were some irregular edges, possibly tool marks. Will didn't talk while I worked. He could see I was focused, and he didn't want to interfere. He had known this boy and to stand here by this empty grave; it was taking a toll on him. I could see he fought the bile in his throat, his color was sallow, and his demeanor was one of defeat.

"I can't imagine how you can do this work without crying," he said. His eyes were full of tears he tried to blink back.

I hunched back on my heels, and it looked as though I had found all I could. I was looking around at the surroundings close to the grave now. Will seemed lost in his thoughts. I asked, "What access to this place do you think the killer had? What was the point of entry?"

He thought for a moment and then answered, "The closest town is west of here. So, based on the presumption that the killer didn't want to be near town or any populated areas in order to stay hidden in these surrounding areas, he would have come from that direction to this spot." He pointed in an easterly direction.

Dr. Sampson always taught, "Look down, look to the sides, and do not forget to look up." I noticed a formation of rocks to the right of the grave, near a larger boulder, easily missed. Formation is not really the right word. These rocks were balanced on each other intentionally. It didn't look natural. I've heard of people doing clusters like this, cairns, if they were lost or wanted to leave a message for someone who might have been following or looking for them. I took pictures hoping there would be more to indicate a message.

"What do you see?"

I pointed to the cluster of rocks.

"Damn it, how did I miss that?" he fumed. "I see these clusters all the time. Campers leave them along trails, and hunters use them to show where they had a deer fall." He looked at me with hope. "This has to mean something, right?"

I took additional pictures and shrugged, "It could be important, I need to bag it." I stood up on stiff legs, reached for the cairn, bagged it, then detailed the information on the tag. "I've done all I can here."

I could hear him berating himself. When he stumbled upon Samuel, he didn't see anything else, and he didn't look up. The brain protects and helps you survive in bad situations. It doesn't always let you see everything in stress-mode. It wasn't his fault, but that's who he was. He felt he had let Samuel down. This is how survivors react to their own despair at not taking the victim's place.

We covered the site with the tarp again, and Will used sage to cleanse the area once more. It was now a sacred spot, with or without Samuel's body.

We headed back to the campsite. I looked forward to getting a fire roaring. I was stiff from the cold and needing aspirin, some food, and maybe some sleep. Today had gone better than I thought it would. I might have found something useful at the site. We found the horses in good condition when we returned. Will found water buckets in the cave to put snow in to melt for the horses. Hunters and campers often leave things behind to help the next person who comes along. Camping is a lot of work.

I immediately became upset at myself. "Could the killer have used this cave around the same time, you discovered Samuel? Have we disturbed any possible evidence?"

Will took me by the arm. "No. There was a bear in this cave the last time I was here with the hunters. He moved to a more secluded area after my hunters tried to shoot him. We didn't ruin anything, unless he slept with the bear. I swear, Sam, the killer did not use this cave."

I excused myself and went outside to rebuke myself for not taking the cave into account when Will first pointed it out to me. "Shit." I had been distracted.

Will was in his element with this outdoors stuff. He had the fire going, melted snow for the horses, and made coffee for himself, tea for me. It was getting comfortable, for a cave. For dinner, we shared a can of beans, some jerky, and a protein bar. Soon after the beans I realized I hadn't gone to the bathroom all day, but nature was calling now. I stood up and cleared my throat. "I need to use the facilities, where, and how do I do this?"

Will looked in his pack, pulled out a roll of toilet paper, a small shovel and indicated, "There is a small area under the tree to the north of the cave. You should be okay there."

I took the toilet paper and shovel from him and left the cave. It took awhile for me to get my jeans, long underwear and regular underwear down, then I had to squat, balance, and avoid getting anything on my clothes or boots. Finally. Clean and buried. I walked into the cave and Will shook his head. "I was getting ready to come look for you." He smiled. The first one all day.

I reached into my backpack, found the aspirin, took two for my ongoing headache, and the pain in my legs. Will watched me. He had already cleaned up the campsite and put out his sleeping roll. I realized at that moment I didn't have my sleeping bag. I tried to think when was the last time I saw it? It was at the stables. "I think I have a problem. I can't find my sleeping bag. I think it's back at the stables."

Will smiled. "Mine is a double-wide. I'll let you share so you don't freeze. Don't get any ideas."

Will hoped she did have ideas. He had never felt this way about a woman. He already felt possessive of her. He already had feelings for her. He felt his eyes follow her, not wanting to miss anything about her.

"Thanks." I murmured, embarrassed. Time passed and it got quiet again, except for the sound I made walking around trying to get the muscle cramp in my leg to relax. My legs always create a problem for me in frigid weather from the scarring and nerve damage that I still had as a reminder of that night six years ago.

Will looked as though he was getting ready to ask me something. His eyes were red and had tears in them. "How do you deal with death all the time like you do, and the terrible people that do these things? That boy, Samuel, was of my Tribe. My child in the Tribe. I know his family. He may not be my child from my body, but he is my child. Everyone in the Tribe is responsible for every child." Anger was present in his voice. He glanced at me again, and asked, "Do you become cold inside dealing with death and killers as often as you do, not to react to it? Is this just a job to you? You act distant from it. This was a real child not some case study in one of your books. I mean, I thought I was a tough guy, but this has shaken me to the core. I can't get my emotions in check."

I felt as though I'd been hit with a brick. The hurt from that comment stung. I stood up and crossed my arms in front of me in defense. "I deal with death, and these killers, because my voice is for the victims who can't speak for themselves. They were victims because they were powerless. I bring their power back by finding out who killed them. I speak for them. You don't. Having been a victim once, it's incredibly important to have someone speaking for you. I'm as much Samuel's and the other boys' mother, as you are their father. Just because I'm white doesn't give you a moral high ground, because I am from a Tribe too, the Tribe of human beings. We are all responsible for the children of all Tribes, not just yours. Because I'm white doesn't mean they don't belong to me, too. I am responsible for them too. Those boys are mine until I can let them rest in peace." I hadn't realized I was crying as I spoke.

I could hardly breathe. Will was standing now and staring at me with tears running down his face. He was inches from my face and said softly, almost in a whisper, "I am sorry. I didn't mean what I said. I was just lashing out because I hadn't seen that cairn you found. You got in my line of anger towards myself. I would never think that of you. Please forgive me."

I felt Will's breath on my face, but I just couldn't look at him. He reached to hold me by my upper arms, but I was still hurt by him and backed up. "I'm tired and need to sleep," Choking the words out. I went over to the sleeping bag we were to share and laid down with my back to him. I was trying to calm down, so I could sleep, and forget. I think Will thought I had fallen asleep when he finally slipped into the sleeping bag, but I was still awake.

Will sat up, kept the fire going for hours. How could he hurt Sam like that? He felt sick and couldn't stand the thought of what he had implied.

Sleep did not come to Will. He could feel Sam's back against his side. He was angry at himself. The last thing he wanted was to ruin something he thought might be starting between them. He felt something for her. Maybe it was the beginnings of love. He didn't know much about love, but he wanted her. He really wanted her. He'd had the vision again, and he couldn't ignore it. He believed in visions, and this one showed a future with Sam.

I had an uncomfortable couple of hours of wakeful sleep and had the same dream I'd had at The Lodge. I didn't know the dream's meaning, but this was the second time I'd had it. Will was in it, and he meant something to me.

It wasn't yet morning. I couldn't wait to get out of here. I could feel Will, asleep next to me. I needed to turn over. My arm was asleep, and I had to find some relief for a few hours more. I was tired and sore, regretted forgetting my sleeping bag and being vulnerable to this man, who had gotten inside of my head.

I turned on my other side and found myself face to face with him. I started to turn back. "Don't, please."

I turned halfway and ended up on my back with his hand on my shoulder. He stopped me from turning the rest of the way. His eyes were soft and gentle. I could see his face in the glow of the fire. He had kept the fire going all night to make sure I was warm. He looked in my eyes as though he could see into my soul, and I felt a little weak. I didn't want to cry again, and I was afraid my voice would crack if I tried to talk to him.

"Sam, I am so sorry for hurting you," he whispered.

"I know," I said, barely audibly. "It's okay. I know you were just upset. Get some sleep."

Will looked at Sam. He didn't want to push it any further. He didn't want to risk screwing it up. He wanted to kiss her, but not here, and not at this place. Not yet. He would have to fix this somehow.

Morning finally came, and I couldn't wait to leave. The snow from last night had stopped, leaving an additional six inches on the ground. It was cold but not as brutal as it had been. Will busied himself with breaking down the camp while I went to find the tree again to relieve myself before the ride. By the time I returned, he had the horses ready. He stood there waiting to help me mount Laney. We weren't saying much to each other. I hadn't eaten breakfast, and neither had he.

"We should make better time going back. The weather has cleared a bit."

"Okay," I mumbled.

By the time we got back to the stream to water the horses, the silence was deafening, wearing on both of us.

Will asked, "Can we talk about this?" He dismounted Bear Boy and looked pleadingly at me.

I answered reluctantly, "No need to. You're not the first person to say something like that to me. It's the line of work I'm in. It is, what it is. I shouldn't have gotten so emotional." I slid down from Laney carefully. I didn't trust my legs right now. I also knew I was emotional because I wanted him to like me.

A minute or two passed in silence again.

"Damn it, Sam, I'm sorry," Will said more forcefully, his hands on his hips, looking at the ground. "I don't want something like this between us. I care about you. When you were in the briefing, you made those boys come alive, real, to those hard asses. You brought them to tears. They are now going to relate to those boys, care about them. They'll find the killer, because you made those boys more than just autopsy photos. God, I'm sorry. You have to forgive me."

I walked over to where Will was standing, watching the horses drink. "Thank you. I'm sorry too, for letting this drag on. I was hurt, because I didn't want to think you felt I was that kind of person. Cold inside. I'm not." I leaned back against a tree because I felt a little off-balance talking to him like this. I wanted to lighten things up. "I heard you don't curse. You seem like a man who doesn't need those kinds of words to get his point across."

"That's usually true. Apparently, you bring it out in me." Will winked at me as he blushed.

He just looked so good out here in the woods with the trees and branches hanging heavy with snow. The horses, and the quiet, made him seem formidable in these surroundings. He was at home and confident out here.

He ambled over and stood in front of me, close enough that my breasts touched his chest. I didn't pull back. He smelled amazing, like a forest and all the good things in it. Scent is the first stage of attraction, and I liked his. I admit it; I was damn attracted.

"I hope he doesn't notice me inhaling him," I thought to myself.

"There's an elephant in the woods I need to clear up now." He tenderly placed his hand behind my head, slowly brought his mouth to mine, and kissed me. Softly at first, then with intensity. He pulled back slightly, looked in my eyes, checked to see if I would protest continuing, and then he kissed me again, a little more probing. I responded and leaned in closer to him, wanting more, my hands at his waist. He released my lips, but still held me close, putting his forehead to mine and whispered, his breath short, "I'd like to take you to dinner when we get back, maybe talk about things, about this kiss." He could tell he had taken my breath away.

Will knew it was the best kiss of his almost forty-two years. He had known it would be. He could have lingered on her lips for hours, and still want more. His heart was beating faster. He didn't want to let Sam get away, but he had to be a better man to deserve someone like her. A man with a foundation who could settle down. Before he met her, he dreamed of the idea of her. The thought of someone like her was always with him, even if he thought it might be impossible. She was the kind of woman to be with for life. The vision was guiding him, and he intended to follow.

I like a man who doesn't have to act tough, to be tough. He's like a gentle bear, I thought to myself. I was weak in the knees. He kissed me with his eyes open. He wanted to look at me—at the woman he was kissing—and to see how it made me feel through my eyes. His lips, well, they were perfect. I took a breath and answered, "I could eat."

We finally rode at a quicker pace back to the stables and to the car that was beckoning with its heat and comfort. The idea of getting off the saddle was foremost in my mind. I had no feeling from the waist down. All I could think about were the heated car seats. Will came over and helped me dismount. He caught me as my legs were a little rubbery. I slid down the front of him thinking thoughts that would have frightened the wildlife.

"You did well out there. I know it was hard, but you kept going. You didn't complain," he said, while noticing there wasn't any space between us. He smiled as our hips grazed each other, and we both had to suck in air.

The horses settled back into their stalls, well-fed, and watered. We grabbed our gear, put it in the car, and headed back to The Lodge. A warm car on a rutted, icy road was better than a cold saddle on a horse. During the car ride back to The Lodge, Will held my hand, his finger running up and down my palm. It felt natural. I liked it. It all seemed too fast, but then again, it didn't.

We would arrive back at The Lodge soon, where there would be a hot shower and food, not-in-a-can, waiting. Charlie would be waiting for me. I'd have to brief him first and answer whatever questions he had concerning the last two days I spent with Will Little Bear. I wouldn't tell him everything.

I t was midafternoon when we got back to The Lodge. "What time works for dinner?"

I thought for a moment and then answered, "I have to brief Charlie first, and then check on any up-to-date information that may have come in. I'm thinking seven by the time I get cleaned up."

Will smiled. "I'll see you in the dining room. I'm looking forward to it, Sam."

Will could still feel her kiss on his lips. He couldn't wait to see her again at dinner. He was nervous. He was never nervous. Just the thought of her place in his vision made him impatient for his life to get on with it.

I was looking forward to dinner, too. I headed to my room to drop my gear off when I saw Charlie coming towards me. He had a look on his face I wasn't feeling inclined to deal with but had to.

"Charlie, do you have time for a briefing on what I found up at the site?" I questioned, as I continued walking to my room.

"We can go to the Murder Room now, and I'll fill you in on what has come in from the Tribal Police and the Fed's reservation birth records. Unless you have other plans?" Charlie said it in a way that I thought would be catty if he had been a woman and if it hadn't come out in such a roar.

"I'll meet you in the Murder Room as soon as I stow my things." It was three, and I figured a couple of hours, and then I'd get that shower I needed. I was also thinking of steak for dinner.

The Murder Room looked like the aftermath when the circus leaves town. Tables and chairs were in disarray leaving the feeling of a rushed exodus. Charlie was standing there with some printed emails and faxes in his hands, making it feel awkward, because he had morphed into my boss again. I had left our personal history on the floor in tatters since kissing Will. "We've got a lot of data to go through on the birth records, as well as the toxicology results on the victims."

"When did this information come in?"

"Yesterday," Charlie verified as he looked at the documents.

"Has anyone gone through these birth records to see if any boys fit the dates and ages we're looking for?" I was upset that crucial information had been sitting around for a day when time was so critical. "Were you waiting for me to do it?" I was livid.

"Let's get to it now. I thought you'd be back sooner," Charlie growled at me.

"Listen. I'll take all the data and go over it myself. I'll check the toxicology reports and update the boards. I'm tired, need a shower, and a meal, but I'll handle this."

"Wouldn't want you to miss dinner with the mountain man," Charlie spat out.

"Really, this is what it's about? Who's got the bigger one? Why don't you just whip them out and find out? Is this about me not letting you in my room? That isn't what we're here for." I was pissed and continued ranting, "That part of our history has been over since we left DC."

I grabbed the papers out of Charlie's hands, scooped up the reports on the table, and left the room as quickly as my tired ass would allow, heading to my room.

Charlie felt like Sam had slapped him. He hadn't seen it coming. He could feel the air leave his lungs as he tried to grapple with what she said. He rubbed his forehead as if he felt a loss, no different than death, engulf his heart. His legs went weak as he slumped into one of the chairs and tried to fight back the urge to run after her.

"What the hell." I didn't care what he thought, even though he was my boss. That alone could cost him his career. Our relationship had been a rule breaker, and I no longer wanted it. I hadn't wanted it since we left DC, maybe even before, but I hadn't been truthful with myself.

I thought it best to take a hot shower to loosen my muscles, to be more alert for the data I had to go through. The hot water raining down on my head and shoulders felt terrific, just what I needed. While in the shower, flashbacks ran through my memory like a collage of things Will had said, but mainly of what he did. I found my fingers between my legs and thought, he gets to me. I pulled myself together, stepped out of the shower, and toweled off.

I spent the next two hours going over the data, making notes to add to the board, and looked at the toxicology reports. There was something I couldn't put my finger on—it gnawed at me, and I couldn't pull it out of my head. I went to the Murder Room and decided I'd update the boards to see if that might trigger what was bothering me about the information I had just gone over.

The boys had peyote in their blood, a hallucinogen from a cactus that grows in the Southwest of the country. I wasn't surprised there was a drug in the reports, because the killer would have to make the boys compliant, but I thought this drug might have caused them to act out and be loud. One of the side-effects of peyote is that it makes people believe they can taste colors, similar to a LSD derivative called mescaline. This would have been counter-productive for the killer, unless he was the one taking it. Maybe the boys, to ease their pain, took some when he wasn't looking. I needed the Tribal Police to find out who has been dispensing peyote, and to see if we could make a connection that way. This wasn't what was just at the edge of my mind, the thing I couldn't get out. Evidence like this sometimes doesn't take you where you want to go. Sometimes it doesn't even fit into the reality of the case. I was thinking that based on the weather and cause of death that the peyote didn't leave their systems as quickly as it should have or it could have been combined with some other drug, maybe an anesthetic, that was masked by the peyote. I needed to call the ME's office and get more details or have them do other tests. I wasn't satisfied. The toxicology test was a dead end unless the lab came up with something more conclusive.

I wrote the details from the data on the map of all the reservations in the United States. The dates of birth of boys coming to the age of twelve didn't make sense, based on where the previous killings had taken place and the distances between them. The harsh weather had to play a factor, considering accessibility to each site, and how long it would take to travel from state to state. It was driving me crazy. There were a handful of boys who would soon be turning twelve that we knew of, spread out in several different states, across different reservations. Who would the killer pick next? I was missing something.

It was nearly seven, and I thought a good meal might help me think more clearly and help me figure this out. I knew I had something, but I just couldn't grasp it. It was an itch I couldn't scratch.

After my earlier shower, I had dressed in black jeans, a gray sweater and black dress boots. I decided to put my earrings back on and to wear my long hair down to feel less like a Special Agent. The sweater showed my assets, and I think that was the effect I was going for. I didn't know why I was so nervous about dinner. Maybe I was hungry for things other than food.

Will was nervous. When he showered earlier, his thoughts went to Sam. That kiss, these feelings, he had never experienced this before. He changed clothes twice and wasn't sure whether to wear cologne. But then he remembered Sam seemed to like the way he smelled. He had noticed. He headed to the dining room, hoping she would show up. He picked a booth in the corner of the dining room so they could talk and if things didn't go well, no one would notice. Not many people were registered at The Lodge this time of year.

Will was already at the table when Sam walked in. His breath caught. She looked even more beautiful with her long hair worn down. It swung as she walked. Wow, he thought. Intimacy begins in the mind, and Will was feeling intimate. He felt himself stir. He needed to regain control before she got to the booth. He'd never had this visceral and physical reaction to any woman before.

As she walked through the dining room, heads turned to watch. She was oblivious to the attention, but Will wasn't. How can someone so drop-dead gorgeous not even know it about herself? A self-confident, smart, and caring woman was new to Will; he was going to need to see if he could measure up. He couldn't stop staring at her.

I spotted Will and walked towards the table. My legs were shaking, and I hoped I wasn't walking funny. He showed such confidence in his demeanor—it could be a little intimidating sometimes. He stood up until I was seated. Manners. "Hi." I smiled. "I'm starving. You clean up nice." I really was thinking he looked amazing. He was wearing well-fitted jeans and a white thermal shirt his muscles were trying to escape from. The top buttons were open, and showed smooth, flawless skin, no tats I could see. This guy could wear clothes, and his clothes liked being worn by him. His hair was still a little damp from the shower. He looked comfortable in his own skin. He looked good enough to eat.

As soon as I sat down next to him, I felt at ease. I relaxed. The booth was in the corner, back of the dining room, and we sat next to each other, thighs touching. I hoped we would be able to talk about the trip without interruption. Not many people were dining, and there were only a few at the bar. No one was trying out the Karaoke, so it wasn't very noisy. I felt Will might still be upset about hurting my feelings, and I wanted to clear the air.

Will leaned into me, looking at me with a sly smile, and kissed my cheek, lingering a bit, grazing my lips as he moved back and whispered, "You look great. I like your hair down."

A shiver ran through me, and I could feel myself moisten. I could smell the same scent I remembered when he kissed me on the trail. I liked it. I more than liked it. I wanted to put my face in the nook of his neck and breathe him in for about an hour, maybe more.

"You look distracted."

Will knew what he had just done to Sam. She was trying to catch her breath. He had gotten to her. He saw her face blush and watched as she tried to regain her composure.

"No, just remembering a scent from the trip," I sighed.

He knowingly smiled back, touching his finger to my hand while asking, "Would you like a drink first or should we just order dinner? Have you eaten anything today?" He couldn't take his eyes off me, and I could feel myself flush.

"I haven't eaten, and I'd rather order dinner, but please order one for yourself if you want one. Like I've said before, when the case is over, you can buy me a drink."

Will signaled to the waitress and she came to take our orders. I decided on having a filet, medium-well with the baked potato, butter only, and green beans.

"I'll have the same." Will said to the waitress.

That comment, my Columbo moment, set electric charges off in my brain.

"What did you say?" I asked in a nervous way, my heart racing.

Will looked at me confused and repeated what he had said, "I'll have the same as you're having."

The waitress was standing there looking at me impatiently, tapping her pen on the order pad, and asked, "Should I put the order in?"

"No, wait. Not yet," I mumbled as I was calculating something in my head.

"God, that's it!" I was remembering the birthdates, the locations, the weather, the distances, and I said to myself, I have been looking at it all wrong! I was looking at the killer all wrong! I had seen one killer going in a straight line, but that's not it. I got thrown a curve. I missed it. It's not one killer. They plan on doing these killings forever, unless I stop them. I think the WHY is—they just like to kill. It's that simple. It is easy for them to kill in these desolate areas. It's a game they play. There is no grand plan, they aren't smart—they just like to kill. The only missing pieces of information are the "why" on the victims' ages, and the "how" on accessing their birthdates. My head was spinning as these thoughts raced through my mind.

Will was watching me. I'm sure he thought I was having a stroke, but he waited. He didn't say anything. He wanted me to say something.

"Will, please come with me to the Murder Room." I quickly walked out of the dining room. Will followed and everyone in the dining room watched. I unlocked the door to the Murder Room and ran over to the boards. I stood there staring, talking to myself. Will was watching me, afraid to say anything. I probably looked a little crazed.

"Look, Will. See the dates? These states, the distances, the locations of the scenes, and the weather—the DNA is the same everywhere, but it is impossible for one person to do this. God, Will, IDENTICAL TWINS! Serial killer brothers with the same DNA," I shouted.

Will looked at what I had pointed at, "You're right. I'll have the same. That's what they're doing. Doing the killings, the same. Having the same. Twin brother serial killers. Is that even possible? Two crazy people thinking the same and acting the same?"

I didn't answer right away. My mouth was trying to catch up to my thoughts.

"Over here. See these birthdates coming up? It's going to be these two boys—Brandon Lewis here in Montana, and Morgan Little Deer in Wyoming. Both Cheyenne reservations. I just know it. We have about three days to get to these locations and stop the abductions. The killers are probably there already, just waiting for the birthdates to get closer. They've probably already found their shelters and planned how to get the boys there. I don't know how they know this, but right now it doesn't matter. Now we know what's next. The why and the how can come later." I looked at Will, and he looked at me stunned. "Charlie needs to take the team to Wyoming, and we'll stay in Montana. It's going to come down to us because the Tribal Police are shorthanded due to tracking down all these boys on the list and the local LEOs can't work on the rez. Please look at the maps and tell me what locations near the boys you think are the next targets that might resemble those of previous sites."

Will studied the maps for several minutes knowing from the briefing what the previous sites entailed. He looked up and pointed, "Here in Montana and here in Wyoming."

"Tell me I'm not crazy about this before I get Charlie down here," I pleaded.

"You're not crazy. You're brilliant."

I grabbed Will by the hand, and we ran out of the room. I knocked and knocked again on Charlie's door. A twenty-something young waitress eventually opened it. It was the same young woman who had touched Will's shoulder in the bar after the briefing. The next thing Will and I see is Charlie at the door in his boxers, looking like we had interrupted something. "Put your pants on. Drink some coffee and get to the Murder Room. I know who's next and we know where," I ordered, not hiding my impatience.

Will looked at the waitress, shook his head in disgust, "Not in my Lodge. Get dressed and get out."

Will and I headed back to the Murder Room. I was pacing, rechecking everything. I had to be sure. Ten minutes later, Charlie came in looking embarrassed. He was drinking his coffee and sat still as I went over everything. When we finished an hour later, Charlie stood up rubbing his head. "We'll meet in the morning at seven, set teams, give a heads up to the local LEOs and the Tribal Police, and we'll leave by eight. Good job, Sam. You may have just saved a couple of lives. Will, thank you too."

Charlie left to begin organizing the meeting for tomorrow morning, and to try and notify the families we felt were targeted. That would be a task in itself since the reservations are large and not all families could afford phone services of any kind and rely on neighbors to pass on the messages. He also needed to get his head together. Before exiting he turned and looked directly at me. "Sam, the bosses won't like it but considering everything, you should take point. Will is an asset and you should rely on his expertise. I'll take my team of three to Wyoming. I'd rather not get the local LEOs involved since we aren't following protocol. We'll firm things up in the morning. I doubt there will be any dissent in the ranks with the plan."

It was almost nine, and I was starving. Will looked at me, "You want to try dinner again? There's nothing else we can do until morning?"

I smiled and took his hand. "Room Service."

TWELVE

Will took my key card and opened the door to my room. I still had hold of his hand. When we were inside, he asked, "Are you sure, Sam? I don't want to rush you, and I don't want you to do something because of Charlie. Don't get me wrong, I want you. I think you're amazing. You take my breath away, but I want you for all the right reasons, and I want you to want me for all the right reasons too. I'm not looking for just a one-night stand."

I regarded him, ran my fingers in his hair. "I don't care what Charlie does with your waitress. It just makes things clear for me. There's no me and Charlie. I want other things. I want more. Besides, why would you assume 'Room Service' meant sex? I'm hungry. I want dinner and conversation. I thought we could do that here without distraction."

Will smiled. "Shall I order?"

"Yes, I'm starved."

Dinner arrived, and we devoured everything on our plates. I would've licked my plate if Will hadn't been there. We had not eaten anything all day, and it showed. There was little conversation while we ate, but it wasn't awkward. It felt normal. Will was a polite eater. He had excellent manners. When we finished, he pushed the food cart out into the hall. He came back and sat on the edge of the bed. "Are you still up for talking because I would like to. I know we have to get up early, but I'm a bit wired."

I glanced at Will from across the room and couldn't help myself from commenting, "You look like you'd be a good dancer. Do you like to dance? Your moves are fluid."

He chuckled a bit. "I come from a long history of dancers. My people have danced for rain, for crops, for war, you name it, we dance. I would dance with you as foreplay. I'd be a good dancer with you." He pushed himself off the bed and held his hand out to me as if asking for the next dance. It was tempting.

I laughed. I hadn't laughed in a long time. It felt good, if only for a moment. His comment stayed with me. I knew it was true. I'd like to dance with him.

"I digress. I want to talk." I took my boots off and sat in the middle of the bed with my legs crossed. "You wanted to talk about the kiss, as I recall."

"Well two kisses to be exact, but yes. First, though, I am blown away by how you put all those pieces together. Now we have a chance to save two boys' lives, and get this crazy killer: correction, these two killers. I can't tell you how impressed I am, and proud that I've been included. It would mean a lot for me to help find Samuel's killer, it would mean a lot to his family, and to the other families. I don't want to make this all about the case, tomorrow will come soon enough, but I just needed to tell you that I understand it now. I get why you do this, and I see how brilliant you are at it."

I smiled at him. "Why don't you take your boots off, put your feet up, and get comfortable. Lean back. I'd also like to state an observation. You really need to put chairs in the rooms that aren't made of branches and twigs. Some upholstered pieces would be nice."

Will laughed, "Clients like the typical Lodge run by an Indian to look a certain way. It's not my taste either. They usually come for hunting, fishing, or camping, and they don't spend much time in the rooms."

It was around eleven now, and I wasn't tired, neither was Will. "So, do you want to go first? Ask me a question, or make a comment about anything? I can see the wheels turning in your head."

Will felt like he was on the spot. He wanted to talk to her but was afraid he'd say the wrong thing or make things uncomfortable again. He wanted to know everything about her and wanted her to know everything about him. For once in his life, he wanted to know someone before being intimate with them.

"When we were at the cave, and you were reacting to the comment I had made, you said something about knowing what it was like to be a victim yourself and having other people speak for you. I want to understand that. Mind telling me?" He touched my hair, placing it behind my shoulder.

I peered down for a moment at my hands. They were shaking. I was trying to formulate how I would tell him. "Well, that's a start, and a bit difficult, but I'll tell you because you care enough to ask." I paused a minute. "You may not enjoy hearing this but getting to know someone isn't always about just the nice stuff, it's also about the stuff that makes us who we are." I took a breath.

"Anything that's happened to me at the Bureau I don't consider as my being victimized. I chose this work, and there are inherent risks that go with it. When you carry a gun and deal with unsavory types, you can physically get hurt, and I have been hurt in the line of duty. The victimization I was referring to, relates to when I was five. I was molested by a family member several times. At first, no one believed me because I was so young. My babysitter had seen changes in me and even though she was only thirteen, she was brave and went to the police. She told them I had been hurt, the police came and brought a social worker. The offending family member was removed from the house, and all because of a brave girl who noticed something, and spoke for me when I couldn't. She saved my life, or at least prevented it from being worse. I think her act of bravery made me want to speak for those who couldn't—either by writing, or when I received the opportunity to be in Law Enforcement, it seemed a good way to accomplish that."

Will seemed stricken. He took my hands into his, looked in my eyes and said in the softest voice, "I'm sorry that happened to you Sam, I can't imagine how hard that must have been for you."

He felt the impulse to kill whoever it was that had done that to her. He already felt the need to protect her. The more he heard, the more he wanted her, not just for a night but for a lifetime.

I looked at this man. HHe really meant what he said, and in some way, he was probably sorry for asking. I felt better that I told him. "It was a long time ago; I came to terms with it. I had to. To be honest, I never knew a man could be like you, until now. I always thought a man like you was an urban myth." I touched his cheek as he took my hand and kissed it softly.

"Urban myth?"

"Someone too good to be true with all those attributes women look for. The one that got away. The guy dreams are made of." I shook my head embarrassed, as he tilted his head and smiled.

I needed to ask something of Will, but I was nervous. "I guess it's my turn to ask you something. Tell me more about who Will Little Bear is. I read that you like to date twenty-something women—like your waitress—and that you're quite the man about town. I may be too old for you. I personally don't see that in you—you're too self-assured. You seem to know who you are. Are you a person who doesn't like commitment?" I caught myself, stopped, and retracted. "You know, I'd like to suck that question right back into my mouth. You don't need to answer that. I'll ask something else," I backtracked like an apology.

"No, I like that question. I really do want to explain it to you. I'm almost forty-two years old, and I've avoided commitment and marriage my entire adult life. I've dated younger women because it's easy and they're not complicated. I've dated a lot, and I haven't gotten close to anyone. I come from a fractured family. My father drank, and my mother took the brunt of it. This is a common problem on the reservation, and people don't get help. I was an only child and couldn't protect my mom. My father killed her in a domestic dispute, then killed himself. I was eight. I told myself I would never get married, never have that kind of life. I thought it might pass down to me, but that doesn't mean I've never dreamed what the right person would be like. I ended up living with my grandmother until I was eighteen, and then enlisted in the Marines. I reveled in the structure and getting strong, so that I could stand up to those like my father. I guess in some ways we both started out on rough footing."

He continued, "Recently, I've decided I'd like to have permanence in my life, something I didn't think was attainable. Maybe it takes a mature man to see the quality of a real woman he can make a life with—a better one than he knew existed. I think you're the perfect age. I guess that brings us to the reason why we were going to talk in the first place—about the kiss."

He smiled at me with those soft brown eyes. "Do you mind if I keep going with this, because I've been needing to say some things."

I nodded. "Please go on, I see that it's important." I sat on the edge of the bed now, getting closer, but giving him space.

Will edged off the bed and started moving around the room, hands in his pockets, looking at the floor. I could see he was weighing his words before he spoke. Once words come out, it's impossible to pull them back in. He moved so smoothly, and despite his demeanor, well, I couldn't help but notice his ass, which was fine.

He turned towards me, and said with real clarity, "I'll never lie to you, or keep secrets from you, and will be faithful to you. I am not, because of fear, ever going to hold back, or be afraid to tell you my feelings. I don't want to miss what could make my life wonderful because of something I didn't say to you."

He was emotional and his voice was wavering. "We're going after a killer tomorrow, and if I miss my chance to say something, well then, I'll regret it for the rest of my life. That kiss, Sam, that meant everything to me. I gave you everything I am in that kiss. I'm betting everything on that kiss."

I started to say something. He put his hand up, "I've got to finish this."

"I've never known anyone like you. You are kind — the way you talk about the boys. You're brave—the way you face things and know you need to go to dangerous places to save others—and you're the first in line to do so. You're smarter than anyone I've ever known. You never give up. From the moment I saw you, something was tugging at me. You don't even know how beautiful you are, when I'm around you I can't breathe, and I want you more than I thought was possible, more than sex, you. I know I need to be a better man to deserve a woman like you, I can be, and will be. I've drifted my whole life trying not to make permanent connections, and now that's all I want with you. But I need to know if that kiss meant anything to you. I know we haven't known each other long, three days, a moment really, but my heart beats as though I've known you my entire life. I've wanted this dream of you my whole life."

I got off the bed and walked over to where he was standing. Tears welled up in my eyes. I touched the front of his shirt with my hand. I looked in his eyes, "Will, let me answer you now." I touched his chest and could feel his heart pounding. He had his hands at my waist, his thumbs in my belt loops, his cheek to mine. I felt his breath in my ear as if he wanted to say something more but couldn't. "Please sit down, you're trembling, and you need to catch your breath." He nodded while looking at me, removed his hands from my waist, wiped a tear from my cheek with a kiss, and sat on the bed. It was as if he didn't trust himself to speak.

I knew this man who was in front of me. Reading people is my line of work, I make instant decisions with regard to who someone is, and my heart was open to him. "Will, you are the most amazing and self-assured man I've ever known in my life. You're kind, gentle, strong, smart, and tender. I'm wildly attracted to you. Handsome doesn't even touch what you are." Taking a breath to continue.

"I'm around a lot of men in my work and need to portray a certain persona to do my job, not knowing where the job persona ends and where I begin sometimes. I've had disappointments in my life, and I've been with the wrong people. You say you don't deserve me. I feel I don't deserve someone like you. I don't fully know who I am. You're able to see me, and that helps me to begin to know myself more clearly. I watched you when we went to Samuel's grave. You're a man unafraid of his emotions, at least around me. That makes me feel like you trust me. I trust you seeing my emotions and want to trust you with more of me. That kiss to me was the Super Bowl of intimacy, something I've never experienced in my life. You looked into my eyes. That kiss showed me who you are. I hope it told you something about me. That kiss made me hope for a future with you."

Will was staring at me, his eyes soft, then he held his hand out to me. I walked over to the bed where he sat, took his hand as he pulled me closer. "You were in the Marines, you understand, a mission can go either way, and I have to be a realist about what could happen. I want you Will, and if we don't die in the next few days, a future with you. I'm afraid, and don't want to go so fast that we pass ourselves going the other way. I want to savor every minute, every day, every year, by going slowly then I can be the person you deserve. I want us to know everything, good and bad, about each other, and still love each other at the end of the day. That's what that kiss meant to me."

I stood as close to him as I could without becoming a part of his very being. With him sitting on the edge of the bed we were almost face-to-face. Taking his face in my hands I said, "I don't know how the next few days are going to play out. We'll be in danger. Anything can happen, something bad might happen, but I want you to know that since we've met, I've not been wondering about what I want for my life. I've figured it out, it's you."

I draped my arms around his neck, put my face in the curve where his essence lives, and inhaled him, wanting to remember it. He was holding on to me tightly, as if to prevent me from disappearing. I whispered in his ear, "Just sleep with me tonight. Nothing else, not yet. Just be here, hold me, and talk to me."

He pulled back slightly to look at me, tracing the outline of my face with his finger, touching my lips, and putting his forehead to mine. He smiled. "This is just where I want to be." He took me in his arms and kissed me as if everything counted on it. Maybe it did. For me it did.

That night he held me, we talked about what we wanted in this life, and we touched each other through our clothing, wanting, but being patient. Kisses ebbed and flowed until morning.

THIRTEEN

Will got up a few hours later. Neither of us had slept, thinking of what was ahead and what we needed to do. The next few days were going to be brutal. He kissed my forehead. "I'm going to start getting the supplies and provisions together. I'll meet you at the briefing at seven."

I held him back for a few moments. "Are you sure you want to do this? You didn't sign up for this like I did."

He looked into my eyes and kissed me deeply. "I'm very sure." He turned and went out the door. I sat up and was suddenly afraid for him. Will had been in the Marines, but he was going into this situation with emotional baggage. He wanted revenge for Samuel and justice for Samuel's family. Something like this could change him.

I showered—as if it would matter—since I'd be wearing the same clothes for the next few days. I ordered up some breakfast and planned the briefing. Charlie had better support my plan, and because he was walking on thin ice professionally, I figured it would be moot. I wasn't a Field Agent; I spent most of my time in the office. But this case mattered to me, and this case had mattered to Dr. Sampson. I was going to see it through.

I needed to pack more efficiently this time. I looked at my shotgun and thought, no matter what, it's coming with me today. I made quick work of packing for the trip and dressed, wearing the warmest things in layers. I had my FBI-issued vest to wear under my jacket, and an additional one for Will to wear, too. I couldn't wear a long coat since it would impede me from having immediate access to my gun and the other things on my belt. My ass was going to freeze. This time, Will, was my responsibility, and I had to be prepared. All my training and experience needed to work for me now. My case, my risk.

The weather would be worse than last time. Blowing snow was expected and temperatures hovering around zero, depending on the wind-chill factor it could feel like twenty below. The extremes would push us on this operation, emotions would be running high, and the fear of not finding our killers before they found their next victims was palpable.

I checked myself. My service revolver was in my waistband behind my back, extra bullets and shells were in the waist belt pocket with more in the backpack, along with a knife in my left boot, my Kel-Tec P-32 in my right boot, a two-way radio, a cell phone and portable charger just in case were noted. My handcuffs, along with my shooting gloves, were attached to my belt. I put two Maglites in my backpack. They're more than just flashlights; they can be weapons. A first-aid kit. I had to consider all possibilities. I didn't know what weapons the killer might have, or if there would only be one of them.

I headed over to the Murder Room with my gear to be ready to leave as soon as the meeting was over. When I arrived at the room, I saw the agents were dressed and ready. We nodded to each other. They were taking this seriously. I looked around the room, and then saw Charlie and Will walk in together. Will winked at me as Charlie walked to the front of the room to address the team.

"I'm turning the strategy of this operation over to Special Agent Wright. Give her your undivided attention. The sooner we get done, the sooner we can get on the road."

Charlie knew he looked a little beat-up with his bloodshot eyes, and lack of sleep. A sense of loss permeated his being. His shoulders were slack and his usual perfect attire unkempt. He felt himself trying to hang on after his conversation with Will earlier sent him into a downward spiral. Will had asked him to step away from Sam and to allow him a chance with her. Will told Charlie he loved Sam. Simple enough words, but ones Charlie could never say to her. He agreed to stay out of the picture.

I walked to the front of the room, to the side where Charlie was standing. Will stood in the back of the room, hands in his pockets, looking ready to go.

"I want to go over the process as to how the final analysis came about, how we know where the perps are going to strike next, and who their intended targets are." For the next thirty minutes, I laid it out, detailed and exact. These agents were ready to put their lives on the line for an educated gut feeling. I told them everything I knew. When finished, they were in total agreement with my findings that we had twin serial killers. "The teams will be myself and Will to pursue the Montana connection, the rest of you, except for Special Agent Randall Johnson, making the Wyoming connection. Special Agent Johnson will base here handling communications, making sure we can all talk to each other. He'll track us by GPS using our radios, phones, and the ones imbedded in our vests. Everyone, please keep your phones and radios on. Turn your radios to Channel 18. Randall will be our lifeline in case we need air support or Medivac. I for one, Randall, appreciate you standing post here for all of us.

"I'd like to bring Will Little Bear up here, so he can fill you in on what it's going to be like out there. He'll tell you what you need to be cognizant of, so you're safe, and so that you can get where you need to go. He'll also go over the maps with you, explain how he pinpointed the areas we are heading to, and where the perps are headed, or may already be. Will may not be one of us, but he has a military background, and this is his turf. He's the expert here on the reservation."

Will walked to the front of the room, went over the maps, and showed each team where they were headed. He passed out maps to each Agent that he had marked with the route he felt best about; based on weather, possible road closures, and accessibility to the target. "I've arranged a guide for the Wyoming team. He'll meet you later today at the designated spot on your maps, marked in red. His name is Stan Willow Bird. Next to me, he's the best," Will said without being prideful. "When Special Agent Wright and I went to Samuel's site a few days ago, she was the one who noticed the rock cluster, a cairn, that you need to be mindful of. Will handed out photos. Rock clusters, intentional formations made by individuals to help guide, help establish a lifeline if they become lost, and can also signal someone who might be looking for something or someone. I think the killers may be using these to communicate with each other, or at least establishing a trail for themselves."

"Stan will give you more information, but there are shacks, huts, covered trenches, and rock openings where supplies are cached should you find yourself in a dire situation. These provisions are often left by people like me; hunters, hikers, and those who live around here. They're safety nets, should anyone get caught in severe weather or find themselves stranded. Here in Montana, I know where most of them are, and Stan will know where they are in Wyoming. If you want to survive out there, listen to Stan. He might just save your life. The weather in both states is going to be bad, expect extreme winds, blowing snow, limited visibility, and below zero temperatures. Dress appropriately, eat protein, and stay hydrated. Lastly, avoid going into any caves. Bears are currently hibernating and don't like being disturbed." Will signaled he was done and went to the back of the room. I could see the agents were impressed with Will and his knowledge. They trusted the information and the findings.

"We are under time restraints based on the birthdates. The Wyoming team has four days to find the perp, and the Montana team has three days.

Good luck to everyone, be safe." I concluded my words and nodded at Charlie as I started to the back of the room where Will was standing.

Charlie came up to me, looking a little worn. "I'd like to apologize, Sam, for my behavior. I don't want bad feelings between us when we have this job to do. Will told me about his background in the Marines. He's made a real impression on me, n you'll be in good hands, better than mine. You know, we could both be fired over this—you in charge, and not a Field Agent. It would be more honorable than some of the other things I've done. Don't almost die again, I hate the paperwork." He smiled, seeming to reflect on something, and joined his team.

Will walked over. "Are you ready?"

"As ready as I can be."

"Are you afraid?" He asked as he grabbed some of my gear.

"Just for the others who are relying on insights, and best guesses, who trust this is the right thing. I'm putting good agents in harm's way. I pray I'm right."

Will was afraid for Sam. He was afraid of what might happen out there, but he didn't want her to know. He was afraid he wouldn't be able to keep her safe. He couldn't lose her after just finding her.

I handed Will his vest and said in a firm tone, "There's no negotiation. You will wear this, and you will follow my orders with regards to the operation. Likewise, I will follow your orders as to how we get there. Are you okay with that?"

"You're a strong woman, a great agent, and you are correct about this. Don't second guess yourself. I'd be proud to follow your lead, to hell and back."

"By the way, what was that all about, you and Charlie coming in together? It looked like the two of you had words."

Will smiled. "I just filled him in on my military background, and explained I was more than capable of making sure you were safe on this operation. He ended up agreeing with me."

"Is there anything else I should know?"

"Not anything you'd want to know—plausible deniability." He winked.

Will and I got into the SUV that we would take as far as possible, depending on road closures and deteriorating conditions. There was a horse trailer hitched, with three horses inside. Hiking into this unforgiving country would be a last resort, and Will didn't want to leave any necessary equipment or supplies behind, which was why he brought a pack horse along. I noticed Will had his rifle, an M40A3. He wasn't taking any chances. We were either stopping this killer before he killed again, or if we were too late, we would finish this one way or another—tracking and killing him. He would never kill again, if I had my way, leaving this detail out when I talked to Charlie.

Will started the car, and off we headed towards Muddy, a little northwest of Lame Deer. We had maybe twenty-five miles to get there, but the first road closure was about twenty miles out due to weather. Will knew a place we could leave the SUV and trailer, where it would be safe and available to us for the return trip. He knew the water sources, shelters, and trails near the area we were headed to. I felt hopeful we could get there in time. It was snowing, and the wind had picked up, rocking the SUV and the trailer as we rode along. The weather wasn't going to hold us back from this mission.

We reached the end of passable roads. The ice and snowdrifts had covered what were asphalt roads and turned them into treacherous avenues only navigated by horse. We were at the destination where Will planned on storing the SUV and trailer. It looked like an abandoned barn from the outside, but the inside was secure. We pulled in, exited out of the car, and went back to the trailer to ready the horses. He already had them saddled, but we had to get the gear from the vehicle onto the pack horse. The wind was whipping up and it was getting colder outside by the minute.

Will wore a flannel shirt over thermals, with a sweater over both. He had his hunting knife on his belt, as well as the radio I's given him at The Lodge and reminded him to turn the radio to Channel 18. He had a Beretta M9 holstered on his right side. I handed him the FBI-issued vest, which he put on, then he put his long shearling coat on over that. Lastly, he put his felt cowboy hat on, tightened with the drawstring. He would stay warm on this trek. Compared to my down jacket, scarf, and wool hat, I was jealous of his attire.

I tied my hair in a ponytail to keep it out of the way and shoved it into my hat. I kept the ear flaps down to keep my head and ears warm.

Will looked at what I was wearing and asked, "Are you going to be warm enough in that short coat?"

"I've got my granny underwear on, thermal long johns, and flannel-lined jeans. I think I'll be okay. I've also got a thermal shirt and two sweaters on under the coat. It's just my ass that's exposed."

"And what a fine ass it is." He smiled.

I smiled back, remembering his hand had been on it last night.

Everything we thought we might need was secured on our pack horse, a pretty, black mare named Girl, with a white star on her head. We were ready to go. We put on our gloves, and Will helped me mount Laney. With so many clothes on, it was hard to lift my legs high enough to get on her back without help. He handed me both sets of reins while he locked up the barn doors, which looked like they might be ripped off their hinges any minute by the wind. Will mounted Bear Boy, grabbed the reins for Girl, and we headed out into the storm.

We were riding into the icy wind. It felt as if sharp pins were hitting our faces. The snow had started back up, but it was icy, and stung like a mother. It was going to be a long day.

It felt like hours before we stopped to water the horses, have a drink ourselves, and eat some jerky. When I dismounted Laney, I could hardly feel my legs, despite the layers of clothing I had on. Will checked the horses' hooves, picking out ice pellets that had formed. We needed these horses and didn't want them to bruise their feet. He pulled carrots from his coat pocket, and gave each horse one, along with alfalfa cubes to give them some nourishment. They were burning off calories by the second in this cold.

Will came over to me and loudly asked so I could hear over the wind, "Are you doing, okay?" His face was close to mine, yet I could hardly hear a thing.

Despite the fact I was frozen, I answered, "I'm fine, just a little stiff." Handing him some lip balm. "Protect your lips. I like them the way they are, I don't want them falling off." Smiling, he did as I asked.

"We're going to make camp within the hour, since we're losing light, and visibility is only about fifty feet. I don't want to take any unnecessary risks," he explained, as he tightened his grip on the horses' reins.

"Sounds like a plan." He helped me mount Laney. I was grateful for Laney, planned to thank her later for carrying me, and for knowing more than me about this riding thing. With Laney, I only had to hold the reins and be easy on the bit. She did everything else. She got back into step behind Bear Boy and Girl, and off we went. We were marching into hell, despite the cold.

This area of Montana is largely open space consisting of gently rolling plains, but there are pockets of woods and rocky areas. Unlike at the Custer National Forest, we were more exposed out here.

Will knew of a place we could camp. It was a small clearing with boulders behind and trees on the other three sides. This would help with the wind. There wasn't any water, but Will would melt snow for the horses to drink. Tonight, might be the only night we would have a fire, since tomorrow we may be too close and too easily detected. Enjoy it while you can, I thought to myself.

Will stopped, dismounted Bear Boy, and looked back at me. "This is where we stay tonight."

I pitched in and in a brief time we made a campfire, made sure the horses were taken care of, and started digging what Will called a sauna ditch for us to sleep on so we wouldn't have to lay on the frozen ground. We dug as far as the frozen earth would let us, then laid hot coals from the fire in the hole, covered them with dirt, and green branches. Will then situated the double-wide sleeping bag over the whole thing. "We're sharing tonight to stay warm.

I wouldn't be able to get to you with all those clothes on anyway." He smiled, probably because he knew that if I gave the word, he'd find a way.

"Where did you learn this?"

"Saw a movie about a mountain man played by Robert Redford, and he did it. Seemed to work out okay for him, but unless you dig it deep enough, you can set your pants on fire," he explained, laughing.

I looked at the smoking hole, then at Will. "Those would be your pants."

Will made coffee for himself and tea for me. We ate his famous canned beans and jerky. I knew I would have to relieve myself before sleeping, and I was studying the surroundings to figure out how it was going to work. It's much easier for guys.

Will watched me and examined his pack. "I think I know that look." He handed me the roll of toilet paper and the shovel. He pointed to the other side of the tree behind us. That other tree over there belongs to me."

I've flown on transport planes the military uses. They give you a plastic bag, and you pick a corner of the plane to handle business while there's turbulence. This was harder because of all the clothes, and it was cold and snowing, an ordeal at best. My new favorite luxury was indoor plumbing.

After being reminded everyone needs to go and squat behind a tree, I came back, and sat by the fire. "You said no secrets," I quipped handing him the shovel back.

It was almost eight at night, but it felt later. My body ached, and my thoughts were anxious about tomorrow. I wanted a distraction, and two aspirin.

I slowly stood up from my log, went to find the pills, and saw Will checking on the horses. He gave them treats and talked to them. It was a dark night that might reveal millions of stars, if the wind and snow ever let up. Sitting amongst the trees, the heavy snow filtered through the branches.

"Will, do you feel like continuing our talk from last night? I think it is my turn to ask a question."

"Sounds like a very good way to pass the time to continue our journey of discovery about each other. I think it matters now more than ever. I want to know everything about you."

"Is it a problem that I'm white?" I asked plainly. "My ethnicity, will it be a roadblock for us to having a life together? I know some Tribes would frown on me being white and wonder why you would cross over, so to speak."

Will half-laughed, "Boy, you don't hold back, do you? I get where you're coming from, but I think times have changed a bit within the Tribes. We've become more open to who people are, and not what color they are. Obviously, I don't find it a problem. There will always be those who cling to the old ways and distrust anyone who is white, but that's the same in any race of people. People in general distrust those who are different." He got up and sat closer to me. "I've been waiting for you my whole life, Sam. The essence of you. I didn't know what color you'd be when you showed up. If someone asked me, Will, why are you with a white woman? I'd look at you and say to them; I just don't see it."

He stretched his back. "My turn."

We were shoulder-to-shoulder in this desolate place, and for the moment I felt safer than I ever had. I knew Will wanted to keep me safe, and he was as worried about tomorrow as I was.

"Let's hear it."

"What would your family think of me?" Will asked in a way that made him appear younger, wanting parental approval.

"I don't have any family, Will, and no they wouldn't have liked you. They didn't like me, because of what happened when I was five. It was as though they blamed me. The closest I ever had to a real family was Dr. Sampson, and he's gone now. He would have loved you and been proud of us."

"What happened? Do you want to tell me?" He put his arm around my shoulder, as if he was trying to deflect some of the sadness.

"It's okay, it's been a long time. Around my seventeenth birthday, my family and I had gone to a ski lodge in Colorado for Christmas. It was the dead of winter, like this, but I kept my window in the bedroom opened a little. Apparently, there was no carbon monoxide detector. The pilot light to the furnace went out and everyone died in their sleep. I was saved because of the open window in my room. Barely, but it saved me. It was one of those tragic things. For some reason, I didn't die. I guess that's why Christmas isn't big on my list of holidays."

Will was silent. He took my hand. "In the last two days, I've made you talk about the two most horrifying things in your life. I feel terrible about that. I don't know what to say. Maybe I should just stop talking."

"It's fine. Believe it or not I was seventeen and in college at the time and my female professor took me into her home, so I wouldn't have to go to Child Protective Services. She was a terrific person to me, and I owe her a lot. Focusing on school brought me to where I am today—sitting with you on a log, freezing in the middle of nowhere, and feeling very lucky that fate, destiny or something, brought us together."

Will kissed me softly. "You are so strong."

I smiled and proclaimed, "Will, I'm beat. Can we get into the sauna double-wide sleeping bag, and see if sleep will come to us tonight?"

He stood up, reached for my hand, helped me get my frozen ass up, and stifled a yawn. "Sounds good to me."

The sauna worked, and we were warm. I laid there with my head on his shoulder, feeling comforted that he had his arms around me. I fell asleep.

Will watched Sam sleep. He thought about the things she had told him about her life. He couldn't believe she had been able to become the person she was with the tragedy she had experienced. "She's so much more than I had originally thought." Will promised himself, "I'm going to make a life with her whatever it takes." He kissed her forehead and went to sleep.

FOURTEEN

I woke up. It was still dark except for a bright moon that hadn't shown itself earlier because of the blowing snow and low visibility. Tonight, would be a full moon. The snow and wind had slowed down, but it was extremely cold. Will had his arm around me, and I could hear his soft breathing deep sleep brings. Any other time it would have been a romantic situation, but in a few hours, the reality of why we were here would become apparent.

Twenty minutes passed, and Will started to wake. He opened his eyes and smiled. "Did you get any sleep?"

"Some."

He tightened his embrace as I snuggled into him. I wanted to make the most of these precious moments and to remember them always. I had no idea what would happen when we caught up with the killer, putting my face into the curve of his neck—my favorite place—and breathing him into my memory.

"What are you thinking?" He looked sleepy and so inviting, it was hard to pull my thoughts together.

"I was thinking that right at this moment, this is all that matters. I want to tell you that I love you. I don't know how all of this is going to turn out, but I don't want there to be any words left unsaid between us." I wanted him, but it couldn't be here.

"Sam, I love you, too, more than I ever thought I could love anyone." He turned towards me, took my face into his big, strong hands and kissed me. His kiss, deep with all the intensity and feeling he had inside. I returned the same to him, trying to live a lifetime in this moment.

Stressful situations can make a person feel things in a heightened way, but this felt real. I wanted it to be real. I needed it to be real. Sometimes people come into your life at just the right time, but they don't fit all the conventions you think are supposed to be in place—in a specific time frame—but damn, sometimes lighting strikes and you can't deny it.

The sun was just starting to come up. We had no choice but to get moving. Will got up and helped me out of the sleeping bag. "We need to thank Robert Redford for this sauna idea," I laughed. "I'm not as stiff as I thought I'd be."

Will brought me to him and wrapped me in arms that made me feel safe. I wanted this embrace to last a forever, but I'd take what I could get for now. He whispered, "Whatever it takes."

I knew what he had just said meant many things. Whatever it takes to be together. Whatever it takes to get the killer and to save the boy. Whatever it takes to get through this. I nodded and hugged back.

I needed to check in with Charlie by radio and hear what their status was, as well as needing to inform him at some point today we would go radio silent if we were getting close to the perp. The static on the radio could be picked up easily out here in the stillness, and we needed every advantage to surprise this bastard or double bastards. The radios had to be patched through central at The Lodge making reception iffy at best and would be a limited resource of communication.

"Charlie, this is Sam. What's your status?"

"Sam, I was just going to contact you. A Cheyenne boy was abducted last night in your vicinity. Even though he lives in Muddy, he was visiting an aunt in Lame Deer. It's Brandon Lewis. His twelfth birthday is tomorrow. You were right; this is the boy you identified as the target in Montana."

"God, Charlie, my timing was off." The weather made the killer open his window of opportunity. I hadn't taken that into consideration, because I focused on the previous analysis of the kidnappings and the patterns within the timing, forgetting to factor in the weather. "Will and I need to find him today. He is going to have a twelfth birthday, if I have anything to say about it." I was feeling sick. "Charlie, what about the boy, Morgan Little Deer?"

"Nothing yet, I'll keep you posted. You and Will stay safe."

Will listened to the exchange. "Let's eat something to keep us going. I've already taken care of the horses. We can get out of here in twenty minutes. What's the plan? I don't want to mess this up."

Over beef jerky, a power bar, and some water, Will and I made a couple of plans to implement once we found the killer and the boy. This was no different than battle plans in the military that were subject to immediate change and flexibility depending on circumstances out of our control. Will knew a place where he thought the killer would hole up since the sky indicated more snow for the day and the perp would be looking for similar settings as in the previous murders. Out here in the wilderness there are only so many places to find minimal shelter.

I made it clear to Will the boy was his priority. "Get the boy out and keep him safe." I would have Will's back and take the killer. We weren't going to debate this, and it had to be settled now.

He looked like he wanted to argue.

I stared at him with determination and repeated, "Here's the priority in terms of necessity—of who needs to be saved—the boy, then you, and then me. Don't fight me on this Will. You said you would follow my lead."

"I will, but I don't like it. I won't let anything happen to you."

One rule Dr. Sampson always taught, "Don't get emotionally involved in cases, it can rob you of your life." I understood now more than ever.

I understood the anguish in his face. "Please Will, don't make this harder than it needs to be. I promise to do everything possible to keep myself safe, but I have a job to do. I have all these dead boys in my head saying to me they want justice, and I need to give it to them so they can rest in peace. There's a boy out here somewhere who is scared, hurting, and needing us to save him."

Nothing else had to be said.

We broke down the campsite. We took everything in case it stretched to another day. Will figured we would ride for several miles and then hike in to get closer to the shack. He knew they had to be there. There was nowhere else out here for the killer to take the boy, Brandon, this close to Lame Deer.

The snow complicated matters for us. We weren't making good time, but it was beneficial in another way—the killer had to stay put. I didn't know the perp's name or why he chose twelve-year old boys, but I knew who he was, what he was, and where he was. Will and I were going to take him down and get Brandon out alive.

Several hours later, Will stopped, dismounted Bear Boy, and walked over to me. "I think we need to make a light camp here until nightfall. We can use the moon to get close after that. We'll have little to no cover out here so silence and the sparse darkness will be all we have to limit our visibility. Sound carries out here, and he might be able to hear us approach if we're on horseback. We're about a mile or so from the shack—we can hike in after dark. The horses are safe here, and close enough to get to them after." He talked quietly. We needed to be careful now.

I nodded to the affirmative and gingerly got down off Laney with wobbly legs. I needed to find a place to relieve myself. Cold weather and nerves seemed to accelerate my need to pee, stretch my legs, and take a couple of aspirin to make sure I could run later. I really needed to stop taking aspirin—it was a crutch, but today was not the day to stop.

We didn't want to take a chance and start a fire, so we sat in the sleeping bag to stay warm for the next few hours. Waiting is the worst part. You start second guessing yourself, and you forget to breathe.

I didn't really notice the cold. The adrenaline was starting to kick in, pins and needles in my body, reminding me that fear could keep me alive tonight, and keep Will and the boy safe. Will was watching me, no doubt wondering what was going on in my head. I was impatient and nursing my own fears of dying because of my miscalculations on time. It was on me if things went badly. It was so still that I could hear both our hearts beating. Looking straight at Will I said in a whisper, "Here's how I see it. Tonight, could change everything, put what we want for ourselves on hold. I promise, no matter what happens here this night, I will come back to you. I love you more than my life. Will you be waiting for me?" My voice cracked, choking back tears, "If I get hurt bad, I don't want you to have to take care of me. I couldn't bear that, I want to come back to you whole, strong, and better—that may take a long time before we can be together."

Will didn't want Sam saying things like this. Everything would be fine. We'll be together. We haven't made love yet. This was all new for Will, his willingness to wait for sex with love. He needed Sam, he couldn't lose her, the promise of her. He didn't want to face the possibility.

Will seemed to have a difficult time talking. He pulled me closer. I could feel him trembling. "For as long as it takes, I will wait for you. You come to me when you can, when you're ready. We have unfinished business." He tried to smile. "I love you Sam, the kind of love that will make me a better man. I will wait. I promise."

I believed him. He leaned in and kissed me. It wasn't passion, or lust, it was simply love, along with the need and desire for this love to go on.

FIFTEEN

I looked at my watch. It was four in the afternoon, and turning dark, December in Montana dark. There appeared a full moon we could use it to our advantage. We had to be careful not to let it announce us before we were ready. The wind was still, and the lightest of snow was falling. I had turned the radios off earlier. There was no sound except for the horses nickering and snorting out their breath.

Will and I got out of the sleeping bag and stood. I was feeling like a boxer before a bout, shaking my arms and legs, trying to get them to limber up. I'm not a Field Agent, and I didn't have experience in killing, but I had made a commitment to the dead boys—Jon, Chad, Tommy, and Samuel—that I would do this for them, and prevent another boy, from the same fate.

Will stretched his back and went over to the horses. He saddled them for the ready, just in case. For later. He had treats for them, and alfalfa cubes. They knew something was going on. They were picking up on our emotions, fear. He was giving them comfort. I went to relieve myself, and so did Will. We couldn't have any distractions. I returned as Will checking his rifle and his M9 Beretta sidearm seemed lost in his own thoughts. He had his hunting knife on his belt, the sharpness glistening in the moonlight. He was wearing his shearling coat over the FBI-issued vest, but he left his hat and gloves behind. Less to deal with.

I checked my Glock 9mm and extra clips, my radio and handcuffs were on my belt even though I knew I wouldn't be using them. I grabbed the Maglite and put it through my belt loop just in case. I reached for my shotgun, checked that it was ready, and braced it against a tree. Finally, I zipped my coat, put my hat and gloves in its pockets, and checked my ponytail, pushing it inside my collar. I had my P32 in my right boot and a knife in my left. In the end, Will and I decided to leave the shotgun and rifle behind, thinking this was going to be up close and personal. We would need our hands free, shivering me with a last-minute dose of reality. Guns and shooting are different things to me. No one should ever have to shoot a real person, even a bad person because it is a grave responsibility that you will carry with you forever. It's the knowing when to shoot, who to shoot and at what time to shoot when seconds count. I was good at the knowing and the seconds, but I wasn't a field agent, never dreaming I'd have my chance to be tested. I felt the fear inside and hoped I was up to this responsibility. I took a deep breath, looked over at Will, thought of the boy and readied myself.

It was time to start hiking to the shack, time to finish this. The snow was deep, and we weren't using snowshoes. You can't really run with them on. We needed to be fast and quiet. It was completely still except for our breathing. We'd been walking for some time when Will put his hand out. I stopped in place, and he quietly spoke, "It's about a quarter mile over there. Let's take a rest and then get going." I could see our breaths. The temperature was dropping.

"I haven't seen any rock clusters, cairns, or signs the killer has been this way. Maybe when the boy wasn't in Muddy, he changed plans and came closer to Lame Deer." Will was thinking out loud, barely whispering.

There was nothing to talk about. We knew what we were about to do. We said all the important things we needed to say to each other. The next thirty minutes would shape our future and that of the boy were here to save. There's no amount of training for this. There's always the unknown, and you just use your best instincts. When you're dealing with a crazy killer, things can go bad fast; they are completely unpredictable.

Will and I looked at each other. He kissed me, "For luck." We crouched back up, slightly stopped, and started towards the shack. The trail was rocky, hidden by snow cover, and I tripped. My ponytail having come out of my collar became stuck in a prickly bush, and there was no way we had time to deal with this. I looked at Will and whispered, "Cut off my hair. Now!"

He took his knife and cut my ponytail off. He looked as if he had done something to hurt me. I looked at his apologetic eyes, and whispered with a smile, "It'll grow back." He looked older just then. The magnitude of this operation showed in his eyes.

We were about one hundred yards from the shack. I didn't see or smell smoke from a fire, and I didn't see any light. The shack was silhouetted by the moon, it looked deserted. We squatted down and listened. It was so quiet. There wasn't much cover for us. Will put his finger to his lips. I wondered what he was hearing that I didn't.

"I hear a horse. It must be behind the shack," he whispered.

I had my Glock out, and Will had his Beretta ready. It was now or never. He eased up and went towards the back of the shack. I started towards the front. We had to be careful so the perp wouldn't kill the boy if he heard us. A shot rang out. I was hit in the upper left arm. It didn't knock me down but spun me a bit. The killer must have heard us, or the moon gave us away. I didn't think the wound was bad. It was so cold that it helped to dull the pain, and it wasn't bleeding too much. Will glanced at me, but wasn't sure what happened, or if I'd gotten hit. Before I could look over at him, another shot rang out. Will was hit in the front of his right thigh. He was down but managed to get a shot off in the direction where a glint off the killer's gun shone in the moonlight. I heard a moan. It made me think Will had hit the perp and prayed it wasn't the boy.

"This isn't happening," I cursed to myself, and ran to the front door. I kicked it in and rotated with my gun pointing from my outstretched arm around the small enclosure. I looked for the perp and Brandon. The back door was flapping as if someone had just run out. I ran through the doorway and saw Will on the ground, just outside to my left. He had just gotten there. He was alert, but bleeding from his leg. I ran to him, took my scarf off, and tied it around his leg. Another flash, and another bullet hit the rock near my foot. I returned fire in the direction the flash originated from. I figured the killer had the boy on the horse, and because the killer was small in stature, I aimed low, shooting twice hoping it would hit him and not the boy. A curse word rang out, and I knew I hit meat. "Will, are you alright? Are you able to run?"

"I will run when you need me to, no matter what," he groaned.

I took off running to where Will had heard the horse earlier. I could still see Will in my line of sight. I'd need him soon. I pulled up, stopped in my tracks, and realized I was facing the killer. He was maybe thirty feet in front of me, pointing his gun at me, and I pointed my gun at him just like on TV. I was thinking, what a pitiful example of a human being. Here is this killer, 5'2", a scrawny 120 pounds, missing teeth, dirty, and wild hair, thinking he's going to do whatever he wants to do to another boy. Not this boy. Not this night.

The gun was in his right hand, and the leash connected to Brandon's wire neck collar was in his left. The boy was sitting on the horse. He looked to be in shock from fear and the cold. If the killer pulled the leash the boy would die. I knew Will was about twenty feet to my left, and in relative darkness. I didn't think the killer could see him because he and his gun were fixated on me. Will had been shot in the thigh, and I was hoping he had the strength to get up on my "ONE," run and grab the boy before the killer could pull the leash. We had worked out a similar scenario back at camp. One of many with no guaranty of success.

The killer stared at me, swayed a bit from the two bullets I had put in him and the one Will had, but he refused to go down. He was still standing.

I tried to stand steady despite the gunshot I'd taken in my left upper arm. It took a huge effort to use both my arms to hold my gun up. My gun was steady, but I was not.

The killer grinned. "Who are you, girlie?"

"I'm with the FBI. Drop the leash and put down your gun, NOW," I spoke as calmly, and as loudly as I could.

The perp looked at the leash. "Or what?" He smiled his toothless filthy grin at me.

"I'm going to count to three and shoot you, you duplicate piece of shit." He laughed.

"Hey, how's your twin brother?" I asked, trying to give Will extra time.

The killer looked surprised, "You know about my brother?"

This was Will's signal from Sam that he only had seconds to be ready to get to the boy. He put the pain of his leg out of his head and focused on her next words.

The killer was glaring at me, laughing, a low crazy laugh. I counted, "ONE." and pulled the trigger shooting him in the head. It was loud, reverberated in my ears, and shook my arms. I could smell the gunpowder and feel the heat. I don't know why they always wait until "three" in the movies, and I kind of laughed. Immediately realizing he didn't drop. "Crap." I knew I'd hit him. I could see the damn hole in his head, and the blood running out of the other holes he had.

Will ran and was almost to the boy when I saw the killer raise his gun and point it at him. I wanted to yell and warn Will, but I didn't want his attention off the boy. I was running with everything I had and heard the shot. I felt something hot hit my right side, but my first thought was that the vest took it. I continued running when Will caught the boy just before his neck could be severed. The leash was still in the hand of the killer, who was falling to the ground now, and in one swift, precise motion, Will, cut the leash with his knife, and grabbed the boy, saving his life.

Stopping I saw the killer was still alive. He was lying there twitching as if the Devil himself were trying to crawl out of him. He tried to raise his hand, the gun still in it. I walked over to him, stepped on his hand that held the gun, and shot him in the head again. He wasn't going to get up. I wanted him dead and this to be over. I confirmed to Will, "He's dead now." I bent over and took the gun from his hand and holstered mine. The boy was on the ground looking at me while Will removed the wire from his neck. "A little blood, but not bad. It could have been a lot worse. Brandon, he can't hurt you anymore. It's alright now."

I walked over to Will and Brandon. The boy was naked and freezing. I took off my jacket and put it on him, found the gloves in the pocket and tried to cover his hands. I could see some of his fingers were broken and he had cuts on his palms. The bottoms of his feet were bleeding, but everything else was intact. We were damn lucky. I pulled my wool cap from the other pocket and put it on his head. I urged, "Carry him inside your coat until we can get back to camp to keep him warm."

Will had shed his coat before he ran for the boy, and it was on the ground. As Will stood up with Brandon in his arms, he leaned against me for leverage, and I cried out in pain. When Will took his hand away, it was covered in my blood. The bullet had struck between the opening on the right side of my vest, the only vulnerable spot it had. I'd been so high on adrenaline that I didn't realize I'd been hit. The blood was coursing down my side onto my pant leg. I fell to my knees, a look of surprise on my face. Will had the boy in his arms now, wrapped in his coat. "Get back to camp. I'll follow. We need to keep him warm. Can you walk?"

Will, nodded in the affirmative, got a better grip on the boy, and started limping, but at a pretty good clip.

"I'll try to take the horse. I'll be right behind you. Just go!"

Will didn't like walking away from Sam, but he had the boy. Brandon was the priority. Sam had been clear about that. He got back to the camp, checked the boy over and determined he would survive. He had cuts, bruises, probably some exposure, and frostbite, but he would make it. Because of Sam.

I was finally feeling the pain. The bullet must have hit a rib or two, and maybe something else that might be important. It looked bad for me. My hand was covered in blood and was icing up from the cold as I stared at it.

There was no saddle on the horse, only a rope around its neck. With the last bit of strength, I could muster, I managed to get astride the horse. I grabbed the rope and tried to guide it with my legs. He started moving, and I thought if I could just hang on until I got to camp. I made it about ten minutes after Will and the boy had arrived.

Will had Brandon wrapped in our sleeping bag, and he had put his coat back on. It was freezing. I think the cold reduced the flow of blood and eased the pain a bit for me. Every part of me hurt, so I didn't concentrate on one thing. I was doubled over on the horse and had lost a lot of blood. Will caught me as I slid from the horse's back. He leaned me against a tree and went to get bandages. My breathing was shallow, and I wondered if Will was going to see me die.

Will saw the blood, lots of it, and the fear of losing Sam gripped him.

He hustled back with first-aid pads, opened the Velcro closure on my vest, pulled up my sweaters and thermal shirt—I cried out. The pain was gaining on me. I was covered in my own blood. I remembered the feeling of losing too much blood from the last time. Been there, done that. Will put several pads on my wound and wrapped his belt around me to keep them in place, and to apply pressure, trying to control the bleeding. I thought the damn aspirin probably thinned my blood. I was going to stop taking aspirin after this, promising myself.

Will looked at me, choking back fear, and trying to sound positive. "You're going to be okay. Fight. You fight now."

He grabbed the radio from my belt and turned it on once the boy had been seen to, the boy had been the priority and Will didn't deviate from my orders. His voice betrayed him. "911. Charlie, come in."

Randy broke in, "I'm patching you in, Will."

I could hear static, and I could hear Charlie respond, "Will?"

"We've got Brandon. The killer is dead, but Sam is hit, and it's bad. I need the local Medivac for the boy and Sam STAT. The pilot's name is Christian Soaring Bird. He lives in Lame Deer."

Charlie asked, his voice shaking, "Is there a clearing you can get to?"

"Yes, in maybe twenty minutes. Randall can track me on GPS and give coordinates to the pilot. Hurry!"

Will had to get us to the clearing fast. He put the boy on Laney, strapping him on so he wouldn't fall off, and made sure he was warm. He gingerly lifted me onto Bear Boy and then mounted up behind me. He covered me with his shearling coat, grabbed Laney's reins, and started towards the clearing.

He had his arm around me and whispered in my ear, "You can't die, Sam. That bullet was meant for me, not you. You saved my life."

"And what a great life to save. I won't take it back. How's the boy?"

"He'll live, thanks to you."

The radio crackled, and Will grabbed it. "Charlie?"

Charlie spoke through static. "We have the Medivac heading your way, should be there in ten. What's your ETA?"

"Maybe ten or fifteen." Will's voice was choked by tears, "Charlie, it's bad."

Charlie's voice broke, "Keep them alive."

Will was trying to stay calm. He had to keep Sam alive, as well as any future they were going to have. He knew he loved her and wasn't going to lose her. This wasn't supposed to happen this way.

Will managed to get us to the clearing. He dismounted and easily got me off Bear Boy. He laid me on the ground, then ran over and eased Brandon off Laney. He laid him next to me. I looked up, and it was snowing a bit. I could smell the snow. I could hear Dr. Sampson's voice, "Look up to find your answers."

The boy looked at me and whispered, "Don't die."

I knew it was bad by Will's tone of voice. I was trying not to think the worst, but I was getting colder, shivering, and going deeper into shock.

Will was behind me, holding me close in his coat to keep me warm. He heard the chopper and stood up to make sure they saw him. We were lucky.

The Medivac had been at Lame Deer where the pilot lived. It was a private, local company and Will knew Christian, the pilot, from Iraq. I lay there with the boy's hand in mine. I looked at Brandon and tried to smile. "If I don't see you tomorrow, Happy Birthday."

Will knelt down and put his hands on my face. "Sam, can you hear me?" I nodded.

"This is not your time to die. You will not die on my watch, you hear me? We have unfinished business. I love you, and we're going to have a future together. You fight."

I looked at Will's face, so I'd remember him. "I was saved before, so I could save you now, so you could save the boy. I love you." I saw darkness and thought, it's not dying I'm afraid of, it's leaving Will. His face faded from me. I couldn't see and I couldn't speak. My mouth was so dry. Things went black.

Will yelled, "We are not done! I love you." He put a medicine bag in Sam's jeans pocket that he'd pulled from his own. "We are not done," he cried, like a prayer.

Will helped Christian and his partner load Brandon and Sam. He told them where Sam had been hit.

Christian pointed and yelled, "You've been hit in the leg."

"I'll be okay. You don't have room. I've got to get the horses out of here and load up the dead man before the animals and the weather get to him. The Feds will clean up the rest later. Please, Christian, call me on the radio as soon as you know something." It was loud under the rotors and Will didn't know if Christian had heard him. He shouted, "Don't let her die!" Christian gave him the thumbs up. Christian and Will had been the only Cheyenne in their unit in Iraq. He trusted him with Sam. The man had treated more than his share of gunshot wounds and worse.

The Medivac took Brandon and Sam to Denver where there was a first-rate trauma center. It was her best bet with this kind of wound. Christian had her stabilized for the flight. He had been a medic in Iraq and a chopper pilot. He ran this Medivac for hunters and tourists in Montana. Anything could happen out here. It was lucky he had been home and gotten the call. The next closest service could have taken an hour or more to get there. Brandon continued to hold Sam's hand on the flight.

As soon as the chopper lifted off, Will dropped to his knees. The sounds of possibly losing Sam that came out of him were like those of a wild animal caught in a trap. Will was overcome with despair, and he sobbed for a long time—until he couldn't. He prayed in his own way, and begged, "Sam, come back to me."

There is evil in this world, and there are those who fight it. Sam had stared evil in the eye and had sent it back to hell without hesitation—for the boy, and for him.

Will's leg was bleeding, but he had a job to finish. He put his coat back on and mounted Bear Boy. Along with Laney, he headed back to camp to collect the dead killer and the rest of the horses. He tied the killer over one of the horses and made sure the piece of shit wouldn't fall off. On the way back he saw Sam's hair on the branch where it had become entangled and where he had cut it off. He walked over, took her hair off the bush, and put it into his coat pocket. He loaded Girl up with everything else back at camp.

Will's leg was bleeding too much with the bullet in it. He had to get the bullet out or he wouldn't make it back to the barn. He sat on the ground with the first-aid kit, took out his knife, slit his jeans open, and dug into the wound to remove the bullet. He screamed from the pain but felt as if he deserved it for letting Sam take his bullet. He dug it out, poured antiseptic over the wound, packed it with gauze, and covered it with bandages. Good enough to get me to the barn, he thought. He tied Sam's scarf around his leg. It helped to stop the bleeding. He put the bullet slug into his coat pocket. Charlie might need it. He could smell Sam on the scarf, and a rush of tears ran down his face.

He turned the radio on and called for Randall. "Randall, come in please." Will could hardly talk.

"This is Randall, Will."

"Call me every thirty minutes and tell me how Sam is doing," he pleaded.

"Roger that Will. How's the leg? Christian said you were hit."

"Doesn't matter," Will answered hoarsely.

He didn't know how long it took to get back to the barn. He was there lying on the ground near the doors when he came to. He must have passed out and fallen off Bear Boy. What he didn't know was that Randall had tracked him and called the local LEOs to the barn when Will stopped moving. Will looked up as the Sheriff was looking down at him.

"He's alive. Let's get him into the ambulance," the Sheriff barked.

Will could hear people shouting orders. "Take care of the horses. Take his car. Bag the body." He kept seeing it play out in his head—what Sam had done for him, and for Brandon.

As he was being put into the ambulance, he grabbed the Sheriff's arm. "Is Special Agent Wright still alive?"

"She's hanging on is what I hear. She's at Denver Trauma with the boy. Quite a thing I heard she did out there. What you both did."

CHAPTER

SIXTEEN

I opened my eyes and squinted at the bright lights above me. It was too bright in here. "Shit, is this heaven? I must have died. Why the fuck is '1+1=1' stuck in my head?" I was spinning and couldn't focus.

A voice that sounded faraway said, "Her eyes are open, doctor."

There was a light flashing in my eyes. A man spoke to me, "Special Agent Wright, I'm Dr. Franks. Do you know where you are? Are you in pain? We'll be taking you up to surgery in a minute."

Everything seemed so far away, like echoes. I could hear a beeping sound. There was talk about blood, words I didn't understand, and people running around me. "Where's Will?" I asked in a whisper.

The doctor turned to the nurse. "Who's Will?"

The nurse answered, "The Cheyenne guide she was with." The nurse came over to me, "Special Agent Wright, can you hear me? He was shot in the leg and is in the Billings Hospital. He should recover. Did you hear me Agent Wright?"

I smiled. A tear ran down my cheek.

The beeping on the monitor went to flatline.

Sam felt great. She was in a beautiful house surrounded by horse stables and pastures. Will smiled at her. "Want to go for a ride later? It's a beautiful day."

She felt great love for him and an immense need to keep him close. She looked down, saw a wedding ring on her finger, and smiled. They would ride out to the low grasses, take a blanket, and make love as the sun went down.

Weightless, and floating on happiness, she felt loved and safe. The taste of Will and the scent of the nook of his neck was in her memory. She smiled.

Suddenly feeling herself being pulled back by something forceful, something strong, made her recoil because she didn't want to leave this lovely place.

She heard Will as he ran towards her. "Come back to me Sam. Don't go there yet. It's not your time. We have unfinished business here."

With a start, and an electrical impulse, Sam's heart was beating again. The medical staff had worked on her for three minutes and she was back. She was rushed to the operating room to remove the bullet and to repair the damage it had caused. The bullet wound in her arm wasn't life threatening, but the side wound, now that was another story.

Will bolted up from his hospital bed the instant Sam's heart began beating again. He nearly pulled the IV out of his arm. "Sam, come back to me," He cried out. He had simultaneously experienced the same vision Sam had.

The nurse ran over to restrain him to prevent him from moving his injured leg. He had just come out of surgery. The bullet had broken the femur in his thigh, and it was in a splint. He had lost a lot of blood, but he was strong and would recover.

The nurse ordered, "Mr. Little Bear, please lay back."

He was crying. "I need you to call Denver Trauma and find out how Special Agent Samantha Wright is doing. Please. Now please."

"I'll be right back. Please lay back and stay calm."

It seemed like a lifetime before the nurse came back. Will's heart was pounding, his blood pressure had spiked. The nurse held his hand and said, "They nearly lost her in the ER but brought her back. She's in surgery right now. That's all I know."

Will pleaded, "I need to get to Denver. Transfer me to Denver."

Just as Will was planning to release himself and head to Denver on his own, Charlie walked into the room. "I'll get you to Denver, Will."

Charlie and Will weren't friends. Hell, they didn't even like each other.

"I need to go there. Can we go there now?"

"I've got the Bureau's plane. We can leave tomorrow as soon as they get your blood pressure down." Charlie could see the distress on Will's face. He understood. He felt the same. "Maybe I can take your statement during the flight. I need, to know what happened out there."

"The bullet slug I dug out of my leg, it's in my coat pocket. I thought you might need it."

"Thanks for bringing the body out since the weather would have prevented my team from getting in there for a few days. He's the best evidence we have."

"Have you heard anything about Sam?"

"Denver Trauma will call me as soon as Sam's out of surgery. I'll let you know as soon as I hear something. That was a good call your medic made taking her there."

"How is Brandon doing?"

Charlie dug his hands into his pockets and replied in a cadence so as not to reveal his emotions. "He has cuts on his hands and feet, but they'll heal. He has lacerations and some bruising, but they'll heal. He has a deep cut on his neck, but it will also heal. He has broken fingers, frostbite on his hands and feet, and he suffered from exposure and dehydration, but he will heal. He still seems to be withdrawn, I don't know how soon that will heal, "Charlie said it in a way that made Will think he might have feelings, after all. Charlie continued. "He did ask if the white lady was still alive, but that's about it. I don't think he'll be able to give a statement, anytime soon."

"His healing may be connected to Sam's healing."

Will looked at Charlie. "The other boy, Morgan. Did you get to him? Is he safe?"

Charlie smiled. "Sam had it right on both accounts. We managed to extract the boy before contact and picked up the twin before he struck. We have the brother in *custody. Maybe we can get some answers out of him, try to understand all of this. Sam managed to save both boys."*

Will looked at Charlie. A tear ran down his face. "Sam saved my life, Brandon's, Morgan's, and now she's fighting to save her own. I feel so helpless."

Later that night, Charlie came into Will's room. "Will, are you awake?"

"Who can sleep? Did you hear anything about Sam?"

"She was in surgery for six hours. It was touch and go for a while, but she is stabilized and in ICU. She's in critical condition. We leave for Denver in the morning. Get some sleep." As Charlie was leaving Will's room, he admitted something he didn't want to face, "She loves you. You know that, don't you? I don't think she ever loved me. Don't screw it up like I did. They don't come any better than Sam. I've known her for a long time, and I can see it on her face and in her eyes that you're it for her." Charlie put his hands deeper into his pockets, took a step, and turned again towards Will. "You, your Marine friend, and the freezing cold probably saved her life. Thank you."

SEVENTEEN

I was early. The FBI's jet left Billings with Charlie and Will onboard, headed for Denver, and for Sam. The two stud bulls, who loved the same woman, had an unspoken pact that whatever happened going forward everything would be in Sam's best interest. Sam's life and well-being were all that mattered. Everything else was put aside.

Charlie took Will's statement on the flight. He asked every question there was to ask and honed out every detail. Only Will, Sam, and the Cheyenne boy, Brandon, were there that night. Sam couldn't talk, and no one knew if Brandon ever would. Will honored Sam in his statement—her unselfish bravery, her focus on saving the boy, and himself. He gave every detail to Charlie as if Charlie were looking through a window, watching every moment.

The flight went quickly because Charlie kept Will's mind and thoughts occupied with the interview. Neither of these big, tough men wanted to think about what they were about to see or find when they arrived at Denver Trauma.

When Will had finished, and Charlie had run out of questions, he looked at

Will and said, "thank you." He was thanking Will for the statement, but more importantly, for his part in getting Sam and Brandon out.

The jet was about to land, and Will felt like time had slowed to a crawl again. He was on crutches but felt he could walk faster than the plane was moving. His heart raced. Every minute he wasn't with Sam was one minute more he had to relinquish of their time together. His doctor in Billings advised against his leaving the hospital, but he understood Will would leave one way or the other. The doctor sent him off in the ambulance that was headed to the airport with a morphine drip, antibiotics, and painkillers, but Will felt no pain except that which was in his heart. No pill was going to fix that. The doctor in Billings called a nurse he knew at Denver Trauma and requested she look after him. He explained everything to her, and she promised she would "make certain he took his meds and to watch over him."

Will and Charlie went into the Denver Trauma Center and headed to the ICU. Charlie went to look for the doctor. A nurse stopped Will at the door. "Only family is allowed."

He thought to himself, I'm more than family to Sam. We are each other's heartbeats. Sam has no family except for me.

Just then Charlie came back with the doctor. They stopped where Will was outside the ICU. He looked like a caged animal, trying to pace, only with crutches.

The doctor spoke conditionally, knowing Charlie and the FBI had the authority to hear his patient's status, since she had no next of kin and had signed a DOPA (Durable Power of Attorney) with the Bureau. "Before I let you in, you need to know her physical condition. The surgery was rough on her. Before taking her up to surgery, they had lost her in the ER for three minutes; it severely weakened her. The bullet entered her intestines and bowel. She is septic, now on high doses of antibiotics. A small artery was severed, causing most of the bleeding. She has not awakened and may not for days. She is on a ventilator because of the blood loss and full arrest she experienced in the ER. We needed to make it easier for her body to repair itself. The next forty-eight to seventy-two hours are critical. If she makes it through that time window, then we have hope. She is physically strong and in good shape; that will be to her benefit. Quite frankly, she has a hard road. After she wakes up and begins to heal, she may need additional surgeries. Her upper arm where she took a bullet will heal well, but she will need extensive rehab in order to get full range of motion back. The bullet fractured and struck her shoulder as it exited."

The doctor continued, "I hear she saved some boys' lives. Now we need to save hers."

Will didn't tell the doctor she had taken a bullet meant for him. He felt a great deal of guilt.

Charlie looked at the doctor and explained, "This is Will Little Bear. He is Sam's only lifeline for coming out of this. Since she is my Agent, I'm putting protection on around the clock for her. Will has been assigned to do that. I don't want any argument. Her only hope is for Will to be in there with her. He won't be in the way, but he will be in there." Charlie knew Sam didn't need protection but made sure Will was going to be in the room.

The doctor looked at Will. "Before her heart stopped in the ER, she asked for you. She was smiling." Will couldn't respond. He didn't trust his voice.

The doctor saw the intensity in Special Agent Falken's face and the words he had spoken. He saw neither would budge, so he relented. "Only one of you in the room at a time. I will inform the staff, so there'll be no problems." He motioned for them to enter the ICU area.

Will blinked back tears. "Charlie, how can I thank you?"

"Bring her out of this. You're the only medicine she needs. She needs to want to live, the rest the doctors will handle."

Will offered, "You can go in first, but please tell me where the clothes are that she was wearing when they brought her in?"

"The nurse might know, probably in a locker. Why?"

"I need to get something I put in her jeans pocket."

"If they don't have them, I'll track them down. Is it important?"

"Very."

The charge nurse showed Will where Sam's clothes were. They were in a plastic bag in a locker near the ICU. He took the bag and opened it. He could smell her blood. Everything in the bag was covered in Sam's blood. He had to choke back tears. In his mind's eye, he saw Sam and the killer facing off. She had stood up to him, never looked away, and she had done what she needed to do—twice.

He managed to get to her jeans pocket, found what he was looking for—the medicine pouch. The pouch of lamb leather showed wear but was powerful with years of prayers and chants. He would need it—Sam would need it. Her garnet earrings were in a separate plastic bag. He took them as well to use in his healing prayer for her. The stones would keep her earthbound while he pulled her back from the darkness.

There was a small, dog-eared, crumbling notebook in the back pocket. He guessed she used it to make notes in. When he looked at the contents, he smiled. She kept a list of funny words—perhaps words other people used incorrectly—or maybe she had made up. He read a few: animation concentration (seeing ideas develop in your mind), beared (having a bear run after you), crisper (an FBI burn out), cattle call (beef up the document), cratering (digging yourself into a hole), creatitude (a creative attitude). This was just up to the "C's." She had a ton of them. He had no idea she was so funny. He wondered what she planned to do with them. He would keep it safe for her. The notebook also had blood on it. Maybe the nurse had something that would clean it.

While Will was going through Sam's clothes, Charlie went in to see her. He was usually able to hold his emotions; he had lost people in the past, but fear gripped him when he saw her laying there. She was so still and vulnerable. He felt guilty about the distance he had put between them. Maybe, if he had shown her the love he felt for her, just maybe he'd be the one she wanted, instead of Will. He came closer to the bed and touched her hand. It was slightly cold. He looked at her and moved closer to her face. "Sam, this is Charlie. I brought Will here for you. He'll be staying with you. You live for him, let him bring you back. You're in good hands, Sam." He walked out, not realizing tears were running down his face. The nurse asked him if he was okay.

Will was outside waiting when he saw Charlie leaving Sam's room, saw the look of anguish on his face, and he didn't know what to say. He gulped in air—he'd stopped breathing. The two men looked at each other. "Take care of her, Will. I need *to get back to DC. I've arranged for Brandon to come to see her if he wants. It might help them both." Charlie left, and Will headed into Sam's room.*

The nurse stopped him, "Are you Will Little Bear?"

"Yes."

"My name is Nurse Sally Adams, your doctor in Billings asked me to watch over you and to make sure you took your medications." She handed him two pills. "You can't help her if you don't take care of yourself. She would want you to. You need to elevate that leg."

Will took the pills.

CHAPTER
EIGHTEEN

The second Will limped in on his crutches into Sam's room he could feel her life force. The tether that connected them to one another was weak, the one he would use to pull her back to life, and to him. He went over and stood by the bed. Tears welled up in his eyes. Seeing Sam, his Sam, lying there with all the tubes, bags, and monitors beeping, reminded him she was only one beep from danger.

He didn't know how long he'd stared at her before he noticed how short her hair was. He had cut her hair, (how ironic for an Indian) and recalled it was in his coat pocket. He would need it for the medicine bag. Anything that might help her. He remembered she had smiled. "It will grow back." He reached to touch her hair and had a memory of her when she had walked into the dining room at The Lodge. It was the night she had her hair down, and he could visualize how it swayed when she walked. "It will grow back," he assured himself.

Will reached into his pocket and pulled out the medicine pouch. Her blood was still on it. He rubbed his fingers over the old beading. It was smooth from years of his meditating on it. Will had used this bag when he was in Iraq, and today he needed to make sure Sam had it. He kissed the bag, put the garnet earrings, along with some of her hair into the pouch, and began a Cheyenne prayer over it. He placed it over Sam's heart. The ventilator prevented him from putting it around her neck. He lit a small piece of sage to cleanse the room, himself, and Sam—to make way for healing spirits.

The nurse came in and reprimanded him, "No more of that, Mr. Little Bear."

"Forgive me," Will said to her, but thought better to ask forgiveness than permission.

Will would stay here in this room with Sam until she came back and was out of danger. He would sit here with his leg up. He would stand here. He would—if sleep came—sleep here. He would live here. Sam was his priority. Without her, he would have no life.

He leaned his crutches against the wall as he sat in the chair next to her bed with his leg straight out under it. He took her hand and placed it on his face. "Sam, this is Will, and I am here for you. You fight, you hear me? You reach for me. I'm staying right here until you come back to me." For a long time, he stayed like this. He looked at her perfect face, the lips that he'd been blessed to kiss, and prayed he'd be able to see her open eyes again. That's were Sam lived. In her eyes.

Time moved slowly. He achingly stood up and occasionally would limp around the room, smooth her covers, put balm on her lips—the ventilator dried them out—rub lotion on her arms, hands, and feet to stimulate feeling for her. He wiped her face and arms with a washcloth and made sure she stayed warm. He watched intently as the nurse checked the monitors and made notes in her chart. He was versed on everything they did for her and to her. Doctors and nurses came and went, checked her vitals, replaced her bandages, and all this time he never left her room. They never asked him to. From time to time, Nurse Sally came in and made him take his medicine. He did so without complaint. It was as if, he was unaware he was doing it. His eyes never left Sam's face. He told her Cheyenne tales and personal stories so she would hear his voice. Sometimes he chanted a little as he prayed for her.

Will looked at the clock on the wall and whispered to her, "You've made it thirty hours past surgery. You're doing great. Keep up the fight. Just keep reaching for me. I'm not going anywhere without you. I love you."

For another eighteen hours, Will kept his vigil. When he slept, his head was on Sam's bed near her hand in case she moved. When he was awake, he took care of her needs; told the nurses if he noticed anything, made sure her gown was clean, her bed was changed, and she didn't get bed sores. He'd eat occasionally, only when they forced him, but always kept his eyes on Sam. The nurses and doctors saw his pain, and the love in his face. They knew this was what the patient needed, just as much as all their medical help, if not more. She needed a reason to come back.

Her vitals and stats were getting better, stronger. The doctor decided to remove the ventilator in the next twelve hours to see if Sam could breathe on her own. He was betting she would. He thought Will might have something to do with it.

It was evening. Will sat next to Sam. There was only one nurse on duty this time of night, and she was with another patient. The lighting was low. Will had let his guard down, and tears came.

He was looking at Sam's face when he felt a hand on his knee. He turned, and Brandon was standing next to him. Will thought, he seems so small. He was barefoot and in his hospital gown. His hair had started to grow in, and the outward signs of the ordeal had started to heal. "Still so small." Without saying a word Brandon sat on Will's good knee and leaned over to the bed to take Sam's hand. His broken fingers struggled to make contact with her. He rubbed her hand tenderly and put her fingers to his forehead. Will could hear a muffled chant. Brandon smiled a little smile.

"She will live," Brandon whispered to Will. "For you." The two stayed like that for a long time, Will's one arm around the boy and his other touching Sam's face. After a while the nurse noticed. She smiled, and then took Brandon back to his room.

The doctor removed the ventilator and Sam began to breathe on her own. Will could finally breathe too. He would breathe for her. She was not awake yet, but the doctor reassured him, "Give her time. She's healing. She will know when it's time to wake up. Just be here when she does." Will kissed Sam's lips, lingering there to make sure she could feel him. Her lips were warm to his touch, and he thought he felt the smallest movement.

Charlie had been calling the nurse's station every day. Will could tell when he heard the conversations. He knew Charlie cared, and he knew that Charlie regretted what he had lost, and what Will had gained.

NINETEEN

There are flashes we see in our lives, and they predict, warn, wake us up, and make us think. They make us change our lives if we are paying attention. That flash was Sam the first night Will saw her in the Meeting Room looking at the whiteboards.

Will once heard it takes three days for a brain to adapt. If you'd hang upside down for three days, your brain will think it is right side up, and vice-versa. Sam's brain finally adapted to her new reality, and she came back three days later.

When Sam woke, Will's head was on her bed near her hand. Her fingers touched his hair, and he raised his head up. He saw Sam's fingers moving and that her eyes were looking at him. He pulled himself up and came closer to her face, tears running down his. As she looked at him, a tear fell from her eye, and she touched his face. "I saw all the boys. They are at peace," she said in a whisper. "Don't forget your promise."

Will had his hand on her face, "I love you, Sam. Welcome back." *She smiled and fell back asleep. Will's emotions were all over the place. He was laughing and crying at the same time. He felt exhausted. For almost six days he* had hardly eaten and barely slept. He felt it now. Sam was back, and that's all that mattered.

Will called the nurse and told her Sam had woken up. The nurse called for the doctor. A few minutes later, the doctor was checking Sam's eye movement and other vitals.

The doctor explained to Will, "She may wake and sleep for a few days until her body catches up with her wanting to be awake. Her body's been through a lot, and rest is the best thing she can do for now. She may or may not remember that she saw you. Her mind may think it was a dream. Give it a few days. For now, she will sleep more than she will be awake. It looks like you did a great job bringing her back, Will. Why don't you get some rest now, maybe take a shower, eat something?"

Will took a minute to call Charlie. "Sam's back. She woke up briefly, but she's coming back," Will's voice cracked with emotion.

Charlie responded shakily, "Thank you, Will, for everything. I'll come to see her tomorrow."

Will mentioned to Charlie, "If I'm not here when you come, I had to leave. I made a promise to her I need to keep, to let her heal on her own. I'd like to call you from time to time to check in. Just between us if that's okay." Will had promised Sam back in her room at The Lodge—no secrets, but he felt this was an exception. It was his lifeline. The promise was the beginning of his self-renewal and becoming the man he wanted to be for Sam.

Charlie didn't quite understand but finally said, "A promise is a promise. Call me anytime." He didn't need the details, he just wanted Sam to be happy. He knew now that Will only had her best interests at heart, and that he loved her. He could trust that.

Will knew he had to keep his promise to Sam. He would let her heal herself from today forward, and he knew she would come to him when she felt whole, when she was ready.

That night, she woke again for a few minutes and told Will she loved him. He kissed her, and she kissed him back. It was brief but meant more to him than anything. She slept again.

Her sleep time would shorten; she would steadily improve and be awake more. He left the medicine pouch pinned to her gown and left her a winter cactus on the bedside table. Nurse Sally had picked it up in the gift shop for him.

On a note card he wrote, "Sam, come to me when you are ready. I will wait for as long as it takes. We have unfinished business. Love, Will." Sometimes you need to turn yourself over to the universe and have faith.

The cactus bloomed for Sam the next day. When she saw it, and read the note, she smiled, and knew this must be the hardest thing Will ever had to do—to walk away from her. She knew she would go to him when she was ready, and worthy of him by being physically whole and free of the Bureau and its aura of death.

Charlie and the nurses told Sam what Will had done for her. She said to them, "I know. I heard him. I felt him, and I came back to him. I heard Brandon, too." Her eyes welled with tears.

Charlie felt happy Sam was back and would recover, but he felt a great void in himself, and it was his own fault. He'd had years of chances to tell her how he felt, how he loved her, but Will had been able to express himself to her, and in the end, he won her heart.

CHAPTER

TWENTY

Nearly two years had passed since Will left the cactus and the note for me at the hospital. We had saved each other from more than death; we had saved each other from the lives we were living. I remembered the dreams. I still have them. I remembered Will calling to me to come back. I could still hear him, and it was getting louder.

After Will left, I spent three more weeks in the hospital and Charlie came to see me often. He was carrying a lot of guilt about us but didn't need to. I explained that to him. We're working on being friends, nothing more. He doesn't understand why Will isn't here and I told him, "He is keeping a promise to me." Someone like Charlie would never understand even if I explained it.

I spent twenty months since getting out of the hospital, dealing with rehab on my arm and shoulder. I had two additional surgeries on my shoulder and had a long recovery to heal from the infections and the complications from the bullet wound to my intestines. After everything was said and done, I went to a plastic surgeon and had my scars reduced to something that with years of fading, might be tolerable. I was done with all that now, and healthy. I had almost full range of motion in my shoulder and an all clear on everything else from the doctor. Finally. The hardest part was not taking the pain medications they pushed on me. I didn't want them. Pain helped me work through what I did that night. Pain can bring clarity. I stopped taking aspirin. It was always about my legs, and the pain from the scars and the nerves that were damaged. It all seems to have dissipated.

I was clear-headed now and had to make some decisions. I, sort of, resigned from the FBI. Charlie didn't try to talk me out of it. He knew the case had taken a toll on me physically and mentally. The FBI was still trying to clean the mess up. We had broken protocols, rules, and regulations. Needless to say, they didn't appreciate how the operation in the field was handled, even though the results had been positive. Charlie was in hot water, having had me take charge of things in Montana. He knew it had been the right decision, even if his bosses didn't.

Counseling was required for killing the Devil. It's hard to counsel someone like me, a PhD in Forensic Psychology, but it's protocol. They had to make certain the killing was "justified," and I wouldn't have residual effects from it, like PTSD. After a while, I was given all clear. Charlie had been concerned and told me that he felt I needed more time. I assured him I was fine. He didn't want me to rush it, but I had plans. Maybe Charlie had other plans, too, and was trying to stall my departure. My sights were in Montana, not on Charlie.

Those twenty months were filled with statements, depositions, and an inquiry as to why I had been put in charge of the operation and almost gotten myself killed. I explained in detail what happened that night. It took hours to dictate, and then I came to find out Will's statement and mine matched exactly. Except for me having to explain the two shots to the head of the Devil and the counting to "ONE" thing. "You had to be there," I said, "He just wouldn't die."

Charlie and I were in the newspapers and on the news. It was embarrassing, but we managed to keep Will out of it. He didn't deserve to have his life turned upside down for what he'd done for us—for me. The Bureau did send Will a letter of thanks for his part. Charlie told me that Will checked in on me with him from time to time. In some strange way, they had become friendly. I never told him that I kept tabs on Will, too. There were times I wanted to call him and beg him to come to me, but it wouldn't have been fair. I hadn't been whole until now.

The Bureau was proud of us for saving the boys and getting the killers, but to save face, they had to dole out some punishment. I didn't care. I had more important things to do.

Charlie was reprimanded, almost lost his job. Somehow, he too, was saved by Will, in a letter written on his behalf to Charlie's boss. I don't know what was in it, but it must have been strong. It saved his ass. Will knows important people.

The Bureau changed my status to Profiler Consultant. That meant I could get my twenty years in and collect a pension in a couple of years. I'd been on full pay until recently because of medical leave, but that would end soon. It was a bone they threw me, but I was grateful to end on a high note. I would be the "profiler of last resort" for them just to keep me on the books. I kept my badge and still had a gun. They also put some letters in my file, praising me for bravery, for saving the boys, and Will. I think I got some sort of medal, but it's in my file. I don't need that. I have other plans. I need something else. Someone else.

The twin brother Charlie apprehended killed himself in jail, either to keep his and his brother's secrets, or because he missed his brother. Life alone must not have been enough for him. Their DNA wasn't in the system, and both brothers had removed their own fingerprints prior to their crimes. Dental records weren't a lead, neither brother had many teeth, and it looked as though they had never been to a dentist. Facial recognition through computer generation also came up with nothing. Photographs were circulated in the media and through all channels the FBI had, and they came up empty. We may never know who they were. It was as if they never existed, except for the death and pain they had left behind. There would be no answer as to the WHY or the HOW of these crimes. It was literally a dead end. I didn't need to know. Sometimes, not knowing is easier.

I'd met with Brandon soon after I was released from the hospital, and even though he was still coming to terms with it all, he smiled at me. "I knew you'd live, for him." I feel there will always be a bond between us. I thanked him for holding my hand in the hospital, and for being so brave. That was nearly two years ago. He was almost fourteen now. He got to have his birthday the day after everything went down. That's all that mattered, and the fact he continues having them.

Brandon's and Morgan's families offered that if I ever needed them, they would be there for me. As for the boys who died, well, their families were grateful for justice being served. They have given me gifts; tokens of love for their boy's peace in the spirit world. To refuse the gifts would be an insult, so I said, "Thank you," in Cheyenne, "nia'ish" and hoped it translated to all of them.

Six months before, I was inducted by proclamation into the Cheyenne Tribe for saving the boys, bringing some peace to the families, and for killing a white man twice; first his spirit, then his body. Whenever I would get to Montana, they would have an official ceremony for me. It helped answer the question I had asked Will, about my being white, causing a problem for the Tribe. Sometimes the Universe makes sense of things in its own time. I was proud I was now Cheyenne in their eyes.

The Bureau, because of this case, had better relations with the tribes, and that's always a good thing. No doubt, they'll mess that up in the future.

My house in Georgetown, with all the furniture included, was sold and was scheduled to close soon. The buyers wanted to renovate before moving in, so I packed up what I wanted of Dr. Sampson's things and the little I had personally. I put everything into an 8'x10', temperature-controlled pod storage unit, hoping to have it delivered somewhere in Montana. I didn't know where just yet—weather permitting. I'd been living in an extended stay hotel, trying to clear up the last things from my life here in DC. I was moving on with my life, and it was about time. It was fall, and I needed to get to my future before the weather turned.

I'd written a book since being released from the hospital. Writing was my first love and the thing I thought I'd be doing before I was recruited by the FBI, by Charlie. Of course, the FBI had content approval, which they reluctantly gave due to the amount of information that was already out in the public forum. It has come full circle. I wrote under the name Dr. Samantha Wright. I had never used the title Doctor before, despite the PhDs, even though I was entitled. I liked Dr. Sampson having that title to himself when we worked together, but after he was gone, I changed my thoughts on using it. My first book would be out in the next two months. I had some advance copies, and my publisher said it looked promising. Maybe, because of all the headlines and all the coverage, people would buy it out of curiosity. I hoped once they read what's inside that they would be satisfied spending the money on it, especially after the final chapter. It was certainly cathartic for me.

The house sale concluded thirty days later, and I did well financially. Dr. Sampson had left me a house with no debt, and it now afforded me freedom for my future endeavors. He had owned the house for years, which had been passed down from his family, and he passed it down to me, his surrogate family. I bought a new, white SUV with 4WD, and seat warmers, a car that would be useful in Montana. I bought a new camera and lenses. I felt there would be a lot to document in the future. I got a new laptop to write books on, and a watch for Will. Will didn't wear watches, but he'd wear this one. Time matters now. The remaining proceeds were enough so I wouldn't have to work, and for once in my life, I felt like I was free to live my life. I was getting impatient. I had unfinished business waiting for me.

I went by the bank with Dr. Sampson's safe deposit key. I had found it in his desk drawer a couple of years earlier but hadn't been in a rush to open it. The woman at the bank looked at my paperwork and took me back to the boxes. I opened the box, and there was ten-thousand dollars in cash, and a note that read, "For a rainy day. Always look up." I put the cash in my bag and told the clerk to close out the box. It was no longer needed. I said a little prayer for Dr. Sampson and told him how much I missed him. I looked up.

I stopped by to see Charlie on my way out of town. We met for coffee, and for a moment it was awkward. Charlie stammered, "I don't know what to say, Sam, except be happy. You deserve it."

He ended up being a friend, but there was always an undercurrent of something not defined, something held back. All the years I'd known Charlie, I never really knew what he was about. He was good at hiding himself, his feelings.

"Do you think my scars will bother Will?"

Charlie shook his head. "If they do, he's the wrong guy. Is he the wrong guy?"

I smiled. "He's the only guy. He's the right guy."

FedEx was my next stop, and I sent a two-day package to Will. I hoped he'd get it before I got there. I was driving. I figured it would take me three days. I was scared and excited at the same time. It felt like I was jumping off a cliff, but I believed the landing would be soft.

All I loaded into the car were four suitcases, one backpack, a cactus plant, a medicine pouch, and a notebook of Dr. Sampson's "funny words." I still had an FBI badge with its limited shelf life. I had a license to carry—in Montana, it's wise to have. I had an envelope with my personal papers, just in case, and ten thousand in cash. I packed my gun, some ammo, Maglite, my new laptop, the new camera, and some CDs for the drive. I was on my way. I continued to keep a knife in my boot. Some habits die hard.

It was the longest drive of my life. When I was a day's drive from Ashland, Montana, I had trouble breathing, my hands shook as I gripped the steering wheel, and my body ached from the healing I had done. I hoped Will had gotten the package I sent before I left DC. Will and I didn't know everything about each other, but like he said in my hotel room that night before our future changed, "We know what matters. The rest of it, we will find out over the course of our lives together."

CHAPTER
TWENTY-ONE

After leaving Sam at the hospital, Will obtained a release from his doctor and went straight to The Lodge. The Lodge would be closed until March. It was quiet and empty except for the few people cleaning, repairing, and painting for when it reopened. Will went to the room Sam had occupied at The Lodge. He noticed something sticking out from under the bed. It was her thermal shirt. He remembered. He could smell her on it. It was the shirt he noticed her being cold in. Randall must have missed it when they packed up everything after the FBI left. He smiled and caught himself, choked back the tears. This was going to be hard, but he would wait. He would become a better man, someone who deserved her, who could be faithful, patient, committed, and selfless. The promise put him on this path, and he wasn't about to get off of it.

He needed a plan. He walked around The Lodge. His leg ached. He was tired of the crutches, and for four more weeks, he would need to use them. He caught himself and chastised himself, "I'm complaining about crutches, and Sam has had so much to go through. What am I doing?"

He hobbled to his unit, the one he lived in at The Lodge. He didn't feel he really lived here, not anymore. He didn't expect Sam to live here. Every day he looked at her picture on his phone, the one he'd taken while she wasn't looking. She was looking intently at something way out in the distance and had a slight smile on her face. He still had a braid of her hair, and he could smell her on it. He would wait, and she would come. He had faith. He had the vision. She had made him a better man; a man who could love—a man who would be worthy of her. Sam had done this for him, but he had further to go.

Sam has her hand inside my heart, and she keeps it beating, she keeps me alive, he thought.

New Year's Eve was cold, and it was snowing. Will was trying to devise a plan, a future that could be ready by the time Sam was ready. He sat there drinking a Pepsi, her favorite drink, and thought of her. One New Year's they would toast and remember what they came through to be together. The value of that was something that pushed Will forward.

I'm going to sell this place, he thought. It isn't me anymore. I can't become better being here; I won't be moving forward. I'm selling this place and building Sam the house I saw in the vision, at the place she liked. Our vision.

He spent the rest of the winter preparing drawings for their house and for everything that would be there. By Spring, he was ready to break ground, with or without a buyer for The Lodge.

He had enough money to start the build. He knew people with money, they often came to hunt, and they liked him. He found a buyer, and four months later started construction on the house—Sam's house. It was the best he had felt in a long time; he had a sense of purpose again. Brandon's, Samuel's, and the other boys' families pitched in and helped. They had their own reasons. They got it under roof before that winter so Will could work on the interior, despite the weather. By the time Will had finished the house, barn, stables, and moved his Guide business, it was October. It had been nearly two years since he left Sam at the hospital. He had kept in touch with Charlie and had a feeling about things. A hard winter was coming, but he was ready. He built the new house by the old stables where he and

Sam had picked up horses the day they went to Samuel's grave site. She had said she loved the area, and now it had come full circle.

The victims' families helped Will from time to time. They knew what he was waiting for, and they wanted to help him, to thank both Will and Sam. They knew he didn't live in the house, he lived over the stables in a small apartment. He would not live in the new house without her. Everyone hoped it would be soon. Will needed her. He hadn't really smiled in nearly two years.

It was a good, strong, log house, befitting Sam's, and his vision. The front of the house was unbreakable glass. One couldn't look in. It reflected trees and the surroundings as if the house was covered in them. The roof was green metal so the snow would easily slide off. He had made it open concept so Sam could see every-thing no matter where she sat. The spacious kitchen had state-of-the-art appliances where they would cook together. He built an island he knew they would spend most of their time sitting around talking. There was a mudroom, a laundry, and full bath. The large master bedroom and bathroom suite was on the main level. Upstairs Will created an office for Sam to write in with views of the entire property. There were decks on all sides of the house. Fireplaces were in the living area, the master bedroom, and her office. He set up a gym. There was a guest room with a bathroom, and plenty of closets everywhere. He installed a security system and a safe. There was no furniture except for the chairs around the kitchen island and the king-size bed he would not sleep in until she was there with him. He wanted Sam to choose everything else. She would make this house their home.

Will had a part in having the Cheyenne induct Sam into the Tribe, and he was proud they agreed. She had been worried they wouldn't accept her because she was white. He'd kept track of her the entire time. He stayed in touch with Charlie, read the papers, and watched her on the news. He was sure she hated the public attention, but it was over now.

It was October, and the weather was starting to turn, but the next few days were supposed to be beautiful. The new owner of The Lodge called that a package from FedEx had come for him, a S. Wright from DC had sent it, and did he want to pick it up? Will was at The Lodge within the hour. He looked at the package in his shaking hands. The front desk clerk stared at him. He decided to take the package to his car and open it there. He kept staring at the return address. His heart was pounding, and he was afraid to open it. With trembling hands, he tore the package open. Inside was a book by Dr. Samantha Wright, titled "The RESERVATIONS Case." He opened the book and looked at the picture of her on the back, inside cover. She was so beautiful. Her hair had grown out and was long again. He touched the picture and ran his finger around her cheek. He wanted to feel her face in person. He missed her more every day. He thumbed through the book and saw a "Dedication" in the front of the book. "To Will Little Bear, you saved my life in more ways than one." Will had tears in his eyes. He would read her book and see if she was able to find peace from her experience. He had found his peace in her. He looked at the smaller square box and opened it. It was an expensive, waterproof watch with a compass. It was beautiful beyond description. He looked at the back of the watch. It had an inscription: To Will: Whatever time I have left in this life, or any other, now belongs to you. Love, Sam.

He never had a reason to wear a watch before, but he did now. He loved it. He set the time, and as he put it on, his hand went to the little box he had carried in his pocket every day for the last almost two years. Soon.

He almost missed it. There was a small note card in the package. He opened it. It read: "Will, I've missed you so much. I'm coming home and will see you soon. I Love You, Sam."

Will's breath caught, and he was overcome with emotion. The wait was over. He checked the date on the package and figured if she was driving, she'd be there sometime tomorrow. He had to get things ready. A sob escaped his mouth, a smile appeared on his face. Something no one had seen in a long time.

He realized she must think he was still living at The Lodge. She didn't know about the house. He'd get here early in the morning to meet her. He couldn't contain himself, his happiness. The only piece of furniture in the house was the king-size bed. He needed to get fresh, clean linens, towels, soaps, and other things. He needed to fill the fridge. He couldn't catch his breath. They weren't going to wait any longer. Will found a backup guide to take his hunting party out because there was no way he was leaving with Sam on the way.

TWENTY-TWO

I drove up to The Lodge. It was ten in the morning on a beautiful, crisp, October day. The Lodge looked like it was doing a brisk business. I walked up to the front desk, "I'm looking for Will Little Bear."

"He doesn't own The Lodge anymore. Would you like to talk to the current owner?" The stunned look on my face caused the clerk to ask, "Are you okay?"

I was shaking. "Does Will still live around here?"

"Yes. Out by the old stables. Do you know how to get there?"

"Yes, thank you."

"Crap, I should have done more checking". I got back into my car and drove out to the old stables. I didn't know Will had sold The Lodge, and I wondered what he was doing out by those stables.

Will arrived at The Lodge at 10:15 and ran into the lobby.

The clerk at the front desk asked, "Can I help you, Will?"

"Has a beautiful woman been asking for me?"

"Yes. I sent her out to the old stables."

Will took out like a light and jumped in his car. He was fifteen minutes behind her. He had run late this morning with a sick horse, and now he hoped she wouldn't leave the stables until he got back there. They must have passed each other on the road.

I drove up to the old stables and couldn't believe my eyes. There was a beautiful new house, a barn, new stables, and paddocks. A sign on the front of the stables read, "Will's Guide & Tracking Services." It was amazing. I looked around, and it hit me. These were the buildings in the dream, the house in my dream. This was the dream. My dream. How did he know?

The weather was cool but sunny, I didn't need a jacket. I went to the stables and saw the stable hand in the shed row. I immediately recognized him. It was Brandon. He looked so good—healthy, and happy. He had grown but had a little bit more to go before being called handsome. I hugged him for the longest time. He whispered in my ear, "I knew you would come home to Will."

Will and Brandon had formed a bond while watching over me in the hospital. Now, Brandon worked for him.

"Is he here?"

"No, he went to The Lodge to look for you. You must have passed each other on the road."

"Is there a horse by the name of Laney here?"

"Yes ma'am. She is in the paddock, over there on the other side of the stables."

"Do you mind if I go see her?"

"No ma'am." I gave Brandon a kiss on the forehead and smiled.

Walking over to Laney, I called her name, and she came up to the fence. I blew my breath into her nose. "Do you remember me, girl? I came by to thank you for taking such good care of me and leading me in the right direction." I spent time just talking with her and petting her, wondering when Will would show up.

I had new jeans on with a pull-over pink sweater. I thought I looked good. I hoped Will would think so, too. I had been working out to get myself back in shape after so much time in the hospital and months of physical rehab. My hair had grown out, and I didn't have any makeup on. I was turning forty soon. Will would be forty-four. We weren't kids, but I felt like a young girl feeling love for the first time.

Will pulled up to the stables and saw a white SUV, with DC plates. The doors were unlocked. He took Sam's bags and backpack into the house, along with the box of things she had brought. He noticed the cactus and smiled. She wasn't going anywhere. She might need them later. He lit the fireplaces in the house to take the chill off. His heart was going crazy. He didn't see her. He went inside the stables, saw Brandon, and asked him where Sam was.

"She wanted to see Laney. I sent her to the paddock." Brandon smiled. Because of her, Will knew Brandon would grow into a better man and would choose the right woman one day because she had saved him.

Will started walking towards the paddock. He hoped he still looked good. He wore black jeans and a white shirt today. He'd been taking better care of himself for her. He checked the little box in his pocket, and then decided to take the ring out, putting it in his pocket. The ring was platinum, with two carats of baguette-cut diamonds. He thought it looked like Sam—sleek, and beautiful. On the inside, he had engraved "W + S = 1." There were matching wedding bands in the safe. He turned the corner and saw her looking at Laney. He just wanted to run to her but stopped.

"Hey, what are doing with my horse?"

I turned, "Just thanking her for taking care of me a while back. Besides, I thought she was my horse." I winked, and then noticed the watch on Will's wrist. He looked more handsome than ever, with his gentle eyes and easy smile. He looked happy, and that's not overrated—not after what we've come through. We earned this happiness. It would be valued.

Will couldn't believe how beautiful she looked. She looked about nineteen. She looked happy, as happy as he felt.

"Well, that can be negotiated."

They took a step closer.

"This place looks like the dream I had in the hospital. How is that even possible? It's so beautiful out here, Will. Is it your house?"

Will took another step closer, as did Sam.

"No, it's your house, soon to be our home."

They were about a foot apart now, and one could feel the electricity—the magnetic draw.

I smiled at him, looking into his eyes. "I love you."

He looked at me trying to believe I was really here, brushed the hair from my face, and took me into his arms. "I love you, too. Welcome home, Sam."

The word love seemed too simple to express all that we meant to each other, what we felt for each other. It was more than love. It was what starts in your soul, edges its way into your heart, triggers your brain to send pulses to every fiber of your being, and makes it impossible to have one life without the other.

We kissed for a long time; softly, deeply, intensely, and we held each other—neither one of us wanting to let go. I could smell Will's essence, and I smiled with the remembrance.

"I want to show you something in the house." He took my hand in his and led me to the front door. He handed me a key. "It's yours."

We couldn't stop touching each other, kissing each other, and it would be like this from now on. Our eyes said everything. I turned the key in the lock, walked in, and was home.

Will took me to just outside the open double doors of our bedroom. He had put my book on the bookshelves he had made. The only book on them for now, and I saw my luggage and backpack there for me. The bed had new linens, all white, beckoning us.

He looked at me. "You are so beautiful. You are so much more than I see with just my eyes. I've missed you." Choking back a tear, he held out his hand, "May I have this dance?"

I remembered what Will had said about dancing with me. He said it would be foreplay. I smiled at this man who had waited for me. He never doubted it would happen, and with a tear escaping my eye, I took his hand. "Yes, dance with me. No more waiting."

He took a ring from his pocket and slipped it on my finger. "Forever."

The ring looked like the one in my dream. "Yes. Forever."

CHAPTER

TWENTY-THREE

Sam and Will's Dance

They melt into each other's eyes. There is no music, just the sound of their hearts beating in time, and the rhythm of their breathing. Their faces touching, teasing lips. He pauses, looks at her lips. They are going to be home to him now; welcoming, smiling. They're soft, yet firm enough to handle his need. There are no words needed. They've told them all.

She is touching the front of his shirt, inhaling the smell of his neck. He takes her in his arms, and they are dancing. She has her hands in his hair, much shorter since she last saw him. The smell of him is intoxicating. They softly and gingerly touch each other through their clothing, tracing the curves of each other's bodies. They explore each other, never losing eye contact, all the while slowly dancing. Close, tight, dancing. He has his face in her hair, her neck. He kisses her softly. Dancing: slowly, intensely, but keeping in step, as if they have danced together before.

They are acting shy with each other, wanting to savor each moment, each touch. They want time to move more slowly. Looking at each other, their eyes are where they live. Where the future lives. Butterfly kisses, a soft coming together of their mouths. Their tongues are tempting each other, for now.

They keep dancing, caressing, and kissing as if it's a prayer. Slowly dancing into the bedroom—their altar—where they will join themselves forever. His hand is at the back of her neck, pulling her into him. Her mouth meets his mouth, exploring, tasting tongues.

As if time is standing still, she starts unbuttoning his shirt, and with each open button, she kisses his skin as it comes into view. Smooth, warm skin. They continue to slowly move, to dance. She removes his shirt, slipping it off like she is unwrapping him. His arms reach for her. His muscled chest calls to her mouth. She uses her lips to kiss and her tongue to lick him softly, so lightly he moans. She kisses the scar on his chest from Iraq and the one by his eye. His scars make her emotional. She looks at him sadly for what he has gone through. He kisses her. It's alright now.

They look at each other, and he slowly pulls her sweater over her head dropping it on the floor. Her hair is mussed, and it sends a shiver through his body. They haven't missed a step of their dance. They look into each other's eyes, and neither can breathe. He looks at the beauty in front of him and slowly touches her, running his fingers, his hands over every inch of her. She marvels at him; at the love she feels for him. They are still moving and swaying in their dance.

He kisses the scar on her shoulder, the one she got saving the boy. He kisses the scar on her throat, the one that saved her the first time. He touches softly, kisses the scar on her side, the one that saved him from a bullet. His hands slide down over her bra. She shudders. His touches and kisses are honoring the strength that made it possible for them to be here. His love knows no bounds for her. The dance continues.

They touch, caress and marvel at each other's exposed skin, their bodies moving. Feather kisses that linger, and fingers pressuring the softness. He kneels on one knee, unzips her boots, and removes them. He takes off her socks. Her hands are on his shoulders for balance, as support for her quivering legs. Her hands run through his hair. He slowly stands. His hands move up her pant legs, tracing the shape of her curves, to the top of her thighs, the place he wants. He is looking into her eyes again, swaying to their own unheard music. Dancing.

Short breaths, building up the need. She kneels in front of him, removing his boots, his socks—making a simple task sexy and alluring. She slowly makes her way to her feet, leaning into the front of his legs, bringing her hand over the maleness of him. She cups him in her hands. She is hungry for him, craving his coming climax. Her hands travel up and down his thighs. She can see him moving inside his pants, his gift for her. She shivers. He wants her. He takes a breath and moans. The dance continues.

Kissing; this time urgent, devouring, probing. They pull back, look into each other's eyes, it calms her a bit. He unzips her jeans, putting his hand down the front. She is natural and she is wet, waiting, anticipating. He tastes her, savoring her. A cry escapes her lips, and longingly he looks at her, slipping her jeans down, and off. He admires her long, beautiful legs. Long enough to wrap themselves around him tightly when he is in her. Soon. He softly pushes her legs slightly apart and runs his hands down the scars on her legs, now mostly faded, flawed by her courage to live. He kisses them as tears well up in his eyes when he thinks of how she got them. He loves them. They belong to her, and she belongs to him. She is so beautiful to him.

She is swaying as he stands. He takes her in his arms, slowly dances with her while kissing and nuzzling her neck. Calming her, patience for the long night ahead. It's still daylight, and they can see everything of each other, no secrets. The dance is getting warmer; they couldn't get any closer.

She unfastens his belt, unzipping his pants while watching his eyes. She pulls them down, he steps out of them, exposing his need, all that wants her. She is again kneeling in front of him, and with her hand feels the scar from the bullet he took to his thigh. She kisses the reminder, putting the side of her cheek to the man that he is, and presses against him. She can smell the sex on him now. She stands, and the dance continues with him now behind her. His arms embrace her, his hands needing her. He moves himself behind her into her firm fullness; not entering, just teasing. She turns to face him, while her hands caress his strong back. She forces him towards her to kiss him with such love; he moves against her, his hardness pulsating. How much longer? He needs her. They waited so long. They dance.

He is hard, throbbing against her legs. She is wet with anticipation, but the dance isn't over yet. They both want to beg, but there's more. He wants to give her everything, and she wants to take it. She offers her breasts to him. He takes her lacy bra off, and with a tongue hot with passion, licks her hard nipples. He puts his mouth over her large breasts, kissing and fondling them. She has the most beautiful breasts, and she gives them to him. He presses his chest into her, they both quake with desire. They continue the dance, looking into each other's eyes. Not a word has been spoken. They dance.

He bends her back, holding her with one hand and runs his other hand over the flesh she has offered him; the furrow between her breasts, the slope of her neck, and her firm stomach. She belongs to him. She is offering it to him, everything to him. She is shaking, trying to catch her breath. They continue the dance; closer, tighter, each wanting more.

She kneels in front of him, impatiently pulling his knit boxers down, dismissing them, and freeing him to her. He is beautiful. Strong, thick, and long. He is throbbing, pulsing, calling to her. She opens her mouth and takes him in. His taste is sweet. She flicks her tongue slowly around him and then stops, knowing she will finish this later. She releases him from her mouth by kissing the tip and tasting his wetness. He lets a soft cry escape. He can't finish yet. He tries to focus on controlling his need. They dance, looking in each other's eyes, using their hands to feel each other; every curve, every scar, every muscle, every memory. They will know everything about each other in this dance.

He has his hand in her white panties and pulls them down. She steps out of them. He quickly puts his fingers inside her, massages her need with his thumb. She comes, shuddering. She can't stop. She has no control. She looks at him, her eyes saying she can't wait any longer. She surrenders. Her look is pleading. He holds her and kisses her with urgent need. He picks her up, carries her to the bed, their bed—the one he wouldn't sleep in without her. Foreplay is over. The next part of the dance continues.

He is lying slightly to the side of her, kissing her, and she is kissing him. She is begging him with her eyes to take her. He has his mouth everywhere on her. She is lying there breathing deep, arching with need, with want, pulling his head to her, biting his neck. A tear escapes.

He opens her legs gently, running his hands along them. She is so wet with desire for him. He loves her need for him. She has already come for him. He is on top of her now, guiding himself inside of her, trying to control himself. Her legs wrap around him so tightly he cannot pull back. He lifts her hips to accommodate everything he wants to give her. He belongs to her now, in every way, just as she belongs to him. The moment is filled with sounds of lust, desire, and love, coming from their lips without words. He is moving slowly and deliberately, deeper, heightening her pleasure, taking her higher. They don't take their eyes off each other. Faster. Panting. He is ready. The first words spoken since the start of the dance come from her, "Come with me now," and her moan, like an animal cry, is returned by him. It seems to last forever, lingering, with shudders, quakes, and ongoing surrender. Wetness is everywhere—sweat, come, and tears from their satisfaction of the release of love that had been kept waiting—for so long.

Hours pass. They've taken each other over and over, in every way, every position, to satisfy each other—to touch, and find every pleasure. He is on his back now, trying to breathe, to calm himself, to recover. She moves down his body, kissing, licking, touching, and admiring. She takes him into her mouth, all of him, to finish what she started earlier during the dance. He awakens and grows as her mouth slowly goes up and down on him; her tongue flicking, licking him, and circling his girth. Cupping him in her hands, she is hungry for him; she needs to be in control of him in this way. She wants to take him to places he hasn't been before. She is amazing; he is writhing. He wants to touch her hair, but she takes hold of his hands and builds what he needs to give her. He is helpless, he can't hold on, and she lets him release. She takes his juices in her mouth, and swallows. Sweet, salty, the taste of them both, together.

He pulls her up to him and kisses her deeply, intense with wanting to taste what she tastes. Passion builds, and she is faint with love. He eases her on her back. Her breasts are high, her nipples hard, and big. His mouth is caressing them, kissing them, massaging them. He softly touches her clit. She is arching her back. She is starting, inviting him. Please. He moves, and all the while, traces her body with his tongue—from the small of her neck to her essence which is hard and pulsing. He kisses those lips as though he is kissing her mouth. Deep, penetrating, probing with his tongue. He bites her softly, and a groan escapes her. He is at first gentle with her, then slightly rough as he takes her to another place. She is heating up, moaning. He raises her hips; she climaxes so intensely she sees the night when she saw all the stars in the Montana night sky and could smell the snow. She is home; he brought her here. He lays himself behind her, his arm over her, holding her, calming her from the continuing spasms, protecting her, and keeping her near. His face is in the curve of her neck, smelling the heat that he made her feel. He would never be done with her. She would never be done with him. They've given each other everything in their dance, to the completion of the last note.

He lays his head on her stomach, she smooths his hair. They are married in flesh, heart, soul, and mind. They are married to each other's eyes, bound by a love neither thought they'd experience in their lifetimes. They will marry officially soon, but it won't change anything. They are a blending of cultures, yet they are the same. They waited, sacrificed for each other. It was worth it. They came to each other whole, better, and without other burdens. Everything this day had been exposed, shared, and put out there for them to reach for—to take and to consume. They knew everything about each other that mattered. Each day forward they would learn the other things.

No two people could get any closer. Any other road taken, any other choice made, any other time, they would not be here, but they would be looking for each other, the dream of each other, longing for this night. The visions were true, and now they understood. He has his watch, full custody of her time, and she has a ring, that is engraved "W + S =1."

Sleep comes. They sleep entwined in each other's arms. The best sleep of their lives. When they wake, he will bathe her, take care of her, and they will dance again. They will need each other to get to that place again. They know they will dance for the rest of their lives. They will grow old together, dancing.

The adventures they encounter will come and go, she will write more books, and they will love each other forever. She had a Dream, he had a Vision, and it brought them to this place called home.

TWENTY-FOUR

After almost two years of recovering from my wounds and detangling myself from my old life in DC as FBI Special Agent Samantha Wright, Profiler, I had come home to Will Little Bear as just Sam. We spent the first week of my homecoming sequestered in our new house, getting acquainted again in our king-size bed; our lips and our bodies almost never disconnecting. We were insatiable for each other and just looking at Will, handsome and muscled as he dominated the bed in all his 6'2", 210 pounds of Cheyenne male glory kept me wet and waiting for his every move. The man at almost forty-four years of age was a stallion and I could barely hold onto the reins.

It was Saturday, mid-morning, we were running low on food and Will needed to see if his guide business was still intact. We had to leave the house. Will wouldn't have gone out at all if I hadn't agreed to go with him into town for groceries and down to the stables to see how things were going. We were having trouble disengaging from each other and having to put clothes on again felt strange. We had become more comfortable with each other naked, unrestrained, and available to each other.

Once Brandon told everyone I had come home, they gave us space and privacy. Will and I had nearly two years to make up for and they understood. We weren't even close to catching up, but it was time to surface, at least for the day. I had put DC behind me, along with my profiler job with the FBI for the moment, and I reveled in my new life with Will.

Today was also a big day for me. My 8' x 10' storage pod was supposed to be delivered, and I would have the balance of my worldly possessions with me again. There hadn't been much snow for October in Ashland, Montana, so the truck should be able to get down our road without mishap. If the hay truck could make it, the pod truck could, too. Will had built this home for us but wouldn't live in it without me and he now had ambitions to move his personal items from the apartment he had lived in over the stables into the house — especially now that he would need clothes. We started making our house a home — combining our lives — our stuff. The only furniture we had were the chairs around the kitchen island and our king-size bed. For now, it felt like enough until we could blend our tastes and pick out furniture that we would both like. It meant something for the new life we were building together.

We stepped outside where the temperature was brisk and in the low twenties, prompting Will to button my coat and put my collar up so I would be warmer. We stood at the doorway for a bit, not really wanting to leave our sanctuary. He looked at me; I smiled back at him, "Let's do this so we can get back in time for the delivery of your things. While we're in town I'll make sure the guys stay here in case the truck comes before we get back."

Will still could not believe Sam was here. He had to keep reaching for her to make sure it wasn't a dream. He had waited so long for her to come home, and unable to take his eyes off her. Sam was his wife in all ways except for the paperwork — all 5'9" of her — slim, long legs with a body to die for. Sam's beauty ran deep; she was the total package, inside and out. She had beautiful long, dark hair, the face of an angel that defied her almost forty years and had no clue as to her own looks or the effect she had on men. Will always described her as a natural, unconceited beauty.

Will took my hand in his as we headed to the stables. Brandon and Jess were inside cleaning the stalls and putting the horses in the outdoor paddocks to get some exercise. The colder weather made the horses playful, and they were running and bucking. Jess Gray Feather was Will's partner in the guide and tracking business. The security business Will operated was his own. Jess was fifty years old, Cheyenne, like a brother to Will, and medicine man to the Tribe. He was a little taller than me, his long black hair had some gray showing but he had a great smile, and I would describe him as affable.

Brandon ran up and hugged me. I kissed him on the forehead, and just as quickly he ran back to his work. Will smiled at me, shook his head and laughed, "He loves you. He missed you." Will called Jess over, "Jess, I want you to meet my wife, Samantha Wright."

I smiled at Will when he introduced me in that way. I felt complimented. I could see he was happy, and I didn't object. I put my hand out to Jess, "Please call me Sam. I'd like to thank you for making it possible for Will and me to have some time together this past week."

Jess shook my hand, smiled at me, half laughed, and remarked, "Will talked about your beauty, but I did not believe him until now. I thought he was imagining you." He turned to Will, "You are one lucky Indian, my brother."

Will smiled at Jess while looking at me. "You have no idea."

I blushed, took Will's hand, while looking in his eyes. "I'm the lucky one."

Jess looked at me again, seemed a little contemplative. "I want to thank you for saving Will and Brandon, they are family to me and now so are you. Welcome to the Tribe, we will give you a proper Cheyenne name that befits your courage at the ceremony."

"We saved each other." My eyes welled up with tears and I hugged Jess because I couldn't speak any further. He wasn't quite sure what to do for an awkward moment but then his arms went around me, and he hugged back. Will came closer, smiling, "Jess, that's enough of that for now. I need you and Brandon to stay here until we get back from town. A truck is coming to deliver Sam's personal boxes today. I'd also like to go over schedules tomorrow for the coming weeks if that works for you."

"Brandon and I have it covered. I will call my sons, and when the truck arrives, we will unload it for you and put the boxes in the house. Since you are going into town, would you order shavings for the stalls? We are running low, and yes, tomorrow is fine to go over schedules. There is a lot of work lined up until we close down in December."

Will was appreciative. "That would be great about the boxes, the door is unlocked. Thanks Jess, it gives Sam access to the boxes when she wants. I'll order the shavings and alfalfa cubes before we hit the grocery store." Will patted Jess on the shoulder and we left for town.

Will held my hand while we walked to the car and as he opened the door for me, "Why didn't you say anything when I introduced you as my wife?"

"Why would I? I thought I was your wife."

Will pulled me to him, kissed me deeply and agreed. "Yes, you are, and that makes me your husband."

I held on, taking in his scent that always brought me comfort. I couldn't wait for this life with him to continue. "Precisely. I just need to get a ring on that finger of yours so everyone will know."

"Let's talk about a date at dinner. The sooner the better." He kissed me again as he gestured for me to get into the car.

"I have no traditions Will, but you must have some that you want to adhere to — ceremony, tradition — something?"

"We can discuss that tonight. Let's get done with our errands in town so we can come back home to figure it out. Later I want to show my wife how much I love her."

Everyone in town must have been told I had returned. People waved and said hello everywhere we went. Some thanked me for what I had done and welcomed me to the Cheyenne family. Will looked so proud, and I was happy to be part of a family, a Tribe. One elderly Cheyenne man walked up to Will and me, put his arms around both of us. "The sweat is set for next Sunday to initiate your woman into the Tribe. It's at the usual place." He turned to walk away, stopped and half-turned back towards us and said something in Cheyenne to Will.

"Who was that man? What did he say to you, Will?"

Will laughed, "That is Matthew Silver Hawk, an Elder of the Tribe. He said I was one lucky Indian to have a woman like you. Seems to be the consensus in the community and I agree." He came closer and kissed me saying, "Let's get our groceries and head home. I miss being alone with you."

"I miss you, too." I smiled and looked at my husband - - physically strong with kind, soft brown eyes, an easy smile, and the whitest teeth you ever saw. I have never known a better man, and I adored him.

Will was so happy, so proud to have Sam in his life. He loved her more than he thought was possible and he was having trouble sharing her with the rest of the world right now. He never thought this would be his life. He silently thanked the spirits. She was his new life, the life he dreamt of and would never give up now that it was real.

When we arrived back home, there was a lot of activity. The truck had arrived with my pod and since no one called me for the lock combination, Jess had used bolt cutters to take the lock off. Brandon, Jess and his sons were carrying my boxes into the house and a couple of other men, maybe Jess' sons, were carrying boxes out of the stables I assumed came from the apartment above containing Will's personal items. Brandon ran over, took the grocery bags I was carrying and toted them into the house. It was a whirlwind of organized chaos, and within a brief time everything Will and I owned was in the living room ready to be unpacked. Jess came into the house with his sons and introduced them to me before they left for the evening.

"Sam, this is my eldest son, Clarence. My next son Frankie. My middle son James. My next son Grant, and my youngest son is Ethan." Jess said each name with pride. I did notice most of his sons were in their twenties and Clarence looked closer to thirty. Jess had quite a family of men. His wife must be a very special woman with a strong constitution, and someone I wanted to meet in the very near future.

As I shook each son's hand and thanked them for their help, they smiled and then said something to Will in Cheyenne as they walked out the door. I was going to have to learn this language, so I could keep up. Brandon had put the groceries away and ran to me again with a hug and said, "I like that you are home." He ran to get a ride from Jess. I stood there a bit amused and again looked at Will and implored, "Translate please."

"I will paraphrase for you: Clarence said you are too beautiful to be human, Frankie asked if you had a sister, James offered to stand in for me if I ever was unable to do my duties as a husband, and Grant said that you are the most beautiful woman he has ever seen. Ethan, like his father, agreed I was one lucky Indian." Will looked at me, softly touched my cheek, and winked, "We may not be able to leave the house again."

I laughed. "I'm going to make dinner since we didn't have lunch. If you want to talk later, I think I feel ready." Will had been wanting to talk about that night, almost two years ago, when we put our lives on hold. He needed to because he still feels guilty about my getting shot. I wanted to talk about what happened to me that night, when I went inside of myself to do what I did, what I needed to do. We had each given our statements to the FBI back then, but we still needed to talk to each other now.

"I know you wanted to talk wedding dates, but I'd feel better if this talk was behind us, and we could look to the future without it hanging over our heads, clouding things up."

Will glanced at me nervously, "I'm glad you're ready. I didn't want to push." I could see he was anxious about it but he, too was ready to get this behind us.

Dinner conversation immersed us in Will's upcoming work schedule which he would go over with Jess in the morning. He was not looking forward to leaving me for days at a time and I wasn't sure how I would start assimilating into this new life on my own. I would need to find my place in it, and in the Tribe. I had to be more than a writer after being an FBI Special Agent and Profiler. I had to be useful, integral to something. I wanted to be Will's wife, but I couldn't completely lose myself, my identity. I needed to find a balance that could make Will comfortable, happy, and still feel fulfilled myself.

It was almost eight by the time dinner was done and neither of us ate much. We were both thinking about the coming resurrection of "that night." I needed to shower and then I'd be ready to talk. I was terrified that once I started telling him about that night it would become real again. I owed this explanation to him, but I wasn't looking forward to it. "Will, do you want to share a shower and then have a beer before we talk?"

Will came over to me, took my hand in his, and led me into the bathroom. He didn't need to be asked twice.

CHAPTER

TWENTY-FIVE

After our rather lengthy shower we toweled off and I began to put sweat-pants and a thermal shirt on. Will looking confused and disappointed, "Clothes?"

"I can't have this conversation naked. I need to focus on that night, not on how much I want you right now," I explained, hoping he would understand. He looked at me and started to get dressed.

I could feel myself start to tremble. I struggled to find the words to start. Will needed this and I would never begrudge him anything. I would give him whatever he wanted or needed — and he needed this. He handed me a bottle of beer and I took my usual couple of sips. Feeling uneasy, I suddenly drank half. He looked at me, knowing I wouldn't drink that much unless I was trying to steady my nerves. He took the bottle from me, finished it, and placed the empty on the floor. It was time to open the steel door that had been bolted for the last two years and to let in some air.

The only place we could have this soul-bearing conversation was on our bed. This wasn't kitchen talk, and that added to the difficulty. I didn't want this place — the place where we connect — to be sullied by the words I was about to say.

Will was watching Sam try to gather her thoughts and he could see she was afraid of dredging this up, but to move forward they had to talk about it and finally bury the past. He loved her and this conversation wouldn't change that. He knew she loved him so much that she would do this for him.

Will broke the silence. "I haven't read your book yet but did writing about that night give you some peace, help you work through it?"

Instead of answering him, I volleyed it back. "Have you and Brandon found peace since then? I was cleared by all the FBI-mandated doctors. I've processed it." I couldn't let Will see that peace had alluded me since that night and I wouldn't let myself feel weak because that would allow the killers to win, and all the pain and suffering would be for naught. I wanted to stay numb.

Will saw what I was trying to do — deflect, protect myself, and not make eye contact with him. If I looked in his eyes right now, I wouldn't be able to talk. He was being patient with me, but not for long.

"Sam, look at me. Always look at me. Look me in the eyes. Stop skirting the issue and stop avoiding my question. No matter what you say it won't change my love for you. Don't be afraid." He moved closer to me, put his hand on my shoulder and whispered, "Talk to me."

"I don't want to make things about the past. It can't do any good. Maybe I'm not ready like I thought I was. This is baggage I brought here. Do we really want to unpack it now?"

Will moved closer to me, leaning against the headboard, and reaching for me to move closer to him. He kissed me with understanding and kissed me again.

"Please Sam, don't be afraid. We need to share our feelings about it. I need you to hear what I want to say, too. This is about both of us. This isn't baggage you brought in, it's already here. It's in me, and in Brandon. We all need to heal from this, to help each other finally heal."

He understood. They had been there together that night, and he had never seen such strength, even in Iraq, like what Sam showed that night. She loved him so much she was willing to die for him and almost did. She didn't know Brandon then, but she was willing to give the boy a chance at life — even if it meant she would lose her own. Will would always feel the depth of her love and he would spend his life showing her the same depth of love so she could again feel safe.

Will got up from the bed and went to the kitchen to get another beer and a bottle of water. When he came back, I reached for the beer and took the first few sips before handing it back. We always shared our beer, we always shared what we tasted of each other. He stood by the bed looking at me, and I reached again for the beer and took a bigger drink. "Okay, how do we start?" Will sat closer to me and pushed my hair back giving me a memory. "I remember my hair getting caught when I tripped and you having to cut it off. I think the killer heard me stumble and that gave us up. I did that. That's on me."

Will sat even closer, so close I could feel his breath on my face and said, "No, there was a full moon. We didn't have much cover and every sound carried that night. It could have been anything, don't take that on. That's not yours to take. Start with the first gunshot that hit. Let it come. I'm here and you're safe."

I took a breath and began. "I heard the shot and immediately felt it hit — the sting of it on my upper arm. It spun me a bit but didn't knock me down. It hurt, but that night was so cold it numbed quickly and quelled the bleeding. Then I heard the second shot, the one that hit you in the thigh. You went down, and I was overwhelmed with the fear of losing you. Before I could get to you, you were able to get a shot off and your bullet struck the perp. Another shot missed both of us, hitting near my foot. I returned two shots. I hit him. That was my tipping point, I was enraged."

Will handed me the beer again and I took another drink. I offered it back for him to finish. We were both showing the strain of the accounting, but I could tell he wanted me to go on. I was shaking. The sounds, the smells, the sights, the feelings of that night, were rushing back at me. My breath was coming hard. I was sweating even though my skin felt cold. I felt like I was being sucked down by an undertow, fighting to keep my head up.

I looked at Will and he nodded for me to continue. "I was so high on adrenaline at that point, so filled with anger that I ran to the front door of the shack, kicked it in, but saw nothing. No one. I couldn't let anything else happen. I had to find the boy. I had to stop this. I no longer cared about myself. My only value at that point was to get the killer and to stop him before he killed Brandon or you. You made it to the back of the shack. There was no stopping what was already set in motion. I started running again to where you had heard the horse, and I remember suddenly being close enough to see the face of the killer. He was about thirty feet away. Brandon was on the horse, in shock or worse, and you were waiting for me to give you the signal. I know I talked to the killer. He called me "girlie." His very existence nauseated me."

Will put his hand on my arm. He wanted me to stop for a moment, to calm myself a bit. He got a cold cloth from the bathroom to wipe the tears running down my face. He tried to cool me with it. He put it to my head to keep the memories from being too much for me. It gave me a break. He handed me the water bottle and I drank. My mouth was dry. I felt hoarse. He kissed my forehead and sat back down on the bed facing me, holding my shaking hands.

"Can you go on Sam, or do you want to stop?" he asked out of concern.

I reluctantly went on. "I wanted to pray, to ask for help or forgiveness, but I didn't think God would listen because of what I was about to do next. I remember saying "ONE." Pulling the trigger, I shot the killer in the head, but he didn't go down. Those seconds when I saw you running for Brandon, the killer aiming his gun at you — I just couldn't let you be killed or have Brandon lose his life because of this maniac. I was the only one expendable. As I started running towards you, that's when the shot sounded. I felt the hit on the right side of my vest, not realizing I had been wounded, not really feeling it. You had Brandon by then and I was free to do what I had to. I had no feeling about it one way or the other, my senses numb. I see myself walk over to the piece of shit. He was laying on the ground, his filthy hand still holding the gun, trying to lift it — trying to kill with it. I knew I was gone by then. I wasn't there anymore. Whoever I was before had vanished and been replaced by darkness. I should have taken his gun. I didn't need to shoot him twice, but I did. I shot him in the head again, and then took his gun, not feeling anything. I killed him, and I liked it. I liked seeing the light go out in his eyes. I would have unloaded my gun into him if I hadn't seen the boy looking at me. I felt dead. I had become an animal, a void. I was just — nothing. Maybe I still am."

Will sat closer. He had tears running down his face. He put his arms around me, but I pushed him away. "No. Don't comfort me. I need to finish. I don't deserve forgiveness for this." Tears filled my eyes as shame engulfed me.

Will gave Sam her space. He understood. He'd done things in Iraq that still haunted him, and he had gotten a Silver Star. She needed to empty herself of this. She wasn't a killer. She only did what she had to do. He needed her to let it go so it wouldn't haunt her, haunt their new life together.

I started to talk again, but my voice was hoarse. "For a moment, I was able to get myself back to the reason we were there that night — Brandon. We needed to get him warm and take care of him. He was our priority. You saw my blood. I saw my blood. It was bad, but I didn't want you to see me die. The rest is out of focus for me. I heard your voice but couldn't make out the words. I could smell the snow. Brandon was holding my hand when things went black."

I drank more water. My hands were shaking uncontrollably. Will had to help steady the bottle for me.

"That's enough. You've said enough." He put his finger to my lips.

"No, I need to finish this. I need to say it. I became a cold, dark animal that night. I didn't know it was in me. What if it still is? If that wasn't in me, how could I have done what I did? I don't deserve someone like you, I'm not what you thought. I thought I had forgiven myself, but I haven't. Brandon can't see me like this. He can't know." I was sobbing so hard I couldn't stop. Will took me into his arms and held me until the sobs subsided.

Will regretted taking Sam down this dark path. He hadn't realized how it might affect her. He loved her and wanted to take this pain from her. He had watched her that night take the life of the killer to save the lives of Brandon and himself. It had taken more from her than he understood.

Will was forcing me to look at him. I didn't want to — I was ashamed. Would my eyes show what I had become that night? I kept hiding my eyes from him, looking away.

"Damn it, Sam, look at me. Now." He was getting angry. I had never seen him so upset. He was yelling at me. "You are not cold inside. What you had to do didn't come from the darkness, it came from love. You didn't kill a person, you killed something evil. You did it because you loved me. You did it because you wanted the boy to have a life. God Sam, I've never seen such love, such strength, such selflessness. You let yourself go to that deep place — not because you were dead inside — you went there because of love. There's nothing to forgive. There's nothing to be ashamed of. Everything you did was out of love." Will shook me a bit, "Do you hear me? Do you understand?"

Will held on to me for the longest time, until we both calmed down. He looked at me with my cried-out eyes, smoothed my hair, and eased my mouth to his. He kissed me so tenderly that I felt the love he was offering me. He was wanting but waiting for me. Always waiting for me. "Are you disappointed in me?" I whispered, afraid.

"Never. I'm so proud of you. I love you." With that, he kissed me more intensely. He wanted to comfort me, but he needed comfort too. I could see it in his eyes. I needed to know his feelings hadn't changed towards me. He knew I needed him to show me it was okay now. He took my sweatpants and shirt off, and then removed his own.

CHAPTER
TWENTY-SIX

I was lying there, facing this sweet man. I looked at him, "We're not finished yet. You need to talk to me. I don't know what you felt that night. I don't remember what happened after you took me and Brandon to the clearing. I need to hear your part. The part I wasn't there for."

He looked in my eyes. "I have to go back further to when we were sitting in the sleeping bag waiting to make our hike to the shack. You told me how you felt and the promise you wanted from me. You wanted to know if I would wait for you even if it took a long time for you to come back to me. At that moment, I didn't know if I would be strong enough to keep that promise, to wait for you. I wanted to force us to be together because I was impatient. I wanted to grab you, to beg you to leave with me right then. Forget the mission, forget the boy. I wanted you and I didn't care how I was going to make it happen. Then I looked in your eyes and saw there were things more important than what I wanted or what you wanted. At that instant, I knew I could do it. Could do it for you. I could keep that promise, I could wait. You made me a better man at that moment. I would have waited forever for you after looking in your eyes that night. When I saw how brave you were, and the love you showed, I made a commitment to you right there that I would be worthy of your sacrifice."

Will's voice was shaking. He took a drink of water. We were both still naked and I think he felt that much more exposed — vulnerable — that he couldn't hide anything from me. I touched his face. "Breathe."

He was hesitant but went on. "The rest is pretty much as you said, until I realized how badly you had been wounded and that you had taken a bullet meant for me. The guilt I felt — the rage and fear — shook me to my depths. I was running on fear the rest of the night, trying to get you and Brandon to the clearing to meet up with the Medivac. When the helicopter took off and you and Brandon were on the way to Denver, I thought I would die right there. I didn't know if I would ever see you again. It was as if your hand was ripped out of my chest, and you were no longer making my heartbeat. I had failed by not keeping you safe. I had failed, and because of that you might have died."

"Will, it wasn't your responsibility to keep me safe that night. Brandon was our priority. You didn't fail me. Don't go there."

I eased out of bed and went to the kitchen for another beer. Will and I never drink more than one beer, and we share that one. Tonight, was different. We needed another one, maybe more. I came back to the side of the bed, standing there, naked. I took a couple of sips and offered the beer to this strong but fragile man. He took it, looking at me as he touched the scar on my side from the bullet meant for him. His eyes welled up with the memory. He drank more than half the beer and wiped his eyes. I slid under the covers sitting near him but still giving him room. He handed me the remaining beer and I drank it down.

Will's voice was weaker. "Those days in the hospital, trying to get you to come back to me were the hardest of my life. The doctors and nurses saw the fear on my face, but they also saw that I loved you so much I would defy the Universe to bring you back. When Brandon came to your room one night, touching your fingers to his forehead, he smiled. I knew then you would come back — Brandon knew you would come back. My fear left. The only thing I had to bring you back with was love, and that's all it took."

I smiled at this man who had brought me back from the brink of death. I knew what it cost him. I would give all that back to him.

"Sam, in my whole life I never knew love. Until you, I never would have believed I could love someone so deeply — that my very life — depended on it. Keeping my promise to you — to let you heal on your own — was the most consequential, significant, and hardest thing I have ever had to do. It forced me to be who you needed, and forced me to become a better man, a man you would come home to. The vision was my lifeline and I believed. I had faith. You see Sam, out of our darkest moments, when we hated ourselves the most, is when we became our better selves and were able to experience the purest part of love. We became what we needed and deserved from each other. Hell gave us heaven. We saw evil that night, but Brandon was able to see that love was what saved us all."

The Chinese have a saying that if you save a life, you are forever responsible for that life. Will, Brandon, and I saved each other, and we would be forever bound.

I smiled at Will. He smiled back at me, and that's when the past was buried. One day we knew Brandon would want to talk to us and we would be here for him. He was our child, as they all are. Love won over evil. We didn't lose ourselves but found each other. From that baring of our souls to each other we knew we would always be able to talk to each other about everything and anything. That was new for both of us.

It was two in the morning. "I'm hungry."

Stifling a yawn, he nodded. "I could eat."

TWENTY-SEVEN

It was Sunday morning. We felt the clouds had dissipated from the past and the future looked bright. Will had to get down to the stables to talk to Jess about the scheduled trips on the calendar. It was a busy time for hunting and fishing trips. Some of the trips were for a day, some were two or three days in duration or until the hunter "bagged" his prey. Will wasn't happy about the prospect of having to leave but he had made commitments before he knew I was coming home. He eventually realized it would be the first time he would have someone waiting for him at home, and he liked that. It made leaving more tolerable. The day would be filled with getting things organized, stocked and packed up. Will and Jess would both be heading out tomorrow for a few days with different hunting parties. The hunters and fishermen paid well for Will and Jess to take them into the wild and to bring them back safely.

I would get used to my new life while Will was away. I'd take a closer look at our home and start going through some of my boxes while I mused about my second book. I had trepidations about being alone in Montana, but I could do it. I'd have to do it. I wanted this life. What I needed, was a one-hundred-and-eighty-degree change, at least for a while. I needed to be normal, not a profiler, not an FBI agent, just a regular woman.

I made a lunch of man-size sandwiches, chips, salsa, and homemade cookies for Will, Jess, and Brandon, and took it to the stables for them. They appreciated the food; they had worked up appetites with all the tasks they had. Will liked that I would do that for all of them. There was a lot to do preparing for these trips, and I never realized what a well-oiled machine it had to be not to forget something crucial. They had to be prepared for anything and to provide some creature comforts to tolerate being outside in the cold. I went back to the house and left them to their work.

A few hours later, Brandon came up to the house smiling. "Will would like some more of the cookies you made last night, so would I. Jess too, I guess."

I smiled at this Cheyenne young man, almost fourteen now, though older in his heart. He seemed wise for his years, was much taller and more filled out. Soon he would be a handsome young man, and the young girls would be chasing him. He was polite and not afraid of showing affection. His black hair was pulled back into a braid and his smile was infectious. He wore a bandana around his neck like a cowboy, but I knew he was trying to hide the scars. I understood that. I packed up the cookies and handed them to him, "Enjoy. Tell Will I'll help you in the stables while they're gone and in return you can give me riding lessons." Brandon nodded in the affirmative with a cookie already stuffed into his mouth. He ran out and I laughed. Brandon had helped Will pull me from the precipice of death. That young man and I were connected for life.

Darkness came earlier as the months progressed, and I could see the lights come on in the stables. I received a text from my love, "One more hour. I miss you." I sent a smiley face in return. I shivered as a noise came from the roof but shook it off thinking it was just the wind. I'd heard a lot of noises lately and had feelings of dread that I kept to myself. Noises were easily dismissed but the ill feelings came from a deep, dark place that hadn't yet healed. I hadn't really felt at ease since the case ended without a satisfaction that things were done, closed as they say. Lose ends, a need for tying up everything that plagued my dreams seemed illusive. This wasn't something to share with Will since all I needed was to accept that the case was over.

Around six Will came through the door. He looked tired, but happy. Coming over to me, he took me in his arms, and kissed me as if he had not seen me in days. I liked my new life. This life had substance, value, and love. I was happy. Well, happy with slight trepidation as to if I'd ever feel safe again. I had good instincts and they were keeping me up at night.

Will was half-laughing. "Those cookies were great when we could pry them out of Brandon's hands. Brandon mentioned that in return for riding lessons you would help in the stables. You know you don't have to, it's his job."

"I know but I want to if it's not a problem. I want to get to know him better. I want to be able to ride and not count on the horse knowing more than I do. I need to be a part of things around here. It's a small start, but I'd really like to. I'm not afraid of getting my hands dirty."

"Okay, but make sure he does most of the work." Will winked at me and came over to kiss me again. "How can I say no to you?"

Will went to take a shower while I finished making dinner. I wasn't very domestic, but I could cook some things. Others I would learn. Cooking is just chemistry and I liked cooking. It soothed me and gave instant gratification. Sitting and eating at the kitchen island was one of my new favorite things. Will and I would talk, make plans, and cherish the time we had with each other. We had a dishwasher, but we enjoyed washing dishes by hand together because it gave us more of what we had missed before — "time" together.

I had gotten cleaned up before Will came back from the stables. We were still in so-called honeymoon mode, and I wanted to look good for him — especially since he was leaving early in the morning for three days. I had my hair down, wore form-fitting jeans, a v-neck, light blue sweater that didn't disguise the fact that I was a woman. One could see the furrow between my breasts, a favorite place of Will's. I noticed him looking at me on his way to the shower. Twenty minutes later Will had his thermal boxers on when he came out of the bathroom and was trying to find some clothes in the boxes from the apartment over the stables. I went to help and finally found some clothes for him to wear on his trip and some sweats for tonight. I promised, "I'll bring some order to this while you're gone."

Will laughed. "I was getting used to the "no clothes" routine, but I'll adjust. It will just make foreplay a little longer."

We had eaten and were sitting at the kitchen island talking about what Will's trips were like, and he showed me on the map where they were going. He also showed me the two-way radios in the mudroom in case I needed to get ahold of him along with all the contact numbers for people I might need — like Christian, the Medivac pilot, and explained how to operate the satellite phone for emergencies. He told me where the guns and ammunition were stored wanting me to be safe. We went over the codes for the security system and the combination for the safe, which was the date I had come home. When he had filled me in on everything I needed to know, for living out here and being on my own, he looked at me, reached over and ran his finger up and down in the furrow between my breasts. He smiled and took a deep breath.

"Have I told you how beautiful you look today? You make that sweater look good." He pulled out his cell phone. "I need a picture of you to take along with me. I have one I took when we first met, but I want a newer one." He took my picture, satisfied he liked it, he showed me the other picture he already had. "What were you looking at in the distance that made you smile?"

"I think I saw an eagle that day, and I thought of Dr. Sampson because he always told me to look up. You can really see things when you look up. I can't believe Dr. Sampson has been dead almost two years now. I remember him in his tweed suit, white shirt, and clip-on tie. I still have a notebook full of funny words he made up. He respected me, and in the end, he loved me like a daughter. All those years we worked together at the Bureau are in my memory. He was the closest I ever had to a real father. I miss him and I'm sad you won't ever be able to know him. You would have liked each other. His death brought us together on the case and ultimately saved Brandon's life. One life for another." Tears threatened my eyes.

"He'd be proud of you Sam, for everything you did. He's watching over you, I know it."

Will compared the two pictures and commented, "You look younger now. How are you doing that? Is there a painting of you somewhere that is aging?"

We both laughed. "My turn to take your picture." When I looked at the result of my handsome man with his sweet eyes, my eyes welled up again, and I looked at him, stood up, went over to where he was sitting, hugged him, breathed in the scent of him at the base of his neck, and whispered with a catch in my voice, "I'm just so happy. I'll miss you. We're going to take a lot more pictures with the new camera I brought with me. I'm going to document our life together. I want all new memories for my life. Our home will be full of photos."

We spent the rest of the night in bed creating wonderful memories to hold onto. He'd be gone for three days and it would seem like a lifetime until he returned. It was my turn to wait. I would.

TWENTY-EIGHT

We were up at five. I made lots of coffee for Will's thermos and for Jess'. I made breakfast sandwiches for them and for their parties in case they got hungry. They could easily eat them while riding their horses. I made sure Will had the clothes he needed for the trip and some of the cookies he liked. I was being domesticated but I was alright with that, for now, it gave me a sense of purpose and calm, after the past that brought me here. Every day things gave normalcy to my life, something I had never experienced before.

I saw the van from The Lodge pull up with the hunters inside and realized that some of the business Will booked was through The Lodge. Will and Scotty, the new owner of the Lodge referred people back and forth to each other. Will came through the door. "I guess I have to get going. It's tough leaving you for three days." He touched his watch, the one from me that gave him custody of my time. He embraced me, looked at me so closely. "God, Sam, I love you." And he kissed me so hard it would linger on my lips for three days.

I handed him the coffee, breakfast sandwiches, and cookies. He was surprised I had gone through all the trouble for him. I picked up his backpack and asked, "May I walk you out?"

"Just to the door. It's hard enough leaving, and with all those men out there — well, you know."

"I get it. I love you, and please be safe."

Will went out the door and just as I turned to think about what I'd do with my day, he ran back in and kissed me. "See you soon. You're so beautiful, Sam. I miss you already." And that quick he took off out the door and headed to the stables.

"What is it about the men around here always being in a hurry?" I laughed to myself and then counted my blessings that the men in my life showed me love and if I got it on the fly, I'd take it.

For me, the next few days were full of activity from helping Brandon in the stables, taking riding lessons, working out in our home gym, organizing Will's boxes, getting his clothes into the closet, and cooking meals in advance. I looked at the many boxes I needed to unpack and just couldn't muster up the enthusiasm to go through them yet. The winter would be long for doing a few at a time. I filled every minute of my alone time, so Will would be home that much sooner in my mind. The house was too quiet with just me in it, getting used to all the sounds at night I wasn't accustomed to here in Montana and the king-size bed just didn't bring comfort without him. I missed his scent most of all.

Will had taken out a hunting party of four men. It was a lot to handle, and the weather was getting colder. Snow came and went and made one aware winter was upon us. The biggest part of Will's job was safety. Trying to keep these people from hurting themselves or others with their guns and knives was a full-time job. Will had never had any accidents or mishaps on any of his trips and he wanted to keep it that way. He handled everything — setting up camp, caring for the horses, preparing the food, tracking prey, and dressing it once they had killed it. One of the men in the group was a regular, and always asked for Will to take them out on these excursions. His name was Tad Collins, a loud, full of life, extroverted man who enjoyed life and the money he had. He was almost seventy-five, average height, gray hair that was thinning, and he had given up physical exercise after his last divorce ten years prior when he gave up on love. He was a very wealthy man from New York with holdings all over the world. He was interested in having Will do some security analysis for him on some buildings he was constructing in Las Vegas. The man also had four ex-wives, six lazy children and treated Will like the son he had always wanted, but never had. Will liked him and talked about him a lot.

It was late. It was the last night of the trip and Will was sitting by the camp-fire, rubbing the watch Sam had given him. He hadn't realized he would miss her as much as he did, so much he physically ached. He was missing the part of himself that Sam had filled. He really wanted to get home. He saw Mr. Collins walk over to the fire and ask, "Is there any coffee left, Will?"

"Yes Mr. Collins, about a cup or so."

"That'll be great, thanks. Anything wrong Will? You look distracted."

"No, not at all, just missing Sam."

Mr. Collins asked, "Do you have a picture of her with you?"

Will pulled his cell phone out and showed Mr. Collins the picture he had taken of Sam the other night.

"Will, she is one gorgeous woman." Handing the phone back.

"Inside and out," Will added.

"I've been married four times and I never looked like you do when I was away from any of them. This the real thing?"

"Yes sir. Forever. I waited a long time for Sam and I'm not letting go. I never thought I could love anyone like I love her. It's changed my life."

"I'd like to meet her sometime. Anyone who can make you smile like that I need to meet. Well, I'm off to sleep since we're heading back early. Thanks for a great trip, Will. Next time I come out I want to talk to you more seriously about doing some freelance security work for me. Good night."

"Good night, Mr. Collins, I look forward to that." Will took one last look at
Sam's picture and tried to get some sleep.

It was Thursday mid-morning and Will was coming home today. I wasn't
sure what time, but he would text me when he could, as soon as he got a
signal. I was down at the barn finishing cleaning the stalls with Brandon.
We were talking about his home-schooling, and I was anxious to get Laney
saddled so I could ride her in the indoor arena before Will got back. I was
getting more proficient at riding and really enjoyed it.

The text came. "See you in about an hour. Love you."

I texted back. "I'll be in the arena riding. I love you, too." My heart started
to beat faster, and I couldn't wait for Will to get home.

I didn't hear Will and his party ride up, but Brandon ran in and shouted,
"Will's home." He ran off to help with the horses. I was having Laney lope
around the perimeter of the arena and started slowing her pace in order to
dismount. As I was dismounting Will grabbed hold of me, put his hand
behind my head and brought our mouths together. We kissed as though we
hadn't seen each other in months. Laney took her nose and pushed against
us. She was focused on getting to the fresh hay in her stall. She'd done her
job and wanted her reward. Will stepped back a bit, smiling, looking me up
and down. "Hi." He said, breathing harder.

"Hi, I've missed you," I returned, while trying to catch my breath. Will
pressed closer to me and I could feel that he was hard against my hip, pulsing.
"Will, you can't go out there like this." I put my hand to him, and he looked
at me like he had a plan. He took my hand in his, "Walk in front of me to
my office." When we reached his office, he closed and locked the door, shut
the blinds on the window, and looked at me for my consent to ease his need.
I could never say no to this man. I tried to get my jeans off, got out one leg,
but the other pant leg wasn't going over my boot. Will pushed my panties
down my free leg and felt me. I was wet with wanting and he shivered. I had
his belt undone and was working on the zipper when Jess knocked on the
door. "Uh, Will, we need to check out Mr. Collins' party on your computer."

192

Will answered back in a breathy way, "I'm looking for something. Just give me a couple of minutes, Jess." Jess, Mr. Collins, and his party were all snickering, I could hear them, but I didn't care at this point-of-no-return. Mr. Collins spoke loud enough for Will to hear, "Take your time Will, I'm in no hurry, but I think you are."

By this time, I had Will's pants down, had access to him now as he sat down on his office chair. We weren't wasting any time, I mounted him, and we both shuddered when I slid him into me. We were in rhythm, and trying to be quiet, but damn it was great — quick, but great. We climaxed in unison as Will put his hand over my mouth. I could be loud and I'm sure it was no secret what was happening in Will's office. We finished breathless, and Will whispered in my ear, "Sam, I saw you and I couldn't wait. God, I wanted you. I just couldn't control it." He kissed me deeply and then we tried to get dressed.

Will opened the door and saw all the guys standing outside of his office smiling at us. They noticed his shirt was half out of his pants and his hair was mussed. I tried to hurry out of the office while smoothing my hair as I quickly walked away. I wanted to get Laney back to her stall, but Mr. Collins saw me attempting to escape and said, "You must be Sam. Will told me a lot of good things about you. The picture he showed me doesn't do you justice. I've read about you and what you did a couple years back. I'm impressed and honored to meet you."

"Thank you, Mr. Collins. Just doing my job, sir. It's nice to meet you."

Mr. Collins attempted to shake my hand, but I hid my hands behind my back, "Oh, Mr. Collins, my hands are dirty from riding." And as I realized what I had just said, everyone including Will started laughing while still trying to tuck in his shirt. I was red in the face, backed out of the hallway, and quickly headed to the arena feeling over-exposed. I hoped I hadn't embarrassed Will. Having worked in a man's world most of my life, well, it's not the first time I'd found myself in a situation and it wouldn't be the last.

Mr. Collins was finally able to stop laughing. "Tell her I'll take a rain check on that handshake, Will. She's a beauty. I don't know how you were able to leave home at all." Will checked Mr. Collins and his party out, but before they loaded into the van from The Lodge, Mr. Collins turned back and said to Will, "Take her out, show her off." He slipped two hundred dollars to Will and said, "No need to shake. See you next time." Mr. Collins was chuckling as he got into the van.

I maneuvered an impatient Laney out of the arena and was walking towards her stall to get her settled in when Will caught up and walked along side me. He was slightly laughing and inquired with a snicker, "Are you okay?"

"How long do you think it will take before that story is the laugh of the town?" I asked as I shook my head, trying not to laugh myself.

"Well, it probably already is." He came closer. "You know I wouldn't do anything on purpose to put you in an uncomfortable situation. I saw you and I just couldn't stop myself. I didn't think they'd be at the office that soon since I had ridden ahead."

"I know you wouldn't. I was your accomplice, wanting you too. I was afraid I embarrassed you in front of an important client. Jeez, Will, did you hear what I said? "

Will snickered, "It was classic. You scored a lot of points for me with Mr. Collins. He slipped me two hundred dollars to take you out for an evening. I think he likes you."

I had taken Laney's saddle off, brushed her, picked her hooves, got her settled into her stall so she could enjoy the hay while Will and I were talking. I walked over to him as he leaned on the stall post, pulled him close by the front of his shirt, and firmly whispered, "We're not done. That was an appetizer, not the whole meal, and I'm still hungry. You didn't even get above my waist. Get your work done and come find me." I looked at him, softly touched the front of his jeans so he had to adjust himself, and as I walked away, I slapped my own butt and smiled over my shoulder to him.

Jess walked up to Will at that moment, "That is how I got five sons. I will take the day trip tomorrow for you. I think you are going to be busy." He patted Will on the back and walked to the office laughing to himself.

Will had his hands on his hips while he continued to watch Sam walk to the house. He watched how her hips swayed in her fitted jeans, and her ponytail bounced up and down. "God, I am one lucky Indian." Will got his work done in record time and went to look for Sam.

I had dinner nearly ready. I made Will his favorite, chicken enchiladas with cornbread. Just as I took dinner out of the oven Will walked in the door. I looked at him and couldn't believe how good my life was.

"Dinner in ten. You have time to get cleaned up and share a beer with me before we eat."

He walked over smiling, "Not so fast, first things first." He kissed me tenderly, lovingly, then licked my lips. "Now, I'll be back in ten. Dinner smells great and I'm starved."

When I heard him coming back to the kitchen, I grabbed a cold one from the fridge, handing it to him. He handed it back opened. "You first, like always."

I took my sips from the bottle and held it out to him. He drank half, put it on the counter, and came up behind where I was standing. He wrapped his arms around me. "That was a great homecoming, Sam. Having you here when I come home, well, it doesn't get better than that. I have plans for you after dinner. I've missed you." He turned me around and kissed me. We couldn't get enough of each other.

During dinner we talked about his trip and what Mr. Collins had said about some security work he wanted Will to handle. I told him what I had done during his absence, and out of nowhere he asked, "May or June?"

"What do you want, Will?" I knew what he was asking.

"June, it is for our wedding." He played with the engagement ring on my finger, looked in my eyes and said, "It means a lot to me that you'll wait. The traditions and ceremonies mean a lot to me and need to be a part of our marriage. That you respect me, and my heritage is so important to me."

What Will didn't say was that he was scared to death to marry because of his family history of abuse but he never wanted to lose Sam. He prayed that he never became his father. Abuse and alcoholism took his family from him at an early age, and he feared he had the genetic disposition.

"Teach me, Will. This Sunday is the induction sweat for me. I'll be Cheyenne in your eyes, and I want to learn and to have you be proud of me."

"I'll be home until Monday, so we'll talk about that, but I have some other things I want to teach you first, especially tonight." He took my hand in his and led me to the bedroom. The night was full of surprises and new things Will thought of those last few days he was away. We tried them all. I couldn't say no to this man.

I woke with a start hearing a thud somewhere near the house. Looking over at my man, he was sleeping deeply, not noticing. I took a tour through the house checking windows and doors until I was comfortable that nothing or no one was there. I couldn't shake the feeling of fear, of being watched all the time but I kept reminding myself that every sound was amplified out here in the wilderness and I just needed to get used to things and let the past go. I eased my way back under the covers and nestled myself into the crook of his neck convincing myself that if it didn't wake Will there wasn't any cause for alarm. His arms went around me, and I finally fell asleep.

CHAPTER

TWENTY-NINE

he sweat ceremony is tonight and I'm beyond nervous. Will hadn't told me what to expect or what I'm supposed to do. I wondered what Cheyenne name they will give me. He was down at the stables, so I decided to Google the ceremony. It wasn't long before Will came through the door. He came over to where I was working at the kitchen island and saw what I had pulled up online. "I didn't forget," he smiled, kissing my forehead. "Jess' wife sent a loose-fitting dress for you to wear at the sweat, and she suggested you braid your hair. It gets very warm. You'll need to hydrate before it starts."

"Who will be there?"

"Matthew Silver Hawk, the Reservations Elder you met in town, the parents of the four boys you gave justice to, even though some are from different tribes — Brandon and his family, Morgan's family, Jess and his family, Christian, and me. There could be more, but that's all I know for now." Will could see I was a bit shocked at the number of people who would be at the ceremony. "They want to honor you, Sam, for your bravery and for what you gave all of them that night. This is what they have prepared to show you their thanks and their love."

I felt overwhelmed. I had never felt such an outpouring of love and affection "en masse," and it was a lot to process. Will could see tears welling up in my eyes. He hugged me and whispered in my ear.

"We are all family now. Let us love you, honor you — you've earned it. You deserve it."

Will gathered his thoughts and remembered there are many kinds of sweats: purification, healing, transformation, and sometimes prayers for special requests. Prayers can be for guidance, acceptance, accepting loss, forgiveness and so much more. Women have sweats, men have sweats, and sometimes they are combined. Will would teach Sam more traditions as time went on, but this sweat was to honor her and give her a Cheyenne name, making her a member of the Tribe, family.

Will pulled up the chair alongside me. "Now I will teach you, so you will be ready for tonight. Most of the guests coming to the ceremony will not be in the sweat itself. They will stand outside the lodge. They will be praying, chanting, or preparing a light feast for after. There will only be a few of us in the actual lodge: you, of course, I will be there as your sponsor. Elder Matthew Silver Hawk will lead the ceremony and control the steam with water on the hot rocks, Jess is the medicine man and brings good medicine to attract the spirits for you. Christian will keep the fire. I asked Brandon to beat the drum because he is connected to your spirit."

I watched his face as he talked to me, and I could see the centuries of tradition that was part of his very DNA. He was a proud man

"The lodge is covered in buffalo skins and other pelts. It will be dark inside when the flap is closed. Do not be afraid, I will make sure you'll be okay. Prayers will be chanted, and songs will be sung. As your sponsor, I will tell the Elder why I brought you here and what you have done to earn such status. We will pass around a sacred pipe, and you must draw from it, as we all will. There are no drugs involved — I don't want you to be nervous about that. If you were on your moon, we would not be able to do this until such time that you were not. Your moon would neutralize the ceremony since you would be going through your own personal purification. "You're not, are you?"

"No, like it matters to you." I winked at him.

Will winked back at me and blushed.

"Do not eat for a few hours prior to the ceremony, but keep hydrated before going in. If you start to feel faint, reach for me and I will make sure you get some water. You will want to bring an offering, such as tobacco. I have picked some up for you to take. At some point during the ceremony the Elder will give you your Cheyenne name — usually towards the end — so that when the sweat is formally over, he can introduce you to all participants waiting outside the lodge."

"Do you know what my name will be?" I asked anxiously.

"No, I will find out when you do."

It was time for the sweat, and I admit I was endeavoring to remain calm. I wore the loose-fitting dress Jess' wife lent me and had braided my hair as suggested. I took off all jewelry as Will instructed, including my engagement ring. I said my own internal prayer, asking for guidance and a plea I wouldn't pass out. The men wore loose fitting shorts, some had wrapped a cloth around themselves, and had removed their shirts. It seemed like hours, and I was feeling the effects of the steam. Will must have sensed I was starting to fade after the pipe. He touched my hand for support so I would endure.

It came to the point in the ceremony for Will to state why I deserved the honor. His words were beautiful and heart-felt. "For bravery and selflessness with no thought for her own mortality in pursuit of saving those from a different Tribe than her own. For killing one of her own race in order to bring peace and justice to those from many Tribes who had perished at the white man's hand. Samantha Wright is an example that cultures can cross barriers and that love can vanquish evil. I nominate this white woman to become one of us — to become Cheyenne and a full-fledged member of our Tribe."

I was feeling emotional. My eyes were full of tears. There were prayers and chanting. I was starting to reel.

Will touched my hand again, gave me a small cup of water and then the Elder announced, "It is agreed that Samantha Wright, a white woman, will be admitted into the Cheyenne Tribe and will be given the name "She who stands with the warriors."

After the pronouncement, everyone exited the lodge and the Elder introduced me by my Cheyenne name to those waiting outside the lodge. Will had hold of me. He could tell I was a bit faint, but I was still standing. We all put our coats on since we were now outside in the weather and didn't want to get chilled. I was surrounded by those who came to welcome me, offering me food and water. Will took my engagement ring out of his pocket and asked in front of everyone, "Will you, "She who stands with the warriors", commit to marrying me, Will Little Bear?"

I replied with a smile, "Yes, Will Little Bear, I commit to marrying you." He slipped the ring back on my finger where it belonged. I vowed it would never come off again.

Two hours later we were home in the shower, consummating our commitment to each other.

THIRTY

For the next month Will was totally booked with hunters and fishermen wanting to get in the last of their gathering for the season. The weather started getting harsh the first week of November and hadn't let up at all. Snow, winds, and low temperatures made everything harder to do, especially for Will being out in the thick of it. We still had trouble with our goodbyes when he had to leave, but the hellos were always worth the wait. Whenever Will arrived home, everyone got out of his way. They knew better than to get between us for at least thirty minutes. Things had been quiet around the house and in my head giving me the feeling that those bumps in the night were normal and not a threat to me or to the life we were building together. Just when I calmed my mind, my thoughts went to the fact that the bad weather may be keeping the thing of my nightmares away, but not forever.

On the last day of his final trip of the season — the last day of November — I received a radio call from Jess. Bear Boy had thrown Will after stepping in a hole breaking his leg after being spooked by a gunshot. Will had to put his horse down immediately. Will had sustained broken ribs, cuts, bruises, and a dislocated shoulder, maybe a concussion. Christian's Medivac service had picked him up and they were on the way to the Billing's Hospital. Jess relayed that Will was traumatized about having to shoot Bear Boy to put him out of his suffering. He would not allow anyone else to do it even though he could hardly stand from his injuries. He had owned the beautiful horse since he had come back from Iraq, and the connection had been strong.

I firmly said to Jess, "I'm heading to Billings. Tell Christian to make sure Will knows I'm coming."

"The roads are bad, Sam." Jess reported, knowing it wouldn't matter.

"I have to be there for him, Jess. He'd do it for me."

Jess knew better than to argue with Sam when it came to Will and vice-versa. "Just be careful."

"Jess, who shot their gun that spooked Bear Boy that started the chain of events?"

"I do not know, no one in the group was responsible. Maybe other hunters."

My heart started pounding out of my chest. My mind went back to that night and the shots I heard. I couldn't breathe for a moment. Getting myself in control I grabbed a set of clothes for Will and myself, some toiletries, his medicine bag, a piece of sage, and headed out the door. Hours later, I arrived at the Billings Hospital. I found the doctor and inquired to obtain an update on Will's condition. I wasn't in legal terms his wife, but Christian had put me down as such on the hospital forms.

Will was asleep after having his shoulder repaired, his ribs wrapped, and his cuts and bruises attended to. The doctor said he had sustained a minor bump on his head that would give him a headache, but no worries about a concussion, the scan confirmed that. He would be laid up for five or six weeks while he healed.

Christian stopped me at the hospital room door and made sure I understood what he wanted to tell me. "Will's blood pressure was high, and they couldn't get him to settle down. He went crazy when they tried to take his watch off. That's why they gave him something to sleep. I told him you were on the way and that helped to calm him down a bit." Christian was Will's childhood friend, the one he had gone to Iraq with and the one who flew me to Denver Trauma when I'd been shot. Christian had Will's back, and mine. "He's going to need you when he wakes up. I already received permission from the doctor for you to stay in his room overnight." This was the same doctor who had taken care of Will when he'd been shot in the thigh that fateful night two years before. He knew who I was from stories he had heard.

Christian didn't tell her that Will believes if the watch comes off Sam's time will stop. Will has always felt he was responsible for Sam's life and the watch only made that more apparent to him. He took this responsibility to heart; Sam was everything to him. Christian ached to have a relationship like Will and Sam's, but he knew he could only love Sam from afar, she loved his best friend.

Christian hurriedly said, "I have to get back to the camp. Jess wants me to get Bear Boy back to your property. I need to get the cables attached to the chopper in order to fly him out. Will wants Bear Boy buried behind the stables before the ground freezes. I'll take care of that, and you take care of Will."

I nodded and hugged Christian, my eyes welling up with tears. "Christian, thanks for everything."

"Take care of him, Sam. Jess said it was hard to watch Will put down Bear Boy, it broke him as soon as that horse took his last breath."

I walked over to Will's bedside and saw he was having a fitful, drug-induced sleep. I smoothed his hair and touched the side of his face. He felt warm. I surveyed his injuries, seeing the scraped bump on his head. I saw his watch was still on his wrist and hadn't sustained any damage. I kissed him as he slowly woke. He saw me, and began to cry, grabbing my hand and not letting go. The nurse came in because when his vitals had gone up on the monitor. She wanted to give him more medication. I stopped her, "I want to talk to the doctor before you give him anything more. Stop." I blocked her access to Will. She left the room, and the doctor came in immediately. He checked Will over and as he read the chart. "His blood pressure is too high."

I looked at the doctor and promised, "I'll get it down. If I can't then you do what you need to. I can do this without you giving him more medication. This isn't physical, this is emotional, and your drugs aren't going to help him. He will just get more agitated."

The doctor inquired in a cynical way, "How are you going to get his blood pressure stabilized?"

"Help me move him to one side of the bed doc."

Will had a tight grip on my hand and I could feel him trembling. "Will, babe, let me have my hand for a minute so I can help the doctor get you more comfortable. I'm right here. I'm not going anywhere."

Recruiting the doctor to do physical labor didn't sit well with him, but he knew Will's and my story and didn't challenge me. The doctor did as I asked, we made Will comfortable and situated him in the bed so I wouldn't be putting any pressure on the side that had taken the brunt of his fall.

I removed the medicine pouch from my pocket and put it around Will's neck as I kissed his forehead. He touched it. I knew he had missed it. He needed it. I lit a small piece of sage, blew it out and let it smoke for a couple of seconds letting it encircle and cleanse him while the doctor gave me a warning look. I gave Will a drink of water, took my boots off, and laid next to him in the bed. He immediately grabbed my hand and held on as if he were falling. I was calming him with my presence, talking softy to him, wiping his tears away. His blood pressure stopped spiking. The doctor left the room confident I could handle this.

Will fell asleep for the next four or so hours with his head on my shoulder. His blood pressure normalized. I watched him through the night and never left his side. Even though he slept, he held my hand tightly.

The next day the doctor found me still in bed next to Will. He asked me to move from the bed in order to check Will over, but Will wouldn't release me. "You'll just have to work around me doc, give me a minute."

"Will, babe, I won't let go, just let me stand by the bed so the doctor can check you over. I'm not going anywhere." Will relented but his grasp on my hand was still strong and his look pleading.

I knew it would take time for Will to come to terms with what he had to do to Bear Boy. It would take longer than it would for his shoulder and ribs to heal. I understood that. I would be there for him.

The doctor explained, "He can go home tomorrow, but a car ride on those back roads is going to be hard on him, painful. I want to see him back here in three weeks for x-rays, but if you can't because of weather, have your local clinic take them and forward the pictures to me. He's strong and in good health but the first two weeks are going to be extremely painful. I'll give you antibiotics and pain medications to take with you. He may need some physical therapy for his shoulder if he doesn't get full range-of-motion back."

"I can handle that doc. I spent months in rehab for my shoulder and we have a home gym. I'll get him back one hundred percent. Christian will fly us home to avoid the roads." The doctor nodded, knowing I had everything under control and that Will was in good hands.

I managed to get Will to drink some broth the nurse brought, as well as eat some Jello. I held the straw as he drank some water. I eased back into bed with him, and he fell asleep still holding my hand. As Will slept I thought about the gunshot Jess said they heard, the shot that brought us to this point. Was it another hunter or someone else trying to get to me and mine?

Christian was more than happy to fly us home. The next day he brought Jess along to drive my car back so I could ride in the Medivac with Will.

Will wasn't ready to talk about the incident and I wasn't going to push him. I lowered him onto our bed, semi-sitting up with Christian's help, made sure he took his antibiotics and offered pain medications to him if he needed or wanted them. For the first week, he was in a lot of pain and could hardly move. His sleep was fitful. Getting him to the bathroom required my and Jess' assistance. When Jess wasn't available, he used a jar. He didn't want to eat, but I made beef stew and that seemed to work. I fed him because he couldn't use his left side and his right hand was always holding onto me in some fashion. He didn't resist. He'd let me do whatever I needed to for him. There was no embarrassment between us.

Brandon would stop by from time to time and tell Will what he was doing to help Jess at the stables and sometimes he would read to Will from his schoolbooks just to distract him from his thoughts. He hadn't said much since we arrived home. He knew Jess had buried Bear Boy as soon as they got him to the property because before long the backhoe wouldn't have been able to dig a deep enough hole due to the cold weather, and frozen ground. I knew it bothered Will he'd not been able to do it himself, to be there to say goodbye to his friend.

I rarely left the bedroom unless Will slept, then I would cook or take a shower. Every other day I'd give him a sponge bath, and if Jess could help, I'd change his bed clothes. I would sit next to him and work on my laptop or read, just waiting for him to tell me about what happened. I was there for when he would be ready to talk. When he couldn't hold my hand, he would touch my leg or hold onto my clothing. He needed the contact, it kept him calm and kept his blood pressure down. From time to time I would walk the house checking window locks, making sure doors were secured and trying to pick Jess' brain for his recollections of that day, especially about the shot that inadvertently killed Bear Boy and injured Will. It was difficult to remain rational when my instinct put me on alert and made me think that Will had been the target. What did I bring to Montana from my past to put Will in danger?

On day ten I was reading in bed next to him. He looked at me and spoke with tears in his eyes. "I loved that horse Sam. When I got back from Iraq after getting wounded, I needed something to fill the void in me. A rancher was trying to sell Bear Boy in the local paper, and as soon as I saw that horse, I knew I had to have him. I didn't have much money then, but I begged, borrowed, and worked two jobs until I got the money pulled together to buy him. He figured me out from the start and knew exactly what I needed from him. I feel like I've lost my best friend. I didn't think I would be able to put him out of his suffering, but I had to. He looked at me, pleading with me, but I had to do it."

I had tears running down my cheeks. I looked at this compassionate, caring man next to me and said softly, "I know how hard it was for you, but you thought more about him than yourself at that moment. You knew you had to do that for him. He loved you and trusted you would do the right thing for him. You had to give him peace from the pain. He counted on you. Will, Jess told me a shot rang out that spooked Bear Boy causing him to step in a hole, do you remember that?"

"I heard something. It happened so fast that I had little time to react while I was trying to handle Bear Boy. Other hunters are out there, we hear shots from time to time, things can happen. I don't know what I would do if you weren't here with me, Sam. You stood up to the doctor and nurse. You've been here, taking care of my needs and being so patient. You've done everything for me."

"I'm here. I'm not going anywhere and that's something you don't ever have to worry about. If you want, tomorrow Jess and I will take you down to the area by the stables and you can say your goodbyes to Bear Boy. I think we should order a marker for him, honoring his service to you."

Will looked at me with his sad, soft brown eyes. "How do you always know what to do, what I need, and what the right thing is?"

"It's just what we do in this family." I smiled at him and ran my fingers through his hair. "Can you eat something now? You need to get stronger. I always like breakfast at night — how about an omelet and a bacon side?"

Will shook his head indicating yes. "That sounds good. I'd like to try and eat at the kitchen island if you help me get up. We need to get some more furniture. Something in between a bed and a kitchen chair."

"We have the next three winter months to talk about that. It takes time to pick the right things. Anything worth having is worth waiting for."

Will laughed, "Just like you."

CHAPTER

THIRTY-ONE

It was now mid-December. Will was still recuperating, and the two-year mark of that night came and went. We had buried it and that's where it was going to stay. At least that was the plan. Brandon had another birthday and we felt he had come out on the other side of that night — or so I thought — sometimes I wasn't sure. I tried to hide within the normal, mundane things of each day, but there were times a noise, a smell, and a word would take me back. The other day I knew I heard a whisper calling to me. Maybe Charlie had been right back in DC that I needed more time to get my head straight. Writing the sequel to my first book wasn't helping since it brought up questions that I had thought were long answered. It was beginning to take a toll on me by always making sure Will didn't see my fears and concerns.

Spending a lot of time with someone during three months of winter weather sounds daunting, but Will and I took comfort from each other. Will and I talked, played card games, watched movies, listened to music, cooked together and yes, had lots of creative sex. My fortieth birthday, January eighth was on the horizon, and Will was insistent we celebrate in some way. He felt much better, received his release from the doctor, and returned to "doing" all the things he wanted — which was usually me.

The Lodge stayed open year-round with the new owner, Scotty Dickson, an Irish rogue on his mother's side, and an Italian flirt on his father's. At the age of fifty-one his hair was snow white. He was my height at 5'9", stocky and freakishly strong. He was recently divorced and had no kids. He had moved from Chicago, after he sold his bar, fled his ex-wife, and set up his future in Montana. His philosophy was," If I have to keep the heat on, might as well keep the doors open." Will had usually closed from the end of December through February when he owned The Lodge, Scotty didn't.

I wasn't sure I wanted to celebrate crossing over into another decade, but Will kept telling me I looked half my age and should savor it. He really wanted to do something for me, to show me off, and slowly let other people into our bubble. Age never bothered me until now. It made me reflect on time and how I wanted to hoard it.

The roads were passable, so we planned on getting out of the house to celebrate at The Lodge for my birthday. Jess with his family, Brandon and his family, Christian with whomever he was dating, and Scotty would be there to help me traverse from the thirties to the forties. Good friends, food, drinks, and Karaoke awaited me. What more could a girl want?

While I rummaged through my closet, I realized I had nothing appropriate for the occasion and was frustrated, standing in my underwear with nothing to wear. Will came into the bedroom with a gift-wrapped box. "Maybe this will help, Happy Birthday Sam." He was smiling as if he had a secret.

I couldn't have been more surprised when I opened the gift and found a dress with matching shoes. I unfolded the dress from the packaging and saw it was quite daring for Will's tastes and mine. Will usually didn't want other people to see my assets — he wanted to keep me to himself. He didn't like the idea of other men looking at me in an inappropriate way. I looked at Will as he encouraged. "Put it on, let's see if it fits. I checked the labels in your clothes and that's the size I told the store clerk." I was a bit tongue-tied. I went into the bathroom, closed the door, and jumped off the sexy dress cliff.

The dress was amazing. Dark eggplant purple, with a little shimmer to it; a light gauge knit that wasn't going to disguise anything. A moderately low front, a very low back, and long sleeves made it sexy, hitting right above my knees, but even though you really didn't see anything, you noticed it hugged me in all the right places. I looked in the mirror after I put it on and thought, "Wow." I put the new shoes on that were not made for snow, a little bit of makeup, and took my hair out of my ponytail, fluffing it into place. I looked in the full-length mirror again and wondered who was reflecting at me. "Damn, girl," I said to myself.

Will was getting restless and called to me, "Is everything okay in there?" I opened the door and came into the bedroom. Will had no words to say, but I did see the whites of his eyes. I don't think he realized how different the dress would look on me as opposed to a hanger.

I looked at him, he had changed into black, ass hugging, dress pants, a black form-fitting shirt, black polished boots, and a silver belt buckle. He looked like he stepped right out of GQ into our bedroom. He was so handsome with so much sweetness exuding from his face. He had his hair cut a little shorter and it took ten years off him. The presence of him took my breath away.

"I don't know what to say." He adjusted himself. He was stirring, getting hard, and wasn't quite sure what to do about it. We had to leave in a minute. "I knew you would look great in anything I bought, but I've never seen a more beautiful sight. You look more beautiful than anyone has a right to see." He motioned with his finger for me to spin around and as he saw the plunging back of the dress and the way it hugged my ass, I heard him clear his throat. "If we didn't have to leave right now, I don't think we'd be going anywhere. I'll get the coats."

I glanced back at the mirror and thought, "I wonder how this will go over tonight?" I heard a ping on my computer screen and glanced at the new email that came up marked Urgent, I clicked on it. I wish I had never done that. A few words, but the wrong ones came up. The words on the screen screamed at me, "You didn't kill me bitch." My breath caught, and I started shaking. I closed the laptop so Will didn't see the screen as he walked back into the room."

"Are you ready to go? Are you alright? You look like you've just seen a ghost."

"I'm fine, just have never seen myself in a dress like this. I'm a bit nervous about what everyone will think." Will came over, helped me with my coat, made sure my hair was out of the way, and kissed me as I turned towards him.

"I have one other gift for you." And with that he held out a new pair of deep, red, garnet stud earrings for me. They were beautiful, set in white gold with small diamonds around the stones. I put them on, and my outfit was complete. I had missed my garnets, but they were still in the medicine bag that attracted good spirits during my recovery the past two years. These were perfect.

It was a great evening. Lots of fun, laughter, great food, a little dancing and then everyone insisted I sing Karaoke. I hadn't sung in a long time — years. Didn't know if I could anymore. I looked at Will and whispered, "I might embarrass you. Are you okay that I sing in this dress?"

"I think you should go for it. It's your birthday and I've never heard you sing. I would like to. These are friends, they won't give you a hard time. Just have fun."

Jess came over to Will, and seeing him teary, put his arm around his shoulder and asked in a barely audible voice, "Is there anything she cannot do? She is really great."

Will said quietly, "The more layers of her onion I remove, the more I am amazed by her."

Moments later the song concluded, and I was relieved. Will walked to the stage, took me into his arms, and kissed me as if he'd forgotten we weren't alone. Everyone clapped and yelled, "Get a room!" It was time to go home, and I hadn't had so much fun in my life, but the email came back into my head making me feel chilled to the bone. All these months my instincts had been correct, someone was out there coming closer to me, to Will and to our life.

I was quiet on the way home, thinking about how to handle that email. Will took my hand in his and ran his finger up and down my palm. He was concerned. "Everything okay, Sam? Did you have fun?"

"Yes, it was a great night. I have so many emotions going through me right now because of all you did for my birthday and what our friends did. Will, I can't find the words. Do you know this is the first time I have ever had a party for my birthday? I love these new memories."

Will, hadn't known that Sam was new to celebrating things in her life. She'd had too much tragedy. He was going to change that. He'd give her the life she deserved.

"That song, you were amazing, I didn't know you could sing."

I laughed with a remembrance. "I sang in a band when I was in my teens. We weren't very good, but it was fun."

"The evening isn't over yet and I have plans for you and that dress. You looked so beautiful tonight that Scotty wants to hire you as a lounge singer — you were that good." He smiled and looked at me like it was the first time he'd ever seen me.

I don't know how he does that. I also don't know how he comes up with new ways to please me. I would deal with the email tomorrow while he helped Christian work on the Medivac. As far as tonight was concerned, I would be completely present for him. I loved this man. We went through so much to get here. I was afraid of an email, but not enough to ruin his plans for us tonight. I leaned over and whispered in his ear, "You make me so happy; I never want to lose you." We pulled up to our home and I said a silent prayer. "Keep us safe."

THIRTY-TWO

Will left early the next morning for Lame Deer to help his friend Christian with the Medivac helicopter. Will could do everything technical, anything mechanical, and was always in demand because he was always accommodating to anyone who needed him. Will was a man of many talents, especially with his hands. I marveled how smart he was, smart in a worldly-way, and his tech savvy blew me away. This man who was most comfortable out in the wild of Montana had talents Silicon Valley would envy.

Christian had two heavy Airbus twin-engine helicopters. Not only did he run his private Medivac service for medical emergencies in Montana, Wyoming, and Colorado, but he air-lifted people out of dangerous circumstances, as well as situations like transporting Bear Boy. Christian was always trying to modify his crafts to get more and more out of them. He wanted them faster with more medical equipment inside and room for the injured. The inside of these helicopters were marvels of technology linking Christian to hospitals, medical personnel, and every life-saving device there was.

Christian Soaring Bird was an interesting man. He had some demons, but when your life depended on him, like mine did two years ago, he was your lifeline. He had been in Iraq with Will as a chopper pilot and medic. He saw a lot of disturbing things and he saved a lot of lives. He had been awarded medals but never wanted to talk about them. To look at him you might not think he knew what he was doing, but you'd be wrong. If your life was on the line, Christian would save it — if it could be saved. He was a brilliant man in his field. He owned the Medivac service, and I believe he was trying to somehow balance the scales of life and death — making up for those he'd lost in Iraq.

I was slowly getting to know Christian. He was a little shy around me, but not around other women. He was Cheyenne, six feet tall, maybe 195 pounds. He had long black hair parted in the middle, usually covered by a black baseball style cap. He always wore fatigue trousers, army boots, and a black knit shirt emblazoned with his company logo. He was muscular, and each muscle had some sort of tattoo depicting his service or his heritage. His strength carried many of his fallen comrades as he had carried me when I was wounded. Lately he's been chewing nicotine gum and was trying to slow down on his off-duty drinking — looking for his forever woman. The only problem was, he'd been going through a lot of women looking for her. He is a charmer, and at forty-one years of age needs to settle down. He's restless and needs someone to give him stability. He'd make a good husband if a woman could look past his bravado and help tame his demons.

I opened my laptop as soon as Will left. He'd promised to be back for dinner. I had kissed him as if I didn't want to forget his lips, his scent, or his touch. I was holding on inside, hoping he didn't see how worried I was. Brandon was taking care of the horses today, so things were covered down at the barn, and I could do some investigating on my computer. The email was still open, sitting there, mocking me, threatening me. I didn't want to lose it if I closed it, so I grabbed for my cell phone and took a picture of it. I also printed it out and tried to backtrack a bit to see if I could find an

IP address in the header section, and then look up the location of origin. Nothing but dead ends; I could only get it nailed down to a city, Bozeman. When I did close it out, it disappeared from the email list as if it had never come at all. It's possible the sender used a self-destruct button on their end or a program like "Burn Note" that pre-sets a timeframe from the sender to have the email disappear. It wasn't in any folder, so my next step was to see if it was still in the cloud network of servers. It wasn't. I put up a firewall to prevent other emails originating from this same party from getting through and to prevent unauthorized access to my network. Part of me wanted to believe it was received in error, but it had my name on it, my email address, and was sent on my birthday. Maybe it was a fluke. I couldn't get crazy over one email. Someone was playing games with me. I needed to calm down and get myself more prepared. My thoughts ran back to Charlie. "Would he do this? Why taunt me?"

I went to the safe and checked my gun which hadn't been fired since that night two years ago and hadn't been cleaned either; it still had my blood on it. I needed to get it operational again. Pulling up the internet, I looked up firing ranges in the area and printed them out. Maybe it wasn't anything, but I had to be ready if it was. I cleaned the gun and loaded it, put it back in the safe, housed in my holster, which was also stained with my blood. I saw two small boxes in the safe, took them out and opened them — our wedding rings, with the infinity symbol inscribed inside the bands. Tears welled up in my eyes as I carefully put them back and locked the safe. How could I tell Will about everything I'd been feeling and now the email? After everything we had gone through, I was afraid of what had come to Montana because of me.

I needed a plan in case another email came or if something else more physical made its presence known. I didn't want the FBI involved though I was still in their employ with one year to pension like a carrot on a stick. If this had to do with "The RESERVATIONS Case" it was going to be a problem. They had closed and classified the files right after I left DC, and I didn't have access to them anymore. I still had a few allies at the Bureau, but would any of them put themselves in jeopardy to get me the files? I had to think — couldn't be careless — I needed to be deliberate, I had to be smart, lives could depend on me, including my own and Will's.

I didn't want to tell Will yet. It was just one email. I'd wait until I had more information, more justification to rock our world.

Will called to say he'd be home early. They hadn't finished what they planned because Christian wasn't in the right frame of mind to do any more work. Will sounded impatient with him, "He'd been drinking a lot today. His latest broke up with him and he's feeling sorry for himself. I've been trying to keep him from calling her and making things worse. I've taken the battery out of his cell phone, but he still has his two-way. He's in no shape to drive or to fly. Christian's partner is on the way to take over on-call so I can come home. Good thing there's a backup copter."

I could hear Christian in the background yelling in a slurred voice, "You should have waited for me Sam! Why can't I find someone like you? That was some dress you had on at your party. God, you've got a body that doesn't quit."

Will, in a frustrated voice, yelled. "Christian stop, that's my wife you're talking about. Sorry Sam, this is the worst I've seen him in a long time. I just heard his partner drive up. I'll see you soon."

By the time Will arrived home dinner was about twenty minutes from completion. He came in looking beat down. He walked over to me, embraced me and lamented, "I'm so glad to be home with you. I'm sorry for what Christian said, he stepped over the line and I'm not happy about it."

"Will, he's drunk and probably won't remember a thing tomorrow. He's your friend and he's going through a difficult time. He helped save my life so give him a pass. He helped you when Bear Boy threw you. He's just sad. He just needs someone. He's lonely."

"Sam, he has a crush on you — that's why his girlfriend left. She got tired of being compared to you. You're all he talks about. When he's sober, I'm going to discuss this with him. He's my friend, but you're my wife."

"Will, I'm just flesh and blood with scars. Christian using me for comparison just doesn't make sense. He doesn't really know who I am. He barely talks to me when he's around. The only real conversation I've had with him was at the hospital and it was about you. He wants the relationship we have, not me."

I opened a beer, took a drink and offered him the bottle. He took the bottle, put it aside, and pulled me closer. "How do you always know what I need? You know how to put me in a better perspective without hurting my feelings. I get how I came across and I'm sorry." He kissed me, ran his free hand through my hair and looked intently into my eyes. "I love your eyes, one hazel the other, darker brown. They draw me in. You live in your eyes — I'm home in your eyes." The oven timer binged, and Will implored, "Feed me, and then I want to talk to you later in bed. I have a question I've been thinking about since you came home."

"Should I be worried? You have that glint in your eye and a sly smile going on." I couldn't imagine what he wanted to ask. He smiled as we sat down to dinner.

Will was hungrier than he thought, two helpings, along with a piece of cake. "Good thing we have the gym, or I'd be fat the way you cook for me. You spoil me." He reflected on something and asked, "Is this life we have enough for you Sam? Is it what you thought it would be?"

"It's all I've ever wanted, Will. I've had the other kind of life. Don't I seem happy? What's on your mind? You're in a funny mood and it isn't all about Christian."

Trying to misdirect me from further inquiries, "I'm planning on helping you with the dishes and then I'll ask my question." Will smiled. Staring at me, looking me over in my yoga pants and sweater, and then kissing me like he was leaving for a trip. He was so tender and intense at the same time. "I love you Sam. I'm crazy in love with you. I want you all the time, not just for sex, but for who you are. You are everything to me." The dishes went undone.

Something was going on with Will. He started the shower to get the water hot and came over to me as I took my shoes off. He kissed me and started undressing me slowly, looking at every inch of me like when I had come home that first night. He wasn't talking — just kissing and caressing me — my breathing became rapid, he stopped. Still close to me, he undressed but never took his eyes off me. I could see he wanted me. He was hard, bigger than usual, and I wanted him. I loved his body. I reached for him, but he stopped my hand, "Not yet, babe."

He washed me as though I was fragile and might break in his hands, lingering on my breasts, I was wet and not just from the shower. I started to become urgent for him as I washed him. He looked at me, and said, smiling, "Slower Sam, we have all night. I want to build it up for you. I want you to beg just like you did the first time." I was going to say something, but he put his finger to my lips and shook his head "no." He shut the water off, grabbed a towel to dry me, combed through my hair and towel-dried it. He wasn't concerned with himself. Never taking his eyes off me he took my hand in his and led me to our bed. My towel dropped to the floor as he touched me so softly with his fingertips. His lips touched my lips, and they were so soft, so light and then his tongue licked them so lightly, I couldn't catch my breath. He smiled and laid me on the bed looking at me as if he'd just realized he loved me, that this was new, and that he wanted to show me how he felt.

I was wanting him inside me. I was starting to get impatient, and he could see that. He kissed my nipples, lingering, making them hard, and he ran his kisses, slowly to my stomach. He looked at my stomach, touched it like he was fascinated by my firmness, and started feeling me through my wetness. I couldn't hang on any longer. "Will please, please babe, don't make me wait any longer, I want you."

"Call me that name I like," He demanded, continuing to enhance my desire, stroking my clit.

"Husband?" I questioned, as my words started missing syllables.

With that word said Will guided himself inside me and filled me up, lifting my hips so I could take all of him. He was so focused tonight. I cried out. He moaned while he slowly, with intensity, made my climax heighten.

He went as deep as he could, seconds turned into minutes, then he hit the spot and I lost myself in a world of lightness and a pulsing, dizzy release. There wasn't a word for this climax, maybe the "big bang". I made sounds I didn't think could come from me. I felt pins and needles all through me and I begged again. "Will, I can't, it's too much. God, it won't stop." Will reached his climax after he knew I had gotten everything he wanted to give and together we went to a place only this man could take us. I have renamed that spot the "Geeeeeee spot." Some scientists say it doesn't exist, I'm here to tell you they are wrong, and my man found it.

I had heard once that there is a plane of existence where sex with love takes you beyond yourself — where two souls meet and find eternity in each other. The pleasure goes beyond physical or human — it goes to its purest form of love — as it was meant to be, pure energy. Will and I found that place and I reveled in it.

It's never just sex, even when it's quick; it's heart, mind, soul and body wrapped in love. That is why we never just have our lips meet — we have our mouths meet. It's more than lips, it's tongues, taste, breath, talk — never just lips. It's all or nothing with us. Just lips are for foreheads and cheeks, kissing for us is everything. Sex for us is all-consuming, it's how we talk to each other.

We lay spent, face to face, in our bed. Cooling down, managing our breathing. Will traced my face with his finger until he got to my lips, and then he kissed me softly and asked, "What if I reversed my vasectomy? You're not on anything, and we could try, to see if, if you wanted, to have a child with me."

We had never talked about this. I thought he didn't want children at this stage of our lives, but I was wrong. I could see it in his face, his longing for a child with me, the natural next step in his mind. He would no doubt be a great father, but what kind of mother would I be?

"Will, I'm forty years old. What if it doesn't happen, can you handle that? My body in the last couple of years has gone through a lot. I don't know if it, if I, I'm afraid to fail you. I don't know if I would even be a good mother. Am

I not enough for you if we can't?" I started to blink back tears out of fear of failing him. How could I say no to the man who waited for me to have this life with him? I'd do anything for him. Then I remembered the email, and fear gripped me tighter, like a punch to the stomach. "How could I bring a child into this?"

Will wiped the tears from my eyes. With his soft, calming voice, "Do you want to try to have a child with me, Sam? That really is the only question I want you to answer."

"What is that name you call me Will?"

"Wife?"

"Would there be another name you would call me if this would happen?"

"Our child's mother."

"My answer is yes." I knew I would try to do this for him even if something happened and I wouldn't be around to have his child.

Will reached over to me and kissed me with a love that came from a deeper, truer place than before. Emotion ran down his cheek. He wanted this so much. "The trips start soon, I want to take care of this procedure before then, okay? I want us to start trying."

"Okay," I whispered.

"Why do you seem hesitant, even when you say yes, Sam?"

I took his left hand in mine, I rubbed his empty ring finger, and looked at him.

"I'm working on that, trust me." Will said, understanding. "I know what you want, the same thing I do. Let's move the date up."

I kissed this man I can't say no to, snuggled into the curve of his neck, breathed in his essence, and as he held me, fell into a distracted sleep.

THIRTY-THREE

February's cold, frigid days were still here. The month has been unbearable because of the weather, and Will's forty-fourth birthday was tomorrow. He didn't want a party or a fuss; he just wanted to be with me since his business would open in a week and he would be gone on trips. He hadn't been able to make an appointment to have his procedure done, but it was still our plan. I hadn't received any more emails and was feeling like maybe it had been a joke, a fluke. Hopefully it had been nothing. I put it out of my mind and finalized the details of my gift for Will.

Ever since Will lost Bear Boy, I had been talking to people all around the state, trying to find Will another horse. Replacing Bear Boy was going to be difficult for him, but he needed another horse. I finally found one at a ranch near Bozeman. The owner knew, Will, and was surprised I called because Will had looked at a horse there last year, but didn't buy it because, and he quoted, "He was waiting for his future to arrive first." I met with the man, when Will assumed I was running errands. I made a deal with the owner to deliver the horse the next day by eight am for Will's birthday — along with all new black tack, saddle, horse blanket, vet release papers, and verification of its lineage. The horse was completely black. Black as the darkest Montana night, not one marking, five years old, sixteen hands, thirteen hundred pounds, and trained for the type of work Will does. The horse's name was Sampson, a beautiful gelding. The horse was expensive, but I used some of the money from selling Dr. Sampson's house. It felt, "meant to be." I looked up to the heavens and said a little prayer to my mentor whose namesake this horse was and knew he was watching over me, and my life here with Will.

It was morning and I busied myself making a birthday cake. I was jumping out of my skin with excitement. Will was down at the stables with Jess and Brandon, getting organized for the full work calendar starting the next week. I heard a truck coming, looked out the window, and saw it was pulling a horse trailer with "Landan Stables" written on the side. I grabbed my jacket, a gift box, and headed down to meet the truck.

By the time I got there, Will, Jess, and Brandon were outside wondering who was coming down the road. The truck pulled up by the stables and the driver got out. His name was Gerald Landan, he walked directly up to me and inquired "Little lady, where do you want your delivery?" Everyone had their eyes on me and wondered what I would say and what I was having delivered.

I looked over at Will and smiled. "Will, would you help Mr. Landan unload your birthday present?" Will looked at me, then at Mr. Landan, and then at the horse trailer. "No way Sam, how? It's too much."

Mr. Landan headed over to the trailer with Will in tow and unloaded Sampson. Sampson pawed his right hoof on the dirt, shook his head, and snorted a little hello to his new home. Will remembered the horse. He had wanted it but had been hesitant until I came home, and his business had picked up. He had the money back then but felt the money was for us and not just for him. Will was smiling as he looked Sampson over from head-to-toe. He couldn't believe I had gotten him "this" horse for his birthday. Mr. Landan said to Will in front of everyone, "Your lady here drives a hard bargain — got me down five thousand — had me throw in new custom black tack, saddle, blanket, full vet certification, free delivery, lineage verification, and notarized ownership transfer papers." Then Mr. Landan looked at me, smiled, looked back at Will, and asked "Would you be able to say no to her? I couldn't." With that, Mr. Landan went on his way. Jess and Brandon took Sampson into the stables, and I waited to see if Will was happy with his new horse — this horse.

Will headed over to where I stood, stopped in front of me close enough so that I could feel his body temperature. He brushed the hair from my face, kissed me and whispered in my ear, "Thank you, Sam. I can't thank you enough. How do you always know?"

I ran my hand through his hair, looked at his smiling face and said, "Happy Birthday Will, Sampson's not a replacement for Bear Boy, he's just a transition in your life. He's here because you need him now, and because you need to get to know each other before next week, before your next trip." With the name Sampson, it seemed perfect. Then I handed Will a box, he looked at me like it was all too much.

"What is this, Sam?"

"Open it. We talked about it — life is about the bitter and the sweet."

Inside the box was a bronze marker for Bear Boy's grave I had ordered back in December. Will had already built the platform for it, but it had remained empty. Will needed to finish that good-bye, then he'd be able to ride Sampson without any reservations.

Will opened the box, saw the marker, and tried to blink back tears. He looked at me, "I need to do this first, it's only right. How do you do it?" He reached for my hand, "Come with me." We paid our respects to a trusted beautiful creature that had served Will well. Will attached the marker and his face showed a sense of peace that he had done right by his friend.

Will asked Jess if he had told Sam about this horse, but Jess hadn't even been aware that Sam was looking for one. Will knew when Sam had her mind on something, she made things happen. He didn't know how she always did what was needed at the right time. She was amazing, and she was his wife.

I texted Brandon towards evening. "Will's birthday dinner is almost ready, but you and Jess come up for some birthday cake." It wasn't ten minutes later when they came in the door, smiles on their faces and a desire for chocolate cake. They all knew to wash their hands first, and then each received a big piece of cake to take home, even though Brandon had a big bite of it in his mouth before I could get it wrapped. We all laughed and sang, "Happy Birthday" to Will.

After dinner, cake, and stories of Sampson. Will came down to earth a bit and asked me, "Sam how could you afford that horse? I know how much he cost, even if you got the price down by five thousand. Is there something you want to tell me?"

"Tomorrow. I'll show you mine if you show me yours, okay?"

"What do you mean? Is that code for what I think it means? I think, we've done that already."

"Financials," I laughed. "We're getting married, trying for a child, and merging ourselves in every way there is. It's time to have the money talk."

"Tomorrow then." Will looked at me like he'd just peeled another layer of my onion away.

It had been quite a day. Will was in a deep sleep and as I got up to get some water, I heard a ping on my laptop indicating an email. I walked over, my hands shaking as I opened the Urgent marked email that said, "Soon Sam." I reached for my cell phone and took a picture. I didn't close the email, just the lid of the laptop. I could print it in the morning, check the cloud if it disappeared, and see if I could trace the IP address to someone more specific than last time. Apparently, my firewall had failed. Whoever was doing this had skills. An email for each of our birthdays — how did they know? Now I was scared, not only for us but for Brandon as well. Sleep eluded me the rest of the night.

THIRTY-FOUR

I wanted to go over Will's and my finances — not just because we were merging our lives, but because I feared the emails were a precursor to possibly more up-close and personal threats. If something happened to me, I wanted to make sure things were in order — that Will would have enough money to go on. I could pursue in earnest what was going on when Will left next week for five days.

I had a productive day of writing and didn't realize it was nearly five when I took a break. Will would be coming up from the stables and I hadn't even thought about dinner. Just as that thought crossed my mind, the door opened, and my man waltzed in with his laptop and some printouts. He had remembered. He came over to the kitchen island where I'd been working all day, kissed me and set his things down in preparation for our talk.

"Will, I lost track of time today. What are you hungry for?"

"Pizza sounds good."

"I can do that — the usual?" I rummaged through the fridge trying to figure out what ingredients I had on hand to accomplish this.

"Sure? I can help."

"Not necessary. Why don't you get cleaned up and I'll prepare dinner?"

I always keep pizza dough around. For some reason, it's often requested, and we're a bit out of the way for delivery. By the time Will was finished and back in the kitchen looking for a beer, pizzas were in the oven.

"Can we talk and eat at the same time Sam? I'm beat and want to get to bed early tonight."

"We can put it off to another time, if you want."

"No, I think it's important, especially since work is going to consume a lot of my time in the next few months. It's always like this, right after the weather clears. Clients want to take a break from their lives."

"Do you need a break from yours?" I went fishing for the answer.

"Never, I love the life we have. Everyone wants what we have but would never be willing to pay what we did to have it. I value what we have, Sam. Never think I don't."

I took the pizzas out of the oven and cut them into squares. Will likes everything on his, and I'm basic with cheese and sauce. He cracked the beer open and offered me the first sips. As he was chewing his first bite, he opened his laptop and pulled up the summary spreadsheet he had prepared. He squinted a bit and confessed, "I'm going to need reading glasses soon." He looked at me straight on, with a bit of defiance, "Whether it's old-fashioned or not, it's my job to take care of us — our family. I won't debate this issue." He looked at me and saw me trying to hide a smile.

"You'll have no trouble from me on that point, sir, despite the fact, that I'm your equal, and have a right to contribute. I concede the point to you." I said as I took a piece of pizza. Will was a man of contradictions — liberal, yet traditional.

He winked at me and continued. "I sold The Lodge for a net of $4.6 million. I used funds from that sale for our land, construction of our home, the stables, offices, the indoor arena and the paddocks — $3.1 million in total. We have no mortgages or debt; I have added you to the Deed on the house."

"The other facilities: barn, stables, paddocks, and indoor arena were split out as part of the business. Half of the remaining money was used to set up the operating account for the two businesses, and the other half went into a money market account. I have added you on as a signer. Jess and I pay ourselves $5K a month, plus health care coverage. Here's the checkbook on this account, we just need to add you on as a signer. It doesn't sound like much, but our expenses are low and when I subcontract out with the security business, well, I can make a lot more than that in a week. I just haven't focused on it lately. I've been waiting for you to partner with me on it."

"Brandon gets $15 an hour, half of which goes into a school account for him to help his parents out. Jess and I have key man insurance policies for $1 million each for the guide and tracking business. I have a $1 million key man insurance policy for my security business in which I have named you the beneficiary, and I plan to put you to work for that. I want to add investigative support to our resume'. I also have a life policy for $500K I recently added with you as sole beneficiary."

Will picked up the printouts, "Here are the upcoming receivables, the jobs for the coming work year we have booked. Each one shows a deposit at time of booking. Our expenses and fixed costs are itemized here. We have a positive cash flow each month some of which goes into a maintenance account and some of that goes into retirement accounts for Jess and me."

Will folded the papers up, closed the lid on his laptop, looked at me with satisfaction and said, "I showed you mine, now show me yours." He grabbed another piece of pizza and settled back in his chair.

"I'm impressed that you built everything from nothing, Will. You are amazing. It shows me another side of you. You are a very talented business-man," I said in a very proud way.

I opened my laptop to my accounting page and began. "I sold the Georgetown, DC house Dr. Sampson left me for $1.7 million. After commissions and closing costs, I received $1.564 million. There were no mortgages on the house when he left it to me. I bought the SUV before I came home, a new camera and lenses, a new computer and other things." I looked over and Will smiled at me tapping on his watch, knowing I had bought that too. I smiled back. "So, after that I had almost, $1.5 million left. It is sitting in a money market account and CD's that you need to advise me on. I added your name to the account prior to coming home."

"The Bureau gave me a settlement of $250K so I wouldn't sue them after Charlie had wrongly put me in the field. They called it "Unreasonable Risk Created By a Superior to a Subordinate." It's supposed to be confidential, so you didn't hear it from me. That money just sits in an account I have named "only to be used for good," since it came from a bad place. I've added you as a signer. For my first book, I received a $30K advance, and have since earned royalties to date of $117K. I recently received a $50K advance for the second book which isn't done yet, and an option for a third. Those are in an account I call, "Rez." You are also a signer on that account. Next year I should receive a pension of $50K a year, which you will have access to at its inception. I don't receive a paycheck from the Bureau because they've classified me in such a way that I don't get paid, but I accrue time, and I have my badge in order to get my pension next year. I also have a life policy with the Federal Government for $250K that you are the sole beneficiary on. I have government health insurance for now — that may end when the pension kicks in so I'd have to go on your policy then." I paused for a minute to take another bite of my pizza.

Will was looking at me with surprise on his face and asked, "Anything else?"

"I could use another beer. What about you?"

"Sure, I'll get it." He got up and went over to the fridge, opened the bottle and handed it to me. I took my drink and offered it back to him.

"I just want to tell you what I want to do, uh, have been doing, with some of the accounts if you agree. For the "only to be used for good" account, I've been paying for prescriptions for the elderly or anyone on the reservation who can't afford them. I worked out a deal with the pharmacist to tell these people he'd found them a supplemental program to help them. They save face that way and get their meds. I was thinking of starting a meals-on-wheels for those same people and I, — I mean we — would pay for the food. I'd prepare it and deliver it myself. It's a way for me to get to know these people and see what else they need. It's bad money going for something good. It comes to about $1,500 per month just for the prescriptions, with food maybe another $500 per month."

Will looked at me, taking a drag from the beer. "Go on."

"With the book money, from the one I call the "Rez" account, I'd like to set up a college scholarship fund for Brandon. I also want to send Brandon to a Math Camp during Spring break. He's so smart, and I want to give him some opportunities. I've already checked with his parents and they're okay with it. I talked to Jess, and his sons can take turns helping at the stables while you and Jess are on trips. I could pay them out of our "only to be used for good" account. We can talk about this further at some other time."

"So, you already talked to Brandon's parents, as well as Jess?"

I looked at Will and I knew I had probably stepped over the line. My fear for Brandon being here until I could figure out what was going on, well, it wasn't an acceptable risk. I looked at Will and tried to see if he was aggravated or just pushing my buttons. "I over-stepped, and I apologize," I said sheepishly.

"That plan works for me. No apology needed."

He could see how much Sam cared about Brandon. They were connected — it came from a good place. He would support the decision. She sure knows how to get things done, he laughed to himself.

"The money I used for your birthday gift, Sampson, I took from the proceeds of selling Dr. Sampson's house. It seemed to be the right thing to do. I got a good deal, and I don't think we should talk about the price of gifts."

Will smiled, nodded to the affirmative, and finished the beer.

"Next year my pension will come direct deposit and will go into the "only to be used for good" account, because I feel anything from the Bureau is tainted money and the only way to wash it is to have it do some good."

I looked over to Will and he gestured with his hand to mean "Anything else? Go on."

I jumped up and ran into the bedroom to find my backpack. I came back into the kitchen and put down the ten thousand in cash on the countertop next to him. Will looked at it and then back to me.

"When I closed out Dr. Sampson's safe deposit box this was inside with a note that said, "For a rainy day, always look up." I guess we can keep this in the safe for a rainy day."

"Is that everything Sam? Are you finished?" Will looked proud and bewildered at the same time.

"That's it. Why are you looking at me like that?"

"I had no idea that you had all that. It's going to take me awhile to process."

"Will, we have all that. It's yours, too. Most of what I have I didn't earn like you did. There's a difference."

"Oh Sam, you earned all that and more from the Bureau and your writing. Don't ever think you didn't. Those things you want to do with the money, uh, already have been doing, well, all I can say is I have no problem with any of that. You're always thinking of others. With everything you've been through, you have such a big heart. Is there anything you want for yourself?"

"I have everything I want already. Maybe some furniture."

"Let's plan a weekend for that. Anything you want, but right now I need some sleep. What about you?"

"I want to clean up and then I'll be in. Okay?"

"Don't be long. I sleep better with you." Will was yawning as he walked to the bedroom. He turned around, came back, kissed me, and then headed to the bedroom again.

As Will walked to the bedroom he said to himself, "Who knew?" and shook his head.

I was attempting to formulate a plan in my head about the emails while I did the dishes. Did someone from the Bureau, who had been on "The RESERVATIONS Case" send the emails? Should I try to contact my friend at lock-up at the FBI to find out if the twin brother had really killed himself? Maybe I could try and hack the classified files to see what they might be hiding about the case. I hated not telling Will about this, but I needed more to go on than the two emails. He was leaving soon, and I didn't want this hanging over him when he was going to be gone for five days. I also didn't want to admit that trouble had followed me here and I wanted to get rid of it before Will had to be told.

I finished the dishes, got ready for bed and crawled under the covers next to him. As if by instinct, his arm went around me and pulled me close without waking up. I had an uneasy sleep and was even more tired when I woke up the next morning.

CHAPTER
THIRTY-FIVE

Will and Jess were preparing to leave the next day and I needed to go into town to run some last-minute errands. I planned to talk with the pharmacist without violating HIPPA laws about any new prescriptions needing coverage for the elderly on the reservation, pick up the mail, shop for some groceries, magazines, and books to occupy myself with while Will was away. I had gotten everything accomplished and was just loading the groceries into the car when I noticed a flat tire. I went for my cell phone, then remembered leaving it on the charger at home. I looked around to see where the auto repair shop was located when I saw a slightly built white man looking at me from the end of the alley across the street. He smiled at me, pointing his finger at me like a gun, and for a split second, he looked just like the twin brother I had killed, but better groomed. My heart was racing as I kept my eye on him. I took off running towards him. By the time I ran to the end of the alley with daylight ebbing away, he wasn't there. I checked the other street off the alley, checked some doorways and store fronts, but he had disappeared. It unnerved me and I was sick to my stomach and shaking.

Was he real or did I just imagine him? I was out of breath walking back to my car — not from running, but from fear and because I had gone after him without a weapon. I had been careless. The car keys were rattling in my hand, my mouth was dry, and I had the sweat of panic running down the furrow of my breasts.

It was getting dark quickly. I walked down the block to the auto repair place and asked the attendant if he could change my tire, all the while checking over my shoulder. The guy indicated it would take twenty minutes before he could get to it, but that he would if I could wait. He finally came to the car, removed the flat tire and looked at me. "This isn't a normal flat. It looks like someone used a knife and slit your tire, ma'am." He pointed to the slash, "I can't repair this tire, but I can order a new one for you, put the spare on, and put it on Will's account."

"I can pay you now to order it and for changing it. Can you put this damaged one in the trunk to show Will?" I had no intention of showing this to Will before his trip and didn't want this attendant talking to Will. I was trying to shut the situation down before it escalated.

"Shit," I said to myself, "May I use your phone? I don't have my cell with me." The attendant nodded and offered his phone to me.

I called home and Will answered. In a controlled voice, I said. "Hi, sorry I'm running late."

"Hey babe, where are you? I was getting concerned. It's dark out. I see your cell is here on the charger."

"I was running errands and when I was finished noticed a flat tire. I had it changed and I'll be heading home now. I'm calling from the auto place. Sorry I worried you." I was trying to level the tremor in my voice, but my emotions were running rampant, and my hands were shaking.

"Are you okay Sam? You sound upset." Will sounded more than concerned, he sounded as if I had scared him.

"I'm fine. I just have a headache — and forgetting my phone — uh, I just, uh, anyway, I'll be home soon." I noticed some of the groceries were defrosting, the ice cream was melting, and my nerves were raw. I blinked back tears and tried to pull myself together before I headed home.

I arrived home, took a cleansing breath, and pulled into the garage. I was coming in through the mudroom when Will came to meet me halfway to help with the groceries. He could see I was out of sorts.

Before he could say anything, I blurted out, "I didn't mean to be gone so long. I don't have your dinner, stuff is melting, my head hurts, and I made you worry. I'm so sorry."

Will could see I was on the verge of a meltdown. "Hey babe, you're home and safe. That's all that matters. I'll put the groceries away for you and I can whip up some breakfast for dinner. You don't have to do a thing, let me do this for you."

I felt like I couldn't think. "Will, I think I want to take a shower. It might help my headache. I'm not hungry. I love you for offering."

Will looked at Sam with concern in his eyes as she walked to the bedroom. It had really unnerved him tonight when she wasn't home. He got a little scared until she called him. She was everything to him. The house without her — well, he didn't want to think about it.

I stepped into the hot shower and found myself trembling, feeling chilled with foreboding. I put my forehead to the cold tile and tried to calm myself. I stood there until I could function again. I toweled off, put on my sweatpants and a sweater. I felt sick like I was coming down with something. I didn't want Will to be upset the night before he left, I had to find my game face and put it on. I walked out to the kitchen. "Let me make you something to eat."

"Not necessary, I grabbed a sandwich left over from lunch. Does your head feel better? Come here, you look a little flushed." And with that, he kissed my forehead to see if I was warm. "A little warm, maybe from the hot water." He drew me closer, and as he held me with a firm embrace, he whispered in a low, soft voice, "I was really worried when I came into the house and you weren't here. I didn't know how to get hold of you. I didn't like how that felt. I love you." He took my face into his hands, looked deep into my eyes, and kissed me tenderly. "Five days is going to feel like an eternity being away from you."

My eyes started to well up with tears, fear was rising like bile into my throat as I tugged him closer to me by his shirt front. "I've become spoiled having you around. I'm going to miss you so much. I'm so sorry about tonight, I wanted it to be special for you." I kissed him with intensity and urgency not allowing him pull back for a breath. He could feel my physical strength, my demanding that he takes me. I put my hands on his shoulders, jumped up, and straddled him where he stood. He hadn't seen that in me before and neither had I. He tightened his arms around me carrying me to the bedroom with my legs wrapped around his waist. I was locked onto his lips and clinging to him as if he was going to be lost to me forever. He eased me down trying to unlock my legs. I was standing now, in a frantic attempt to get his clothes off, as he was with mine. I had started a heat with him that was all-consuming. He was caught up in it now, and neither of us could stop. Things got a little rough — not hurtful, but demanding and insistent. For the next hour or so we took everything from each other and gave everything we had. When there was nothing left except exhaustion, he lay facing me, softly running his fingers up and down my every curve, every mound, every valley, memorizing my shape to take with him tomorrow.

"I want a picture of you just as you are now, just for me to see. God you are so beautiful." He leaned off the bed, retrieved his cell phone from the floor and took the picture. The picture didn't leave anything to the imagination, but I couldn't say no to him, not now. His phone had a code to unlock it so I didn't think anyone else would see it and Will would never show it to anyone. I belonged to him — only him.

I couldn't look at him. I felt embarrassed that I had been so aggressive. I knew where it came from — fear — but he didn't, and I couldn't tell him that the next time he came home I might not be here if the threat got to me first.

He said so sweetly, "Look at me Sam." I resisted. "Babe, please look at me." I looked in his eyes and saw love followed by concern. "Are you okay?"

"I'm a little embarrassed."

"Why? That was unbelievable." He ran his fingers through my hair while he looked at me.

"You're not thinking, who was that woman?"

"I was thinking my woman loves me so much and she wanted me so much that she didn't hold back for a second. That's going to give me a lot to think about while I'm gone. It was amazing, Sam. I felt things I never had before." He softly laughed and as a compliment, added "You really are physically strong." He got up, started picking up the bedding and pillows that somehow ended up on the floor. He was shaking his head and smiling. "I'm spent, and we have to get up early. Ready for sleep?"

"You cured my headache and I'm already asleep with my eyes open." I rolled onto my back, stretched, and made my way into the arms of my sleepy man who, for tonight, could not say no to me.

Morning came way too soon, and as I pulled myself out of bed, I noticed a few bruises. Will was up a little earlier to shower, and when he came into the bedroom, he also showed signs of our roughhousing last night — including a bruise near his eye. "Oh shit, Will, it looks like I beat you up last night. I'm so sorry."

"I think I hit my eye on the corner of the bed. You know, when you were trying to, uh." I put my hand over his mouth. "Was that Kama Sutra?" Will started laughing as he touched the bruise near his eye and winced.

He shook his head as he looked at me," I think it was mutual. You've got some marks from my love too. Last night was memorable."

I figured I had time for a shower before he got back from the barn and ran hot water over my sore muscles and bruises. Before I had finished, Will opened the shower door, "Sam, I've got to leave. Come here and kiss me." I came to him soapy and wet putting my arms around him. We kissed long enough for it to last five days. When he turned to leave, we noticed wet, soapy imprints on his clothes from me and they were distinctive. "I love you Sam. I don't mind you marking your territory. Mr.

Collins is going to enjoy this." He headed out of the bathroom smiling and shaking his head.

"I love you too, Will. Be safe." I missed him already and wondered if I would ever see him again.

Will walked up to the group and everyone turned to look at him when Mr. Collins started laughing after seeing the soapy water marks on his clothes. When he saw Will's bruised eye, his laughing turned into hysteria. Everyone was laughing. Will mounted Sampson and ordered like a trail boss. "We've got a lot of miles to cover, so let's get going." He could feel his face turn red, but he didn't care. They didn't have what he had. He had Sam.

The laughing and snickering lasted a few miles until Mr. Collins rode up alongside Will and asked him in a reflective way, "What's it like to be with someone like Sam? I'm not trying to get personal, it's that kind of smart, capable, beautiful woman is new to me, and I've been around awhile."

"She's a miracle. Every day is a miracle." Will answered in a way that was like a thankful prayer.

Mr. Collins slapped Will on his back and said, "Don't ever fuck it up. That's rare, I never found it. Most people never find it."

Will smiled at Mr. Collins, thought about last night, and realized he'd better think of something else, or he wasn't getting off Sampson anytime soon. He touched his watch and smiled.

Jess's son Clarence was covering the work at the stables this week. Brandon was taking quarterly finals, and after that would be on Spring break at the math camp, I was sending him to. That took one worry off my shoulders; I went to the safe and retrieved my gun and holster. I grabbed my backpack and pulled out my badge and ID in case I needed it. I took the notebook of funny words Dr. Sampson had made up and put them in my back pocket. I needed that connection with him to look after me. I checked the list of shooting ranges in the area, picked one and decided to head there as soon as I found the medicine pouch. I wasn't sure in detail what the pouch did, but I knew I needed something to help get me through this week. I put it over my head and tucked it inside my shirt. Before I got into the car, I opened the hatch to look at the tire that had been slashed, about an inch in length, maybe with a serrated edge. I took some pictures with my phone and then turned it over so that side wouldn't show. I needed to find something I could make an impression of the slash using putty or something. I'd get that later. A mental note was made.

I picked the shooting range farthest from town not wanting to run into anyone who might mention it to Will. I went in and was assigned an alley. I hadn't used my gun since shooting the killer. I put on my ear protectors, loaded my weapon, and took aim at the target — not seeing the silhouette but the face of the piece of shit I had killed back then. I fired the full fifteen rounds into the center of the target. I reloaded and discharged the next fifteen rounds into the head of the target. When I turned the decimated target in to the attendant with the remaining ammunition and ear protectors, the man at the desk gave me a look and quipped, "You must practice a lot. This is topnotch shooting. You didn't miss once." The clerk noticed the blood on my holster but didn't say anything when I showed him my badge. I tucked my loaded gun into the back waistband of my jeans — my jacket hiding it — and headed out to my car.

I eased into the car while pulling the camera case up to the front passenger seat to access its contents. I checked the lenses, made sure I had a full SD card. I drove into Ashland and went to the location where I had seen my "mirage." I walked the length of it, trying to find anything that might indicate a white man had been standing there, taunting me. I took photos to get a perspective of the alley and how it junctured into the street at each end. I took pictures of the store fronts, alley-way doors, and a dumpster; anything and everything that might seem out of place. I went into the stores and questioned people if they had seen a white man; no one had. They would have noticed a white man.

I went back to the car, took out a notepad and wrote down everything about the day I had seen him — an estimation of the time, weather conditions, his description, what he was wearing, and if anyone else had been in the vicinity when I looked around for the auto repair shop. I wrote down what I did that day, retracing my steps and searched for areas where he could have hidden to watch me, without my knowledge. "Shit, he looked like the twin dead by my own hand. Could someone been put up to this? Perhaps, made to look like the twin to put me off the real intent? Too many questions and not enough information."

I stopped at the dental office and asked the dentist if he could give me some of the putty, he used for making dental molds. He thought it was a strange request but gave me a package of it. For reasons I didn't understand fully, people in this town don't question me much or want to know what I am up to.

When I returned home, I printed out the photos and tried to analyze what I had seen. I went down to the garage, opened the rear of the car, turned the tire back over where the slash was and tried to see if I could find any prints on the rim or any residue from the blade. I didn't have a kit, but I used my blush brush, pencil lead shavings crushed into powder, scotch tape, and white copy paper. I found a few prints on the rim, they could be from the guy who changed the tire for me, they could be mine, or they could be whoever slashed my tire. I took the dental putty and made a mold of the slash to try and figure out the size of the blade, tool markings, or type of knife.

The next thing I did was to go over the car entirely; I dusted for prints, took pictures of the car, and checked for any tracking devices that might have been attached. I did everything I could think of. I then washed the car to clean it of the print residue. I was covering my own tracks. I didn't want to believe what was in my mind and if I erased my investigation it wouldn't exist, and I would be fine.

It was late afternoon. I headed down to the stables to see Clarence to ask if he needed anything. Laney was gone on the trip with Will curtailing my riding for the week. Everything was under control at the stables. Too bad it wasn't under control for me right then.

When I arrived back at the house, I emptied the mail from my bag I picked up the day before, along with the magazines and books I bought to occupy my time while Will was gone. I had gone all day without eating, and still wasn't hungry. I was feeling flushed and a little queasy. "The RESERVATIONS Case" always made me nauseous, not only because of its heinous nature, but because I had killed. I separated the mail between Will's and mine. In the mail was a white, invitation-size envelope with fancy writing on the outside, made out to me, but no return address. It looked like someone sent me an invitation or announcement. I opened the envelope and inside was a lock of hair. I dropped the envelope and fought back the reflex to vomit. Along with the hair was a small piece of paper that had block writing on it: FROM THE BUSH IT WAS STUCK ON, GIRLIE."

"Crap. This was my hair. I put on the gloves I do dishes with, picked up the envelope, and attempted to find some prints by dusting it with cacao powder and using clear tape. I didn't find prints. Maybe DNA would be on the back of the stamp or the closure of the envelope. I couldn't do anything but put it into a plastic sandwich bag to preserve it.

I needed to think. Who could I trust at the Bureau to run the tire prints for me? I couldn't come up with anyone. Then I thought, maybe the Tribal Police or the local LEO's. They know me, maybe they could run them for me under the radar. I would make a visit to the Tribal Police tomorrow. I didn't sleep all night with my gun was under my pillow and my thoughts blocking my rest.

Will and Jess were cleaning up camp and getting things ready for the night. The first trip out of the season was always hard to get used to, getting back into the rhythm of how you usually do things. The weather was colder at night, they would take turns keeping the fire going for their clients. Will would take the first shift.

Will was drinking coffee to stay awake, tending the fire when Mr. Collins walked over and sat across from him. Mr. Collins quipped, "The older I get, the less sleep I seem to need." Will handed him a cup of coffee. They sat in silence for a bit and then Mr. Collins asked, "When we get back to town, I plan on staying at

The Lodge for a couple days and I'd like to go over the security plans I talked to you about on my last trip. Do you think you'd have time? It'll be the weekend. Bring Sam and we'll have dinner and talk."

"I don't see any problem with that. I've been meaning to take Sam out to dinner. I did tell her we were probably going to talk about business the next time you came out. Let's plan on it."

"That black eye you've got, were you in a fight?"

"No sir, not a fight." Will kind of laughed, "I really don't want to say if you don't mind."

Mr. Collins was reticent, "Do you mind if I ask, does Sam, give you a hard time for being gone so much? I think I have four ex-wives, mainly because I was never home."

"No sir, she doesn't. She's very understanding. A full five days is tough, but then going home to her is the best thing I could ever imagine. We went through a lot to be with each other, and I wouldn't trade our life for the world." Will was a little choked up. "Mr. Collins, may I ask you a question?"

"Sure Will, let's hear it."

"We're getting married in June. I'm the one who wants the whole traditional ceremony because of my heritage. Sam doesn't really have traditions. She doesn't have any family, and I'm having a difficult time, because this is turning out to be very one-sided on my part. She hasn't said anything, and never would, but I don't want that day to be about just me, about what I wanted. Do you have any suggestions?"

"Will, I've found that if you ask women what they want, they will usually tell you. You may not always want to hear it, but it will be the truth. Have you asked her what she wants?"

"I think she would tell me she wants what I want. Sam always gives without taking — she never depletes me — but I feel I'm not giving enough back."

Mr. Collins stretched his back, "Will, I was terrible at being married, but I did learn something in the process. Real love, the love you have with Sam, is something everyone wants. You know in your heart what she wants. Give it to her. She's probably been giving you hints, and you haven't been paying attention. Is what she wants what you want? Answer that, and you'll know what to do."

Mr. Collins went to his tent as Will continued to sit at the fire, thinking about Sam. He looked at the nude picture of her on his phone. He couldn't believe this woman was his and how gorgeous she was inside and out. He thought about last night, touched the bruise by his eye and smiled. He hadn't seen that side of her before. He wasn't complaining — it had been unbelievable — his thoughts and her picture made him stir, but where did it come from? He'd been trying to keep her in a small, little world, not wanting to share her. He loved her so much. He touched the watch on his left wrist and then he looked at his hand. No ring. He thought about the things she would say occasionally, about him not having a ring on. "I'm asking her for so many things and I haven't given her the one thing she really wants, a ring on my finger."

Jess came up to Will. "It is my shift now, Will. Get some rest. Are you okay?"

"Just missing Sam."

"Will I know you. It is more than that. What is going on?"

THIRTY-SIX

I didn't sleep all night. I was exhausted, and my mind was trying to forge a plan that wouldn't land me on the Bureau's radar while I investigated. The boxes — I hadn't unpacked them yet — we didn't have any furniture to put the stuff in, had been on my back burner. The files on "The RESERVATIONS Case" I had used in the field and Dr. Sampson had worked on before his death should be in those boxes. I had used them while writing my first book. I started looking for the boxes labeled "Case Files." They were on the bottom of the stack of course, requiring me to move everything out of the way. The files were there, dumping them out in no particular order, maybe starting in an abstract way I would see something new. It was four in the morning as I was sitting on the floor amongst the boxes going through files. There had to be something in there I had missed before. A note Dr. Sampson left, anything to point me in a new direction. Six hours later, there was nothing I didn't already know. There must be something in those classified files in DC I hadn't seen and hadn't been told about by Charlie. He had put me on the case: why would he conceal things from me? It had been my case, the one I had solved when I was with the Bureau; the case that almost got me killed.

I wasn't feeling well, like I had the flu, but I knew it was the situation eating at me as it did last time. I decided to get up, get dressed, put my gun in the middle of my back waistband and head to the Tribal Police Station. Franklin Running Deer was the Chief — a real stand-up guy — and I hoped I had enough influence with him to run the prints for me on the down-low. He didn't like the Feds much, maybe he'd do this just to spite them. I walked into the station after I arrived and saw Franklin at his desk. I waved, he stood up and walked over to me.

"Sam, to what do I owe this pleasure? You're looking beautiful, as usual."

I liked Franklin, maybe it was because he seemed to have an affection for me since his mother had been white. He was my height, 5'9" and a svelte 155 pounds. He kept his hair length just below his shoulders, but what was striking were his eyes — the darkest, deepest brown — almost black eyes. His eyes enabled him to easily get confessions from perps because if you didn't know him, he used those eyes against you. He could be scary. Franklin had been married but several years before his wife left him, due to her addictions. Since then, he's put himself into his work. Will had helped him through those hard-times, and Franklin was a friend who remembered.

"Franklin, can we talk in private?" I asked in a quiet tone.

"Sure, come into my office." He closed the door, gestured the offer of coffee, sat at his desk, and asked, "What do you want to talk about? I see you are wearing your weapon. Is Will in town?"

I was pacing a bit and didn't know the correct approach without coming off too vigilante. "Uh, no, Will's on a five-day trip. I had a flat tire the other day, someone used a knife to slash it and I managed to pull some prints from the rim. Some might be mine or the guy who changed my tire, but maybe they could be from whoever did it. I was wondering if you could run these prints for me — under the radar, so-to-speak."

"May I see the tire first?" Franklin queried, looking at Sam's nervous pacing and constant reaffirmation that her weapon was there by constantly touching it.

"It's in the back of my car outside." I answered with my eyes averted, wondering why he needed to see the tire — unless he just wanted to talk outside, away from internal ears.

Franklin got up from his desk, grabbed his jacket and followed me outside to my car. He could see the trembling in my hands as I opened the back of the car. He pulled on gloves and picked the tire up to get a better look. "Yep, that's a knife slash alright." He put the tire back, looked at me, and seriously asked, "Does Will know about this?"

"I wanted to get some answers first, Franklin. I didn't want to distract him before his first trip of the season. Can we keep this between us until I know more before telling him? I didn't want to worry him over something that's probably nothing."

"I'll run those prints for you Sam, but then I'm entitled to know what's going on. This isn't just about the tire, is it? Are you out at the house by yourself? Is that why you're wearing your gun?"

"Franklin, it may be just my imagination if the prints don't bring anything up." I tried to smile a bit, trying to reassure him I wasn't hiding anything.

"You know Will and I are close friends, actually more than that, like brothers? He'd want me to look after you."

"I know Franklin, I'm sorry. Listen, I don't want you to be in an awkward situation. Let's just call it a day, forget I was here." I got in my car to leave.

Franklin came over to the open car window and bent down to look at me. "I'll run them for you. I'll call you as soon as I have something. You look tired, Sam, are you sure you are, okay?"

I handed the prints to him and replied, "Just fighting off a flu bug. Thanks Franklin." I drove off as my heart pounded in my chest.

Franklin didn't like this. There was something more to this than Sam was telling him. He decided to put a deputy on her at the house just in case. He didn't want to know what Will would do if something happened to her. Sam was everything to Will and he'd kill to protect her. Everyone knew that Sam almost died a couple years before working a case for the Tribes. Franklin felt he owed her, but Will wouldn't like being kept in the dark.

As I drove home my thoughts went to finding some solace. In the center of our home is a two-story, thirty-six-inch diameter wooden lodgepole that helps support the entire structure of the house. The beams that run at the roof line attach to it like an umbrella of safety. It gives stability, strength, and allows the house to be fully open without supporting walls. When I can't sleep, I find myself drawn to that pole. I lean against it and try to channel its strength into me. When Will reaches for me at night, and his hand doesn't find me he knows where I am. He comes to me, to see why I need to be there. I always tell him it reminds me of the tree by the stream where we had watered the horses and worked through our first misunderstanding. This lodgepole makes me look up and out through the glass that makes up the front of our house. I usually find answers there. Lately, it's hasn't been speaking to me.

Will and Jess were so busy on this trip they didn't have time to talk as they normally would. Jess knew Will needed to talk to him but until they got back, there would not be much privacy. When there were brief opportunities, Jess would ask a question or two, trying to get at the heart of the matter bothering Will. One such opportunity came at two in the morning during their shift change to keep the fire going.

"What steals your good spirit, Will?" Jess observed Will rubbing the face of the watch Sam had given him.

"I've been foolish and selfish with Sam. I know what she wants and it's all she really has wanted from the day she came home. She never asks for anything and I'm making her wait for it." Will admonished himself.

Jess didn't know what Will was referring to and asked, "What does she want? Is it something you cannot give to her? Do not want to give to her?"

"All she wants from me is a ring on my finger." Feeling the emptiness of that space on his left hand. "I told her I would move up the date, but I haven't. I've asked her to do, to give, so many things, but the one thing she wants I haven't done

because of how I thought it needed to be. The big ceremony and the traditions of our heritage being more important somehow. Hell, I'm also afraid because of the family I came from. What if I'm my father?"

Jess put his arm around Will's shoulder, "Do you want to see yourself reflected in her eyes or in a mirror? Will, you roamed aimlessly for almost forty-two of your years. Sam came to you, gave you an anchor, a mooring in calmer waters so you could find peace. Is a ring her anchor? You may have built her a house, but she built you a life. Will, you will never be your father, stop using that as an excuse."

Will wanted a simple answer from Jess, but the answer shouldn't come from Jess — it had to come from his own heart. "Jess, I want to marry her more than anything. I want to give her what she wants. It's the same thing I want. I don't want to wait. Do I give up my traditions to do that? Do I trust that my very DNA won't harm her?"

"My brother, the sun and moon occupy the sky at the same time as do you and Sam. Do you want the wedding or the marriage? Go to the Courthouse, marry her, then have tradition later as a celebration. Everyone knows you are already married in the ways that matter." Jess put his arm tighter around Will's shoulder and looked in his eyes. "Sleep on it Will, the right answer will come to you. The one that will make you both happy. I will only say this once more my brother, you broke that cycle of your family, your DNA is pure, and you are a good man."

Will tried to sleep. He looked at Sam's picture. He ached for her. His heart didn't beat right without her. He knew what he would do. When he got home, he would give Sam what she wanted, what she needed and it would give him everything he needed and wanted, too.

Franklin called the next day and asked if I could come by the Tribal Police Station. He wouldn't tell me on the phone what he had discovered by running the prints I gave him. I arrived within the hour, and he met me as I drove up, in the parking lot. "Franklin is there a problem that we have to meet on the parking lot?"

"Sam, I ran those prints. One print was yours, one was the auto repair guy, and the other caused an FBI Alert and couldn't get past it on the computer to get any further information. "What's going on? I'm entitled to know. The Feds are going to be calling to find out why I ran those prints."

I started to walk back to my car and Franklin stopped me. "I'm grateful for your help Franklin, but I need to verify something first before I can tell you. Give me the week and then I promise I'll tell you what I know?"

"I don't like this Sam. I trust you, but now the Feds will be knocking on my door for answers. What do I tell them about where I got that print?"

"Tell them I gave it to you. It's the truth and it will stop them in their tracks. They'll leave you alone, I'll make sure of that. By the way, pull your deputy off me, he'll only complicate things."

"I don't like you being at the house alone with Will gone." Franklin said with concern.

"I'm okay Franklin, no worries." I patted his shoulder to alleviate some of his concern.

Franklin watched Sam, her gun in the middle of her waist, walk to her car and drive off. He wanted to pick up the phone and call Will, but he'd give her the week. She earned that. He would pull his deputy. How did she know?

I had no choice now but to make some calls. I had to get into those classified files. I picked up a couple of burner phones to protect myself and those I would contact. They would have "plausible deniability" as to who the call came from. I kept the calls quick and under a minute. Over the next three days, I tried to call in favors with my contacts at the Bureau. I verified one twin did die by his own hand in jail. I verified the one I had killed, along with his brother, were cremated after no family members came to claim the bodies. I called the best forensic computer expert I knew and sent her encrypted copies of the emails and cell phone pictures along with coding she had given me. I had her try to locate the IP addresses of those emails that I couldn't narrow down, and lastly to find out why my firewall hadn't held.

I had one more day before Will would be home. I went into town and picked up the mail. My new tire had arrived, so I picked that up, too. Coming out of the Post Office, I was scanning the mail for anything that might be unusual. I glanced up to see where I was walking and saw a white man putting a note under the windshield wiper of my car. My car was two blocks away. I started running by instinct, my hand reassuring me my gun was in my back waistband if I needed it. The white man looked at me, watching me run towards him. He smiled at me and took off down a side street. Not seeing a small pothole in my path my foot hit the edge of it, twisting my ankle, causing me to fall in the middle of the street inches from the front of a car with screaming brakes barely able to stop. I heard a scream followed by cursing that later I figured was from me full of frustration and searing pain. Several people ran over to me, picked me up along with all my mail that had gone flying. As soon as I put weight on my left ankle, I cried out and felt faint. They helped me hobble over to my car, sat me in the driver's seat where I indicated I could drive myself to the clinic and have it looked at. I thanked them all and apologized for scaring them with my language. I looked through the windshield, saw the note flapping in the breeze under the wiper blade, pulled myself up and reached out of the window to snag it with a Kleenex and held the note by its corner. The words on the note, "You think you're so smart." Those words and the pain in my ankle caused me to throw the car door open and heave on the pavement. My heart was pounding as sweat covered me with panic and disgust. I refused to cry because I was already weak of body, I couldn't be weak of will if I would survive this.

"Fuck." I hit the dashboard with my hand and felt like I was falling down a rabbit hole. I started the car and drove to the clinic. My ankle was already swollen, and the pain was setting in. Two hours later, after waiting my turn while more urgent cases had been seen, x-rays showed a severely sprained ankle. The ankle was wrapped, and I was issued a set of crutches, a prescription for pain meds, which I refused, and was sent on my way.

I headed home knowing I only had one objective — see if I could hack the classified files without setting off any alarms at the Bureau. I couldn't call Charlie. I wouldn't call Charlie. I pulled over to the shoulder of the road, made a U-turn and went to the library. Hobbling into the library, I asked the attendant permission to use their computer. I spent the next three hours to no avail unable to get into the FBI server. Feeling frustrated, tired, in pain, and of the realization that I had to tell Will everything when he got home. I would show him everything. Being at a disadvantage now with my ankle sprained, feeling like the flu was catching up with me, and I hadn't eaten or slept much the past five days made me realize I couldn't do this alone anymore. After talking to Will I would talk to Franklin. I spent the night updating all my notes, putting everything in some semblance of order so I could explain it all to Will and ask for his help and his forgiveness.

THIRTY-SEVEN

I was anxious and worried Will was coming home today, it was Friday afternoon, and I hadn't heard from him. He usually sent me a text as soon as he got a signal close to home. It had been difficult taking a shower with my ankle being so painful, but I needed to look as good as I could for him. My fall had cut my knee and elbow along with spraining my ankle, when the hot water hit, it stung. I dried myself, put on black jeans and a white sweater that said, "Hi, I missed you." It was still cold even though it was March, but I was sweating. I hobbled to the kitchen island so I could sit down and check my email. Waiting on answers from those I had called in favors from made me crazy with impatience.

Will was just about to text Sam and tell her he was an hour from home, but the phone rang, and he recognized Charlie's number. Will thought for a moment before answering, but then did. "This is Will."

"Will, this is Charlie, Charlie Falken."

"Why are you calling Charlie?" Will didn't trust Charlie, even though he had been a lifeline during the two years Sam was still in DC.

"Is everything alright with you and Sam?" Charlie asked in a way that made Will nervous.

"Everything is great. Why are you asking?" Jess could hear Will's side of the conversation and was concerned about the worried look on Will's face.

"Well, I was wondering why Sam was trying to hack into the classified "RESERVATIONS Case" files. An alert went out and I was notified. I didn't want to call her until I knew how to approach this — get some insight from you. I'm trying to keep her out of trouble."

"I'll get back to you Charlie." With that, Will hung up. He noticed he was shaking. He stopped Sampson's forward momentum to text Sam. "Home in an hour." The happiness he felt two minutes before was now replaced by a fear he couldn't control. The same fear he'd felt in the past.

The text chirped, and my heart started to pump faster. I responded, "Can't wait to see you. Love you." I limped to the bathroom mirror to take one last look at myself to see if there were any outward signs of what was going on inside of me. Physically I felt the same way I'd felt giving that briefing on the murdered boys during "The RESERVATIONS Case." I was nauseated by this case rearing its ugly head. Will and I had buried this — I wanted it to stay buried.

Mr. Collins rode up next to Will, "I know you'll be in a hurry to see your lady, so I'll plan on seeing you tomorrow night at The Lodge for dinner at seven." Will confirmed with a head nod. Mr. Collins could see a change in Will's demeanor.

As Mr. Collins hung back, Jess came along-side Will. "I willl handle things from here. Get home, see Sam. Clarence is at the stables. Leave Sampson in his hands."

Will gave Sampson a nudge and headed home at a quicker pace.

As I watched through the window, I saw Will ride up alone without the others in sight. He dismounted Sampson, handed the reins to Clarence and headed towards the house, to me. I opened the door, standing on my crutches, trying to smile a welcome. Will saw me and didn't quicken his pace. He didn't look happy to see me. He wasn't smiling. Will stopped about a foot from me, looked at the crutches, came closer giving me a restrained kiss. He looked at me and asked with a tone of caged anger, "What's going on Sam? What happened this week?"

I felt like my world just fell away hobbling back into the house. It's been five days and that's how he greets me. I was hurt. I tried to keep the tears at bay. "Hi, to you too, Will," I said as I navigated on my crutches back to the kitchen, needing to sit down before I fell down.

Will followed me, slamming the door and finally realized I was in pain and asked. "What happened, Sam? Are you alright? You look thin." Then he noticed I was wearing my weapon and the medicine bag, causing the anger on his face to intensify.

"I twisted my ankle. It's fine. Nothing for you to worry about. I'm sure you have work down at the stables. Don't let me keep you. Sorry you don't like the way I look, but I've been sick all week." I was rambling, trying not to look at him. It would hurt too much to see the look on his face. He was angry at me, and I didn't know why. I wondered if Franklin had called him. If not Franklin, there were dozens in town who could have called him.

Will was pacing, his hands at his belt, thumbs through the loops, looking alternately at the floor, then back at me. "Charlie called and said he was alerted that you were trying to hack into the Bureau's server — the classified files on "The RESERVATIONS Case." Why, Sam? Why do I have to hear this from Charlie? What haven't you told me? You could have called me on the satellite phone. You're wearing your damn gun, WHY?" His voice was starting to shake, and the volume increased. He kicked the empty chair sending it across the room.

"Charlie called you. What did you say to him?" I tried to keep my voice neutral.

Will snapped at me. "Nothing, because I don't know anything! Whatever this is I want you to stop pursuing it. I want you to STOP!" Will's anger was starting to boil over, his blood pressure was elevated. He slammed his fist on the granite countertop. "Damn it, Sam, you're not at the Bureau anymore! I thought we were done with that. I thought we buried it."

"Please calm down, Will. Please, your blood pressure," I implored, as his face reddened, and his jaw clenched.

"Calm down? My wife is doing who knows what behind my back! I thought we promised, no secrets. I want the truth, NOW, Sam, NOW!"

He was yelling at me. I don't even think he knew how loud he was. I was sick of being screamed at and finally fought back. "You want the truth? I'm not your wife Will, there's no wedding ring on your finger, or mine. Check that sense of possession at the door." I was angry now, I got up clumsily, grabbed my crutches. Will blocked my way with his outstretched arm as some sort of gate to keep me in. I started getting louder to cover the screaming physical and emotional pain I was feeling.

"Charlie calls you and you take his side. You trust him, don't even give me a chance to tell you before you judge me. Who are you, coming home after five days and giving me a worthless kiss, full of accusations, all because Charlie called you?" Pointing to all the files on the kitchen island I snarled angrily, "I had everything ready to talk to you about it, you haven't been here in five days. When was I supposed to tell you anything? Now get out of my way." I was crying. I was feeling sick. The pain in my ankle was intolerable — as it was in my heart.

Will looked like I had slapped him. He had tears filling his eyes. He stepped aside. He could hardly breathe. I grabbed my keys trying to head to my car. "You can't drive like that," Will said in a more controlled tone. "Stop, Sam. We're not done here, STOP!" He tried to block me again with his body, not touching me, but making his presence felt. "Damn it, STOP!"

I looked straight into Will's eyes trying to explain, my voice more even and controlled. "I'm not perfect Will, and maybe I handled some things badly, but I didn't deserve how you walked in the door acting like judge and jury before even finding out what I had to say. You've seen the scars I have, the pain I went through? The sacrifices? Do you think I would intentionally want to go through that again? Do you think I want to lose what we have? I've proven I love you more than my life. I don't want to lose you, but I can't be here with you right now. I need some space from all this self-entitled anger you are throwing at me." Suddenly I had a violent urge to throw up. I limped over to the sink, barely making it, and did so. Twice.

Will ran over, pulled my hair back and stroked my back. "Sam, are you sick? You've lost weight. God, what's going on around here? I leave for five days, and everything goes to hell."

"I don't know, the flu, maybe. What do you care?" I rinsed my mouth out and I tried to make it to the door again, pushing past him this time. I turned half-way, "You have a lot of nerve, Will, talking about secrets. What about unfulfilled promises?" I got to the door and fumbled for the knob. Dropping my keys, I struggled to pick them up but couldn't.

Will was rubbing his head, one hand on his waist, pacing in a circle trying to get control, but couldn't. "Please don't leave Sam, not like this, please." Will fell to his knees, the tears were coming. "You're right, I just, uh, I can't go through that again, see you go through all of that again. The fear of losing you — I felt it all over again — like it was yesterday — the hospital, the waiting. God, please don't leave. I can't lose you, I can't. Please stop!" Will sounded like he was having a panic attack, trying to draw air in, then continued through his tears. "I couldn't handle it if something happened to you. I don't want to live without you. I love you with every-thing I am, everything. Damn it, Sam, STOP!" He sobbed, kneeling there on the floor, looking older, hands covering his face, trying to wipe his tears away, to get control.

He finally looked at me with red eyes, tears rushing down his face, and I saw the absolute fear of losing me on his face, the same look he had more than two years before. I stopped, balancing on my crutches, my body trembling, trying to control what I was feeling. I limped over to where he was kneeling and stood in front of him. I was crying and feeling sick again. "I don't want to leave. I never want to leave. You're not losing me, God, I love you. I want to talk to you. I planned on talking to you, but I can't talk to you like this." I said in a small, frail voice. Seeing him like this was killing me and I had caused it.

As he knelt, Will put his shaking hands around my waist, laid his forehead against my stomach and held on tight. I reached down, leaning on my crutches, as I stroked his hair until his panic ceased. It seemed like we cried for an hour. My ankle was killing me, and I needed to sit; I could feel it swelling, tightening the gap of silence with pain. Will took a gulp of air and slowly got to his feet in front of me, so close — an unyielding grip on my waist. I couldn't move. I could feel his eyelashes when he blinked. His breath on my skin. He kissed me, with shame at first, testing if I would pull away or reject him, and then he kissed me again, fear mixed with apology, escalating to panic and then back to deep, unconditional love. He stepped back to look at me, his eyes red from crying. "God, Sam, I'm sorry. I went crazy. The thought of losing you — I couldn't think. I'm sorry. Please, I'm so sorry."

I was really feeling physically wrecked on top of everything emotional. "Will, I need to lay down. I'm dizzy and feeling sick again. My ankle," and before I could finish the sentence, I felt myself falling into a faint.

Will caught Sam as her crutches crashed to the floor. He carried her and gently put her on the bed. He took the gun from the back waistband of her jeans and the notebook from her back pocket. He placed the gun under the bed. He used a pillow to elevate her leg and got some ice from the freezer, gently placing it on her ankle. He could see how swollen it was. He went into the bathroom, got a cold face cloth and put it on Sam's forehead as she came to. He smoothed her hair and saw how beautiful she was, even with red, swollen eyes. He loved this woman; she was everything to him, and he was not going to lose her. He needed to man up and not let fear control him. Not let Charlie manipulate him. He called Christian — the closest thing to a doctor that made house calls.

I tried to get up. I felt the need to flee, but Will wouldn't let me. He held a bottle of water for me, carefully lifted my head up as I took a sip. "Lie still for a bit, you might still be dizzy. I called Christian to come and look at your ankle. It looks bad. He'll be here soon."

I looked at this man who was my life, and I begged, "Forgive me for what I said in anger. I didn't mean it, I'm so sorry. Please forgive me."

"What you said, Sam, was my fault. I caused it by my own inaction. I let you down, and you had every right to say that about not being my wife. I guess in some way I've been taking you for granted because I already felt married to you. I was wrong, I'm the one who is sorry." He played with the ring on my left hand, my engagement ring. "I haven't kept my promises to you and I'm so sorry. I'm ashamed."

I looked at him. "Are you thinking of taking my ring back? Don't you want to marry me? What if I can't give you a child, will I be enough for you?" I started crying again. My emotions were all over the place, ruled by the pain in my heart, and in my ankle.

"God, Sam, you're my life. If I ever gave you the impression you weren't enough, and that's why I asked you to have a child with me, I'm sorry. I didn't mean to make you feel like that. I love you so much, and God, I'm so stupid, asking you before we were married. I've hurt you and I didn't mean to. You're everything to me. With or without a child, you are everything I want, need, and ever dreamt of. You're part of me. I'm so sorry."

Will remembered he never answered her question that night. He had been so caught up with wanting her so much and with asking if she would try to have a child, he hadn't realized how that could have made her feel. One more thing he asked her to do for him without a ring. One more hurt he needed to fix.

"Will, I'm afraid of losing you if I fail, if I can't have a baby. Maybe we should try and if it doesn't work, then you won't have to commit to me. We should find out before we get married."

"I want to marry you more than anything. I want to add one more ring on your finger as soon as possible. No waiting. You and I, we've done too much waiting in this life. Now is what's important. If you can, if you want, we'll go to the Courthouse on Monday. I know the judge and it won't be a problem. No more waiting."

"Will, your plans. Your wants? June is not that far away. You have work."

"That's the problem Sam, those were my plans, not ours. I promised I would move the ceremony up, and I didn't, and I'm sorry. I want you to be my wife. I know now I want the marriage, not just the big wedding. Without you, I'm nothing, this life would be nothing, mean nothing. You are my priority, my center of the universe, my rock and stability. I can't imagine my life without you."

We heard the front door open and close. Christian came walking into the house. "Will, it's me."

Will got up and beckoned him to come into the bedroom. Christian looked at both of us, our eyes red and faces blotchy from crying. "Are you guys, okay?"

Will cleared his throat and showed Christian my ankle. "Looks pretty swollen and bruised. What do you think?" His voice hoarse from crying and yelling.

"Did you go to the clinic for an x-ray, Sam?" Christian inquired while looking closer at my ankle.

"Yes. They told me it was just a bad sprain and wrapped it."

"Well, it looks like you have a green break. You didn't break your ankle bone but bent it with the same resulting pain and the effects of a break. The x-ray may have been taken from a bad angle that didn't show the bend. We need to get the swelling down with ice and put an inflatable clear cast on it for you. It will give a lot of extra support. I saw some crutches on the floor in the kitchen, you'll want to use them for four to six weeks, or until you can put weight on it again."

"Christian, do me a favor and take Will's blood pressure." I looked over at Will and he knew I was serious. He didn't say no.

"Sure, let's take care of that. Will, roll up your sleeve or take your shirt off." Christian kept looking back and forth at the two of us afraid to ask, but then did. "What's going on around here? You both look like you've been crying. What's wrong?"

"Just tears of joy at seeing each other after five days," Will was trying to control his voice. "Sam doesn't feel well. She has flu-like symptoms — she got dizzy and fainted — probably from the pain." Will wasn't going to tell Christian it was from the fight they'd had.

Christian took Will's blood pressure, and it was a bit high. He then took my temperature. "Will, you should consider taking a medication for your high blood pressure, don't take chances. You've got a great life going here. Don't have a stroke or something." Turning to me, Christian said, "You seem to have a low-grade fever. Could be from the flu or the inflammation in your ankle. Have you been eating and sleeping enough while Will's been gone? You look like you've lost some weight."

"Probably not," I answered, wondering why everyone was talking about my weight. "Would you inform Will's doctor in Billings of these results and have him send a prescription for Will? We don't want to take any chances — we have too much to look forward to."

"Copy that, I'll send the doc a message while we wait for the ice to take effect on your ankle. I'm going out to the rig to get the inflatable cast. Be right back. Oh, you may want to get those jeans off because they won't fit over the cast."

Will came to the side of the bed, knelt on one knee, laid his head on my breasts, and put his arms around me. He needed to be close, he needed comfort. He was trying to apologize without words. I kissed his forehead and took in the smell of his essence. "You're still shaking Will, are you alright? I need you to calm down so we can get your blood pressure in check. Please."

"I'm trying to be alright." He picked up his head, looking at me, "Let me help you get your jeans off. I'll cover you with the sheet before Christian gets back."

Will couldn't help but feel himself getting aroused as he took Sam's jeans off, but Christian would be back any second. "God, Sam's in pain, sick, and I still can't control my need for her. It's the way I communicate with her and need her to know we're okay, that I'm sorry for so many things."

"You cut and scraped your knee, too." Will said, trying to regain control of his urges.

"My elbow as well," I added.

"I think I'll go take a shower and scrub five days of the trail off. If you feel better later, can we talk? I need to, if you do." Will stood up from his kneeling stance, looked at me with blood shot eyes, "It takes a lot of love for us to fight like that and come out on the other side. I didn't think it was possible. I get it now — what we have — is more than I ever imagined or thought existed, but we have it."

I noticed the bulge in his pants. "We have more than enough love to get through this. I want to talk after Christian is gone. I love you and I'm so glad you're home. You better get in the shower before Christian sees your need." I touched the front of his jeans to signal I understood.

Will bent down and kissed me deeply, trying to make up for the worthless kiss the night had started with. When he felt I was understanding him through the kiss, he whispered, "I love you so much, I've decided to stay home next week. I want to be with you. I have to be with you." He half-smiled and headed for the shower.

Will cried while he showered. His heart was beating fast. This fear he had felt before, and he couldn't go there again. Whatever she had to tell him, they would deal with it together. He was not going to lose her. This time he would keep her safe. Then he laughed to himself. I want to keep her safe, and I'm the one who hurt her.

Charlie had flipped a switch in Will, not knowing how strong his and Sam's love was, he'd find out.

By the time Will came out of the bathroom, hair still damp, wearing sweats and a t-shirt, Christian had the inflatable cast on my ankle and had dressed the cuts on my knee and elbow. "If this cast feels like it's getting too tight, just deflate it a bit and then call me. It needs static pressure to work correctly, or the green break won't heal. You two look like you need to eat and get some sleep. I'll check in with you tomorrow and see how you're feeling, Sam. Do you have any pain meds?"

"I don't use them." I smiled and thanked Christian.

As if it were a reflex, Will had pulled the sheet lower on my legs, covering me, keeping me to himself. "Christian, I really appreciate you taking care of

Sam." Will meant it even though he and his friend were still a little awkward about things — well, awkward about me. They shook hands, Will walked him out, then locked up for the night. I could hear Will call Jess telling him what his plans were for the coming week and to get his next trip covered. It didn't seem to be a problem. Jess was a wise man.

Will came back into the bedroom laying himself next to me on the bed. "Feeling any better?" he asked tracing the outline of my face with his finger, landing on my lips. "I'm sorry babe."

"I know you are. I'm getting there. What about you?" I asked, trying to breathe through the ankle pain.

"I'll tell you in a bit." And then he kissed me softly, lingering at my lips for a long time. We kissed as if we needed to learn everything there was about each other's lips — their softness, their curves, their taste, their firmness, and if they were still welcoming. As soon as lips had been studied came tongues, and the taste of us. It was never just lips, with us.

Will wanted her so much. He had missed her. It had been five days. Sometimes he couldn't get through one night without having her, but she was in pain, and it wasn't only her ankle. He had a lot to do to fix this. The fear had rushed over him like a tidal wave, and he was caught in the surge. He couldn't believe he had let Charlie get into his head.

THIRTY-EIGHT

Back in DC Charlie Falken was standing in Sam's old office, remembering the times they broke the rules here. He could kick himself for all the times he should have told her he loved her and hadn't. If he had said those words to her, he would have had to let go of his past, be with Sam in the present. He thought about it, a lot. He didn't want anyone else. "Sam doesn't belong with Will in Montana. She belongs with me here in DC. I can get her back — all's fair in love and war." Charlie had no idea it would be war when Will found out.

Charlie thought Will had sounded surprised by what he told him on the phone. Will must have been on one of his mountain man-trips. The guy didn't even know what Sam was doing while he was gone. This was nothing more than a fling Sam wanted — she'll get over it soon — the adventure would wear off, and she'd figure out who she really wanted. She'd understand what he had to do, and he would win her back.

Charlie's cell rang, he answered. "Yes sir, the plan seems to be working. I've got people on her, watching. She has no idea. She was never told about the third brother; those files are sealed and classified. She tried but couldn't. I'm heading to Montana next week. I'll keep you posted." Charlie hung up from his boss and smiled.

Will and I had fallen asleep after a tumultuous evening. We didn't get to talk, but we would. We didn't have our welcome home sex, but we would in time. The thing that reared its ugly head had to be faced first and it had to be dealt with.

I woke around eight in the morning and really had to pee. I tried to get out of bed, but every time I'd made an effort, my ankle screamed, and I gave up. Will wasn't in bed, but I figured he was down at the stables. "Shit. I need one of those buttons that tells someone I've fallen and can't get up."

I heard the door and Will walked into the bedroom. "You finally up? You've slept around ten hours. Feeling better?"

"Will I need help, I really have to pee, and I can't get up, my ankle won't let me." I looked desperate.

"I'm going to pick you up and carry you into the bathroom. Put your arms around my neck." Will lifted me, but just shifting my ankle caused me to groan with pain.

He carried me into the bathroom and was trying to stand me up so I could get to the room with the toilet, it hurt for my ankle to hang down. Everything hurt. Finally, I was standing with my butt facing the toilet, but I couldn't keep my balance to get my panties down, and then sit. "Will, do you mind helping me? Please pull down my panties, ease me into a sitting position so I can pee, and hold my foot up so it doesn't hang down. I can't hold it much longer."

Will did as I asked. He pulled my panties down, eased me to the seat, held my foot up so it didn't hurt as much, and then he stifled a laugh. I finally relaxed and peed for what felt like five minutes, Will kneeling in front of me, holding my foot up. As soon as I was finished, we had to reverse the procedure. I was back in bed now, trying to forget the humiliation, but with the revelation that Will loved me, even seeing me at my worst.

"Did I mention Mr. Collins wanted to meet us for dinner at The Lodge at seven tonight?" Will asked, knowing it hadn't come up, but wanting to change the subject.

"I don't think so. It was pretty loud around here last night." I replied with a wink.

"I called him and explained the situation, so he's bringing us dinner from The Lodge at seven. He really wants to talk to both of us and this is the only chance he has before flying out tomorrow."

"Will we have no furniture, and the living room is full of boxes." I was trying to imagine this very wealthy man sitting at the kitchen island all night.

"I explained that to him as well — there's no problem."

"Well, you're going to have to help me shower, dress, and whatever else comes up." Will could see I was trying to fight through the pain and was exhausted by the strain.

"It's okay, he's a regular guy. I'll do whatever you need, including making you some breakfast now."

"We have to talk today. It can't be put off. What did you do with my gun?" I was trying to organize my thoughts, to put my mind on something else other than my ankle.

Will came over to the side of the bed and sat down. He took my left hand with my engagement ring on it and kissed it. "Whatever this is, you need to tell me. I will help you. I can see how it's affected you, but I'm here now. I've pulled my head out of my ass. As soon as we eat, I'll bring that pile of files in here and we'll talk for as long as we need to. I placed your gun under the bed after you fainted. I didn't want Christian to see it while he was here last night. It's still there. I'm worried Sam, you're scaring me but I'm not going to let my own personal fears get in the way of what you need to tell me. I should have given you a chance last night and I'm sorry."

"I still feel a little queasy, maybe some toast and tea for me. My head feels like I drank last night." I was skirting the issue until we could talk in detail.

"I'll be right back with your breakfast and then we'll talk."

Will situated me in the bed so that I was leaning back on the headboard, my ankle propped up on a pillow, and a tray of toast and tea on my lap. He sat on the floor to keep me company and ate an omelet he had made for himself, along with a cup of coffee. I ate a little, but my stomach didn't want to cooperate. I grabbed the waste can from alongside the bed and threw up. Will went to the sink, came back with a cool cloth, and took the waste can from me. "Jeez Will, can you take any more of the worst I have to offer?"

He smiled at me. "That's what we do in this family. When I was hurt after I'd been thrown, you told me there's no embarrassment between us. We take care of each other."

He felt my forehead with the back of his hand. "You don't feel warm today, but pain can make a person nauseous. You sure you don't want a pain pill?"

"I'm sure. I've done without them before, and I can do this. You'll probably get sick from of kissing me last night." I was feeling emotional again and tried to drink my tea to hide the fact.

"It would be worth it. I thought those were some of the best kisses ever. We made a night of just kissing. I liked it, it's what I thought about the first time I kissed you at the stream." Will bent down and kissed me again, even though I had just been sick. Besides if I get sick, I can stay in bed with you all day. I'll take my chances."

"Would you bring me all the files from the kitchen, my laptop, cell phone and a bottle of water? I want to talk to you before some other horrible bodily issue comes up."

Will brought me what I asked for and organized it on the bed so I could see everything. This way I could point, and he could hand it to me. He took his shoes off and sat next to me leaning against the headboard. "Sam, may I say something first? It's the thing I was going to talk to you about last night before I got the call from Charlie."

"Okay." I answered, with trepidation.

"Sam, marry me on Monday. I don't care if I need to carry you into the Courthouse, hold a bucket for you, or help you go to the bathroom. Will you marry me on Monday?"

"Yes, I will marry you on Monday." I said yes but was worried it would change after I finished briefing Will on the week.

Will put his hand to the side of my face. "I love you, Sam. Now, tell me about all of this."

I pointed to the red file and Will handed it to me. "It all started on my birthday. Before we left for the party an email ping with an urgent notification came up on my laptop. I opened it and there was a message, "You didn't kill me, bitch.""

I showed Will the picture from my cell phone and the printout I had made of the email. "Once I closed the email it disappeared. I tried to trace the IP address but hit a dead end at Bozeman then checked the cloud, but it was as if it never existed. Someone must have had a timed erase on the email. I didn't say anything because it was one email at that point figuring it was a joke, a fluke. I thought I might be making a big deal out of nothing."

"I put up a firewall to try to stop any other emails from that origination point. I thought it worked, but then another one came through on your birthday." I pulled out the copies out of the cell phone picture and the copy I had printed to show Will. "That one also had a message, "Soon Sam.""

Will's stomach was in his throat. He was feeling sick now, too. The emails weren't a joke. He needed to show Sam he wasn't afraid. He needed to keep her safe this time. He wasn't afraid to kill for her.

Will was incredulous. "You know how to trace IP addresses and create firewalls?"

"It's part of forensics, sometimes. I'm not a geek, but I have some skills."

"Another layer of the onion," Will muttered under his breath.

"I called in a favor this week from a friend of mine who is a forensics computer expert to see what she could find but haven't heard back from her yet. I may not if she feels they're watching her."

"They?"

"The Bureau."

I looked at Will to see if I should continue.

"What's next?"

"When you were at Christian's I got my gun from the safe, cleaned it and found some firing ranges in the area on the internet. The day you left for your trip I went to the firing range outside town. I hadn't fired my gun since that night and didn't know if I could, so I went to find out. I needed to protect myself, to make sure I was ready, in case."

"And could you?"

"Yes."

"How well?"

"Perfect. Then I came home to put it back in the safe, loaded."

Will thought for a moment, remembering. "And your sending Brandon to math camp was really about this?"

"I needed to get him away from here, to keep him safe. This may have been nothing, but I couldn't take that chance with him — not with him — not put his family through it again. I needed time to figure this out while he was gone. While you were gone."

"The finance talk was that part of this?" Will was getting emotional again.

"I just wanted to make sure everything was in order. I didn't know what your finances were and wanted to make sure you'd be okay — taken care of — if, uh. That Brandon would be okay, if something went wrong and I got, uh, so everything I have would go to you and you'd make sure Brandon went to college so that you could go on."

Will was starting to see a pattern. A pattern of Sam trying to protect without thinking of her own safety. Putting him and Brandon first again. He was over-whelmed how she readied things in case things went bad. He was shaking with the thought that he could have lost her. "What if she hadn't been here waiting for him?" He felt sick about the way he treated her when he came home. "God, he was a fool. He could never go on without her."

Will's eyes were tearing up. He stood up and murmured, "I need a break." I could hear him splashing water on his face in the bathroom. He came back after a few minutes and sat next to me again. He kissed me, felt my forehead for fever, and urged me, "Go on."

"The night I had the flat tire, I saw a slightly built white man down the alley from where my car was parked. He smiled at me and pointed his finger at me as if to shoot me. He looked just like the killer. I ran down the alley but by the time I got there, he was gone. I thought it was my imagination. I went over to the auto repair place, asked to have my tire changed and when the attendant saw the tire, he said it was a slash made by a knife. I ordered a new tire since he couldn't fix that one and he put my spare on. I also took an impression of the slash so I could try and find out what type of knife was used."

"Where's the tire Sam?"

"In the back of my car under the new one." Will jumped up, putting his shoes on he grabbed my keys, and ran down to the garage. He was gone for some time, and I was starting to feel that this was going badly for me.

Will pulled the tire out of the back of the car and saw the slash. He couldn't breathe. She wanted to protect Brandon and me. That's who she is. He couldn't ask that she be less than who she is. She would never ask that of him. Seeing this, seeing someone did this to scare her, threaten her, made him want to kill them. He'd do anything to protect her. He would kill for her.

Will came back and stood in front of the bed, his hands in his back pockets, trying to be stoic. He asked in a low, hoarse voice, "Why didn't you tell me that night? I wouldn't have left. I would have stayed with you, Sam. The sex, the love that night, it all makes sense now. You thought you might not see me again. You wanted to give me everything you had. You let me take your picture in case it was the last time, wasn't it? Oh God, Sam." Will made an effort not to cry, but some tears did escape.

Looking at the man that was my life, I responded softly, "I didn't know how else to show you how much I loved you. That's how I wanted you to remember me if I wasn't here when you got back."

Will couldn't even think of that. Not having her, God, he'd die. He'd want to die. This wasn't her fault, yet she took on the burden. He needed to carry this for her in some way to show her she could count on him.

273

Will cleared his throat and choked back tears. "What comes next? What else has happened?"

My voice was shaking, but I wanted to keep going. He deserved to hear it all, "I went into Ashland and took my camera. I retraced my steps, took pictures of everything and anything to see if I might have missed something. I asked around if anyone had seen a man of that description. I took notes so I wouldn't forget any details. I snapped pictures of the tire, checked my car for any GPS devices in the wheel wells, all around, and dusted the entire car. I pulled some prints off the rim of the tire and went over to the Tribal Police Station and saw Franklin. He ran the prints for me. One set was mine, one was from the car repair attendant, and the other one set off an FBI alert."

"Franklin helped you?"

"He was hesitant, worried about his friendship with you. I walked away, but then he relented." I tried to explain to Will, wanting him to know Franklin's loyalty.

"How could he say no? He knows what you did for these boys. Everyone on the rez feels they owe you for so much."

Everything I relayed to Will, was backed up with the pictures I took and the evidence I had collected. I showed him everything that was compiled and kept going with the briefing.

"I picked up the mail the day of the flat tire. The next day when I went through it, there was an envelope. I thought it was an invitation or an announcement and when I opened it, a lock of my hair was inside with a note, "From the bush it was stuck on, girlie." I handed it to Will in the plastic sandwich bag I had put it in.

"Is there more?" Will asked in a quiet voice. He kicked off his shoes and came over to sit by me again, but I could feel him trembling. He took my left hand and kissed it taking a deep breath.

"I went through the files that I and Dr. Sampson worked on and that were used for my first book. I reviewed all of them but there wasn't anything new. Nothing I didn't already know. I knew in my gut that the classified files at the Bureau had something in them that Charlie hadn't told me. Something he's let loose on me."

"Sam, what do you mean let loose?"

"Charlie not telling me made me vulnerable, he made me a target. I wasn't prepared. Whoever is doing this knows I'm in the dark. He let it happen or wanted it to happen."

"Sam, why would he? He cares about you."

"I went to town yesterday on some errands and to pick up the new tire. When I came out of the Post Office, I saw the same white man at my car that I had seen in the alley. My car was parked two blocks away, he was putting something under my windshield wiper, a piece of paper. I ran to get to get there, stepped in a pothole, and sprained my ankle. I fell in front of a car that almost hit me. Some people picked me up off the street and walked me to my vehicle. I asked but they didn't remember seeing him. The paper he had left on my windshield said, "You think you're so smart." I handed the note in a plastic sandwich bag for Will to see.

"You were almost run over, too?" Will rubbed his head as if a headache had sprung from out of my comments.

I quickly changed the subject knowing Will was almost at his tipping point so I tried even harder to relay things in a manner that would calm him. Was I scared, absolutely? Could I come out and say that? No, I couldn't. "I bought some burner phones and tried to call in some favors at the Bureau. I found out that both brothers had been cremated because no family member came to claim the bodies. I went to the library in town and used a computer there to try and hack into the Bureau's server to see if I could get to those classified files. There's something in those files I wasn't told about. Charlie hid information from me on that damn case, my case." I looked at Will, trying to read his face, his thoughts, and finally lamented, "That's all I have." I was exhausted.

We sat in silence for a long time. He put his arm around me and kissed my forehead. It was almost one in the afternoon. He was trying to absorb everything I had told him.

"You know how to hack?" shaking his head in disbelief.

"Apparently not that well," I replied, trying to lighten things a bit.

I wasn't seeing any response from him and surmised. "I guess Monday is off. I wouldn't blame you Will. I thought I came to you without burden or baggage, but I was wrong. I never would have brought this to your home if I had known. I'm sorry Will, I really am. I've been trying to find out what's going on all this week so I could tell you, so you and Brandon would be safe even if I wasn't, but then Charlie called you first." I was starting to cry again. "I should leave here. It will follow me and leave the rest of you alone. It wants me."

I started to get up, but Will restrained my efforts and drew me back to him. "You're not going anywhere. This is OUR home. I need you. I love you. I'm not going to lose you. Monday, we're getting married. Don't even think of going anywhere. Now let me think."

I saw Will struggling with something he was trying to resolve inside of himself. He looked at me and said with decisiveness, "I'm going to help you with this. You didn't bring this here, Charlie did. He tried to manipulate me with that phone call. He must have had a reason to do that. The question is why? Go over everything again with me in greater detail. I don't want to miss anything. I want to understand so I can fight with you."

"Will, are you still angry with me?"

"Oh, I'm more than angry. I'm mad, but not at you. I'm mad at Charlie and the Bureau. This is going to get finished. This is my turf, my rules. Am I afraid for you, yes, but I'm no longer going to let fear take control? I'm going to embrace you instead of the fear. Let's retrace your steps again. Start from the beginning and don't leave anything out. I want to look at it differently this time, as if I'm on a mission in Iraq. I also want to look at your laptop and see if I can find something you might have missed."

Will was a serious geek with real tech skills. His security business was the real deal. He had no idea Sam had these skills, but he wasn't surprised. She was the smartest person he had ever known in his life, and she took it all in stride, as if it was normal.

I went over everything again with Will. He looked at every photo, every piece of paper, looked at me with determination, and said flatly, "You're the bait, the lure. Charlie is using you to make something happen here. To solve something, to catch someone, and to bring distance between us by making you vulnerable and by getting in my head with that phone call. He wants us weak to get to you. Charlie set this in motion, not you. Everything you did was out of love to protect me and Brandon, to keep us safe — it's your instinct. Well, now it's time for me to keep you safe. This time, you are my responsibility. This time, I set the priorities. I'm calling the shots. I'll call Franklin and he'll help us. Any problem with that Sam? With me taking control?"

"No, not at all. Thank you, Will. I can't do this on my own, I need you to help me, to handle it. I can't even stand up on my own right now, with this ankle pain, and being sick. I would be easy to get to, like the weak one in the herd. I've lost perspective because of my emotions. I don't want to do this anymore. I can't do it anymore."

"Do you trust me, Sam?"

"With my life, with my heart," I answered as I held his hand.

"I'll take care of you. I won't let anything happen to you. I'm never going to lose you. No one is going to fuck with the life we're building together."

Will checked his watch. "Sam, it's five and we need to get you cleaned up before Mr. Collins gets here. You ready?"

Before Will took me for a shower, he locked the doors and put the alarm on. He didn't want any surprises. He also reached under the bed and grabbed my gun putting it on the bathroom counter within our reach.

"I have to pee again."

Will had his hands on his hips looking at me. "You can do that in the shower, it will save some time." He picked me up and carried me to the bathroom.

Just as Will was undressing me, the phone rang, the caller ID indicated it was Christian. He answered and put it on speaker.

Christian was calling for a follow-up, "Just checking in on both of you. How are you guys doing today?"

Will replied with an update. "Sam is feeling a little better, but her ankle is really painful. She wants to take a shower. Can this cast get wet?"

"Probably not, it's a bad idea, but you can cover it with a trash bag and use duct tape or stick with sponge baths for a few weeks. Hey, your prescription is at the pharmacy Will. I've got a call coming in — just let me know if you need anything."

I looked at Will. "I really need to shower so I can wash my hair and I really have to pee."

"Let me get a trash bag and tape, I'll be right back. Can you balance here for a minute?" Will asked, trying to find me a good spot to lean on.

Will hurried back, waterproofed my cast and helped me remove my sweater and underwear. He put the medicine bag on the counter. The hot water was running, I was standing naked, and said in a pleading voice, "I can't balance in the shower myself and wash my hair at the same time, you're going to have to get in with me, please."

"I didn't think you'd want me naked with you just yet, because of last night's fight." Will sounded apologetic. "I didn't want to assume. Give me a sec to get my clothes off. I need to help you. I don't want you falling."

Will helped me into the shower and continued to hold me. I couldn't hold it any longer and I think I peed on his feet, but he didn't say anything. I couldn't put any weight on my ankle, and it was wearing me out.

He was being shy with me, and his breathing was coming faster. Mine was, too. "Sam, I don't know what to do, how to act right now. I want you, but you're in pain and we haven't totally cleared the air from last night. A lot was said, things that I'm ashamed of. Tell me what to do."

"I want you too, Will, I always do. Do you have any idea how much I love your body and what it does to me? I would never say no to you, even with this ankle, but I don't feel well. Last night took a lot out of me. It's been six days and it feels longer — like starting over. Start by kissing me. Start touching me again. Show me we're okay."

Will looked at me, his eyes were embarrassed. He started to kiss me tentatively, he didn't know what to do with his hard nakedness against me. I leaned back so I could see his eyes. "Look at me, Will. Is this how you want to start moving forward, to connect again? We will not use sex as a bargaining chip in our relationship. I will never punish you by withholding myself from you, and I don't want that from you, either. You and I — our bodies belong to each other — it's one of the ways we communicate with each other, and it's the way we will heal from last night."

Will nuzzled his face into my neck, then rested his forehead on my breasts. I could hear him softly breathing. He made his eyes meet mine, and asked quietly, "How can you forgive me like this? Why would you take care of me after what I did? After last night?"

"Sam, we need to stop letting fear control us. We're stronger than that. We've proven that."

"I love you Will, and we're also stronger than any argument. This is real life. We'll fight sometimes, we'll make up, we'll cry, and then we'll laugh. We get to have it all. We have enough love to get through it and we'll be fine. So, are you going to ask me?" I asked him tenderly as I reached down to touch him. "I also need forgiveness from you. Asking me, that forgives me for the things I said, for the anger I expressed." We showered and forgave each other without words.

The only pants that would fit over the cast were sweats. I tried to dress nicely from the waist up hoping that was all Mr. Collins would see of me at the kitchen island. A few minutes before seven, the time of Mr. Collins' supposed arrival Will was carrying me to the kitchen to get me situated at the island so I could use a second chair to elevate my ankle. I had hoped to be seated by the time he arrived. Before that could happen, there was a knock at the door and Will had no choice but to answer the door with me in his arms. I opened the door while in Will's arms, much to the surprise of Mr. Collins. Mr. Collins smiled, bags of food in his hands, and laughed. "That's a great way to be welcomed into someone's home. Should we trade — you take the bags, and I take Sam?"

"Mr. Collins." I smiled at this force of nature who just blew into our house.

"Tad, please."

"Tad, I am so sorry you had to come out here and bring dinner on top of it. I'm a little embarrassed we have to sit at the kitchen island," I apologized while Will tried to set me down, get my ankle propped up, and take the bags from Mr. Collins.

"Don't think twice, lovely lady. This is a wonderful house. The two of you look happy, why clutter it with furniture? It's perfect. I'd give all my possessions to have what you two have."

Will pulled the plates out and between Tad and Will dinner was served. Tad had brought wine, but I declined since I didn't think it would stay down with the nausea I was having. Will took a glass but nursed it slowly, since he only drinks beer. The meal was great; lots of conversation, lots of laughs, and then it was down to business. Will cleared the island and Tad rolled out some blueprints for security systems that would be incorporated in the new buildings he was constructing in Las Vegas.

Tad explained his plan to Will. "I want to pay you independently to review and analyze these blueprints and tell me where I am vulnerable with this system. The company that drew them up has had some issues with deficits of coverage. Before I scrap these and begin again, I was hoping you could take a look first, tell me where they lack, how they can be improved on, and whether I should pay them for the work they've done. I will pay you five thousand dollars for your time, as long as, I can get your report within the week. If I like what I see from you, I'd like to make an offer for your services on a retainer basis. So, Will, what do you think?"

Will looked at me and I gave him a look that encouraged him to go forward. He's been wanting to build his security business, and this could be the opportunity he'd been waiting for. I wanted him to go for it, especially since I had done a thorough background check on Mr. Collins and his businesses. I felt comfortable with him and what he was representing.

"I appreciate your confidence, sir, and would be happy to accept the job. I want to make it clear that Sam is my partner in this business. She has a Forensics background with a keen eye for detail of what is and isn't there. I would like her to work with me on this project, with your approval."

Tad looked at Sam, "Okay, how about a little preview to help me make an educated decision and to answer Will's request?"

Will was nervous with Tad putting Sam on the spot like that. How could she find something so quickly never having seen the blueprints before? He knew Sam was brilliant, but this was asking a lot.

I pulled the blueprints closer to my line of sight, took a few minutes and said, "I see one vulnerability right away — one that could bring down your entire system."

"Really? Explain." Tad was interested and focused.

I positioned the blueprints so he and Will could see them as I pointed to the ceiling heating and cooling ductwork. "As you can see, the way your design for the heating and cooling ductwork is laid out, at each end of your building where they terminate to the exterior, you could have a breach. The external influence on your equipment could interfere with your entire system. Any type of contraband could be assimilated into your system through this weak access point. The size of the ductwork, and the fact that the grate covering that exterior opening is only galvanized metal. One could expect some perp to use that as an entrance to your building without being detected. Access is easily available with a ladder, sheet metal cutters, and anyone as large as 5"10", 175 pounds could gain entry there.

I would suggest temperature-controlled security devices, or even laser alarms along the runs of the ductwork and at their termination points. I would use steel grates — no more than one-inch grid openings affixed with at least six-inch long bolts with security locks. The openings won't affect your air flow and will keep out other types of intruders, including rats. You have other deficiencies Will can outline in further detail in his report. Some of which he is already aware of by looking at your plans. Instead of giving you everything tonight, let us earn our fee and give you a complete report later this week."

Tad looked at Will, then back to me. "Welcome aboard, Sam."

"Now if you don't mind Tad, my ankle is killing me, and I need Will to carry me to the other room. I am so grateful to you for bringing dinner, since we couldn't come to The Lodge. I hope to see you again, soon."

"No problem. I enjoyed your company, as well, and it never hurts to have a beautiful woman around to brighten up the atmosphere. Will, when you come back, let's talk."

Will carried me into the bedroom and tried to make me comfortable. I was tired, my ankle throbbed, and I was worried about all the other things we had to do this week. Will kissed me and said quietly, "You were amazing, how did you see that so quickly on the blueprints?"

"I looked up. People always forget ceilings, ductwork, and roofs. They don't look up."

Every time I peel another layer off your onion, it's mind-blowing. Is there anything you can't do?"

"Yes, swim."

Will said with a surprised look, "You can't swim? Well, when I teach you, just know that you're not allowed to pee in the pool like you did on my feet in the shower." He started walking back to the kitchen, smiling and shaking his head.

"We'll leave that to another day," I said laughing.

Will went back to the kitchen to finish up the evening with Tad. Tad was having another glass of wine and said to Will "I called for the van, they're on the way to pick me up. I'm impressed. You and Sam really are quite the team. You need to marry that woman, Will, she's the whole package. I'd still be married if I had a woman like that to go through life with. I tried four times, but I'd try a fifth time for someone like her."

The van came and as Tad was leaving, he handed Will a check for half the fee, "I look forward to seeing your full report. Email me at the address on my card here, let's say, by next Saturday." Tad and Will shook hands, and the evening ended on a positive note for the family security business.

Will was stoked and so proud of Sam. She had made that deal work and he was always blown away by how smart she was. She handled Tad with finesse and had locked him into the deal before he even knew he was locked in. She knew we could juggle this deal and work on the case too. I hoped she was correct.

Will cleaned up the dishes, wiped down the kitchen counters, and went to see if Sam needed anything. He was hoping she needed him.

284

I was sitting in bed reading when Will came in from the kitchen. He sat next to me and kissed my forehead. "Thanks, I really mean it. You sealed that deal. This could be our future, a future where I'm gone less and making more money to take care of us and able give you everything you want."

"Will, I don't need material things. I already have everything I want. I do like the idea of you being gone less. I want you to be fulfilled in your work, to be happy and to do what you love."

"I love doing you," he said with longing as his hand drifted over my breasts despite my sweater.

"What time is Franklin coming tomorrow?" I asked while stifling a yawn and starting to arch my back in response to what he was doing.

"Around nine or so." Will replied distracted. "I want to ask you something, and I'm not trying to rush you, but you never asked me for anything in the shower to satisfy you. I hate when things feel one-sided and I'm the one who is ahead."

I told him my desires, though they came up short on what he hoped for, but he smiled, "I can do that. Whatever you want."

FORTY

Sunday morning and my ankle was still killing me, but I'd be damned if I'd take any pain medications. I got through two agonizing years without them and could do it again. The pain makes me sharper, with more clarity and that's what I needed right now.

Will has been taking care of me and it's the first time he's had to. I look at him as he hovers, trying to anticipate what I need, when I need it. He's trying to make up for when I didn't allow him to do anything. I'm still not feeling well either. The last time this case was in my life I felt sick in the same way. Maybe this is just coming from emotion and not physical.

Will came into the bedroom and offered me an update on his activities. "I finished the dishes, swept the floor and put a load of towels in the washer. Do you need anything? Do you need to go to the bathroom? Do you need me?"

"You know you don't have to do all of that. I appreciate you taking care of me, but I think you need some air. I'm good for now."

"Do you mind if I go down to the stables and talk to Jess about things? I need to give him a heads-up. I owe him that. I'm going to put the alarm on when I head down there. I don't want to take any chances." He turned to leave, and I saw his 9mm holstered on his belt.

"That's a good idea. Could you leave me a bottle of water, the waste can, my laptop, and move my gun within reach of my hand?"

Will gathered up what I requested, along with my phone. "Call me if you need something. I'll come right back." Will walked over to the bed and sat on the edge. "I still feel like we need to talk more about all of this. I never thought we could have a fight like that. It really shook me to my core. I need to know that we're okay. I never want to lose you, and I was an ass yesterday. I'm sorry."

I reached for him. "Come closer, I love you. We still need to clear things up. It's been a lot to process, but I'm not going anywhere." I kissed this man I adored and as I was releasing the kiss, he held on and kissed me deeper, lingering still with a little fear in the touch of his lips. I understand this man I plan on spending my life with, he just needs time to figure it out for himself.

"I'll be back as soon as I can, but I really need to talk to Jess. I love you, Sam." As he left the bedroom, he turned around, and said with a smile in his voice, "Tomorrow we get married."

Will put the house alarm on and headed down to the stables. He needed to talk to Jess. Jess was the medicine man of the Tribe, but also like a brother to Will and very wise.

Jess saw Will approaching. "I wondered how long it would take you to come and talk to me. You took thunder into your home yesterday and the earth heard it. You created a storm that is still simmering and could erupt again if you do not take my teachings to heart. I need to counsel you on how to bring the peace back. Your blood pressure only rises because you and Sam are not settled. You cannot have barriers with each other, there can be no closed doors, not even in your house."

Will looked at Jess and agree. "Yes, I broke Sam's heart and I need to heal it. I've hurt her in many ways, some out of fear, and I don't know how to fix it. Please help me Jess. She is everything to me. She is my life."

Jess came up to Will and put his arm around his shoulder. "Let us sit down and I will begin to teach you how to repair what you have broken through fear."

The two Cheyenne brothers sat down, cleansed themselves with sage and said a prayer to begin the lesson of "surrender".

Jess began. "In all of our lives we need to say, "I surrender". The surrender can be to our heart's very beat or to the Universe itself. Surrender is not weakness; it is the realization that strength can sometimes break what we want to keep safe. When you are brought together by Visions, it does not mean that you still do not have to nurture and tend to the Vision's gift. Visions are a road map to your soul's destiny, but if you veer off the road you could change that very destiny written by the spirits. You and Sam had double Visions and the strength of that means you are so tightly bound to each other that you dream each other's dreams. It can last a lifetime depending on the equality of sacrifice of each soul or dream partner gives. When Sam's heart stopped for those three minutes, she lived in her Vision place, then you and Brandon pulled her back to this plane of existence. She has been clinging to the feeling the Vision gave her when she died that she does not feel here."

Will was listening to every word Jess spoke because he knew he had to be the one to mend and stabilize his tether to Sam, just like he did when he pulled her from death. As Jess taught him the lessons he never had to learn before, he touched the watch he never took off, the one Sam gifted him that gave him custody of her time. She trusted him with this, and he needed to show her he had earned her trust.

"You have to understand, Will, that just because we made Sam Cheyenne does not mean the transition has happened for her yet. Sam still has ties to her old life. For her to sever those ties completely she needs to feel that she is grounded in her new life. You call her your wife, yet you have not completed that passage for her, and she is susceptible to the winds that blow. She does not belong here or there. She is in limbo with her own being. It is up to you, Will, to bring her willingly into your world."

"Jess, what did you mean by equality of sacrifice?"

"Let us compare what sacrifices Sam had to endure to come to you, into your world, and then we will see what you have done to draw her here and to make her want to stay. Sam took a bullet meant for your life force to end, she did that willingly and with love. The result of that took her on a two-year long journey of physical *pain, handling the negative forces of the Bureau on her very spirit and eventually giving up everything she knew of her almost forty years to come to you at your place of comfort. She, without complaint, changed her career, her place of residence, and her whole old existence to be with you. Despite her offerings to you, she was still without an anchor from you. Yes, you built her a house, but it was not quite her home with her having no sense of permanence. Do her boxes remain unpacked? Has she nested by acquiring furniture or is this house still empty of her very person?"*

Will had not realized, had not seen, and he felt ashamed. "Jess, can I fix this, or have I lost everything because I have been blind. All I thought of was what my sacrifice had been; waiting almost two years for her to come to me, but that was her sacrifice too. I have really done nothing. I am in the comfort of my native surroundings, my friends are here, the work that I enjoy, and a wonderful woman is here for me, waiting for me to see what she needs. I've been a failure. I've asked her to be Cheyenne, to be my wife on my terms and timeline, to change herself, the very DNA that makes her brave and needing to keep safe those she loves while she asks nothing but one thing of me and I failed to give it to her."

"It is not too late, Will. When a strong, capable woman becomes vulnerable because she is seeking a sign of love's commitment, the love she has becomes weak, it can bring a man to his knees who has relied on her to be the cornerstone of his own strength. A man feels helpless and that is where you are right now. At Sam's weakest, she is still stronger than most. Sam's strength has come at a high price which she has paid many times. She is paying now. You are making her pay. You both need to surrender before another payment comes due. She will surrender her ties to her old life when you surrender your fear and marry her."

"All she wanted was a wedding ring on both of our fingers and I was making her wait, like I waited for her. I didn't even know it, but I was penalizing her. She isn't one hundred percent here because I haven't made it possible for her to be here." Will was distraught.

Jess leaned back in his chair and said "My wife told me a story her mother told her and maybe it will help you understand some things about women. Women float above everything in life, and they see everything. They are like the eagles that fly above us. They see all those they are responsible for; they see the needs of everyone in their care and they figure out how to solve all the problems that are put into their hands. We orbit around our women. They have a gravitational force that keeps us able to stand on this earth. Without women, we would fly off the earth without direction and lose ourselves in the atmosphere. Men are simple, women are complicated. It is one of the great mysteries of the Universe. Their complexities give them abilities we can only aspire to."

Will looked at Jess. "I need a few minutes to absorb what you are telling me. I want to call Sam and see if she needs anything. I also want to take a minute with Sampson." Will stood up and went into the shed row and called Sam. "Hi, are you doing, okay? Do you need anything, babe? I know I've been down here longer than I thought, but if you need me to come back I will. Okay, as long as you're feeling better. I will be back soon. I love you." Then Will went over to Sampson, the horse Sam gave him for his birthday, and put his forehead against Sampson's trying to absorb some of the horse's spirit. Will got his knife out and cut some of Sampson's tail hair off to have a bracelet made for Sam for their marriage. Will came back to Jess' office, "Let's continue."

"What is your worst fear, Will?"

"That I will lose her, and my life will be over."

"Your fear holds her too tight, and she is struggling with that. You cannot marry her with the fear you carry. Your sacrifice to her needs to be giving up your crutch of fear. To loosen your grip on her and give her some freedom to be who she is."

"When you marry her, your fear must be gone. The marriage will then bring peace. Your fear has always made you think that what you and Sam have is fragile and easily broken instead of what it is, bars of steel no one can break except for you. You cannot outrun yourself. You have to accept her Cheyenne name, "She who stands with the warriors." When you can do this, you will both be happy forever. When you give up the fear, she will surrender and hand over what she will no longer need, control of taking care of everything and everyone."

"Jess, I asked her to have a child with me even before we married yet she said yes to make me happy when she still needed what I hadn't given her. She made

the appointment for the reversal of my vasectomy when I should have done that myself. I said I would move the marriage date up, but didn't, because of fear I would become my father and hurt her. I don't seem to follow through on what I promise, but I want things from her. She never says no to me."

"You are a better man Will because of Sam, but you have to stay on that journey, you can still be more. She deserves more because your woman is pregnant with your child. The child will be a girl. She does not know it yet, but she is about two to three weeks. I can tell, I have many sons. Do not tell her yet or it will alter how she lives the next few weeks. She cannot know this, or she will not be strong enough to fight what has come into your lives. When this resolves itself, she will know, and she will tell you."

"That can't be, Jess, I haven't had the reversal procedure." Will's eyes were tearing up, he couldn't believe it. If it was true, he would be so happy and proud. "She's been sick with the flu, dizzy, tired, and emotional. Why did I not see it?"

"Have yourself tested, but when your universe collided with Sam's you became viable again for her, only her. Trust what I tell you. Now go to your woman, make her your wife before this child becomes known to her, and leave your fear behind."

I called Will on his phone and lamented. "I tried to get up to go to the bathroom on my own, but the crutches are in the kitchen, and it wasn't working without them. "Will, is it possible for you come back to the house and help me? I need to get up."

"I'll be right there, don't move."

Will looked at Jess and said, "My future needs me. Thanks for all the wisdom. I know what I need to do now to right the wrongs. Come to the house when Franklin arrives, I need you to hear what Sam has to say." With that Will ran up to the house to take care of Sam.

FORTY-ONE

Will had called Franklin, the Tribal Police Chief, asking him to stop by the house so we could fill him in on what was going on and to see how he might be able to help us. Will wanted Jess in the meeting as well, since danger might come to this place, and he had to be prepared. We all needed to take precautions and with my injured ankle, I was not going to be able to participate as much, at least on foot. Franklin would be here any minute and Will was making coffee.

Since his talk with Jess, Will was seeing Sam in a new way. He looked for the signs that Jess saw of her being with child. Will's world just got larger and the looming responsibilities he would have only filled him with love and excitement. He knew how to make everything right now. He would give Sam everything she wanted and everything she needed. He would bring harmony to this life of theirs. He would be what she needed.

Franklin drove up at the same time Jess was walking up to the house. Jess saw Franklin and inquired, "Chief, long time since we crossed paths. How is your position in life?"

"It is conflicting, but I try to find a middle ground. How are you, your wife and five sons?"

"We are thriving, thank you for asking."

Will had the door open before they could knock. He made his greetings and offered coffee saying, "I'll get Sam, so we can get started."

When Will walked into the bedroom to take me into the kitchen, I was vomiting my breakfast into the waste can. "I can't seem to shake this flu Will."

Will knew it wasn't the flu, but couldn't say anything to Sam, it had to come from her. She gave him everything he's ever asked for from her. He would spend the rest of his life giving her whatever she wanted and needed.

"It will pass, with your ankle and everything going on, it just needs to run its course."

"Can we make a bathroom detour, so I can brush my teeth again? I don't want to speak to our company without doing so." Will waited while I brushed my teeth, then picked me up and carried me into the kitchen, sat me down, and used a second chair to elevate my leg. He gave me a bottle of water, a cup of tea, and had all the files and evidence in piles for me to easily access.

I looked at our guests and apologized. "Sorry for your inconvenience at having to come to the house, but my ankle has sidelined me a bit. I want to explain what is going on, and I especially owe you the details Franklin, since you did me a favor. I hope nothing has blown back on you because of that."

"Sam, nothing I couldn't handle. You did promise to explain things, so I appreciate your doing so. I'd like to think we have an understanding with each other and did not want to affect my friendship with Will." Franklin said it in a way to make sure Will didn't have his feelings hurt by not being told of what I had asked Franklin to do for me.

Will looked at Franklin, smiled, and then confirmed, "She's hard to say no to, I understand. There is no problem, and our friendship remains very strong."

Jess continued to drink his coffee as he looked intensely at me. "Sam how is your flu?"

"I am not sure it is the flu. I think it may be the stress of the last week or so. I'm sure it will pass in time. Thanks for asking as to my well-being."

"You are family."

For the next couple of hours, I went over the story, starting a timeline from my birthday January 8 forward. I showed them all the evidence and Will took them to the garage to see the tire. I could see Jess and Franklin listening intently, each having their own reasons for wanting to help me and Will with this situation. They asked few questions and by the time I had finished, they nodded as to understanding what was at stake.

Jess was the first to talk. "I will make sure the security alarms, sprinkler systems in the stables in case of fire and other facilities are activated around the clock. I will arrange with my sons to take shifts to make sure the horses and property do not come into peril. We will carry our side arms and be prepared. We will not let harm come to Sam. I also have all the trips covered while Will stays with Sam this week and into next week. I will call in help from the families Sam gave justice to and they will be here tomorrow to help any way they can. Even though some are from different Tribes, when it comes to Sam, it does not matter to them."

Franklin added, "I will have my deputies do grid searches for this perp in town and around your property. If the Feds are doing this to you Sam, we will make sure to use that to our advantage. They do not know old Indian tricks and we are proficient at them. I want to put a deputy on the house if Will is not home and will personally get my contact and inside connection at the Bureau to get me the name on those fingerprints that I ran for you. The Montana Bureau does not push their weight as does DC, but we will keep everything under the radar. I and my department will not let anything happen to you Sam. We would not want to see what Will might do if anyone tried to hurt you."

Will made an announcement during the lull of the conversation, "Sam and I will be going into town tomorrow to the Courthouse, so we won't be here in the morning." And he left it at that, but Jess and Franklin knew what it meant and nodded to the affirmative.

We took a few minutes to formulate some plans, covering different circumstances, and then everyone left to enjoy what was left of the day. As they headed for the door, Franklin and Jess took time to hug me and to tell me they had my back. The men who surrounded me were brave and gave me a sense of safety in this new life I was living with Will.

Will washed the coffee cups and wiped down the island. I watched this man I loved busying himself, taking care of all the little things he knows I like to have done. He saw me watching, he smiled, came over and carried me to the bedroom so I would be more comfortable. When he saw I was situated just right in the bed, he sat by me and said in a comforting way, "These are good men, Sam, men who will make sure you are safe. They are family and friends who when braided into the likes of you, are bound by their instincts to protect you."

I wanted to do one final cleanse of the air from the night we fought, to have it put behind us before we marry tomorrow. I urged Will to come closer. "Will, I want you to talk to me about you. I want to understand when things changed for you. How you got past the fear today. When you started believing that what we have is strong. I feel like if we hadn't had the argument, it wouldn't have changed things for you or for us. You can tell me anything. I won't judge."

Will came closer, looked in my eyes, tucked my hair behind my shoulders, and tried to figure out what he would say in answer to what I needed for us to put it to rest, to have a final healing. "I think you're right. That argument broke me, and I had to choose between being who you needed or losing you. I wasn't going to lose you. God, Sam, losing you was not an option. The fear made me weak. Fear of seeing what we had gone through before being repeated, fear that I couldn't protect you, even fear of other men looking at you, and fear that what we had was fragile, too new, too rare to be strong. When I finally got out of my own way and listened to what you had to say, what you needed, I could finally see things clearer. It also helped me talking to Jess, he saw things I couldn't because I was blind to the reality, and he counseled me." Will could see his hands shake and felt himself getting emotional. He felt things more since Sam, that was new and sometimes difficult to control.

I put my finger to Will's lips, "You don't have to go on, you're getting upset. I don't want to push you or force you to feel all this again."

"No, I want to Sam, I need to. I was trying to hold you so tightly that you couldn't breathe. I was trying to keep you to myself, afraid that if you saw that I was just a work in progress trying to be the man you thought you came home to, that you'd have second thoughts. What scared me most was, that as strong as you are, capable, able to handle things, you were vulnerable and needed me to take the control from you, you didn't want it anymore. This was the tipping point for me, I chose you instead of the fear." Will cleared his throat and got up to get a bottle of water.

He sat back down next to me, and I ran my fingers through his hair. "We are all just works in progress, Will. We need to talk to each other more. I need to know when I come up short in being what you need and want. I had always been on my own and had to learn to release the control I thought I had to keep because that's what I always had to do. That was hard for me, but I knew you'd catch me, take care of me, handle things."

Will handed me the water bottle, smiled and continued. "I never thought I could feel the range of emotions that being with you brings out in me. The love I feel for you, and for this life we are living together. I never experienced anything like this, ever in my life, and I was foolish thinking it would slip through my fingers like a dream. After we fought, and we fought so hard, I couldn't believe we came out on the other side and that's when I really believed we were forever. That our love was so strong and could get us through anything."

"We are forever, and what we have is strong. Will, I'd like to put that night behind us. I don't want to keep it as a memory. I want us to move forward. Do we need to talk about it anymore? I will if you need to."

Will put his arm around me, drew me closer, and whispered, "Lessons learned. I'm going to make us some dinner now, you rest here. Every time I think I couldn't love you more, you show me a new way." Will kissed me and looked like he found his peace. I could finally breathe again.

FORTY-TWO

Will woke me at six am. I looked at him and asked in my sleepy voice, "Are you going down to the stables?"

"No, babe," Will answered, excitement in his tone. "I'm going to help you get dressed so we can go down to the Courthouse. Do you want me to help you in the shower?"

"Will, slow down. Are you sure this is what you want? Give up those ceremonies and traditions? Where is this coming from?" I asked, half-awake.

"We're getting married today. You want this, I want this. We don't wait for anything anymore." Will came over to the bed, sat on the edge, looking at my nakedness and whispered, with love seeping out through all of his pores, "I love you with everything thing I am, and I want to be your husband today. I want that ring on my finger, and I want you as my legal, true wife with a ring on your finger too, showing the world, we belong to each other." With that said, he touched my nipples, picked me up, and took me to the shower.

Will was pacing with excitement. He looked so happy. He wore his best black dress slacks, a pressed white shirt, and the boots he was most proud of — special ones from Lucchese. I found a black skirt in the closet so I didn't have to wear sweats, and a pale pink cashmere sweater Will always admired when I wore it. I needed to find one shoe I could walk in. My hair was down and cooperating with my efforts for a change, I put a little makeup on, and stood in the middle of the bedroom on crutches looking a bit like a deer in the headlights, but ready.

My soon to be husband bounded into the room, informed me that he had the papers we needed from the safe, showed me that he had the rings, and then looked at me. "You look really beautiful. Are you ready? I called the Courthouse, and the judge is expecting us in an hour."

"Will, I love you, I adore you. I can never say no to you. I just don't want you to have regrets about not having our wedding the way you hoped."

"I want this. I didn't know how much I wanted this. Christian and Scotty are going to meet us there as witnesses and to take pictures. Do you want this, Sam?"

"Yes, Will, dare I say it, I do. By the way, which one of the guys is the bride's maid?"

Will laughed, helped me into my coat, carried me to the car, put my crutches in the back and off we went to our destiny. The ceremony was brief and personal before his friend the Judge and we said the most standard of vows with Scotty and Christian standing in as witnesses. I didn't even notice the surroundings, only the face of my beloved, Will. The situation with Christian had dissolved away because friendship was strong between Will and his friend and unspoken words were understood. Before ten am we were married legally, husband and wife. A sense of calm was felt in both of us. Will kissed me and I could feel a difference, a happiness and sense of permanence in his lips. I hoped he felt the same in mine. I took his left hand to see the ring on his finger, the one with an infinity symbol engraved on the inside — just like mine — I touched it and smiled at this man I couldn't say no to. He smiled at me. "It's never coming off, just like the watch. Let's go home, I think we're supposed to consummate our marriage so it's legal, Mrs. Samantha Wright Little Bear." He never stopped smiling.

Someone had put a "Just Married" sign on the front door of the house, along with a "Do Not Disturb Sign." Will carried me into the house, locked the door, put the alarm on, and while kissing me as he carried me, took our commitment to the bedroom. I stood, trying to stand without crutches, looking at my husband, "I'm nervous Will, it's been eight days since you've been inside of me and I feel like a virgin."

Will leaned my crutches against the wall, put our coats down and walked over to me. He looked at me for the longest time with his soft brown eyes, drawing me in, and with the sexiest of murmurs said, "I'll be gentle."

My new husband of a little over an hour, with his softest of a bedroom voice said his own vows to me, in our home, in our bedroom. "I am a better man because of you, and I promise to always keep trying to be more, to make you proud, keep you satisfied, and make you feel loved. As I promised on our third day together, I will never lie to you or keep secrets from you, and I will be faithful to you. You are my life, and I will do everything to make you happy." He tugged my sweater over my head and dropped it on the floor. My breath was already coming quicker. I was becoming emotional.

He continued, "I will be the man you deserve. I will take care of you and keep you safe without fear." Will unzipped my skirt and it fell to the floor, he helped me to step out of it. "You are my refuge, my center, and my home." He slipped my panties down and off. "I will nurture and keep safe the visions that brought us to this place, this time, this connection." Will removed my bra and looked at me as if it were the first time. "Everything I am, or have, belongs to you and I will love you forever. You are my heart, you share my soul, there is nothing I wouldn't do for you. I love you, my wife. There is no "until death we do part," we will be together as our rings say, for infinity, this plane of existence or some other, we will never part." His mouth took my lips, then my tongue and all the sacrifice, pain, hurt, arguments, and fear were completely replaced by unconditional, undying love.

I wavered on my weak ankle but stood there facing this man — my man — the man I would go through anything this life sends us to handle. He was my life. I unbuttoned his shirt and removed it from his arms that always embrace me, looked in his eyes, and said my vows. "Will, my life before you had no meaning, no substance or love. Since you have been in my heart, I have been a better woman, more fulfilled and satisfied than I thought possible. I will never lie to you, keep secrets from you, and I promise to be faithful, not only as your wife, but your partner, your friend, and your lover." Will slipped his boots off and stood in front of me again so I could unbuckle his belt, unzip his pants and have him step out of them. My voice was shaking with joy. "I don't know what this life will bring, but you and I can endure it all together. I want to be where you find your peace, joy and love. I want to be your home, your sanctuary. I will be your wife in a way that never makes you feel afraid to be who you are." I eased Will's knit boxers down, freeing him from the restraint and exposing him to me. "Will, there will be times we fight, misunderstand, and get hurt, but I promise you, there will always be more than enough love to heal those times, to make the good times so much more and to always keep us strong. My body belongs to you as does my heart, my soul, and my mind. I will love you in this life and any other. I love you my husband and you will always be the guardian of my time."

I kissed my amazing Cheyenne husband, my eyes showing him he was my world, that his culture was also mine. He picked me up and gently laid me on the bed to protect my ankle. He put a pillow under my leg, opened me up to him, and looked for my signal to enter. We would have foreplay after, this was more urgent. This would make everything right again between us. I reached for him and spread my legs further and guided him in. It never felt like this before. This was binding. Two people, two cultures coming together, leaving just one world, ours, in its wake.

The rest of the day and all through the night we sealed our fates with each other. What happened to one happened to the other. I had a funny dream that night. When sleep finally came after Will and I allowed ourselve's to rest, someone was calling me. I was happier than I've ever been in my forty years of life.

FORTY-THREE

The sun was just coming up and Will reached over for me. "Did you sleep well my wife?"

"I did, but I had a funny dream. I need to think about it; it was a little vague. How about you, did you sleep well my husband?"

"Yes, but I kept getting an erection every time I felt you next to me. You were sleeping so deeply I didn't want to wake you."

I reached under the covers, "I see. I'm awake now."

Just as Will rolled closer to me, the phone rang. It was too early for someone to call. Will looked at the caller ID and saw that it was Franklin. He showed me. "Better answer it," I said.

"Franklin, you're up early."

"Will, one of my deputies saw someone fitting the description Sam gave us of the perp loitering in a back alley behind the Post Office just before dawn. Unfortunately, he was quicker than my deputy. He lost him."

I could see Will was concerned. "We're up and keep us posted if anything else develops. Did you let Jess know?"

"Yes, I called him first, so you'd have a little more time to sleep, or whatever. Hey, Will, I hear congratulations are in order. She's a keeper. Sorry to be the one to break up your honeymoon."

"No, we're grateful to know, I'll be in the house with Sam. Thanks Franklin."

Will hung up and turned to me. "So, it begins." He told me what Franklin had briefed him on. We got up after a quick, but satisfying connection, took a shower, and got dressed. My mobility was improving and with the crutches I was at least not having to be carried everywhere, even though Will wouldn't have minded.

"Okay then," I put my Glock in the back waistband of my jeans. Will had cut my left pant leg open to mid-calf so I could get it over the cast. In my right boot, the only boot I could wear was my knife. I stopped in mid thought, looked at my husband and asked with a lump in my throat, "Will, who put the Do Not Disturb Sign on the door yesterday?"

Will had his 9mm holstered and we looked at each other as if we had just let the reality of the coming day in. "I don't know." Somehow our getting married seemed to make everything possible, that we would get through this, that everything would be fine. Will called Jess to check in, inspected the entire house, make sure everything was locked, then he started making breakfast. I still wasn't fascinated by food and this situation was still making me queasy. I had thrown up again this morning again.

Will knew it would pass and needed to make sure Sam ate. She needed to stay healthy and strong, especially now and because she had lost some weight while he was gone. He wanted to make sure she gained it back. She was always so beautiful to him, but dare he say, he liked a little more flesh on her.

"You have to eat something Sam, if just toast and tea. I need you to stay strong in order to get through this." Will encouraged. "I want my wife to eat, okay? Please."

I crutched my way to the chair at the kitchen island, sat myself down, put my leg up on the opposite chair, and complied, "Yes, husband. I'm hungry, and you're right, I'd like eggs too please. While we wait to see how things develop, we can go over the blueprints and start preparing the report for Mr. Collins. I'll type while you dictate. It will keep us from getting crazy with the waiting." I smiled as Will brought my food over and placed it in front of me. "We missed dinner last night you know?"

"Lunch too," he added with a smile.

Will put his breakfast down and came up behind, put his arms around me, caressing me, and whispered in my ear, "I love you, and owe you a honeymoon when this is over. Where do you want to go? Maybe somewhere I can teach you to swim. I can imagine you in a swimsuit." Will placed a gift box in front of me and had a sly smile on his face.

I opened the box and pulled out a one-piece black swimsuit. "When did you have time to get this? I've never owned a swimsuit. I may have to do some additional grooming for this."

"I'll be the one in charge of that," Will laughed.

I looked at his left hand. I touched the ring that now filled that prior void and nodded in acknowledgement. "Someplace with tons of furniture stores, and I'm going to make you shop until you drop loads of money." I began eating my breakfast.

Will laughed and considered it for a moment, "I can do that because my wife landed the Collins' Account."

Will smiled to himself. Sam was starting to have a sense of permanence — slowly, but finally surrendering, starting to leave her other life behind. Furniture would be the start.

One of the worst things in life, especially for someone in law enforcement, is waiting coupled with impatience. Will and I have done our share of waiting, but this was different. No one wants to stand idle while wondering how some other person with ill-intent is going to affect your life. Will was in charge, riding shotgun and doing all the coordination with Jess and Franklin. I was a bit of a liability with my bad ankle, but I could tell that Will was less afraid, less stressed, by being able to call the shots for us. He was protecting me, he needed to get his confidence and control back. It wasn't his responsibility back then to protect me — his priority had been Brandon, and he always felt guilty about that, but I was his wife now, I was his life-long responsibility, and he would shoulder it. He welcomed it. He reveled in it.

A few other sightings took place during the day and were called in by the Tribal Police, but nothing concrete. It was almost five pm and it had been a relatively quiet day. Just when you lull yourself into feeling that you've dodged a bullet, the phone rings and Will answered it with a look on his face that went beyond pissed, he recognized the number and said with agitation, "What is it now Charlie?" as he put the phone on speaker.

"I just wanted to follow up and see if you were able to talk to Sam about that hacking issue, I had previously called you about?" Will was silent for a minute. "Will, can you hear me?"

"Charlie, I did some checking on that and that hack came from the town library computer, not Sam's, so I think you may have been misinformed. There are a lot of people around here who were affected by that case. People may still want answers to their questions," Will replied as calmly as possible.

"I forgot you're a security and computer expert, Will. Well, perhaps there was an error in judgment based on the fact it came from your locale. An assumption must have been made. Hey, could I speak with Sam just to get verification and close out this inquiry?"

While Will kept Charlie on the line, I was on the laptop trying to trace the origin of his call to see if Charlie himself was in Montana or still back in DC. I pinged his phone number in Bozeman and showed Will.

"I'll get her on the phone. Hold on Charlie."

"Charlie, so how's DC treating you? What did you want to ask me?" I asked in a light-hearted manner.

"It's Spring here, you always liked the cherry blossoms. I just needed to get confirmation from you directly if you tried to hack the Bureau's server."

"What kind of question is that, Charlie? Someone's misdirecting you. I've been busy getting married to Will. So, what is the phrase? I can neither confirm nor deny." I'll put Will back on. I'm making dinner for my husband. Good speaking with you Charlie, enjoy Spring in DC."

"Anything else we can help you with, Charlie?" Will asked while I phoned Franklin. I was hoping he could call his friend at the Montana Bureau to re-verify that Charlie was in Bozeman.

"No, I think that's it. Oh, congratulations on the marriage. Sam's a great woman. She's the best, you're a lucky guy." And he hung up before Will could say anything more.

Charlie threw his phone across the room, and it shattered. "Fuck, she married him. This complicates things for me."

"Good job, Sam." Will came over and kissed me, smiled and laughed, "I'll bet that pissed him off."

Will knew Charlie was in love with Sam, always had been. He wanted me to screw up so he can swoop in and save the day — try to take Sam away. That was never going to happen.

FORTY-FOUR

Will and I took turns sleeping. Jess had the lights on at the stables all night, his sons carrying side arms, rotating shifts. The alarm systems on every structure, as well as the house were on twenty-four hours a day. The horses were never alone, neither was I. Jess went out on a few hunting trips, and when The Lodge van came with the hunters and fishermen, security heightened. The clients never really noticed a change, and business went on as usual, but we took no chances.

Franklin called the next morning and confirmed Charlie was in Bozeman. We also heard from Franklin that the local sporting goods shop had a break in the night before. Climbing ropes, a shotgun, ammunition, camo hunting outerwear and hiking boots had been taken. The security cameras showed a slightly built white man hold up a sign to the camera, "I'm coming for you Sam." This piece of information unnerved Will for a minute, then his anger clicked in, and he was in Marine mindset. Franklin informed us he hadn't heard back from his contact on the fingerprint yet. Seems the Bureau did a lockdown on access to one particular file, my file. There was also no sign of

Charlie, he hadn't called again or shown up, of which both were expected.

By Friday it was getting tedious. Sometimes at night there were noises, Will and I would check the house, outside lights were on and Franklin's deputies were at various places on the property keeping watch. Noises on the roof were usually caused by the sounds a metal roof makes in wind, rain, or expansion and contraction, depending on weather. Friday night was especially loud. Spring here in Montana sometimes brings thunderstorms, lightning, high winds, hail, and cold nights. Friday night had it all but for the hail. Will did an outside inspection but didn't see anything out of the ordinary. Franklin's guys also kept an eye on the roof and the decks.

Will and I managed to get the report for Mr. Collins completed and sent it to him in a secure email. I thought he would be impressed as to the comprehensive and extensive complexities of the report he would receive. The company who drew up the blueprints were so inadequate in their recommendations that bordered on negligence and/or incompetence. I don't know how much they charged Mr. Collins, but he should demand a refund or at least relieve them from their contract. Having our security analysis job helped fill in the mundane gaps of waiting — a favorite of law enforcement when out on surveillance — except they usually drink too much coffee and eat too much fast food or donuts to fill the time.

Will and I tried to get a little newlywed romance in, but our minds weren't one hundred percent there, and we decided we'd rather wait until this was over and done, than trying to short-change ourselves in the love department. We would have our whole lives to catch up. We didn't want our guard or our pants down if something happened.

Saturday came and went with nothing significant to report. On Sunday, Will had to cover security at the barn for a few hours while Jess took care of a horse with colic. It was March, but the weather could still be cold, and today was one of those days. I decided to spread the case files out in my unfurnished upstairs office to see if I could come up with anything, mainly just to fill the time. I like sitting on the floor with my work all around me. My office was cold, so I started a fire in the fireplace to take the chill off. I often came up here to work and built a fire, writing in this atmosphere helped my process. I opened the damper, lit the kindling, and got a nice fire going. Instead of the smoke from the fire venting out it came into the room, covering me with black smoke and as I tried to see what was blocking the chimney, I got a headful of soot dumped on me. I went coughing to the closet, in search of the fire extinguisher to put out the fire, trying to stop all the black smoke. My office was filled with smoke, soot, and fire extinguisher residue. I needed to see what was blocking the chimney. I grabbed my Maglite and as I opened the door from my office to the upper deck without thinking; it was the only exit without going downstairs, I set off the house alarm or by this time the smoke may have set it off, it was a tossup, but the noise was hurting my ears and the smoke was burning my eyes.

Will heard the alarm and started checking the panels at the barn and stables when he realized it was the house alarm. Sam was at the house; he took off running, his heart in his throat. As he was sprinting towards the house, he saw Sam on the second story roof, crawling with her bad ankle and trying to get to the chimney. Franklin's deputy ran up alongside Will, keeping pace and asked, "Isn't that your wife? Why is she all black? Why is she on the roof?"

"Call the fire department and call Franklin." Will yelled as he ran up the front deck and into the house. He had his gun drawn and checked all the rooms in the house only to find them clear. He then ran upstairs to Sam's office, opened the door and walked into black smoke filling the air. He shut off the alarm using his cell and called to Sam.

I had gone out on the deck, coughing, and trying to breath some clean air. I found an easy access to the roof since the roofline sloped down low in this area of the house. I needed to see what was stuck in the chimney to prevent the house from burning down. I crawled up — not easily done — trying not to slip with the inflatable cast on my foot. Yes, I knew this was stupid, but I was climbing on adrenaline and really didn't think of the consequences. I had my gun in my back waistband and the Maglite stuck down my sweater, between my breasts so both my hands were free to climb. I climbed towards the chimney, turned on my Maglite, drew my gun, and looked down into the opening. I had figured an animal might have gotten stuck inside and blocked the air flow, but it was an animal of a different sort. It was the white man I had seen taunting me — stalking me — the third brother. He looked as if he had been stuck in the chimney for a couple of days. For just a moment I wanted to shoot him; fear filled my throat with bile, but I holstered my gun and shut off the Maglite, thinking he was dead from exposure to the cold weather we had the last few nights. The moment I dropped my guard, his hands grabbed the front of my sweater and pulled me forward, then down, closer, until I was eye to eye with the loathsome creature. His smile not unlike his brothers was sinister and empty. I pulled myself back, trying to loosen his grip on me. He was stuck and as I pulled to get free, he lost his grip. I tumbled backward, and as I slid down the roof, seeing the edge coming, I flailed my hands in an effort to grab on to anything to stop my momentum from descent over the edge. I lessened my fall by grabbing onto the gutter with my one hand, bending it with my weight as I went over the side. It wasn't a far drop, but I ended up on the deck, flat on my back with a thud and my ankle screaming and as I was wincing from the feel of my gun in the middle of my back, looked up and saw the third brother staring down at me. He was grinning at me, seemingly superior from where he stood. He had gotten himself out of the chimney and was hell bent on finishing me. Before I could think how incredulous this seemed, he yelled "for my brothers" and leapt on top of me, straddling me, and as I felt his filthy hands coming towards my throat, I heard a gun shot. I don't even know when I pulled the gun from my back, but the sound came from my gun, the blood spatter came from the third brother's brain. The spatter was warm and nauseated me for a moment. He had a surprised look to his face as he crumbled on top of me, taking his last breath in this world. I grimaced, pushed him off and climbed back up on the roof to get away from him and the blood that continued to escape that cavity I had blown in his head. I needed fresh air to breathe – to get the smell of his death out of my nose. I needed to make sure no one else was in the chimney, like another brother.

I saw Will climbing up onto the roof and coming towards me. I sat down, forgetting I was covered head-to-toe with soot, remnants of black smoke, and bloody brain matter. Was I relieved, or just in shock? Either way, I handle life with humor and smiled to myself, what were the odds for a third brother, crazy triplets.

"Sam, are you okay? What are you doing on the roof? You know there's a dead guy on the deck below? What a bloody mess." Will was shouting questions and comments as he tried to catch his breath. He ran his hands over me to make sure it wasn't my blood I was wearing. As he looked at me, he was trying not to laugh or cry, but his emotions came out in a sound that a hurt animal would release. I needed to break the tension, or we would both cry.

"Will, we need a chimney sweep, a cover for the chimney, and some kind of alarm for it in the future. I started a fire in my office because I was cold. I opened the damper, but then the smoke billowed in at me. I tried to check the damper and soot came out covering my head. I used the extinguisher to put out the fire then came out here to investigate," I said in a very weary way and handed him the Maglite. "Look for yourself." My head nodded towards the chimney.

Seeing Sam was calm in a weird, relieved way, and physically alright, Will took the Maglite, crawled to the chimney and peered inside seeing a rope, remants of torn clothing, and a shot gun wedged in. He looked at me and then back down the chimney opening. "You're right we need a chimney sweep." He came and sat next to me on the roof; his hands shook a bit, and he was pale. He looked at my face, "You have a little something and took his finger as to wipe it off. Why didn't you call me instead of venturing up here alone?"

"I figured you would hear the alarm. Besides my phone was charging in the kitchen and I needed some air and to see what was blocking the chimney."

"Are you okay? A third brother? What are the odds?" He was rambling.

"No, I'm not okay." I smiled as a quick tear escaped my eye. "Seems anti-climactic after all these months. I'm feeling cheated out of a real fight. Cripes, he was six feet from getting inside the house and now he will be six feet under. One shot, I only got one shot. You sure he's dead. The deck, well, that's a mess blocking our way back into the house."

Will held onto me and shook his head yes while he answered to confirm my hope, "Yes, he's dead, head shot, I checked on my way up here."

We could hear and see the Volunteer Fire Department coming, followed by Franklin's Tribal Police, fully decked out Suburban, lights flashing, sirens screaming. Will and I both knew that this could have gone "really badly" if the perp had been able to slide the rest of the way down the chimney and get into the house. He must have gotten snagged on a "L" bracket and couldn't get himself loose. He probably had gotten in there Friday night during the storm, it would have masked his sounds, and the deputies didn't see him during the storm. He only unhooked himself when he was trying to pull me in, my backward momentum freed him. We both shook our heads like trying to shake out dark clouds. We didn't want our thoughts to go there because we would fall apart and then on second thought, we both realized this was relatively easy compared to our last adventure together. We were both okay and the bad guy was dead. Will took my hand, looked at me, shook his head again and sighed. I kind of smiled and thought of Dr. Sampson, he was right; always look up.

"Will, I don't think I can get down off the roof — it was easier coming up. My ankle hurts from falling off and from that piece of shit jumping on me." It seemed higher now from this perch perspective and trying to get down with a bad, aching, ankle wasn't going to be easy. The adrenaline that had bolstered me on the way up had run its course, depleted, and left me exhausted.

Will called Franklin and updated him. "There's no fire in the house, but we need the Fire Department to get Sam off the roof." We couldn't go through my office with the dead guy blocking the way. Franklin was now at the front driveway on his cell with Will, he looked up and saw us sitting on the second story roof. We waved to him, and Will gave him some additional directions.

"Franklin, you need to get your team up here, take some prints, photos, and make sure what's in the chimney doesn't fall into Sam's office. It is evidence. I need backup documentation on this in case the Feds play games when they show up. Also make sure your guys know Sam's office is a crime scene now, and not to disturb things in the fireplace, except to take pictures. Get her case files off the floor, boxed, and taken out to the barn. Those are Sam's files. We'll be calling the Feds next. Oh, and check the other two chimneys just in case. Hey, Franklin, Will added, the perp is dead on the deck outside Sam's office, it's going to be tough to clean up."

Franklin answered, "Copy that Will. What? Why is Sam all black and bloody? Is she hurt?"

Will looked at me. I looked at him. "Franklin she isn't hurt but her ankle is causing a problem"

"Will, you have some black on your face from the smoke." I informed him.

Will smiled and asked, while trying to stifle a laugh, "Have you looked in the mirror?"

"How bad do I look?"

"Well, Franklin could see you from down there. We'll get you down from the roof and get a towel for you. I don't know how you do it; you're covered in blood, soot and smoke and yet you still look beautiful?"

"Will, we might be wearing evidence. I can't go into the house with that thing on the deck blocking my office door. Are there any clothes left at the apartment over the stables?"

"Maybe some sweats, possibly some t-shirts," Will replied just as the Fire Department's ladder was placed against the roof and one of the firefighters started crawling up the roof towards us, trying not to laugh at the sight he saw.

I was helped carefully off the roof and down the ladder. I left in my wake black soot on their uniforms and smiles on their faces.

"Will, may I use your cell to call Charlie? You know I'm going to start cursing? I plan on being very dramatic. I'm frustrated and need to take it out on Charlie."

Will handed me the phone and followed me as I headed to the apartment over the stables, limping without my crutches until Will decided to pick me up and carry me to help speed things up. I dialed and waited for Charlie to answer.

"Charlie, it's Sam. Yes, this is Will's phone. Get your fucking ass to our house and get your dead perp off our deck. Don't give me that shit, you're not in DC, you're in Bozeman. Get your team over here and get your manipulative, self-absorbed, abuse-of-power-self over here NOW!" I hung up before Charlie could respond.

Will smiled at me as he opened the door to the apartment. As he carried me in, he remarked, "I like when you talk that way to Charlie." As an aside, Will commented, "I thought you were giving up cursing."

"Yes, but today's not the day. You've cursed in the last week yourself, mister."

"You're right, I'm a bad example. We'll start over tomorrow on that cursing ban."

"Just so you know I liked how you gave out orders to Franklin. I like it when you take charge. You can order me around tonight in bed if you want."

Will put me down and smiled. "I'll think about that."

I went to the bathroom, saw myself in the mirror and just stood there looking at my reflection for a minute. "Cripes Will, why didn't you tell me? I don't have a little something, I've got a lot of something all over me." I was nauseated at my reflection knowing what was on me.

Will laughed and shrugged his shoulders, "I'll check to see what clothes are still around here for you to change into."

"Do you have a trash bag? I'll need to put these clothes I have on in the bag as evidence." I asked, as I started to get undressed. "Jeez, Will, even my underwear is black." I tried to wipe the blood, soot and smoke off my face, but my hair was full of it and kept raining down on my face, and onto the rest of me. "I need to shower. Will, maybe we'd have time for a lifted-ride in the shower before the Feds show." I was feeling like I had a buzz after drinking and needed physical comfort to get myself back to reality. I didn't want to fall apart before Charlie showed up.

Will quickly gabbed my bra and panties from my hands as I was putting them into the bag. He shoved them into his jeans pocket, "They don't need my wife's underwear for evidence. That's really a small shower, it will be tight."

"Right. Got carried away. Thanks babe. My adrenaline is running high again, it's distracting me from the task at hand."

Just as I was going to step into the shower with my foot wrapped in another trash bag, and as I continued my efforts to tempt my husband with a quickie straddle, Jess yelled up to us that the Feds were coming down the road. Charlie must have been closer than I thought. I was standing naked, a trash bag on my leg, blackened by who knows what, and had to get out there to talk to them — well, just to Charlie. Will came over and held out his hand, "I found these sweatpants and this long-sleeved t-shirt. I think they belong to Jess."

I shook my brain infused, sooty hair, out as best I could, pulled it back into a ponytail, grabbed the clothes, and got dressed going commando. The clothes were huge on me, and I had to tie the shirt around my waist, hold the pants up with my one hand, grab the trash bag of evidence, my gun, and badge with my other hand. Will was standing there looking at me with his hands on his hips, and said clearing his throat, "Sam, you don't have a bra on and its cold outside. You know, uh, your nipples, well, they can be, uh, big and it's a white shirt."

"Will at this point no one will notice; I am still covered in muck, and this white shirt isn't going to stay white for long. Please carry me over to the house so I can talk to Charlie when he shows up." I wasn't thinking about what I was wearing, I was thinking about what I wanted to say to Charlie.

Will decided to pick his battles and nipples were low priority, right now. He still remembered that night when he first saw her nipples through her shirt at The

319

Lodge and couldn't get them out of his head. "She has no idea how she affects me sometimes when I just look at her. I'm in a constant state of "wanting" with her."

Will picked me up and had some black soot transferred from me to his face, hands and clothes. He looked pointedly at me and said in a firm voice, "You're done with them Sam, no more Bureau, right? They used you, used us. I can't even think about what could have happened if that guy had gotten in the house, gotten to you. You resign, okay? I don't want to debate this."

"Right, no argument from me. No debate, I'm done with them."

I kissed Will despite the black transfer, and he didn't mind. I said to my new husband, "We fought too hard to have this life of ours, I will not have it jeopardized again. We don't need or want the pension. I'm done with the badge and the gun. I'm done. Just so you know there will be more cursing coming."

Will smiled, kissed me before we headed out the door and whispered, "Thanks Sam, it means a lot that you'd give that up for me, for us."

"Oh, Will, when I ask you to hold my pants up in a little while, do it quickly because I have to make a physical point with Charlie."

Will knew how physically strong his wife was and whatever she did was going to hurt Charlie, and he would deserve every bit of the pain she might inflict on him.

He smiled. "Just give me the word."

Will carried me to the house just as Charlie's line of black government cars pulled up in the driveway, along with the coroner's van. I was surprised that our local news van wasn't here but would bet Charlie cut that off at the source.

I could tell Will was angry from just seeing Charlie, his jaw was clenched and I'm sure if he wasn't carrying me, he would have knocked Charlie out, or worse.

Charlie stepped out of the lead car and sauntered over to us, hands in his pockets. He wasn't quite sure what to make of Will carrying me and that we were covered in soot and black smoke residue. Despite the fact Charlie already knew he still asked, "What happened to you Sam? What I can see of you, you look tempting as usual. That's not your blood, is it?"

I think Charlie using his ill-advised word, referred to my body's reaction to the cold, and this sent my husband over the edge he was already teetering on.

Will, in a low, controlled voice directed at Charlie, challenging him, said, "We can do this now, or later, but you and me, we have something to settle."

Franklin and his deputies were there, Jess and a couple of his sons, the fire fighters were there, as were Charlie's men in black. "Will, please put me down." I held onto my pants, my gun and my badge as I handed the trash bag of my clothes over to Charlie, "Here's evidence you might need. One bullet fired from my gun into the head of the dead guy."

Charlie turned, handed the bag to one of his underlings and in a superior type of voice, "Franklin, you and your deputies can leave now, we've got this covered."

Franklin smiled and retorted in a defiant tone. "No way. I'm not missing this for anything."

I was in a pissed mode, plus I wanted to make a scene in front of all these people and humiliate him. "Charlie, you tell me why you kept "The RESERVATIONS Case" information from me, used me as bait, used Will, put me in danger, and brought this piece of shit to our house, this town, and to innocent people here?"

I took a breath, pulled my pants higher, and continued my tirade.

"Why didn't I know about the third brother? That was my case. I solved that case. I deserved to know. Was this your idea, or did it come from higher up? I want answers NOW!" I was on a roll and if anyone could have seen my face under the soot, they would have seen that it was tinged with red anger.

"Sam, I'm going to need to take yours and Will's statements. This was a classified case you tried to interfere in, and you are not entitled to answers, but I am, and you'll give them to me." Charlie turned to walk away to talk to his agents.

I took a big breath and yelled. "Fuck you, Charlie, you brought this here. Anything I did was defensive and to protect my family, my friends, my Tribe."

Charlie turned around smiling, coupled with a laugh, said, "You have a Tribe now?"

"Yes, ask them. I'm Cheyenne now and you're messing with the wrong Indian."

There was a collective "She's one of us." Heads bobbing up and down in confirmation.

Will came closer to my ear, "Take a breath Sam, you're going to explode, and pull your pants up a little."

I was standing in the cold, wearing clothes that were ready to fall off me, I had no underwear, was holding my badge and gun, and yes, I was wrong; people could tell I didn't have a bra on.

I was fuming that Charlie thought he could talk to me this way in front of my people. "Charlie," I yelled. "I want answers NOW! I deserve answers. You could have gotten us killed. You lured a crazy perp to our town, to our house, and for what — so you can be the big guy who catches him as he tries to kill me or Will and then you, what, uh, bask in the glory, or get a promotion? You don't need our statements, you've been watching and monitoring everything, haven't you? You put this in motion."

"Will, please hold my pants up now." I whispered over my shoulder to my husband and gave him a wink.

I limped closer to where Charlie was standing. I shoved my gun and badge into his chest hard enough to take his breath, and in front of everyone who was watching I continued to rage. "I shot one bullet from my gun into the head of the nightmare you sent here. I am no longer your agent. I am no longer anything to you or to the Bureau. I resign, and you can shove my pension up your ass." As Charlie started to reach for me, I grabbed his hand, "thumb-tapped" him and sent him to his knees crying out in pain. I didn't let go or let up on the pressure. Other agents ran up and Charlie waved them off. As he was still reeling on his knees he pleaded. "Damn it, Sam, let go. Where the fuck did you learn that?"

"Ziva on NCIS, and I'm not letting go until you promise me and Will answers in front of all these people and that you accept my resignation."

I could hear Will behind me snickering and feel him getting a better grip on my pants.

"Fine, let go, that's my gun hand, damn it," Charlie snarled. The thumb tap sent the nerves in his hand to a pain level of ten, and as he stared at my thumb pushing those nerves relentlessly, his face contorted with pain.

I let go of Charlie's hand. Franklin, his deputies, the fire fighters, some of Charlie's own men — Jess and his sons, were all smiling and stifling their laughs.

I looked at Will. "I think I can hold my own pants up now," I smiled at him and went on to another verbal assault towards Charlie.

"Charlie, you get that thing, that piece of shit off our deck and clean it up. Sweep out the chimney, clean my office, pay for any repairs to the house, pay Franklin for his budget overruns, pay the Fire Department for their costs, and then you start talking to Will and me, and it better be the truth."

Charlie's men were standing there, watching us, waiting on his orders. I called to them, ordering them very loudly myself, "Get to work, NOW!" Charlie motioned for them to proceed, and they left to do their jobs while he continued to rub his hand where I had "thumb-tapped" him.

"Shit, Sam, did you need to ruin the nerve in my hand?"

"I could have done worse for all you've done to us, so stop your whining."

By the time the perp was bagged by the coroner, the chimney swept, forensics had done their thing, a cleaning crew of agents dressed in their nice suits cleaned my office, along with the deck, and statements were given not only by Will and me, but everyone on-site, and we finally extracted, a tooth-pulling somewhat-alternative statement from Charlie. Will brought my laptop to me, I typed Charlie's statement, printed it out in Will's office at the stables, and made Charlie sign it in front of witnesses with the threat of something worse than a "thumb-tap" happening and that it would be a little bit lower.

Charlie knew Will had contacts in high places, people whose lives he had saved in Iraq, one being the son of a Senator, and that even his boss wouldn't have a job if Will made that phone call. This was the same person who saved Charlie's job last time and could take it away just as easily now.

Will had been quiet most of the time, he liked how Sam handled things, but at the end of this stress-filled day when Charlie was about to leave Will pulled him over to the side, out of ear-shot and asked him, "Why Charlie? Why do this? If you care about Sam, why put her in danger? Why put her through this?"

Charlie looked at the ground, hands in his pockets, with a half-grin on his face. "If you ever tell her, I will deny it. I love her, always have, for almost twenty years now. Do you think I'd take that shit from her in front of everyone if I didn't love her? I never told her, but I figured the two of you wouldn't be able to sustain your relationship with a problem like this, and I'd pick up the pieces. I'll always be here for her if you ever screw up. I figured I'd catch the perp, save the day and get the girl. I assumed you were just a notion, a novelty for her that she'd get tired of life out here in Montana. I never thought she would marry you. By the way, she can keep her pension." Charlie handed the gun and badge back to Will. Will put them down on the deck stair. Then, as a cruel aside, Charlie added, "Just remember, I had her first. It's hard to forget being with her; it ruins you for any other woman."

Will could feel the rage building inside and in a low, guttural, angry voice hissed at Charlie, "If you ever step foot into our lives again, you can kiss your career and any aspirations your boss has for higher office goodbye. Now get into your car, get off my property and never contact my wife again. She is done with the Bureau, understand? If not, I can make a phone call. You know I can."

With that said, Will put his pent-up rage into his fist and punched Charlie in the face, causing a blast of blood from his nose that stained his nice, expensive suit. Charlie wavered but didn't go down.

Charlie got into his car with his hand to his nose, and as one last statement said "I'll give you this one shot, Will, for free. I think you broke my nose — I deserved it. Take care of her."

Before Charlie shut the car door, Will asked, "What color are Sam's eyes, Charlie?"

"Brown, right?" Charlie off-handedly answered with a now nasal voice.

Will shook his head, "Get out of here Charlie." Slamming Charlie's door for him. Will thought to himself, "You don't have Sam without being in her eyes — knowing the two colors. Charlie never had her. Never would."

Charlie's car and all those who came with him drove away from the house and out of sight.

Will saw Jess and his sons heading back to the stables and waved. They wanted to check on the sick horse to make sure he was still recovering and get things back to normal.

Franklin walked up to Will and said with a smile, "Me and my guys will be leaving now. Tell Sam we're proud of her, how she stood up to Mr. FBI. I need to learn that move she used on him, I liked that. She took him down with just her thumb. I'll make sure everyone deletes the pictures they took of Sam tonight with her black face, her unusual attire, and, uh, you know. How's your hand? Nice punch." Franklin walked away smiling, gathered up his deputies to head out and close his case. Franklin would keep his processing evidence of the scene in a locker should he ever need to use it in the future against the FBI.

Will stopped walking, "Hey Franklin, you send us a bill for all the overtime and whatever else it took. We appreciate everything you and your department did for us. You're a good friend."

Franklin said, with a serious look on his face, "There was no way we ever wanted to see what you would do if Sam got hurt or worse. You're a lucky man, Will. You and your new wife try to have a nice night."

Will walked over to me as I was sitting on the bench outside our front door with my ankle elevated, rubbing my thumb and smiling to myself at seeing my husband punch Charlie. "Why aren't you inside, it's getting colder? For future reference, Sam, everyone could tell you didn't have a bra on, but they all promised to delete the pictures on their phones."

"I can't go in there until you and Jess cleanse the house, along with me and you. Right now, it's contaminated by Charlie and his self-serving ideas. It could have gone bad if that piece of shit had gotten down the chimney."

"I don't want to think about that Sam, ever. I'll run down and get Jess and we'll take care of the cleansing, so you can get in and get cleaned up." Will took off his flannel shirt leaving him wearing only a t-shirt and put it over my shoulders.

"Will, sorry about the no bra thing. I don't want you to think I don't respect you wanting to keep certain things to yourself about my physicality. I just wasn't thinking. Sometimes I just don't get what the big deal is."

Will smiled. "You're with me, my wife, and that's all that matters. You didn't disrespect me. One of the reasons I love you is that you don't get it. You can't see it. We'll put some ice on your thumb when we get into the house. Franklin wants to know how you did that." Will leaned over, kissed me, then shared another bit of information. "Oh, since we don't have secrets, Charlie said he did this to break us up and because he is in love with you." With that Will headed to the stables to get Jess. He stopped in mid-walk, turned to me, smiled with those brilliant white teeth, shook his head, then headed back down to the stables.

I called to him, "Ice for your hand, too. Thanks for doing that." I sat there thinking about what Will had said about Charlie loving me and I quietly laughed. I didn't believe Charlie had the capacity to love anyone, especially me.

An hour later, with a freshly saged and blessed house, I was in the mudroom taking off the over-sized clothes, shaking my hair out in the slop sink and trying to get the worst of what was on my face off without tracking it through the house. Will came in and started taking his blackened clothes off. He retrieved my underwear from his jeans pocket, handed them to me and then tried to clean up what I had transferred to his face. "I'm going to need three showers to get this off and out of my hair," I said, looking at my naked husband and noticing a little activity.

"How's your ankle, you've been on it all day? Do you want some ice for your thumb? I was really proud of you and how you handled things with Charlie." Will was aware I had noticed and was trying to pretend that talking would curb his desires.

"I didn't really think about my ankle with everything that was going on. It's sore, but tolerable. My thumb is fine. That was fun. Thanks, Ziva. Do you want to help wash my hair?"

Will walked closer to me, put his mouth to mine, kissed me deeply with his hands on my breasts, playing with my nipples, eased back to look at me and indicated by touch. "These belong to me." Then his eyes became focused on mine, "I love your eyes Sam — one hazel, the other, darker brown. Your eyes are where you live; I always want to be reflected in them." He looked at me and smiled. "Now let's get your hair washed so we can get a little romance in tonight."

"Whatever you and your side kick want, everything is on the menu," I murmured breathlessly as I limped to the shower, the trash bag still taped on my cast.

FORTY-FIVE

Brandon was coming back from math camp tomorrow, and I was busy making of his favorite cookies. He had sent a post card last week saying how much he liked it, and that he won a trophy. I was so happy, looking forward to his return, but I was more relieved that he had not been here because of what went down yesterday. He didn't need any more bad dreams.

Will came up to me and put my gun and badge down, on the kitchen island where I was sitting. I looked at him and my expression asked, "Why?"

"Charlie refused to take them and said you'd still get your pension. I made it clear to him that you were done with the Bureau just as you had told him. I also threatened that I'd make a phone call and his career would be over if he ever contacted you again. I don't think we'll hear from him. I'm going to lock these in the safe in my office at the stables. Sorry I forgot to tell you last night, but you got my mind on other things." Will grabbed a few cookies and smiled.

"Will, I don't want them around here at all. Let's put them in the safe deposit box at the bank, along with the statement Charlie signed. I don't like that I'm still stuck for another year. What if they assign me a case? I don't want that life anymore. I need to write a letter of resignation and return these. I just want to be done with them. Isn't that what you want?"

Will looked at his beautiful wife sans black soot. "I agree, but let's give it a week for things to die down and then send them by courier. Right now, I don't think Charlie would process the paperwork. Let me think if I can have someone else deliver these on your behalf. End this and be done with them."

"Babe, we can go into town later if you want, at least put them in the safe deposit box, get the mail, have my ankle checked, and maybe have an early dinner at The Lodge." I needed to get out of the house.

"That sounds good. Let me tell Jess. You know, I'm going to have to start carrying my load of trips again starting next week, but I want us to plan a honeymoon, furniture shopping or anything else you want. No more broken promises or delaying anything."

"Let's talk about it at dinner." I smiled at my sweet man.

While Will was down at the stables, I read Charlie's statement one last time before it would be locked away at the bank. It was a whitewashed version of things, but we had to make some compromises to get Charlie to sign it. Like with all bureaucracies, reality and truth are different things. Will and I needed something to have in hand to keep Charlie and the Bureau at a distance. We also knew that Franklin had hard evidence he had gathered, locked away in case we ever needed it, along with any documentation and evidence I had gathered during my investigation — including and not limited to — my tire. All I cared about was that Will and myself, along with those who helped us, would not experience any blow-back or repercussions from the FBI.

AFFIDAVIT

I, Special Agent Charlie Falken, attest and swear to the following:

That this Affidavit of statements is as follows as it relates to "The RESERVATIONS Case" which has now been officially "Closed and marked Classified" as of today's date.

That the FBI, "Bureau" became aware of the third brother approximately three weeks after the case had been solved by FBI Special Agent Samantha Wright, Profiler of record. The case remained open until such time as final statements were accumulated, and all reports had been completed.

That the third brother, known by the alias Eugene Smith, came to collect the cremated remains of his brothers from the Bureau after seeing news reports and photo exhibits of the killers.

That the Bureau never informed or updated Special Agent Samantha Wright of the existence of the third brother as it related to "The RESERVATIONS Case." Due to her on-going medical leave and recuperation from her injuries sustained during the commission of the operation, and until such time she was released after having complied with all Bureau mandated physical and mental evaluations, October of last year she was never briefed.

That the Bureau held the third brother for questioning as a person of interest, and who submitted voluntarily to DNA sampling and fingerprint analysis.

That said, DNA confirmed a familial match, more specifically, he was a brother to the two serial killers involved in "The RESERVATIONS Case." Eugene Smith stated they were triplets, and that the brothers had been deprived of oxygen before birth resulting in mental deficiencies causing them certain pathologies that led to them committing these crimes.

That Eugene Smith stated on record that he played no part in the killings perpetrated by his siblings and had alibis for all the times and dates of those killings. Alibis were verified and confirmed. The Bureau still held the suspicion that he had some connection, incidental or direct to the killings, and would put preliminary surveillance on him. The Bureau could not legally hold him at that time.

That the Bureau concluded the name, Eugene Smith, was an alias. After a more thorough background check found the alias didn't go any further back than seven years. His driver's license and passport were manufactured, and his fingerprints had been altered so he did not appear in any databases.

That Eugene Smith had no dental records and had purchased his false teeth online. It was concluded, he would be placed under continued surveillance and further investigation until such time there was enough evidence linking him to the killings his brothers had perpetrated.

That surveillance found he operated a shredding business which contracted with the federal government and included work for the Tribal Police Stations on all the reservations. We surmised he had access to documents which would have included the birthdates of the boys on the reservations and that he had given said aforementioned information to his brothers facilitating their ability to commit the heinous crimes.

That Eugene Smith had kept a low profile until such time Special Agent Samantha Wright moved to Ashland, Montana in October of last year, near the location of the last killing and the death of his brother at her hand.

That the Bureau had been tailing him extensively since that time due to his computer research on the area, research regarding Special Agent Samantha Wright, and her highly public personal life in Ashland. This suspect had computer skills, and it was one of the reasons it took time to monitor all he was doing. The Bureau discovered his plans to go to Ashland to seek revenge against Special Agent Samantha Wright for both his brothers' deaths.

That without knowledge or permission from Special Agent Samantha Wright, the Bureau set up an operation, with management's approval, to use her as bait with the intent to apprehend this perp before his ability to cross into her safety zone established by the Bureau and to carry out his plan against her. We felt by putting the focus on Special Agent Samantha Wright instead of possible child targets again, that it was an acceptable risk.

That the suspect has since been found deceased by self-inflicted injuries outside of the safety zone. The case is now officially closed.

That, Special Agent Samantha Wright, Will Little Bear, and their associates, listed separately herein, are absolved and cleared from any wrongdoing, participation, interference, hacking, or any other activities or potential allegations in this operation, and will suffer no negative consequences by any party, including the FBI.

That the Bureau, thanks Special Agent Samantha Wright, Will Little Bear, and their associates, for their unselfish and invaluable assistance, even if involuntary to the fruition of this operation.

Hereby Certified, FBI Special Agent, In Charge, Charlie Falken

I folded the specially edited, bureau-cleansed, letter and put it back in its envelope. I put Brandon's cookies in a container and changed my clothes. Will came up from the stables, took a quick shower and we headed off to town. I needed to get out of the house, breathe some fresh air, smell the Spring and feel safe again to walk outside.

Will and I stopped at the bank, put the envelope, my unloaded gun and badge into the safe deposit box. Will then had the clerk add me as a signer on his checking account, the one we had talked about when we went over our financials. I could see Will was trying to handle the things he promised, to set the scales straight in his mind. I adored this man and his heart.

We picked up the mail, Will's prescription at the pharmacy, along with readers he now needed, and then headed over to the clinic to have my ankle looked at. Will indicated he wanted to have his blood pressure checked and to talk with the doctor about the vasectomy reversal procedure while I was having my ankle x-rayed by the tech.

Will pulled the tech aside and told her to make sure I was protected from the x-ray and then went to see the doctor. Will had his blood pressure checked, which was within norms, and he also had his vasectomy checked to see if he had any swimmers. It didn't take long for Will to give the doctor a sample since all he had to think about was what we did last night in bed. The doctor checked the sample and said to Will. "You don't need a reversal, for some reason you're viable. It could be from a physical trauma or just a failure of the duct, a recanalization. It does happen — not often— but it can. Is this a problem for you?"

Will had to blink back tears remembering what Jess had said and replied to the doctor, "No it's not a problem. My wife is in the other room having her ankle x-rayed and I'd like it if we could find out if she's pregnant. She's had some symptoms, but we figured it might be the flu."

The doctor came into the x-ray room and stopped the tech before she took the x-ray and asked me to come into his office, so we could talk about Will. My heart started beating faster as I asked, "Is something wrong, you're scaring me?"

"No, Will's fine, but we want to share some interesting information with you."

I walked into the doctor's office and Will was there. He reached out his hand wanting me to sit by him.

"Are you alright? Is there a problem?"

The doctor handed me a piece of paper with test results from Will's sperm count; it showed that he did, in fact, have a sperm count, even though he'd had a vasectomy. It was a low count, but he was viable. I kept staring at it. I looked at Will and then the doctor. "How long has Will been viable?"

"Will came in last October just before you came home, like he has done every year which is something we recommend as a normal course of follow up. In October, he was not viable, but he is now and there is no way of knowing when his vasectomy may have — in lay terms — reversed itself. It happens in about one in four thousand men, it's called recanalization. Now Will tells me that you've had flu-like symptoms, dizziness, and that you recently fainted. I would suggest we see if you're pregnant."

I couldn't talk. Will was holding my hand and he could feel me trembling. "I guess we should do that," I said, my voice shaking in disbelief.

The doctor handed me an EPT and pointed me to the bathroom. "If it's positive, we'll do an examination and determine how far along you are." I sat down on the toilet. My hand was shaking I could hardly pee on the stick. I finished, put it on the tray and handed it back to the doctor. I sat down by Will, and he could see tears welling up. "Sam are you okay?" I nodded to the affirmative.

The doctor looked at his watch, looked at the stick, and said, "Let's do that exam now. I'll need you to get undressed from the waist down. Will may stay here if you want. I'll be back shortly."

I was caught in a fog and wasn't sure what I felt. Will helped me get undressed because of my ankle cast. I got up on the table, covered myself with the paper sheet, and looked at the stirrups. I was shaking. Will was getting concerned because I wasn't saying anything.

"Sam, please tell me you're okay. Are you upset?"

The doctor came in before I could answer, indicated for me to scoot down, and put my feet into the stirrups conjuring up the past, but I shoved that memory into a box and focused on the now. Will had to help with my ankle cast since it wouldn't fit in the stirrup while the doctor checked me out. The doctor pulled his gloves off smiling. "I'd say you're about four weeks along. Everything feels fine. When was your last period?"

"I can't remember, I'm not that regular, I think five, or so weeks. It's been busy at our house. I've been distracted. Stressed."

The doctor then asked, "Have you had any alcohol, cigarettes, drugs or pain medications with regards to your ankle?"

Will could see I wasn't able to talk so he responded to the doctor, "No, she hasn't had anything. She refused to take pain meds for her ankle."

"While you're here let's do an ultrasound and take a look. I want to make sure none of your previous injuries have caused any problems and we may be able to see the gestational sac. We'll set you up for regular check-ups, and have you leave with a list of dos and don'ts."

Will, still seeing my inability to form words, asked the doctor, "She works out a lot, rides, and is pretty active. I'm going to teach her to swim. Is any of that a problem?"

"Shouldn't be a problem, she doesn't have to discontinue those activities, but have her go easy for the next couple of months. Since she's done it for years, she should be fine; after that and until about the last two months when she should begin slacking off. Swimming would be a good form of exercise for her. No heavy lifting." The doctor paused, and then asked Will, "She doesn't know how to swim?"

Will shrugged his shoulders and being a little embarrassed, asked, "What about sex?"

"Sex is fine."

The doctor winked at him having heard rumors of our homecomings after Will's trips.

Tears were running down my face, but I still couldn't talk. I had so many thoughts and feelings I couldn't get my mind focused. I could see Will was getting scared, wondering how I felt about this. He wiped the tears from my cheeks. I took his left hand, played with his ring and I put his hand on my stomach. He started crying and laughing with me.

After the ultrasound, the tech told us, everything looked normal, printed out a sonogram showing the sac, and left the room so I could get dressed. Will helped me. As I stood there my breath was coming in short bursts. I grabbed him around the neck and started sobbing. Through my sobs, I quietly said,

"We're having a baby, Will. I wanted this, but I was afraid I wouldn't be able to and now, I am, and I'm so happy. Are you happy?"

Will held onto me tight, he was fighting back tears. He eased back a little from my strong embrace and answered, "I'm so happy, Sam. I can't believe it. I'm just so full of love for you and our baby. I know I said we would never wait for anything again, but we will wait now." He held me until the doctor said they needed the room.

When we came out the door, the x-ray tech relayed to us, "The doctor indicated that we could do the x-ray as long as I cover you completely with the shield. Let's do this so we can see if your ankle is healing properly. We don't need to remove that cast since it's clear. It won't interfere with the pictures." Will didn't want to let go of my hand, but the tech said he had to leave the room for her to take the x-ray. As soon as the x-ray was taken Will had hold of my hand again. A little later the doctor came in and indicated my ankle was healing well, but it would be about two more weeks for the cast and crutches to continue being part of my daily chores.

We finally emerged from the clinic and went to the car to drive to The Lodge for dinner. As soon as we were both inside the car, Will took my face into his hands and kissed me with so much love and tenderness. He still had tears in his eyes as did I. We kissed for a long time, our kisses expressing our happiness. My husband finally looked at me, "Let's get some dinner. You need to eat." We headed to The Lodge.

As he drove, I said to him, "Let's not say anything to anyone just yet, let it just be for us for now, okay? I want to make sure everything will be fine."

Will smiled at me, "I think that's a good idea."

We had our usual dinner at The Lodge — filets medium-well, baked potatoes, butter only, and green beans. Will always took half my potato, gave me his green beans, and he waited to see if I'd have any steak left for him. We ate in between kissing and private talk. Scotty came over and commented, "You two look happy. Can I buy you a drink?"

Will answered, distracted, "We're good Scotty, but thanks. Just came for dinner."

Scotty looked at me and smiled. "Sam, you look more beautiful every time I see you. Maybe next time you're in you'll sing again." It seemed like he wanted to say more but didn't like his timing. "Well, I'll let you two enjoy your meal. Oh, Will, when you have some time in the next week or so, I'd like to talk to you about something."

"Anytime Scotty, just give me a call and I'll check my schedule."

Scotty left the table, and we went back into our little world.

"Will, you could have ordered a beer for yourself. You don't have to give up things just because I can't have them right now."

"I don't need it, if you can't share with me, I don't want it. You're the one always making sacrifices, I need to do something, too. We're in this together. This is "our" pregnancy."

Dinner was eaten, and we wanted to get home. Everything felt new being married, expecting a baby, and my past further behind me. Here I was forty years old, a former FBI Profiler, two doctorates, a high IQ and a writer with some success, but nothing has made me happier or more satisfied than what my life was right now.

I wanted Will. I wanted to be close to him, and I could hardly contain myself. As soon as we walked in the door of our home, I grabbed him by his shirt front, put my hand behind his head, and brought his mouth to mine. I kissed him as if I had never had him. He eased back slightly and looked into my eyes. He could see my intent, my want, my quickened breathing.

"Sam, talk to me first. Last time like this it was because you didn't think we'd see each other again, uh, that you wouldn't be here. What is it this time?" Will was a bit emotional remembering.

I wouldn't let go of him, but I looked into his eyes, smiled, and explained. "Marriage, the baby, it's changed it all for me. It's like everything feels like more. I want you more, to feel more, to taste more, and I love you more. I thought I loved you as much as I could, that I thought possible, but I was wrong, it's more now. The same but different. It's all through me, every cell of my body wants more of you, more of our life. It's just better, I'm happier, and I want to share this all with you. I look at you, and I want you more than I ever have. I'm still me, but more. I'm your equal and your wife. I never thought this could be my life." I couldn't seem to stop myself from talking until I finally ran out of breath.

Will, with his gentle eyes looking at me, seeing me differently, said, "Everything you just said, is how I feel. I didn't know how to say it. It's like the fight we'd had broken open everything and what came out was just more love. I sometimes think I'm a tough guy, but here I am feeling all these emotions, expressing them to you, and I don't feel less of a man, I feel empowered by what you've created in me. I have more depth now than when we first met. I'm a better version now of the man I always wanted to be for you."

I pulled Will to me, reached down, massaged him, felt him move, and felt him grow. I wanted him, and I was trying to get his belt unbuckled and his pants unzipped. He picked me up and took me to the bedroom. Unlike the night I thought I was going to be lost to him, this was different, I knew I had him, that he belonged to me, and I wanted all of him. I wanted him now. "Will, please, help me, take your pants off, take mine off. I can't wait."

Will and I were undressed from the waist down in seconds and for now that was all that was needed. I reached for him, stroked him, kissed him with everything I had. I backed him up to the bed, pushed him down, and got on top of him. I guided him into me, and we both moaned. I was moving and so was he, it was faster and then with one move he was on top of me, getting deeper inside of me. We were on a ride we couldn't stop, didn't want to get off. I was making sounds of complete surrender. Will could no longer hold back and climaxed with me. Neither one of us could stop and I wouldn't let him back out, my legs wrapped around him. I couldn't even feel my ankle. Will through short breaths, pleaded, "Sam, babe, relax a little, loosen your legs, I promise not to pull out, but you are so damn strong, and I can't breathe."

I relaxed a little and unlocked my legs from his back. I still had my arms around his neck, and he was still inside me. "I'm not done yet, Will," I whispered. I used my vaginal muscles to tease him, to stroke him from the inside, and I could feel him start to respond.

"I know babe, I know you're not done. Just give me a few minutes, then you can have me again, whatever you want. Unbutton your blouse and unhook your bra for me, while I'm massaging you. I want to get you to that place for when I'm ready again."

Will kissed me intensely and moved his mouth to my nipples as my back arched. He made me insatiable and sensitive; he could feel me getting wet-hot around him while he was in me and it made him hard again. He slowly advanced himself inside me, gaining momentum until he had me full, moving with him, lifting my hips until he took me to that place again, such satisfaction and complete release.

As I laid spent with him still on top of me, still in me, but relaxing, "Babe, have I given you enough, do you need more? I could go down on you," Will offered as he tried to catch his breath but continued to kiss me wherever there was exposed skin.

"God Will, yes, it's enough. Lay next to me, hold me, bring me down a little. I think I actually left my body for a second there, I feel completely satisfied, so satisfied. God, I love you so much. I love you for taking me like this, the way I needed you tonight. You belong to me, and you gave me everything I asked for. Was it enough for you Will? Did you get what you needed? I could do more for you." I was talking like I'd had too much caffeine; except I was just high on love and sex.

"You seem to get everything from me, more than I thought I could give. I am spent, Sam. I have nothing left. You're amazing and a lot stronger than you appear." He laughed a bit.

We fell asleep moments later, Will still wearing his shirt and me still with my unclasped bra and blouse on. I was dreaming, and it woke me. It was almost three in the morning. I could hear the soft, deep breathing of

Will's sleep. I looked at him while he slept and was amazed how handsome he was. Sometimes he would reach for me and pull me to him without even waking up. Sometimes he would say my name as if to make sure I hadn't left or that he wanted to tell me something. Tonight, he had been beyond tired.

I slipped out of bed, took the rest of my clothes off and went to my place of reflection at the lodgepole in the middle of our home. I leaned my back against its strong, wooden presence and tried to absorb some of its power that holds this house up and keeps it standing. There was a crescent moon tonight, and I stared at it as if seeking answers from the night sky.

A little while later, I heard Will coming over to me, bringing me a shawl to put over my bare shoulders. It was cool in the house. I noticed he had taken his shirt off. He was the most beautiful man, naked.

"Couldn't you sleep? Are you feeling alright?' He asked in a sleepy voice, stifling a yawn.

"I'm sorry I woke you. I had a dream and couldn't fall back to sleep. I feel better than I have in weeks."

"I reached for you, but you weren't there. I knew where you would be. Yesterday was a big day for us, I understand you needing to be here in the center of our home, in the center of our universe." Will came closer to me, stood in front of me, taking me into his eyes like he was seeing me for the first time. He makes "us" always feel new.

"You are the most beautiful woman I've ever seen, but there's something more I see now, it's making you have a light in your eyes that wasn't as bright before. You're happy. That love, that unbelievable sex last night, that came from deep inside both of us, an unending depth of love. I can still feel it, feel you. What you do to me sometimes, Sam, is more than I could imagine was possible."

"I am happy Will. I didn't think it was possible — an abundance of love with a feeling of peace. I still feel you inside me, too. Last night you gave me everything I asked for and needed. Everything I love is here with you. Everything I need or want is here with you." I reached up and ran my fingers through my husband's mussed hair, then softy touched his chest, so I could feel his heartbeat with mine and smell his scent from the well at the bottom of his throat. "You know I adore you and I can never say no to you?"

"I know how you feel, how you love me. I see it every day from you, and you have never said no to me. I can't say no to you either, never want to."

"I think I got pregnant the night of your birthday," I smiled.

"That had been quite an acrobatic night." Will smiled with a memory.

"My body will change," I reflected, causing him to look me up and down.

"I know. A different kind of beauty," Will said, while touching my face and looking into my eyes.

'It won't just be us, anymore." I checked his eyes to see if he understood that.

"I know. We'll be a family. Something we both want. We'll have to wear more clothes in the future."

"You'll need to add a room onto the house."

"I know. Just not tonight."

"In my dream, Will, we're having a daughter and her name is Katie."

"I know, I've had the same dream. She looks like you. You know we share dreams, don't you?"

"Yes. I like that. We share a lot of things, my husband."

"Babe, we're connected on so many levels, some we haven't even discovered yet."

"She has your gentle brown eyes. I want her to have a childhood better than we had. I want her to have so much love that she feels safe, secure and part of a family that won't let anything make her ever believe there's ever enough love."

"It's the way we do things in this family," Will said as he traced my face with his finger and lightly kissed my lips, then licked them, sending a shiver through me, and put his weary forehead to mine. I could see how tired he was.

I took Will's left hand, the one with the ring, and laid it on my belly. "My body belongs to both of you now. This ring on your finger means everything to me. I know we both felt married before the wedding, but I needed the outward sign to bring me out of my vision and into your world. I didn't know how much I wanted it. Wanted you. Wanted this life."

Will looked at his ring and smiled. "I'm never taking it off. I didn't know how much I needed and wanted it too. I'm proud to share this life with you. I couldn't imagine it without you."

As I leaned against the lodge pole Will placed his hand behind my head and softly brought his mouth to mine, kissing me just like the first time at the tree by the stream. The first time that brought us on this journey.

"Come to bed now, sleep with me. Right now, I'm only capable of sleep." Will took my hand in his and the three of us went to bed.

FORTY-SIX

I was in the process of making lunch for Jess and Will to take down to the stables when Will texted me. "Brandon's here and he's looking for you."

I replied, "I'll be down as fast as my ankle will allow." I was excited to see him after everything that had happened. To verify in my heart, he was safe. To show him that life continued even when he was away, and that we were all still here to welcome him home.

I was carrying six beef and swiss sandwiches with all the trimmings in a bag (these guys can eat), apples (that usually ended up in Sampson's mouth), jicama sticks, and the box of Brandon's cookies all the while trying to maneuver on my crutches down to the barn. Will knew better than to try and help. I had made it clear that I needed to do this myself because he had to leave tomorrow for a trip, and I had to be on my own. I did miss being carried.

As I walked into the stable area near Will's office, Brandon ran over to me, took the lunch bag from me, set it on Will's desk, and then ran back to hug me hello as I balanced on my crutches — still holding his cookie box. He was all smiles and to me he looked as though he had grown a few more inches for his fourteen years. Will was smiling at Brandon's greeting and he could see how happy I was to know he was safe. Brandon had something behind his back and excitedly said, "I brought you something. Let's sit over there on the bench so your leg won't hurt and then I can give it to you."

Will and Jess started to chow down on their lunches, but they could hear and see me with Brandon from the office.

I smiled and asked in a puzzled way, "What did you bring me?"

"I want you to have the trophy I won at math camp because you're the one who deserves it." Brandon held the trophy out for me to take.

"Brandon, you're the one who earned this, you worked hard for this, you should keep it for a memory." As I looked at the little name plate on the trophy, it said "Brandon Lewis, First Place" I could feel myself blink back some tears.

Out of the corner of my eye I could see Will and Jess covertly watching and smiling while they ate.

"No Sam, you earned it. I know you sent me to camp to keep me safe. You never get prizes for what you do, and I want you to have this. I won it for you."

"What did you hear Brandon?" My voice was unsteady.

"That you sent me to camp to protect me, to keep me safe, and of course, to make me smarter."

Will and Jess stifled their laughs as soon as their emotions kicked in as to what Brandon had just said to Sam. They had not said anything to him. Will didn't know who would do that.

I smiled, half-laughed at this young man, "Well then, I accept this prize with a full heart. Do you want to talk about what you heard?"

Brandon looked down at the floor for a second and then answered, "No, it would make it real, and right now I'd like to think of it more like a dream."

"You can talk to me or Will about anything, you know that don't you? If you ever want to get rid of that dream, we can talk about it."

"You and Will can talk to me too if you need to. Maybe, sometime, but not today. I'm happy to be home and to see you again. I missed teaching you to ride."

Will watched his wife and this young man relate on a deeper level than anyone should have to because of the night we all shared over two years ago. He could see Sam had some plan to figure out how far she could offer herself to this young man. He was always amazed how much she had to give. How she always knew what to do.

I held out the container of cookies I had made for Brandon and said, "Well since you gave me a gift, I think it's only fair I give you these cookies I made for you. Is that a fair exchange?"

Brandon smiled, opened the container and stuffed a cookie in his mouth. "It's fair." He quipped through the cookie.

I laughed and tried to make things lighter to get to a deeper matter, "Did you have any problems at camp? Sometimes people can be unkind. Your mom said someone said something to you. Do you want to tell me?"

"It wasn't much, just that I was an Indian trying to be a cowboy with this bandana on and they tried to take it, but I wouldn't let them. It didn't happen again after the counselor talked to them. No big deal. I'm old enough to handle myself."

Will could see the wheels turning in Sam's head. He wanted to see where this would go. He could see her eyes were on Brandon, weighing things. Seeing if he would trust her. She had good instincts.

"Yes, you are old enough to handle yourself and because of that I want to show you something, is that okay?"

"Sure, what is it?"

Will and Jess didn't understand what Sam was about to do and they stopped eating to watch.

I stood up and took my denim shirt off, leaving me with my tank top on. "Come here Brandon, stand in front of me." I held out my hand to him and he placed his hand in mine with no qualms.

Will and Jess looked at each other and then continued to watch Sam.

I took Brandon's hand and put his fingers at my throat to touch my scar. I moved his fingers to touch the scar on my shoulder. Then I pulled up my tank top on my right side and placed his fingers on that scar.

Will and Jess both had tears in their eyes, they couldn't believe how selfless Sam was. Will knew she was uncomfortable with her scars. He knew how vulnerable this must make her feel. At that moment, he loved her even more and didn't know how that was possible. He looked at Jess and said, "That's my wife."

"You loved Will and me to do that for us," Brandon again touched the scar on my side, put his hands into his pockets, looked at me directly in my eyes, and smiled his understanding.

"I would do it again if I had to," I said, remembering.

That comment stuck in Will's throat, he knew it was true. It's who she is.

I touched Brandon's cheek with my fingers and asked, "Do you trust me?"

"Yes, Sam, I do trust you. With my life."

I started to untie the bandana around his neck, and he looked at me like he wanted to back away, but he didn't. I removed the bandana slowly and touched the scars on his neck with my fingers, gently, and with a half-smile. "Well, I think your scars are beautiful, just like Will thinks mine are. I like to think of them as "life marks." It's like when you get dings or scratches on furniture, it shows that people live there, that life is being lived, leaving its mark. Your scars show you have character, that your life is interesting. They show your strength and who you are, just like mine say who I am. Be proud of who you are, Brandon. A strong, smart, and caring young Cheyenne man who has nothing to hide from anyone." I handed the bandana back to him and kissed the top of his head.

Brandon looked at his bandana, thought for a second and said "Sam, you keep it, I don't need it."

I took the bandana back from him, he smiled, and asked, "Can I have lunch now?"

"You better, before Will and Jess eat it all." I laughed as he grabbed a sandwich off Will's desk and ran outside with his box of cookies tucked under his arm.

Will and Jess had heard and seen the interaction. As I was putting my shirt back on, Jess came over to me and said, "You gave Brandon some of your strength, but it does not weaken you. You will be stronger because of it." This wise medicine man who is not big on demonstrative displays of affection kissed me on the cheek and went to get another sandwich.

Will walked up behind me, wrapped me in his arms, and whispered in my ear so Jess couldn't hear, "See, there are no doubts, never were, that you will be a great mother. It's in you. What you did for that young man will always be with him."

I turned around to face my husband and sighed. "Your love for me makes me stronger than I think I can be. Do you know who told Brandon I had sent him to camp to protect him?"

"No, but he is a young man who knows things instinctively. There is a power brewing inside of him. He will figure it out one day. You'll help him."

I pulled Will by his shirt front closer to me and kissed this man I adored. I catch myself often saying that I adore him. It's just that other words seem flat to me when expressing what I feel when I look at him.

"Sam, I have a five-day weekend coming up after this trip tomorrow; we can go to Denver for a short honeymoon, do some furniture shopping, and Mr. Collins has offered to put us up at the Ritz Carlton as a wedding gift. How does that sound to you?"

"Sounds wonderful. One caveat, I talked to Jess, and he already said he can arrange what I asked him to do."

Jess tried to no avail to hide himself behind his sandwich, looking guilty.

"What have you already asked my now silent partner to do? What have the two of you been up to?" Will asked with a wink.

"A traditional ceremonial celebration of our marriage before we go to Denver. I owe it to you Will, I want you to have it. I want us to have it. It matters."

"Will looked over at Jess and shook his head, "Sam, I don't know what to say. How do you always know what to do, knowing the right thing to do and what I need?

"Because I know you. Because I love you and can never say no to you."

My man is a liberal about many things — politics, justice, fairness, equal rights, our sex, and more — but when it comes to his heritage, he is traditional, except for falling in love with me, a former white woman. The two sides of him make him a blend of what speaks to my heart and I wouldn't change him for anything.

"Will, I do have a request for tonight, if you have time. I know you're leaving tomorrow for a couple of days and you're very busy."

"I had already planned on tonight. I'd never leave without us having a night."

I smiled, "I also plan on tonight, but prior to that I want to burn all the case files I have in those boxes I brought here that Dr. Sampson and I worked on. I thought I was keeping him near me by bringing his work, but I have memories of him, and I don't want those files to keep me connected to my past. I want them burned and forgotten."

As Will listened to Sam's request he remembered some of what Jess had taught him. He could see Sam, in small steps, walking away from her old life and walking into their life. She had a sense of permanence here with him now because he had given her what she needed from him. He looked at his left hand, the ring he proudly wore, and was happy because he had also needed what she had wanted for them both.

"We'll burn them in the fire pit after dark," Will promised, as he eased me closer, kissed me and whispered, "You have no idea how much I love you. Share a sandwich with me before you go back up to the house." I stayed and ate with Will and Jess. I knew Will was just making sure I ate enough. I liked it when he took care of me.

I left Will and Jess to their work, took the trophy and the bandana up to the house with me. I found a place on the bookshelf to display it next to the winter cactus Will had given me while I was in the hospital. I wrapped, then tied the bandana around the trophy that meant so much and put it in its honored spot in Will's and my home. Brandon never wore another bandana, and he held his head higher as a result.

FORTY-SEVEN

We burned the files until they were ashes. I felt lighter and more grounded as the flames consumed my past. I said a prayer to Dr. Sampson to make him understand why I needed to do this, to forget the shackles that had kept my foot in at the Bureau, and to move on with my life with Will. Dr. Sampson would have loved Will like a son. He would have approved of what we did that night over two years ago. I knew he would understand.

Will watched Sam as the fire engulfed years of hers' and Dr. Sampson's work — finding justice for those who found themselves in the path of death and pain. She had spent her last twenty years speaking for those who couldn't, and she tried to stop those from continuing their destruction, sometimes putting her own life on the line. He was proud of her. He was in awe of her. She was his wife, but she was so much more. Everyone he knew had some connection to Sam because of what she did and who she is. They see her outward beauty, but they all know it's her inner beauty that they really admire and gravitate towards.

The cleansing by fire was done. Will and I went into the house to have our night. Will never enjoyed leaving for these trips, but now he wasn't afraid like before. He and Jess planned on hiring another guide so that Will would be gone less, especially with the baby coming, and because he wanted to build the security business, to work with me. He took the watch on his left wrist seriously, and he wanted to spend it all with me.

I went into the bathroom to wash my face and get ready for bed while Will locked up the house and brought in some firewood for the bedroom fireplace. The nights were chilly, and it was romantic. As I stood at the sink in my bra and panties, I could see Will reflected in the mirror. He was leaning on the door jamb at the entrance to the bathroom looking at me and smiling. I dried my face and turned around to look at him. "What are you thinking looking at me like that and playing with your ring?"

"How beautiful you look. You defy your age without even trying. Happiness has made you look even younger. I can never get enough of looking at you and now that you're carrying our child, I can't help but feel so proud and blessed. I love you more than I can express Sam, but I'd like to try and show you. This ring tells me I'm bound to you for eternity, it's never coming off my finger, and that makes me happy."

I reached out my hand to this man who has gone through so much with me to get us to this place, this time, this life, and beckoned him to come to me. He walked towards me, and I could remember the night when I asked him if he liked to dance. That's how it felt tonight, I looked at his gentle eyes as he embraced me, and I asked, "Do you want to dance with me?"

He smiled with those unbelievably white teeth and nodded, "Dancing with you would be foreplay. I'd be a good dancer with you." He remembered, and we started dancing without any music except for what was in our hearts.

Will left the next morning. He came back twice before heading out for just one more kiss, one more hug, one more I love you, and one more touch of my belly. He looked fulfilled and happy.

I busied myself with preparations for the ceremony he had longed for, took pictures of every room in the house so we could furniture shop in Denver, and picked up the belt buckle I had specially made for him as a wedding gift — one he had admired in a catalogue, but that I had a local artisan make.

The night before his return I couldn't sleep. I didn't find comfort in our king-size bed without him. I found myself at the lodgepole looking out the glass front of our home at the night sky, counting my blessings and talking to Katie about the men who would be in her life; Will, Jess and his sons, Brandon, Christian, Franklin, and Scotty. I told her how lucky we were to have all these brave, yet gentle, big-hearted men in our lives who would do anything to keep us safe. I told her in confidence, "Even though we are strong, they like it when we need them." I finally felt sleepy, went to bed, and dreamt of Will.

Will came home the next day and our greeting took thirty minutes before he could go back down to the stables. The day after his return we had our Cheyenne ceremony and celebration. I could see the joy it brought to him, it completed him for our marriage. It gave him his heritage and his traditions. It was the last piece his heart needed to really feel married to me. I understood him. I also felt a closeness to this culture I had been welcomed into and I was grateful having all this family in my life.

Will and I exchanged gifts. He gave me a horsehair bracelet that had my garnet birthstone woven into it, with sterling silver end caps. Sampson had given up some of his hair for this gift and I smiled at the irony of it all. I gave Will a belt buckle that fit with the traditions he cherishes, he loved it and immediately put it on to show everyone there.

We went to Denver and had a lavish, three-day honeymoon, compliments of Mr. Collins, who by the way was impressed by our report and gave our little security business the rest of our payment, a retainer for future business, and a contract for the next five years. Needless to say, we bought lots of furniture for our home that would be delivered by the time we got back.

On the last day of our honeymoon, we were dancing in the club at the Ritz Carlton when I heard a man tell his wife, pointing at Will and me, "They aren't just dancing, that's foreplay."

His wife responded to her husband, "Then dance with me, too."

I laughed and whispered to Will, "We need to get to our room. We're steaming things up. People are noticing."

Our room had a terrace that overlooked Denver, and we could see out to the mountains. Will was watching me, admiring the dress that he had given me for my birthday accessorized by my wedding gift — Sampson's horsehair bracelet. He smoothed my hair that the breeze was trying to control, touched the garnet earrings I wore that were also a gift from him, and put his arms around me. "The last six months sure have been exciting since you came home. We got through a lot together. Every time I think I can't love you more, I do. Every time I think you can't get more beautiful, you do. I can't wait to see your beauty as you get further along with "our" pregnancy. Every time I think we've had the ultimate sex, it gets better. Every time I think I've peeled back the last layer of your onion, there's more to you. I just never thought this would be my life, that what I hoped for would come true. That you, Samantha Wright Little Bear, would be the love of my life and my wife. You made me understand that I can be a man and still have the range of emotions I need to be a human being, and your husband. I am one lucky Indian."

I looked at this man I married. He had his new belt buckle on that I gave him and touching the watch I sent him before I got home that he refuses to take off. Will understands symbols. "Will, why do you not think that I'm the lucky one. That I'm the one who got more than I ever imagined for myself. That all those things you just said are possible only because you came into my life and stole my heart. If you weren't the one to take the first step and kiss me at the tree by the stream, we may not be here. Mr. Little Bear you don't give yourself enough credit for all that you are, all that you do, the things you know, how you love me, and that your body is so arousing to me. You are everything to me, I adore you. Our child will be so blessed to have you for a father. Me and Katie, we're the lucky ones." I put our left hands together and we looked at the rings on our fingers. We smiled at each other, knowing that the infinity symbols engraved inside each ring were as true as it gets.

Will put his forehead to mine and whispered, "How do you always know what to say, the right thing to do, and always know what I need?"

"I watch you. I listen to you. I know you. I always look up to you." Will took my hand in his, looked me up and down, then sighed, "That dress gives me ideas. I plan on taking my time with you tonight."

FORTY-EIGHT

We returned from our honeymoon the day our furniture arrived. I spent that day and the next day having Will, Jess, and Brandon move things around until I had it just like I pictured it in my head. They would do anything for me, but it had now gotten to the point that if I asked for one more "Let's try it over there" I would have had a mutiny. "Done," I announced, and they all sighed with relief.

Will and Jess knew Sam was nesting. One more step closer to what Jess described as "surrender" to her new life, stepping out of her vision and into her real life with Will. Will saw that the boxes Sam had brought still sat unpacked, but he had a feeling he would be recruited to help her with them soon. He smiled to himself. He watched her face as she looked around their home and smiled at how it looked like the both of them morphed into one. They had combined their tastes and it was perfect.

Jess was taking out the new guide — his son Clarence — on his first trip to show him the ropes with a group of four hunters, starting tomorrow, for three days. They hired him after his recent help and because they could trust him. He was family. Clarence was a big guy even in comparison to Will. Clarence had to be 6'4", 225 pounds with a hard body like steel. He could carry two eighty- pound bales of hay, one in each hand as if they were feathers. He looked like his father Jess, just super-sized. He grew up here, he knew almost as much as Jess about the area, hunting, tracking, and was truly a horse whisperer. He was a rodeo bull rider like Tanner Byrne, but last year was the last accident his wife would allow. Jess and Will were particular with regard to how things were done, how the clients were treated, and they felt Clarence had a feel for that. Jess hoped one day his part of the business would go to Clarence, and this was a start.

Will had one more day at home and then he would have a two-day trip. It was time to get down to real life again, and to get back into some structure, balancing Will's guide business, the security work coming in from Mr. Collins, my writing commitments, a required date night, and waiting for Katie. Will had promised to talk to Scotty at The Lodge and wanted to get that done before he left. We planned on lunch with Scotty the next day, to run some errands, and call it an early night so Will could get some sleep before his trip. After Jess and Brandon left Will put his arms around me and kissed my cheek from behind where it felt like he was getting ideas for tonight. "You've really made this house a home Sam. What about those boxes?"

"I've marked them by room so whenever you have time just place them in the middle of the rooms they are designated for, and I'll unpack them while you're gone. I'd do it, but the doctor told me not to lift heavy boxes and some of them are books." I turned myself around within Will's grasp and ended up facing my husband, putting my arms around his neck. I could smell his scent, and he hugged me back.

"I'll make you a deal Sam, I'll get all the boxes moved and you make dinner. Then after all this heavy lifting and after we eat, I was thinking of soaking in a hot bath. What do you think?"

"Deal." And I gave my man a kiss.

The next morning Will went down to the stables early to help Jess and

Clarence get everything ready for the trip and to start the preparation for his own tomorrow. By the time I had breakfast ready he was back. We slowed down our pace, and a couple hours later we left for town – errands, then lunch with Scotty.

I had gotten my appetite back and was anxious for one of the amazing lunches Scotty's menus offered. Will and I sat at our usual booth, placed our order and waited for Scotty to join us.

Scotty saw his friends, hell they were his family here in Montana — waiting for him to join them at their table. They were probably curious as to why he wanted – no, needed to talk to them. How was he going to tell them that when he was in Chicago and trying to find financial backing that a guy sought him out, lent him the money to buy The Lodge from Will. Now this same guy wanted a favor from him because of something that had happened in the past. This guy was with the FBI and Scotty didn't know until recently that Will and Sam knew him – that they knew Charlie Falken. Scotty needed their help and Charlie Falken couldn't find out about it.

We saw Scotty coming towards our table, but he was trying too hard to look like he was happy to see us. Just as Scotty was getting ready to sit down, to talk to us Will's cell rang. It was Brandon.

"Okay, keep him calm, I'll be right there. I'll call the vet."

"Will, what's wrong?"

"Scotty, do you mind that Sam and I take a raincheck on the talk? One of the horses I was planning to take on my trip tomorrow got his leg caught in a broken fence board having a disagreement with another horse and is cut up pretty bad. I'll need to meet the vet at the stables."

"No problem Will, it can wait. Sam, if you're in town while Will's away come in for lunch."

Will put money down on the table and we got up to leave, but before we walked away, I could see a look on Scotty's face that made me hesitate. I looked at Will and he knew I needed a second. I went over to Scotty, and I gave him a hug, a kiss on the cheek, "Call me if it's something that can't wait. Hey, when I have things that I'm trying to work out, I always look up."

Scotty felt like he dodged a bullet. He wasn't ready to talk to Will and Sam. He needed to get his so-called ducks in a row and be ready for the many questions they would have. The last thing he wanted was to lose their friendship. He'd wait. He hoped Charlie Falken would.

ABOUT THE AUTHOR

Theresa Janson grew up in the American Midwest and uprooted to Colorado in the mid-90's. Writing has always been in her blood, and she has culled stories from working as a paralegal with attorneys and law enforcement—knowing everyone's secrets. Her life and work have given her insight into a subconscious collection of experiences prevalent in the words of this novel and all her works. She was given nightly dreams, and those dreams are the words that lead you through these chapters until you can't catch your breath.